SEVEN LETTERS

D0047518

ALSO BY J. P. MONNINGER

The Map That Leads to You

SEVEN LETTERS

J. P. Monninger

St. Martin's Griffin

New York

First published in the United States by St. Martin's Griffin, an imprint of St. Martin's Publishing Group

SEVEN LETTERS. Copyright © 2019 by Joseph Monninger. All rights reserved. Printed in the United States of America. For information, address St. Martin's Publishing Group, 120 Broadway, New York, NY 10271.

www.stmartins.com

Designed by Donna Sinisgalli Noetzel

The Library of Congress Cataloging-in-Publication Data is available upon request.

ISBN 978-1-250-18769-7 (trade paperback)
ISBN 978-1-250-18770-3 (ebook)

Our books may be purchased in bulk for promotional, educational, or business use. Please contact your local bookseller or the Macmillan Corporate and Premium Sales Department at 1-800-221-7945, extension 5442, or by email at MacmillanSpecialMarkets@macmillan.com.

First Edition: October 2019

10 9 8 7 6 5 4 3 2 1

To Susan, who lives by the brook

The sunlight has never heard of trees.
—A. R. AMMONS

Life is tough, my darling, but so are you.
—ANONYMOUS

PROLOGUE

The Irish tell a story of a man who fell in love with a fairy woman and went with her to live on an island lost to time and trouble. They lived in a thatched cottage overlooking the sea with nothing but donkeys and gulls and white chickens to keep them company. They lived in the dream of all lovers, apart from the world, entire to themselves, their bed an island to be rediscovered each night. In all seasons, they slept near a large round window and the ocean wind found them and played gently with their hair and carried the scent of open water to their nostrils. Each night he tucked himself around her and she, in turn, moved closer into his arms, and the seals sang and their songs fell to the bottom of the sea where the shells held their voices and relinquished them only in violent storms.

One day the man went away, mortal as he was; he could not resist his longing to see the loved ones he had left behind. She warned him that he would grow old the moment his foot touched the soil of the Irish mainland, so he begged her for one of the donkeys to ride back to his home for a single glance at what he had left behind. Though she knew the risk, she loved him too much to deny his wish, and so he left on a quiet night, his promise to come back to her cutting her ears with salt and bitterness. She watched him depart on a land bridge that arced to the mainland and then turned back to her cottage, knowing his fate, knowing that love must always have its own island. She raised up the fog from the ocean and she extinguished all light from the island and the chickens went mute and the donkeys brayed into the chimney smoke and the gulls called out her anguish.

After many days of travel, and through no fault of his own, he touched ground and became an old man in one breath. Even as age claimed him upon the instant of his foot striking the soil, he called to her to save him, but she could not help him any longer. In the seasons afterward, on certain full moon nights, she permitted the island to rise from the mist and to appear to him, or to any broken-hearted lover, the boil of the sea stilled for an unbearable glimpse of what had been lost so thoughtlessly. To his great age he lived for the moments when he might hear her voice rising above the sea, the call of their bed and their nights and their love, the call of his heart, the call of the gulls that held all the pain of the world. He answered on each occasion that he was here, waiting, his heart true and never wavering, his days filled with regret for breaking their spell and leaving the island. He asked her to forgive him the restlessness, which is the curse of men and the blood they cannot still, but whether she did or not, he could not say.

Part 1

———

DINGLE

FIRST LETTER

To: Dr. Fowler/Dissertation committee
From: Kate Moreton
Subject: teaching release, spring semester

Dear Dr. Fowler:

As we discussed, I am taking leave of my teaching responsibilities
for the spring semester, 2019. Dean Howell has already given her
permission and the attendant paperwork is attached. Please feel free
to contact me with any questions.

I am using the Brady Milsap Scholarship monies—awarded by
the Dartmouth Alumni Association—to fund a research trip to
Ireland, and, specifically, to the Blasket Islands off the southwest
coast of Ireland. My dissertation, as you know better than anyone
else, centers on the narratives of the Blasket Islanders and their
emigration from the Blaskets to the United States. I hope to gather as
many narratives as I can, including all those already published, and
compile the definitive anthology and bibliography of oral accounts
of the islanders' relocation to the Springfield/Chicopee areas of
Massachusetts. As you know from my proposal, the island is now
abandoned except for a tourist cafeteria to handle summer visitors
who come to explore the remnants of the original village. The Irish
Land Commission ordered the island vacated, and by 1953, this

community of twenty-two people and their furniture were transferred over the sound to four newly built cottages at Dunquin with three acres of arable land attached.

To the extent that it is possible, I hope to compare and contrast the narratives of those former Irish citizens who, in the middle of the twentieth century, found themselves living in a new land in America. It's an ambitious project, and I could not have undertaken it without your endorsement. I will be housed, for at least part of my time in Ireland, at the University of Limerick.

The citizens of the Blasket Islands represent, to many linguists, the purest, and oldest, Irish language constructions. My travel will inform my research and I cannot imagine finishing my dissertation without having this experience. I regret leaving the classroom, but I am energized by the scholarship that awaits me. I grew up in the Springfield/Chicopee region of Massachusetts, and I have long been fascinated by this population. It has been a lifelong dream to travel to Ireland to further my research and interest. It is a part of my heritage.

Thanks to you and the members of the dissertation committee for encouraging me in this regard. I appreciate the letters of recommendation committee members sent on my behalf to the Brady Milsap Alumni Scholarship Fund. I am confident my research will prove invaluable in fleshing out my dissertation and will, perhaps, make a small contribution to our understanding of the Blasket Island populations.

Respectfully submitted,
Kate Moreton

1

I had misgivings: it was a tourist bus. As much as I didn't want to admit it, I had booked passage on a tourist bus. It wasn't even a good kind of tourist bus, if there is such a thing. It was a massive, absurd mountain of a machine, blue and white, with a front grill the size of a baseball backstop. When the tour director—a competent, harried woman named Rosie—pointed me toward it with the corner of her clipboard, I tried to imagine there was some mistake. The idea that the place I had studied for years, the Blasket Islands off Ireland's southwest coast, could be approached by such a vehicle, seemed sacrilegious. The fierce Irish women in my dissertation would not have known what to say about a bus with televisions, tinted windows, air-conditioning, bathrooms, and a soundtrack playing a loop of sentimental Irish music featuring "Galway Bay" and "Danny Boy." Especially "Danny Boy." It was like driving through the Louvre on a motor scooter. It didn't even seem possible that the bus could fit the small, twisty roads of Dingle.

I took a deep breath and climbed aboard. My backpack whacked against the door.

Immediately I experienced *that* bus moment. Anyone who has ever taken a bus has experienced it. You step up and look around and you are searching for seats, but most of them are taken, and the bus is somewhat dimmer than the outside light, and the seat backs cover almost everything except the eyes and foreheads of the seated passengers. Most of them try to avoid your eyes because they don't want you sitting next to them, but they are aware, also, that there are only so many seats, so if they are going to surrender the place next to them they would prefer it be to someone who looks at least marginally sane. Meanwhile, I tried to see over the seat backs to vacant places, also assessing who might be a decent, more or less silent traveling companion, while also determining who seemed too eager to have me beside her or him. I wanted to avoid that person at all costs.

That bus moment.

I also felt exhausted. I was exhausted from the Boston-Limerick flight, tired in the way only airports and plane air can make you feel. Like old, stale bread. Like bread left out to dry itself into turkey stuffing.

I felt, too, a little like crying.

Not now, I told myself. Then I started forward.

The passengers were old. My best friend, Milly, would have said that it wasn't a polite thing to say or think, but I couldn't help it. With only their heads extending above the seat backs, they looked like a field of dandelion puffs. They smiled and made small talk with one another, clearly happy to be on vacation, and often they looked up and nodded to me. I could have been their granddaughter and that was okay with them. They liked "Danny Boy." They liked coming to Ireland; many of them had relatives here, I was certain. This was a homecoming of sorts, and I couldn't be crabby about that, so I braced myself going down the aisle, my eyes doing the bus scan, which meant looking without staring, hoping without wishing.

Halfway down the bus, I came to an empty seat. Two empty seats. It didn't seem possible. I stopped and tried not to swing around and hit anyone with my backpack. Rosie hadn't boarded the bus; I could see the driver standing outside, a cup of coffee in one hand, a cigarette in the other. Two empty seats? It felt like a trap. It felt too good to be true.

"Back here, dear," an older man called to me. "There's a spot here. That seat is reserved. I don't think you can sit there. At least no one has."

I considered trying my luck, plunking down and waiting for whatever might happen. Then again, that could land me in an even more horrible situation. The older gentleman who called to me looked sane and reasonably groomed. I could do worse. I smiled and hoisted my backpack and clunked down the aisle, hammering both sides until people raised their hands to fend me away.

"Here, I'll just store this above us," said the old man who had offered me a seat. He had the bin open above our spot. He shoved a mushroom-colored raincoat inside it. He smiled at me. He had a moustache as wide as a Band-Aid across his top lip.

I inched my way down the aisle until I stood beside him.

"Gerry," he said, holding out his hand. "What luck for me. I get to sit next to a beautiful, red-haired colleen. What's your name?"

"Kate," I said.

"That's a good Irish name. Are you Irish?"

"American, but yes. Irish ancestry."

"So am I. I believe everyone on the bus has some connection to the old sod. I'd put money on it."

He won a point for the first mention of the *old sod* that I had heard since landing in Ireland four hours before.

He helped me swing my bag up into the bin. Then I remembered I needed my books and I had to swing the backpack down again. As I dug through the bag, Gerry beside me, I felt the miles of traveling clinging to me. How strange to wake up in Boston and end up on a bus going to Dingle, the most beautiful peninsula in the world.

2

"How Irish are you?" Gerry asked when we had settled in our seats. "I find there is such variety in the attachments people have to Ireland. American people, I mean. Well, I suppose anyone. I've always thought Ireland is the earth's bedtime story, so to speak. It's hard to put it into words."

"My family is from Ireland. Both sides, actually. I guess I'm about fourth-generation."

"Second-generation for me. Of course, I'm a good bit older than you. Where are you from in the States?"

"I grew up in Springfield, Mass."

"I'm a Chicago man myself. Born and raised. Well, I'm very pleased to be sitting next to you. What fun! You know, my wife died last year, and people say, Gerry, how can you go traveling all by yourself? But I say, on the contrary, it's just the thing. Traveling by yourself you have to meet people. You have to be outgoing, otherwise what's the point of it all? I bet you agree."

It was going to be a long trip, I realized. A very Gerry day. I wondered if I hadn't made a terrible mistake by sitting next to him.

Before I could reply to his last statement, a low whining sound filled the bus. Rosie suddenly appeared near the driver's seat and hurried down the aisle. She had to turn sideways and people tried to ask her questions on the fly, but she held up a finger to delay them. The whining sound grew louder. Then a pair of doors opened in the center of the bus and I realized the whining sound came from a wheelchair being lifted into the coach. The person in the wheelchair was a very, very old woman. She nodded back and forth when the seat came to a stop. She wore a beautiful red boiled-wool jacket and gray trousers. She wore slippers on her feet, but they were stylish and purposeful. She had an exceedingly kind face. Clearly, she felt apologetic for making us all wait while she was loaded onto the bus. A male nurse came up the lift with her. When the lift settled, he supported the old woman from behind as she shuffled painfully forward. He guided her to the seat that I had left empty, with Rosie assenting, saying, *Yes, yes, that's right, there's a darling.* The old woman sat slowly, almost as if she might shatter from sheer hollowness. The nurse spent a few minutes tucking a plaid blanket over her legs and then the nurse handed to Rosie a tote bag filled with articles obviously intended for the elderly woman. Rosie put them on the seat beside the old woman. Then the nurse rode the lift back down.

"I knew that seat was reserved for a reason," Gerry said, nodding as if confirming something important. "Precious cargo."

"Do you know her?"

"Never seen her. She looks like a grand lady, though. Not a tourist, I don't think."

"No, not a tourist," I agreed.

Her eyes had flickered on mine in passing. And while I had boarded the bus and tried to keep my eyes from expressing anything, she had sent her vision into the world to see where a new friend might be waiting. Willing to be a friend, she saw friends everywhere.

People tell you Ireland is green, but they're wrong. It's blue and purple and white and sheep and stone and cloud and sea and sand and a green that can't quite be true. All of that. I looked out the window, my forehead pressed to the glass, my mind empty. Gerry had insisted I take the window seat. He said it would be wasted on him because he tended to fall asleep on bus rides and he could do that in an aisle seat as easily as by the window. It turned out he was as good as his word; he fell asleep before the bus had reached full speed. He snored, but not horribly. Sometimes he made a sound like the suck hose at the dentist's office.

I considered reading, but I didn't think I could concentrate at the moment. I thought about Milly, my best friend and closest neighbor back in the States. I thought about the tidy little apartment I had lived in for two years. I missed it all. I missed the Dartmouth campus, where I taught and worked on my dissertation, and New Hampshire, and maple syrup, and wood smoke. As much as I yearned to know and understand Ireland, and as much as I appreciated the fellowship that had brought me as a visiting scholar to the University of Limerick, I missed the life I had known and made for myself. I felt alone. Not good alone, necessarily, but stretched-out alone, empty alone.

Almost by magic, my phone buzzed. I had it on vibrate. When I pulled it out, I saw Milly's number and a tiny picture of her smiling at a parakeet. The parakeet was named Buster Maximus. He was the fourth Buster she had had for a pet.

"Hi, Milly," I whispered. "I'm on a bus. I can't really talk."

"What?"

"I'm on a bus."

I stood and squeezed past Gerry. He smiled and nodded and then went back to sleep. He was good at sleep. I went to the back of the bus and stood between the two bathroom doors. It was not the greatest place in the world to stand, but I didn't feel comfortable talking next to Gerry. Milly had some Eva Cassidy on her stereo system. She loved Eva Cassidy and listened to it whenever she worked on her sculptures.

"Can you hear me now?" Milly asked. "I can barely hear you."

"I'm on a bus, Mill. Going down to Dingle. Funny, though, I was just thinking of you. How are you? Is everything okay?"

"That should be a song. Going down to Dingle. It sounds dirty."

"I'm on a tourist bus. It's enormous."

"Tell me what you're seeing."

"Right now I'm seeing two bathrooms," I said, but then I took a deep breath. I was Milly's space mission, the probe sent from her earth to send back photos of the planets and asteroids that I passed. She loved stories, loved details, loved anecdotes about anything unusual. I was too tired to be inspired, but I made myself level out. "It's beautiful, though, Mill. It's pretty much how you pictured it. It's how everyone has pictured it. The guy I'm sitting next to says Ireland is the world's bedtime story."

"Is he cute?"

"He's seventy, Mill."

"You're going to the islands today?"

"To Dingle, but I'll probably be able to see them."

"That's so exciting. Take a million pictures. Do you promise? You're so bad about taking pictures."

"You know I don't like technology, Mill, but I'll do my best. How are you doing?"

"Fine, sweetheart. Don't worry about me. I'm fit as a fiddle."

"I do worry about you, Mill. You can't tell me not to worry."

"Well, not to worry so much then. I'm fine."

"Milly, let me call you later. Or maybe tomorrow, okay? Then I can tell you what I saw. Maybe we can Skype if I can figure out how to work the stupid thing."

"Okay, Katie, go enjoy. You're my little Irish traveler. My little Irish colleen."

"That's what Gerry called me. I must look the part. Love you."

"Who is Gerry?"

"The guy, the old man sitting near me."

"Got you."

She said she loved me back. I clicked off the phone. Before I could put it away and sneak past Gerry to resume my place, I saw the old woman standing near her seat. It was a mismatch; the bus was too big and she was too small. She looked frightened and unsteady and unsure of where she needed to go or what she hoped to do. No one seemed to be paying any attention to her. Maybe, like Gerry, the other dandelions were sleeping.

I walked carefully up the aisle and stood silently until she turned and saw me.

"Do you need a hand?" I said when I reached her.

"You don't mind? We are such a bother, we old folks."

"Not at all. Happy to help."

"I need to use the ladies'. I'm sorry to impose. My name is Nora, but most people call me Gran."

"Not at all. Tell me the best way to go about it. My name is Kate."

She was a charming, dear bird. Old people can become softer and kinder, or harder and grumpier. She was the soft kind. She smiled at me; she had beautiful blue eyes—soft and translucent as smoke—that held something about her childhood in them. A childhood of laughter. She possessed the Irish twinkle so many people spoke about. I had made an accurate appraisal of her earlier: she looked to find friends wherever she went. She reached out her hand and grasped my wrist. Her hand had little strength.

She told me to brace her from the front. I held her under her tiny elbows, walking backward through the aisle. She used the seat backs to steady herself. I backed down the aisle and paused by the bathroom door. The one on the left was available. I held the door open.

"I'm afraid I need a hand inside as well. I am embarrassed to ask it. I thought I was all set for the journey."

I wasn't prepared for that request, but I nodded and said of course.

"What a way to get to know someone," Gran said, touching my wrist again. "Well, into the breach. Nature is master of us all."

It wasn't easy to navigate, but we managed. The bathroom was absurdly small. When I had Gran straightened out, she thanked me again and when I got her back to her seat she invited me to tea the next time fortune would bring us together. She said she lived in Limerick part of the year. She had married an Irishman and had lived half her life in Ireland, the other half in Manhattan.

"Promise me you'll visit for tea," she said and insisted I take a small, ivory card that she dug from the pocket of her jacket. "Are you here for long?"

"Six months."

"Well, then, it's settled. Have you been to Dingle before, my dear?"

"No, this is my first time."

"Well, you look as if you could have been born here. Where did you grow up?"

"Springfield, Massachusetts."

She regarded me carefully. Then she nodded.

"Yes," she said, "that explains it."

Then she whispered a phrase in Irish.

"Doors lead to doors," she said, which was a phrase I took to mean it was a small world.

"And an open door has two sides," I returned in Irish.

She looked at me and smiled. She patted my hand. Then I returned to my seat.

3

So now I had two friends on the bus. Gerry woke when I took my seat again. He rubbed his eyes and stifled a large yawn. Then he leaned a little toward me and looked out. Whatever he expected to see seemed to conform with what his eyes discovered. He sat back. He dug a tin of Altoids out of his pocket and offered them to me. I took one. He shook the tin.

"Take another," he said.

I wondered if I had bad breath, but I thought it more likely that he was simply being generous. He took four and popped them in his mouth. They were the cinnamon kind that burned your tongue.

"Now, are you here as a tourist or . . . ?"

He let the ending of his sentence hang so I couldn't ignore it.

"I'm a doctoral candidate at Dartmouth. In New Hampshire. I'm studying women's narratives from the Blasket Islands."

"How fascinating. I've only read Tomás O'Crohan's *The Islandman*. A friend recommended it to me and I loved it. Have you read it?"

I nodded.

"I'm not usually a reader," Gerry continued. "Not like some people. I taught middle school algebra for thirty-seven years, so I tend to stick to measurable facts. But I like a good story. I liked reading about the way life used to be on the island. I wanted to read it before I came to Ireland."

"It's a wonderful story."

"It's tragic, too, of course. Very tragic. They lost an entire way of life when the Irish government moved the Blasket Islanders off their land. Is that your area of study?"

"My father's people lived on the Blaskets."

He leaned back a little to appraise me.

"Oh, I see. But you didn't grow up here."

"Many of the people from the Blaskets moved to Springfield. My father was a fireman as his father was before him."

"I'm starting to understand you now. This is a personal interest as well as a scholarly one, we should say."

I nodded. Gerry had it right. Not everyone I met understood my area of study, but Gerry comprehended it at once.

"Do you speak Irish? I can't quite get the hang of saying *Irish*. It was always *Gaelic* when I was growing up."

"Yes, I do. It was a family language. I'm not fluent by any means. But my father spoke it with his people. Many people in Springfield spoke it. I've studied it."

"Is your father still alive?"

"No, I'm afraid not."

Gerry patted my arm. The cinnamon mints burned the top of my mouth. The bus suddenly gave a wheeze and pulled into a small parking lot. We had only been underway for an hour and a half, if that. Rosie grabbed the mic at the front of the bus. She pointed to her right, up a green, steep hill, at a series of stone huts. The huts, she said, had been built as primitive shelters long before memory. They were laid up without mortar. She said historians and paleontologists held various theories about the exact origins of the people who inhabited the huts. We had a half hour, she said, to explore the site. Restrooms and coffee were available at a small canteen built into the side of the mountain. She said the driver would jingle a bell when our time was up. She said to be careful walking because the morning dew could make the steps slippery.

I was glad for the chance to get off the bus, but given the age and mobility of the passengers, it did not happen quickly. Gran did not bother disembarking. I smiled at her as I passed. Gran smiled back.

"Do you need anything?" I asked when I was almost past her.

She shook her head. I smiled and followed the slow, orderly line of dandelions filing off the bus. I felt tired to the bone. I realized, as I shuffled forward, that I had miscalculated my itinerary. Any halfway intelligent human being would have stayed a day or two in Limerick, got themselves situated; then, when they felt less exhausted, they would book a trip down to Dingle and the cliffs looking out to the Blaskets. But not me. Even after Milly had suggested exactly that course of action, I had assured her that I knew better.

I'll be fine, I told her. *I want to get to see them as soon as I can.*

That much remained true. But when I stepped off the bus into the misty morning light, I realized I had overestimated my stamina. The last step onto the ground nearly tripped me. I caught myself easily, but at the same time I realized I had a dozen loose ends ahead of me. I still had not booked a place (*I'll find one, relax, B&Bs are all over Ireland*) and did not honestly know where I was going. I knew the town and location names; they had been imprinted on me forever. Yet knowing a name, and knowing what it is to stand on a foreign land, tired and wrung out from travel, is a different thing altogether.

Maybe that was why I began to cry. I blamed it on fatigue. But what caught me unawares was the simple beauty of the *clochán,* or beehive huts, that stood just twenty yards up the hill beyond the bus. The *clochán* were simple stone structures, primitive yet beautiful. Behind me the sea spread like a blue bib around the neck of the land and sheep, hundreds, thousands, moved like clouds fallen to land across the green acres that sloped to the sea—yes, a cliché, but how could I not resort to cliché?—and the stone huts of the ancients, the Irish before the Irish, stood quietly and waited for our inspection. I cried because here, almost magically, the land that I had studied, the stories that I had been told from the knee, now began to come true. For practical purposes, I should have stayed in Limerick to compose myself, but instead I stood at the beginning of all Ireland, in a way, and the work of their hands still caught the sea air and morning mist.

"No mortar, can you believe it?" someone—a man in a tweed cap—said beside me. "Can you believe that? And still standing? For six thousand years, they've given shelter to the island's inhabitants."

"Amazing," a woman beside him breathed.

"Makes you think, doesn't it?"

The woman nodded. I climbed higher to get closer to the *clochán*. It turned out Rosie was correct about one thing: the morning dew turned the steps slippery, and I clung to the railing as I climbed, the only passenger from the bus who bothered to test her legs.

When I reached the first level, I felt a jumble of ridiculous emotions. Call it too much travel in too short a span, but I felt emotional when I turned to see the Irish landscape spread before me. The sea sent its air up from below and the hills met it with a chill of their own. My hair blew in the wind, and it was not difficult to imagine other women, women through the ages, standing here to watch the day break on the land or their livestock mowing the green grass or the men plying their boats below. I felt a swell of gratitude that I been permitted to come to Ireland, that I had time in front of me to study the people dearest to me, that the stones of the *clochán* still stood true and proper after all these decades.

At the first hut, I put my hand on the stones and felt them. They were unexceptional stone, thick as dictionaries. Still, I liked putting my hand on them. I looked back around me to make sure no one had followed me, then I closed my eyes and whispered a poem that my father had taught me long ago as he put me to bed. I recited it in the Irish, the old language.

"Bless those minding cattle / And those minding sheep, and those fishing the sea / While the rest of us sleep."

A few moments later the bus bell jingled and called us back. But now at least I knew why I had not stayed in Limerick and grown comfortable. I wanted to be raw and open to this land. I removed my hand from the stones and walked carefully down to the dandelions who stood in a clump at the door of the bus.

4

I slept for part of the remaining ride. But it was an uneasy sleep, peppered with a hundred emotions. I woke frequently to see the landscape passing by, and several times I had difficulty remembering it was not a dream at all, but that I was on a bus traveling to Dingle. Above me I saw fields that had not been replanted since the potato famine of 1845; I saw more beehive huts beside random spears of stone stuck into the hillside as if in defiance of nature. When we rounded Slea Head, the most western point in Europe, Gerry said to me, "The next parish over is Boston." I smiled and nodded and fell asleep, and I didn't wake again until we pulled into Dingle proper, the streets closing on us, a misty rain shutting off the sun and making the village quiet.

"Here we are," Gerry whispered to me. His breath smelled of more cinnamon.

I sat up and rubbed my eyes. The whining sound of the lift being raised filled the coach. The dandelions now stood, most of them opening the bins above them. Rosie came on the public-address system and began talking about lunch, room accommodations, and the attractions Dingle afforded.

"Are you staying here with us?" Gerry asked. He was, I realized, the kind of fellow who waited while others disembarked. It wasn't a bad tactic, but I felt eager to get off, to find a place to stay, to eat a bowl of soup.

"No, I couldn't afford it."

"B&B, then?"

"That's the plan."

"I looked into that myself. I've heard good things about St. Joseph's. It's run by a woman named Mary something or other. Well, of course, it would be Mary, wouldn't it?"

"Thank you. I'm sure I'll find a spot. It's off-season, at least."

Finally we had room to stand. Gran, I saw, had already been off-loaded. I leaned over to see what had become of her, but she had apparently drifted off into the mist. Maybe she was a fairy woman. I would have been more curious if I had not been exhausted.

It took a while, but finally I found myself standing on Dingle soil, my backpack a weight behind me, Gerry shaking my hand.

"Good luck," he said. "It was a pleasure meeting you."

"Likewise. Have a great trip."

"That's my plan," he said, referring back obscurely to the statement I had made a few minutes before. It took me a moment to get it, then I nodded and walked away.

I am here, my whisper said.

I could have wished for a better day, however. Rain fell in a slant, sea-driven and salty. I heard Milly in my head saying something about misty rain being good for my complexion. But it didn't feel that way. It felt wet and cold and I wondered again why I had not been more attentive to details. I should have made a reservation. I should have been walking toward my rest. Something a little reckless had made me travel freelance. It wasn't my typical behavior. I tended to be orderly, or at least levelheaded. Maybe, I thought, Ireland afforded me a chance to indulge fortune in my life.

I stopped in Foxy John's, a lovely pub that doubled, during the day, as a hardware store. It was not a destination; it simply rose up before me and the thought of a cup of tea seemed the perfect thing to ward off the wet. I thought, too, that I could get directions to St. Joseph's B&B, or at least ask the proprietor for a recommendation. It was off-season, October, and the town looked quiet and settled on its shoulders.

"You'll not do better than St. Joseph's," the bartender, a stout Irishman with a handlebar moustache, told me when he delivered my tea. "Would you like me to call ahead for you?"

"Would you do that?"

"Why wouldn't I? I've known Mary Langley these past fifty years. I'll give her a jingle. Shouldn't be a problem."

I sat beside my first peat fire. It could not have been more welcome. I did not feel any less exhausted, but my fatigue had transformed into a thin line of static electricity that seemed to spark and sputter inside my head. It almost felt enjoyable, like being slightly dizzy on wine. The tea was excellent. It tasted darker and richer than the tea I drank at home. For pleasure, I put a dot of cream in it as well. The cream blossomed in what my father called *cows' lungs* of white. I had no idea where he got such a term, but it felt appropriate in this setting.

Before I had finished half my cup, the bartender returned with news that I was welcome at St. Joseph's and expected whenever I came free of the fire. I thanked the bartender and nearly asked him to sit with me, but he seemed to have things to do and I relished the moment to gather myself.

I texted Milly.

> *Sitting in a tavern called Foxy John's. More Irish than you can imagine. Almost settled for the night. I am sending you a picture.*

I turned the camera around and snapped a few photos of the interior. I also leaned close to the peat fire. It smelled of soil and dampness and something else, something elusive and hard to name. Fire and heat, of course. I knew fire from New Hampshire, but this had a different cloudiness, a mood to go along with its warmth. I decided I liked peat fires and promised myself I would sit beside them whenever possible.

I sent the pictures to Milly, then slipped my phone back into my pocket and finished my tea.

5

I woke to the sound of a curved knuckle tapping on my door. To my surprise, I didn't feel the typical dislocation. I knew exactly where I was, and I knew exactly who had knocked.

"Kate," Mrs. Fox said. "I'll be putting breakfast away in thirty minutes. I thought I should inform you."

"Yes, Mrs. Fox, I'll be there."

"I'll hold the tea, then."

Mrs. Fox reminded me not so much of a fox, but rather of a badger, one I had seen once in a childhood book. A chubby, fleshy woman, she had met me at the door of the St. Joseph's bed and breakfast with a great gust of welcome. She had dark hair set in some sort of permanent wave and a crisp way of slashing her hands against the air when she spoke. Mrs. Langley, the inn's owner, was in Italy, she told me, so she, Mrs. Fox, would do for me. Mrs. Fox had shown me to the room, asking at my back if it was satisfactory. It was satisfactory, but not a great deal more. It came with my own bathroom and a window looking out on a backyard where a bird feeder hung askew from a clothesline. It was clean and tidy, and the truth was I would have slept on the floor if that had been my option. The bed, however, had been downy and good, and I slept like two stones under the earth—another of my father's sayings—and stayed under dreamlessly until the knuckle had tapped on my door. I had slept nearly half-way around the clock.

But I was hungry. Sharply so. I washed quickly, patted my hair into the semblance of an electrocuted cat, then bent to the mirror for a closer look. Yes, I looked like an Irish colleen. That was impossible to refute. But my face was narrow and angular, with sharp cheeks that guarded blue eyes. Years ago a boy in my elementary class said I looked like a happy eraser, and whenever I examined my own appearance, the phrase came back to me. No, I reflected, I was not a happy eraser, but he had gotten at something by the phrase. My redness made me smear at the edges as if I joined with the world too easily. I was the mild, flesh-colored crayon in the crayon box. My coloring was a lie, really, because I was definite in my views and opinions. I resembled my grandmother on my father's side. I would have looked at home in a Victorian gown, high-necked and flowing, so that sometimes, wearing jeans and a fleece, I felt like a time traveler.

I blew a stream of air up at my curly hair in exasperation, then tiptoed down the long hallway that led to the best smells within a hundred miles. Mrs. Fox stuck her head out of the kitchen and told me to sit in the guests' dining room, explained that the tea—did I take tea or coffee?—well, the tea was there and I just needed to lift up the cozy. The other lodgers, the Helmootes, a German couple, had already gone out for the day. She was sorry to wake me, needing sleep as I obviously did, but the rules of the inn shut breakfast down at nine thirty and she didn't like to go against Mrs. Langley's orders.

"I appreciate you holding it for me," I said, sitting slowly at a darling tea table. "I'm sorry I slept so long. That bed is magic."

"Irish air," Mrs. Fox called, ducking back in to rattle at something on the stove. "How do you like your eggs?"

"Oh, any way."

"Any way is no way, how, then?"

"Scrambled, I suppose."

More rattling. I sipped my tea and buttered a beautiful scone. Blackberry, I thought. The butter had the yellow coloring of a sunset. I smiled seeing it. My father always purchased Irish butter, his single extravagance, and he claimed he ate his homeland one slice at a time. American butter, he swore, was a mewling, bony-looking paste that a decent cut of bread should reject.

"Here we are," Mrs. Fox said, weaving into the small sitting room with a tray before her. "Eggs and bacon. You have potatoes on the table and scones . . . yes, you've found them. Well, make your breakfast. You're likely famished from travel."

"I am hungry. Thank you."

"And please make sure you sign the guest book. It's Mrs. Langley's passion, trust me. She'll take my hide if I don't have everyone sign."

"I will. Right after breakfast."

"Oh, I nearly forgot," Mrs. Fox said, taking a step back from the turn she had made to leave. "Mrs. Nora Crean rang up. She is going to call for you at ten thirty. I told her you were still asleep."

"Mrs. Crean?"

"She said you would know her as Gran. Everyone knows her, of course."

I paused with the scone halfway to my mouth. How strange it felt to be receiving a message from someone whom I had met so recently, and so briefly. I didn't like it. I had nothing against seeing Gran again, but not on the first morning in Ireland. Not now, not here, not when I had just arrived. All I had managed the afternoon and night before was a brief walk around the town, my main objective to stay awake long enough so that I could go to bed in good conscience. Now I wanted time alone to read and to write and to plan about how I should approach my research in the area. Gran's visit upended all that, but I was aware that Mrs. Fox saw nothing unusual in our meeting.

"Did she leave a number where I could reach her?" I asked, thinking I could cancel the appointment.

"No, I dare say she didn't."

"I'm not sure I'm ready . . ."

"I understand."

"How did she even know where I was?"

"Now that's easier to solve. Nobody comes to Dingle in Oc-tober, after the tourist season, and minds his own business. That I can promise you. If you sneeze three people will offer you a hankie."

Mrs. Fox flexed her badger eyebrows and returned to the kitchen. I shoved the scone into my mouth, annoyed and tired and mostly needing a bath.

A portly man in a black suit came to fetch me. He climbed out of an enormous traveling car, an old-looking thing, and tick-tocked slowly up the stairs to the front door. He wore a chauffeur's cap, though the cap stayed back on his skull as if it could not quite decide to give its service to the wearer. His hair had been red once, but it now had faded into an autumnal wreath that circled his head up to the top of his ears. His face was kind; the crinkles near his eyes gathered in merry chevrons. It is impossible to be in Ireland without hoping to see a leprechaun, and this chauffeur did a serviceable job of playing the part. True, he would have been an older, somewhat wearier leprechaun than I had ever imagined, but his way and his tap on the door before he pushed it open led me to think we could not help liking each other.

"You must be Kate," he said. "I'm on an errand for Nora Crean."

"Gran?"

"Herself."

"Is she in the car?" I asked, going up on my toes to see over his shoulder.

"No, she's got a surprise for you. She wanted to make your first day in Ireland special."

"Thank you, I . . ."

It occurred to me that I was outmatched. How did she know

it was my first day? Had I mentioned it in our brief encounter? I felt gloomy suddenly. The entire point of traveling to Ireland revolved around following my own interests. I had nothing against Nora Crean, or Gran, but neither did I have a special desire to give over my day to her.

All of this passed through my mind in an instant. The chauffeur seemed content to allow me to stack the chips anyway I liked. I let out a long breath. He smiled. I asked his name.

"Seamus," he said.

"Of course it is."

"Will you be coming along, miss?"

"I don't even know if what I am wearing is appropriate. I only had a backpack full of clothes . . ."

"You'll be fine, I'm sure."

Who can resist a leprechaun? Even one as old and faded as Seamus seemed to be? I nodded. I left with a single bag. I followed him down the stairs of the B&B. He held open the automobile's back door for me. I climbed in and he shut the door softly. I looked around. It was vintage automobile, maybe from the 1950s. I was not great about cars.

"Seamus, what kind of car in this?" I asked when he settled behind the wheel. He removed his hat and set it on the dashboard.

"It's a Chrysler. A Plymouth Belvedere. They imported some through Britain and others they built in a factory in Dublin, miss. It was built in 1945 for a British diplomat. Nora Crean bought it at auction."

"It's beautiful. I've never been in a car like it."

"Automobile, miss. You don't want to insult the machine."

He started the engine. I sat back against the luxurious seat. Keep calm, I told myself. Unless I was being kidnapped, nothing too horrible could happen to me in such a car, especially as it was driven by Seamus. He puttered down the road, not topping thirty miles per hour. It was odd to see him on the right-hand side of the car and several times, in the first few minutes of the drive, I clutched at the seat to brace myself for impact.

The landscape took my gloominess away. I would never be able to resist the landscape, I reflected. In the morning light the grass held the last of the dew while the sheep—sheep lived everywhere—grazed and never lifted their heads. I suspected we were driving toward the sea. I took out my phone and tapped the screen to bring up the compass. The car traveled gently south and a little to the west. Just as Gerry had said, Boston lay in that direction.

At last we topped a small rise and the ocean glistened before us. I sat forward in my seat. Seamus did not increase the speed. Gulls called as we lost our slight elevation. I rolled down my window with a hand crank. The air that met me smelled of brine and sand and old rock. My heart lifted. Seamus saw my smile in the rearview mirror.

"Did you know your hair grows redder by the sea?" he asked. "It's true of all redheads."

"I hadn't known that."

"It's a fact. Some say hair like yours is made from leftover Christmas ribbon."

"I think you're full of nonsense, Seamus."

"Did your parents tell you nothing?"

I fell a little in love with Seamus.

And I fell in love with the tiny harbor we approached. *Daingean Uí Chúis*, in the old Irish.

My heart, I couldn't help thinking, had come home.

6

Seamus parked directly on the dock, not far from a number of fishing vessels moored against a wooden seawall. Gulls greeted us and increased their volume as soon as the engine turned off. I knew the rough history of Dingle. I knew that it had been a fishing village for centuries, and that boats from the Isle of Man had plowed the waters off its coast for mackerel. Later, the larger trawlers arrived for herring. But most of that was gone. Now the town fished for tourists, primarily, and the bait consisted of fifty-some-odd pubs offering Guinness and Murphy's Stout and fish and chips.

"Here we are, miss," Seamus said, reaching for his hat and propping it on his head.

"Is Gran here?"

"Down on the boat there. You'll see when you step out."

"Okay. Thank you for the ride."

I started to open the door, but Seamus scrambled out and opened it for me. He was a somewhat haphazard chauffeur. He reminded me of men unaccustomed to wearing suits who you sometimes met at weddings. They did their best, but the clothes never fit. They remained imposters of themselves.

Before he could direct me where to go, or what I should be looking for, he darted to the back of the automobile and opened the trunk. He pulled out a large wicker hamper and tucked it over the crook of his elbow. Then he nodded to me and told me to follow him. The hamper was heavy, apparently, because he stopped to switch elbows twice before we had gone a hundred feet.

The boat he led me to was not much to look at it. I supposed it was a fishing vessel; it reminded me of the lobster boats I knew from Maine. It was larger, though, than a typical lobster boat, with a curved bow that seemed to rise like a horse's neck out of the water. Its engine idled. A pearl-colored stream of smoke came out of a stack on the roof of the cabin. The deck of the boat—was it a ship or a boat, I wondered?—swept back to a wide stern. Across the stern I saw the vessel's name: *Ferriter.* It was a Blasket surname, I knew, but I couldn't place it immediately.

"Here we are," Seamus said, then called out into the wind, "Hello on board. Is there a man with breath aboard who could help an old man with a basket?"

No one answered. Seamus cursed under his tongue and used his chin to point to the ship's center.

"We can board here," he said.

"Can I help you with the basket?"

"No, no, I have it fine. I like to make sure Nora Crean values my labor."

"I understand."

"Step on board. They probably can't hear over the engine."

I did as I was told. The ship, however it was configured, was well cared for. Ropes and gear stood in neatly arranged piles. Someone had swept it recently, because a small pile of litter lay next to the broom leaning against the back gunwale. The sea around the boat sent small cackles of sunlight that flashed and blinded one.

"Here we are," Seamus said, pointing again with his chin to the cabin at the front of the boat. "Nora Crean waits for you there."

I tapped on the door and pushed through. Nora Crean sat at a small table, a steaming cup in front of her. She looked up and smiled. I was reminded again of the kindness of her face. She wore a heavy Irish sweater, a dense, dark-looking garment with a yoke of anchors across her chest. It looked warm and perfect on her. The tightness that had troubled her face at times on the bus had disappeared. Now she was at home, her expression seemed to say, and now she could be herself, not dependent on strangers or tourists to help her on her way.

"Hello, Kate," she said, but pronounced my name in the old Irish, *Ceit*. "Welcome. I'm sorry if I rooted you out too early, but I didn't want you to miss such a lovely morning. We have so few of them, you know?"

"Hello, Gran."

"Where would you like it?" Seamus asked, somewhat rudely, as he pushed through the door behind me. "Did you fix a lunch of bricks, Nora Crean?"

"What I fixed is my own business," she said. "If it's too heavy for you, we could hire a younger man to see to it."

"You'd find no man who would take this job. You can count on that."

"Did you have a restful night?" Gran asked me, ignoring Seamus's last dig. "Don't pay attention to Seamus. He wouldn't know he was alive if he couldn't complain about every turn of the earth. Now come and sit with me. Have you had your breakfast?"

"Yes, thank you."

"And you slept well?"

I nodded and slipped in beside her. She sat on a curved bench behind a table with a sort of liver-shaped top to take up less room. Before I could answer, our attention was diverted by Seamus lifting the enormous basket onto what looked like an engine cover. He steadied it and looked over at Gran. He raised his eyebrows.

"Do you have to wear that hat?" she asked him. "He wears it to embarrass me. He likes to call attention to his lower status, as he says. It makes him righteous and proud."

"I am a chauffeur."

"You are many things, Seamus, we can agree on that."

How had I ended up here? The day before I had been in Boston. Seamus backed away from the hamper. The boat moved hardly at all. To my surprise, he removed his hat and sat down beside me. I was now between them. I couldn't quite read the situation. I knew under their banter they held affection toward each other. But what did they want with me? Gran patted my hand.

"We thought you would enjoy a picnic on the island," Gran said. "If you have the time, I mean."

"On the Blaskets?"

She nodded.

"*An Blascaod Mór*," she said in the Irish. The Great Blasket Island.

Then instead of patting my hand, she took my hand in hers. The kindness in her eyes held me. As simply as that, I was going to the Blaskets.

Nearly as soon as she said it, I heard the sound of a rope being tossed onto the deck. A moment later, a second rope splattered onto the boat. Then someone stepped aboard, because I felt the back-right corner of the boat shift. The man—it was a man— shouted something to whoever remained on the dock. They spoke for a second, their voices loud and deep, and then the man who had stepped on board pushed through into the cabin.

He smelled like the sea, was my first thought. He brought the outside air into the cabin with him. It clung to the deep, heather-colored sweater he wore. He wore a ridiculous-looking hat, a baseball hat with ear flaps that didn't suit him at all, and a pair of canvas pants tucked into large rubber boots that climbed to his shins. I could not see him. By that I mean, he had come in too quickly, and the open door had brought in the brightness of the sea, so that momentarily I was blinded to anything above chest height. But an instant later I saw his face, a sharp, beautiful face that struck me as nearly too handsome for its own good. Some men know if they are handsome, but this one didn't seem to care or put any value on it. He had brown, soft hair under the cap, and an athlete's neck, broad and muscled, and his movements contained a compressed power and grace. His eyes were deep set; his chin had a square cut like the boat he stood on, trim and efficient as if it might cleave the water. He did not hesitate in any of his actions. He knew the boat and he knew his place on it and his large hands did not settle, but seemed to be in movement with a willingness to work. Even in his heavy boots, he seemed quick and fluid. A wrench stuck out of a pocket along his hip, and I saw where oil had clung to it and soiled the leg of his pants. Apparently, he had been working on the boat, or he done a necessary task somewhere with the wrench, because he tossed the tool casually into a wooden box set against the wall of the cabin. The wrench made a loud, metallic twang, which seemed to satisfy him. Then, free of the wrench, he wiped his hand against his sweater and stropped it, front and back, to get his fingers clean. Moving as he did, he looked like a teenaged girl's dream of a boyfriend, impossibly symmetrical, and it occurred to me he might, like a girl's dream pony, be sketched on a notebook or book cover almost in an incantation or spell to make it real. The teacher at the front of the class would believe the girl took notes, but meanwhile she drew a dream-boy, an impossible beauty that she had taken from fashion magazines or the pages of a story.

"This is my grandson, Ozzie," Gran said. "Ozzie, this is Kate."

He nodded. But that was all he did. No handshake, no full recognition. He went to the wheel of the ship and turned back to us.

"Are you ready?" he asked.

He directed the comment to Gran and Seamus. I was not included.

"Yes, if you are," Gran answered.

Evidently, this trip was not his idea. Evidently, taking an American girl on a picnic was not the day he had in mind.

For a while, no one spoke. Or rather, we spoke about how the boat needed to maneuver out of the small harbor and into the Blasket Sound. Mostly Seamus spoke to Ozzie. When the conversation became difficult to maintain over the engine sounds, Seamus rose and went to stand next to Ozzie. Ozzie was at least a foot taller than Seamus. Six-two or six-three, I guessed. Milly would approve, I knew. She thought every couple should be a salt and pepper shaker, with the girl-pepper being just a bit smaller than the boy-salt.

"He's cross that I asked this small favor of him," Gran said, her voice low to keep it obscured by the engine. "He'll get past it. He wanted to fish today, and instead he's taking us on a holiday."

"What does he fish for?"

"Mackerel. Depends on the season. It's not a thriving industry, but he likes it. He likes being on the boat alone. He was in a foul temper when I asked him to clean it up and take us for a ride."

"I hope I didn't . . ."

"No, no, no," she said and squeezed my hand. "It will do him good. He is too solitary. He was a soldier once. This does him a world of good."

"A soldier?"

"He's American, dear. As American as you are, although he has dual citizenship. He returned to Ireland only a little over a year ago. He served in the Navy. He was one of those exclusive ones."

"A Navy SEAL?"

"You'll have to ask him. I honestly don't know. It's the one benefit of growing older. We don't have to remember all the details. We're forgiven more than we should be."

"I'm sorry he feels put-upon."

"It's good for a man to be put-upon now and then. They have things their way too often. Besides, he's been slow coming back from the war."

About at that moment, we cleared the harbor and entered the open sea. Seamus turned to me and crooked his finger.

"You can see them now," he said, "come take a look."

I did. I deliberately stood on the side away from Ozzie, keeping Seamus between us. The islands appeared as dark spots on the horizon; a joke moustache painted across the lip of the sea. I knew from reading that the crossing could be rough. I also knew the Blasket Sound was famous for mist. It gave rise to myths and fairy tales of all sorts, and at times the islands themselves were thought to be merely a fantasy that came and went with the fog and sea air.

"It's true," Seamus said to me.

"The islands?"

"No, that your hair grew redder by the sea."

"You're an old flirt, Seamus."

"It's flirting that keeps me young."

Ozzie asked a question without looking in my direction.

"Where are you from?"

"Originally, Springfield, Mass. Now I live in Hanover, New Hampshire."

"Dartmouth?"

"Yes."

"And you're doing graduate work?"

"I am."

I wondered how he knew even that much. I tried to recollect if I had explained my presence to Gran, but I couldn't recall doing so. In any case, I didn't want to give him any strings to pull or worry. I was aware of him. I had been aware of him since he walked into the cabin. He was too good-looking not to notice. Obviously, we were about the same age. In addition to giving me a picnic on Great Blasket, Gran, I suspected, was playing match-maker. I could have saved her the trouble. I was on sabbatical when it came to men. The truth was, I was tired of the whole dating ritual. So when I spoke again, I tried to keep my language flat and orderly. We were acquaintances, I wanted him to know, and that's how we would remain.

"And you're a fisherman?"

Seamus went to sit back at the table.

"Some days I am."

"Mackerel?"

"Whatever swims."

He kept his eyes forward. His hat, truly, was ridiculous.

"Do you always wear that hat?" I couldn't help asking.

"You don't like it?"

"I'm not sure it likes itself. I see a lot of self-loathing in that hat."

"Is that so?"

"That hat needs therapy. Many sessions, in fact."

He turned his head. He had half a smile on his face.

"Gran said you had red hair."

"And that means I am ill-mannered and brash?"

"It means that your brain is on fire. It means that you have to speak through the smoke of it."

"That's a new one."

"You could be a seal. It means that, too. You're not to be trusted with small fish around. If you have the impulse to dive overboard, I wouldn't stop you."

"A selkie?"

He nodded. He was damn good-looking, I realized for the twentieth time. I had to resist the impulse to take his picture. Milly would want to see him. She would dissect him. But before

I could take a picture or say anything else, he raised his hand and pointed to the south.

"There's a whale," he said. "Do you see it?"

"What kind?"

"Oh, an Irish, magical whale. One that plays a banjo and sings."

"I'm an American who romanticizes Ireland, is that it?"

He turned and smiled. It was a mean, obnoxious smile, but I couldn't help smiling back.

"Not a realist like you," I said.

He smiled more.

By then the Blaskets had risen from the sea.

I reached out a hand and held on to what would be called the dashboard in a car. I didn't know what it would be called on a boat. For a long time, I didn't chance speaking. To his credit, Ozzie said nothing. *These are the Blasket Islands,* I told myself. How many times had I listened to stories about these islands? About the life there, the cottages roofed with felt and rushes, the chickens who lived in the rafters, clucking as if they prayed on behalf of the souls below? How many times had I heard described the trips to the height of the island where the sod could be cut and piled into squares so that they might melt and burn upon a hearth? Here was the taste of seal, I knew. Of mother-cod and gulls that careened sideways in the misty mornings. This was my father's land, and my land, and tears rose and I could not dare speak for fear all about me would guess my heart.

"An easy passage," Ozzie said to Gran and Seamus. "We must have a selkie aboard."

"Mind your manners, Ozzie," Gran scolded. "Bring us in slowly so she can see it as we know it to be."

"As you say, Gran."

He backed off the engines. The islands grew. I knew the

names as I knew the beads of a rosary: *Tiaracht* to the west, *Inis Tuaisceart* to the north, *Inis na Bró* and *Inis Icileain* to the south, and *Beiginis* nearest the mainland. The Great Blasket Island sat in the center, a continuation, geologically, of the Slieve Mish Mountains that ran down the center of the Dingle Peninsula. I felt myself choked with emotion. My father would have given anything to have stood where I now stood, but he was gone and dead four years in August. He had told me many stories of the passage between the island and Dingle, of the seas rising up to tip their hats as the boat plunged deep into the oncoming waves. Now we came slowly toward the land on placid seas. Ozzie nodded to Seamus and then left the cuddy. He climbed forward to ready the lines while Seamus took over the helm.

"You can pilot a boat?" I asked Seamus. "Should we fear for our lives?"

"I'm at home on water," he replied, watching Ozzie signal him to move starboard. "It's on the roads that I feel at sea."

"Did you live here once?"

"My father's father did. We might be kin, Katie. Half the people of Ireland are related to the other half."

"I'm happy to think of you as a cousin, Seamus."

"As distant as that?"

He smiled and moved his hand against the throttle. The boat swung around a large pier and suddenly we were ready to moor against the creosoted pilings. I had read about this small cove. Except for a white strand, *An Trá Bhán*, that ran away from it, it was the only place fit for landing a boat. The Blasket Islanders had fished from canoes called *naomhógs*, nimble crafts made doubly valuable because the Irish government could not tax them. But there were no *naomhógs* on this morning. The tiny harbor, if it could be called that, stood empty and still.

Ozzie jumped from the boat onto the small pier and tied her off. Seamus cut the engine. Nora spoke from behind the tiny table.

"We thought we'd have a picnic," she said. "I've asked Seamus and Ozzie to give you a tour. My legs won't let me tag along. But they know their history. Then when you're finished, perhaps you'll have a bite with me. The island isn't large, when all is said and done. You'll see the better part of it in an hour."

"Thank you. I'd love that."

"Which hat would you like me to wear, Nora?" Seamus asked. "What does the well-turned-out tour guide wear?"

"Be off with you, Seamus, and treat this young lady properly. She doesn't need your wagging tongue."

We climbed out the way we had climbed in. In a count of ten, I stood on the Blasket Islands for the first time.

7

The wind was everywhere. That was the first thing that struck me.

Gulls called and the sea broke, but otherwise everything was wind and silence. My hair pushed and pulled around my head and I had an odd moment of understanding why the actress in any old Irish movie spent a good deal of her time trying to keep her hair from her face. I did the same. Put an apron on me and send a man out to sea, and I could have fallen into the life among the quiet remnants that formed what used to be a village. It was ghostly, but not frightening. It felt more as if someone had thrown a party, a long, long party, and then, at the stroke of an appointed hour, all the guests had paraded from the rooms and banquet halls, leaving everything where they stood. Years had passed and the food had been consumed by birds and ants, the walls slicing away in winter gales, and only the round rocks of the foundations, mortared with a white paste of ground ash, remained to hold the secrets of what had passed. For all of that, the past felt near, felt as if it could be lifted, like a tent pole, and made to stand again. I had never experienced a sensation like it.

We walked for a time without talking. Seamus held his tongue, which was remarkable. Ozzie lagged behind, bored and likely tired of witnessing an American's wide-eyed wonder at the Blaskets. It turned out my friend Gerry from the bus had been correct: Ireland was the bedtime story the world told itself. It was, at least in my romantic mind, the place of rushes and wattle, of peat fires and canoes that struck out in terrible swells to hunt for mackerel and cod, chased seals into the caves around the island and killed them with bright harpoons. At Christmas, the families bled a sheep to death inside their cottages and made all manner of food from the animal, each cottage putting a candle in the window to guide the infant Jesus to the manger. Yet within the story, too, lived privation. Nearly anything of any luxury had to be carried across Blasket Sound on trawlers. The sick died without a doctor's attention if the sea worked against the village. Even marriages and burials waited on the tides to calm so that a priest might visit the small church and preside over the rites. A Blasket Islander lived on top of the sea, beside the sea, inside the sea. I felt its overwhelming presence before I had walked a quarter mile.

"It's a long way to come to see a graveyard," Ozzie said when we had cleared the pier. "All the way from America."

"Is it a graveyard? It doesn't feel that way to me."

"I wouldn't say it's a graveyard," Seamus said. "It's an empty dance hall, it seems to my mind."

"That's exactly how it felt to me," I told him. "Exactly."

"This life is gone," Ozzie said. "I bet they were glad to leave this island when the day finally arrived."

"You look as if you could step into one of these cottages and cook a proper cod stew, Katie," Seamus said, stopping to turn and throw a look at Ozzie. "Don't mind him. Unlike most Irishmen, he fancies himself a forward thinker. That's his American side. He should know we Irish live in the past as easily as the present. We're not even sure the past is gone to us."

"It brings everything to life," I said, my eyes casting everywhere to see the details of life on the island. "All my research. And my father's stories. I see now where they came from."

"The dead have things to tell us, whatever Ozzie thinks about the subject. You see now plainly enough that the island is mountainous, with little arable land. It couldn't support the population. I suppose we're all at peace with the government's decision to vacate the island, but you can't rid the land of what the people rubbed into it."

"Did anyone resist?"

"Oh, I imagine a few hung on, but it wasn't an easy life, now was it? No electricity, no running water, leaky roofs. And the smoke! One old gent, his name was Micheal Carney, did you know him, Ozzie?"

Ozzie shook his head. He wasn't being petulant, I saw. Maybe he wasn't bored, but felt, instead, the poignancy of the loss. He manifested the silence that some people exhibit in a church or synagogue or mosque. Perhaps, I realized, he wanted to be certain that I took the lives buried in the Blaskets' soil to heart as he did. If I were merely a nosy tourist, he seemed to suggest, then I could go hang. From what I could tell in his attitude, his verdict still teetered in the balance. He watched and waited and listened.

"Well," Seamus continued, "he died in his eighties and he lived his boyhood here. Right there by the schoolhouse. He told me once over a pint that the single worst thing about life in these cottages was the smoke. The chimneys never drew worth a penny. They were made of mud and daub, and you couldn't chase the smoke up the stack with a pitchfork. He said his people crouched like cavemen most of the time, all of them glimmering by the hazy firelight. He said his eyes continued to burn for five years after he left the island. People thought he was a drinker for his red eyes, but it was merely the smoke that turned them fiery."

"Maybe they should have brought electricity over for them," Ozzie said, a branch in his hand that he slapped against the stone foundations. "Maybe the government should have done something for them."

"There's some that think so, it's true. But it would have been carried through at great cost and all to the benefit of twenty souls? It made no practical sense. You know it yourself if you would take a step backward, Ozzie."

"Did Gran spend time here?"

"She did as a girl. She came to visit her grandmother during the summer season. She never lived here as you think of it. But she will fill your ears with stories if you care to listen. She is a great one for words."

Ozzie made a raspberry buzz with his lips. He produced the sound, I thought, to remind us all that Seamus was the talker not Gran. To save us from sorting it out, three donkeys suddenly appeared. They ambled down the main thoroughfare at their leisure. They were wild-looking creatures, with fur that collected in dreadlocks and whirls of weathered hair. They constituted the only permanent residents of the Blaskets remaining, I knew from my research.

"Beware the donkeys," Seamus said. "They have gone back to the wild. They'll bite you if you try to handle them."

"You're talking foolishness now," Ozzie said. "Those donkeys are as wild as I am."

"Why don't you try to jump on the back of one if you're so certain?" Seamus asked, obviously enjoying the prospect of seeing Ozzie bucked off the back of a donkey. "You can test how domestic they are easily enough."

Ozzie slapped the stick against the stone foundations again. We stepped back and watched the donkeys pass by. From the accounts I had read, donkeys played an important role in collecting sod for fires back in the day. They would be outfitted with panniers that held blocks of peat, both sides of the animals bulging with fuel. The women tended to that work, walking miles up into the highlands to bring back blocks of peat that they would burn to cook and heat. For light they burned scraws, or top-sods of turf, and sometimes the women harvested great sheaves of heather to boost the fire when the year came wet. They carried the heather on their backs and walked beneath the weight of the grasses.

"All Jacks," Seamus said when we resumed our tour. "If they brought Sallys onto the islands, the Jacks fought and shoved one another off the cliffs when the females came into season. It was a terrible business."

"Not much fun to be a donkey on *An Blascaod Mór*," Ozzie said, deadpan. "A bunch of monks living together."

"Not much fun to be a donkey anywhere," Seamus agreed. "As you know as well as anyone. Although I suppose it's better to be a donkey now than it was in the day. At least they're free. There was one a time back that became quite a celebrity. He was known as Bob Marley. He had his own fan club."

A pair of donkeys came past us, following the first group. I turned to watch them go, and in that moment, Ozzie leaped on the back of the one nearest to him. He did it lightly and landed without making the donkey break its stride. But the poor creature's posture changed in an instant. What had been a quiet, sleepy animal, suddenly felt attacked. It began bucking wildly, kicking its hind legs up and back. It made a terrifying braying sound, then began to run. The other donkeys shied to one side, and I caught a glimpse of Ozzie as he clung to the donkey's mane. Whether it was more than he had bargained for, I couldn't say. Delight touched his features and he looked thrilled and happy, his own impulsivity possibly rising up to surprise him. I wondered in the seconds it took to see the donkey jolt and stop, kick and paw, whether Ozzie had known a blink before that he had intended to mount the animal. It was possible, it seemed to me, that he had sprung onto the donkey out of a crazy notion, one not fully formed in his head. It was like the irresistible impulse to touch an electric horse fence: one knew better, but one did it anyway.

At the same time, I *saw* him for the first time. Of course, I had had glimpses of him before, but now he was unaware of what he revealed to the world, unware of who was near him, and he rode the donkey with an expression of genuine pleasure. He was too big for the animal, too physical, and yet they were evenly matched at least for a few rambunctious moments. The donkey's strength surged beneath him and rubbed Ozzie against a stone wall, trying to scrape him off. But then Ozzie put his hands on the animal's shoulders and vaulted off, cleanly escaping the donkey's thrashing hooves. Whatever else he was, I noted, he was a fine athlete. With his long arm and hand, he slapped the donkey on the rear end and sent it on the way.

"You next," he said to Seamus. "Just as I said, they're not a bit wild."

It was a perfect picnic. The sun came out to warm us. It was an October sun; the wind beneath it pestered the leaves and tucked the grass back to prepare for winter. We ate on the strand, the narrow beach that ran across the front of the island. As Seamus set up the table and toted the basket out to the beach, I wondered how Gran could navigate the walk. I needn't have worried. Ozzie swept her up and carried her easily. She did not protest or pretend she could manage it. He set her down at the head of the small table and fetched a blanket to cover her knees. Whatever else he was—and I was still deciding what to make of him—he was gentle and thoughtful toward his grandmother.

Seamus, despite his protesting against Gran's harsh rule, acquitted himself well as a butler. He laid out the food and opened a bottle of wine with admirable ease. The wind blew his hat off and he merely stood on it until he was ready to bend and pick it up. He popped the cork and gave us each a jelly jar full of excellent red wine. Then he sliced cheese and apples, placed them beside a swarm of grapes, and finished by cutting pieces of a baguette into clever rounds. As a final ingredient, he placed wedges of Italian sausage on a pale, bone-colored plate that I guessed he had selected for its beauty.

"Would you like me to cook a leg of lamb as well, Nora?" he asked when he stepped back from the table. "Or will this do for lunch?"

"It's very nice. Thank you, Seamus."

He bent to pick up his hat and put it back on his head. Then he sat down across from her and took a swallow of wine. Ozzie sat between them, and that left the fourth seat, directly across from him, for me.

"May I take a picture of you all?" I asked. "I'm horrible with these phones, but it's such a beautiful setting . . . and the meal looks so lovely . . ."

I found myself getting emotional.

"Let me take it," Ozzie said, standing to take my phone. "You sit here between these two old birds. We'll take it to commemorate your first meal on the Blaskets."

"Thank you."

In giving him my phone, our hands touched. It was such an insignificant contact, so casual and without meaning, that it stunned me to realize I blushed. *Absurd,* I told myself, but for the tiniest instant we stood close to each other, his body blocking the wind. A part of me realized I wanted a picture of him, too, so that I could send it to Milly to have her analysis. No one had sharper boy-antennae than Milly.

All of that passed in a rush. I handed him the phone. He took it and stepped back a half dozen paces. He bent down to adjust the angle while I sat at the table. Gran leaned to one side and Seamus inched over to make it easier to include him in the shot.

"Take the picture," Ozzie said into the phone. "Take three."

"Do you know—?" I asked, but he cut me off.

"Isn't it Siri who takes the photo?" he asked, looking at me over the phone.

"No, you have to push a button."

"I thought these phones could do it automatically."

"Do you have a phone?" I asked.

"I have *had* phones. I don't have one this minute."

"No, I meant, are you familiar with how phones work?"

"You speak to them, I thought."

"Take the blessed photo," Seamus said, reaching for his wine.

"Why don't I take one to show you?" I asked, rising.

"Siri," Ozzie said, "take a photo."

"It doesn't work like that, Ozzie," Gran said.

"I thought the point of these phones was to get Siri to help you."

"Sometimes," I said, hesitantly stepping around Gran's end of the table to go to him. "It depends."

The whole thing felt terribly awkward. I held out my hand. He smiled—and he did have a damn good smile—and handed me the phone. Our hands touched again. I took the phone and saw immediately that he had been joking. He had snapped four or five pictures, all of them candid because of his bluffing, and the business about Siri had been a ruse. He knew perfectly well how to take a photo with an iPhone.

Was he mean or merely devilish and playful? I wondered. I couldn't say for sure.

"I get you now," I told him, putting the phone away. "I see what you're about."

"Do you? It would help me to know what I'm about. Please tell me when you've made a full study. You're the Dartmouth grad student, after all."

"You Googled me," I said, finally putting it all together. "You researched me."

He blushed.

"No, you did!" I said. "You totally did. I'm flattered. And did I meet your expectation?"

"You're not as tall as I thought you'd be."

"But otherwise?"

He looked at me. I had the sense that he saw me for the first time. Truly saw me. Our eyes met. They did that ridiculous thing that men and women do with their eyes. Like stirring a can of paint with our vision; like looking for a match in the other's cornea.

"Come on now," Gran said mercifully. "Let's have our lunch."

"For once we agree, Nora Crean," Seamus said.

When Ozzie climbed back into his seat, I took a picture of the table. I would put Milly on his case. She would deconstruct his look, his clothes, his body posture. Nothing escaped Milly's attention once she focused on a subject.

A bit of a sea came up for our return journey. It was not threatening, but it lifted the bow of the boat and slammed it back down with many good, solid thwacks. Gran slept, her cheek on Seamus's shoulder. For his part, Seamus stared straight ahead, occasionally closing his eyes. I wondered about their relationship, but I thought it impolite to ask. I had never encountered a couple, if they were a couple at all, whose flow back and forth held such quick wind changes. I knew they shared a deep affection for one another; that shined through everything they did together.

I stood beside Ozzie, my hand out to steady myself as the boat went from crown to trough in each wave. I was grateful for the waves; they gave me a sense of what the islanders had experienced and how the sea had kept them isolated. I could not imagine taking to the rough passage in the traditional canoes they employed, with nothing to propel them except oars. At the same time, the motion of the boat made me slightly seasick. I had tried to remain seated, but somehow standing made the sickness more endurable. Looking through the window ahead, I gauged how long the passage might take and what the strength of each wave might be. It helped to occupy my mind.

For half the passage at least, we didn't speak. It was loud in the boat; the waves tossed foam at us and the wind pulled from the west. I had no feeling for Ozzie in those moments, good, bad, or indifferent. I was too intent on the condition of my stomach to give him much thought. But when we gained Dingle Bay the waves calmed and we moved forward in the lea created by Ireland herself. The *Ferriter* seemed to feel her work had been accomplished, and Ozzie moved the throttle back so that we might not be as jarred by the swells.

"There we are," he said, turning to face me in three-quarter fashion, his attention still keeping the waves in mind, "the great adventure is nearly done. It looks like you'll survive."

"Thank you. Thank you for taking me out to see the islands."

"It was just a hello. To get to know the islands, it takes a great deal more than that."

"Yes, I know that. I take the research seriously, if that's what you're wondering."

He looked at me full-faced and smiled.

"Sorry," he said. "I'm protective of the heritage around here."

"It must be terrible to have your American half at war with your Irish half."

"Oh, it's a great battle inside, believe me. If you put your ear against my chest, you'll hear gunfire."

"Are you sure it wouldn't be harps? How is it that you don't wear a tweed cap and have a bottle of whiskey somewhere easy to hand?"

"I have one," he said and reached forward to pull a bottle of Bushmills from a pile of greasy rags stored behind the wheel. The bottle was half full. "Would you like a drink? This is Irish water. You might as well get used to it."

"Sure, give me a drink," I said, although it was the last thing I wanted.

But I didn't want him to think of me as the prissy sort, an academic who lived on tea and overstuffed chairs. He handed me the bottle. I wasn't sure of the protocol, so I twisted off the cap, rubbed the mouth of the bottle, and took a drink. I had intended merely to sip, but a wave caught me in the middle of it and forced the bottle higher. I drank, my eyes burning.

"Do you know," he said when I passed the bottle back to him, "that if a man or woman drinks from the same bottle without wiping it first, it means they are going to make love? It's an old Irish custom."

"I thought it meant a man couldn't keep a set of glasses clean."

"That, too, of course."

He took a solid drink. He didn't wipe the neck of the bottle. His Adam's apple bobbed twice.

"And the tweed cap?" I asked.

"I have one somewhere, but I can't put my hands on it. Do you like Irish whiskey?"

"I do."

"Well, that's a point in your favor."

"Am I trying to win points? I didn't know we were playing a game."

"I think Gran wants us to play a game. She was born with a caul, you know? She's said to have second sight."

"Cauls were sold to sailors to keep them from drowning," I said, calling up what I knew about the subject. "They were talismans to defend against witchcraft."

"I'd need one on both counts, then."

"And they bring good luck. Are you lucky, Ozzie?"

"I met you, didn't I?"

"Are you sure that's luck?"

"That's to be determined, isn't it?" he asked. "You're different than I thought you'd be."

"And how did you think I'd be?"

"Oh, a rather stuffy American. An American who came to Ireland hoping to find a more authentic version of herself."

"You thought all that, did you? I'm impressed. Here I thought you were a fisherman, plain and simple. But now that you're

speaking, I could imagine you might have even read a book once
or twice in your life."

"I am a fisherman, that's right enough. As to books, they're
the headstones of dead thoughts."

"Where did you get that phrase?"

"I read it on a bottle cap."

"And here I was thinking you weren't a reader."

He took another drink. Then he tilted the bottle neck toward
me. I took a drink, too.

"Sure, I'll go out with you," he said.

"Out with me?"

The Bushmills burned down to my knees.

"It's what you've been wondering since we met," he said.
"Whether I might fancy you. And whether you would go out
with me if I asked. So I'm asking. Why don't I take you to dinner
tonight?"

I looked at him. There it was. Milly called it the moment
of entanglement. You could either say yes and lose all hope, or
say no and lose the same hope. I couldn't say what I wanted to
do in that instant. He was deadly handsome, and cocky, and obnoxiously sure of himself. But he was also a man who lifted his
grandmother tenderly onto the beach of her childhood, and who
skipped a day's fishing to take a stranger to see an island he had
visited countless times before. Nevertheless, I didn't want the
complication. It was all too new, all too foreign to me. I had work
to accomplish. I had to set up my apartment, buy paper towels,
put a grocery in a refrigerator somewhere. I didn't need the complication that he inevitably represented.

"Only if I can buy you dinner," I said. "And if it's on a friendly
basis."

That sounded ridiculous even to me. I looked down, and
when I looked up, he had broken into a full smile.

"I prefer to eat with enemies," he said. "I'd hate for us to be
friendly."

Then he turned to Seamus and called for the old man to take the wheel. We had returned to Dingle and I had not thrown up on Ozzie's shoes. I counted it an accomplishment. But I had no idea if we had set a date or not. The whiskey burned in my mouth and I felt a little dizzy. Gran woke and seemed momentarily unsure of where she was. Seamus slipped away from her carefully and relieved Ozzie at the wheel. Ozzie climbed out by the bow and readied the mooring lines.

"And that's the Blasket Islands," Seamus said with his wonderful lilt, his hands and eyes lively on the docking process. "And your hair has turned red as a morning sunrise, Kate Moreton. If you're not all Irish, I'll eat a crow."

"You're chipper when you wake, Seamus."

"I wasn't sleeping, Kate. I was communing with the fairy people. You have to close your eyes to do it."

Then we bumped fairly hard against the fenders, and through the window I watched Ozzie jump onto the dock and tie his line off. He shouted something back over his shoulder to another boat. Seamus backed the engine for a second, and the boat swung its stern to rest. I turned to see Ozzie set the line there, but instead I caught Gran's eyes. She smiled at me and I smiled back, and I had no idea what we had just communicated.

8

"Of course it's a date!" Milly said over Skype, her image oddly bulging forward in her camera. "Are you kidding me right now? It's a date and he's hot as anything. You've been there one day and you've already snagged an Irishman."

"I've hardly snagged anything. I don't *want* to snag anything. I'm here to work, not to snag people. I've sworn off men forever."

"But there you are. And you have a date. Biology wins every time."

"I'm not some schoolgirl with a schoolgirl crush, Milly. I'm here to work on my dissertation."

"Yes, you are."

"Yes, I am what?"

"Yes, you are there to work on your dissertation. And yes, you are a schoolgirl. We're all schoolgirls, honey. It's the fates playing with us. You can't help it. No one can help it. You don't have to be giddy about it, but you don't have to lock yourself away, either. Think of it as a chance to reach greater cultural understanding."

She made an obscene gesture, a gross pantomime of a sex act. I laughed. I leaned forward and tried to see behind her into the interior of her atelier. She had been working on a painting, an enormous mural of horses and motorcycles and boys in tighty whities. It was a low-level commission from a mysterious woman she called her *benefactress*; she had combined the commission with a five-thousand-dollar grant from the New Hampshire Council on the Arts to keep her above water.

She had her hair in a bandana and a smudge of paint on her lip. Milly worked odd hours. She might stay up all night, then stay in bed for two days. It was how she worked. She called the good working periods her Da Vinci phase. She bristled with energy and competency whenever she hit that stride. In her down phase, she could be alarmingly reclusive, hiding out and refusing to answer her phone or messages until someone—usually me— went and ferreted her out and forced her to rejoin the land of the living. I had no concerns about her for the moment. A glance told me she was living on adrenaline and music and art. Seeing her, knowing what fun it would be to be sitting in the room with her, made me the slightest bit homesick.

"Honestly, Milly, you have to come up with another form of distraction than my nonexistent sex life. I couldn't read him if my life depended on it. I don't know if he's going to show up or not. Or what time. Or anything. I've decided to undate him. I'm calling it off even if it never was a thing."

"He's a broody Irishman. Those are the deadliest of all. You know that show? The one where they go out fishing for Alaskan crabs? That's you. You're way out offshore, fishing for Alaskan crab. And the seas are tossing you and you might get killed, but you might come back a rich fisherwoman. Haul those traps, girl. Or are they pots?"

"He's an American and an ex-serviceman. Don't build him into a mythical creature."

"What are you going to wear? You should be a little slutty. He wouldn't know what to do with a slutty PhD."

"I have a fleece and jeans, Milly. I've got nothing to wear. Even if it were a date, which it is not. Which I have just declared an undate. And I am not a PhD. I am a doctoral candidate."

"Try on something so I can see."

"No. Go paint something, Milly."

"You better. He's going to show up and you're going to be going out all grungy. Do you think you'll sleep with him? You'll definitely sleep with him. First date, right into bed."

"Oh God, Milly."

"Why not? How long have you been in the convent?"

"Since Abe."

"Abe, the dour-faced."

"He wasn't bad."

"Honey, you have a hunk of a man over there waiting to take you out. Put on one thing so I can see. Did you take a shower?"

"When I got back I did."

"Well, doll up a little. You're allowed to have fun, you know?"

"I'm here to work. What about that don't you get?"

But I moved away from my computer and changed shirts after she gave me a look. The transformation wasn't great. I put on some eyeliner and touched up my lips, the whole time talking to Milly about her painting, about news from Dartmouth, about my department. She filled me in on all the gossip and poured herself a drink of Irish whiskey to celebrate with me, and when I finished primping, she made me move the eye of the camera up and down so she could check me out.

"What shoes?" she asked when I finished.

"I have no shoes here. Nothing cute."

"Just go with what you have. Wear it, sister. He's just a man! Poor, stupid saps that they are," she said, and laughed.

She drank some Irish whiskey. I wished I could join her.

We signed off a little later. I spent a few minutes in the bathroom checking my look in the mirror. I thought of Seamus telling me my hair grew redder by being beside the sea. He wasn't far wrong. I looked sunburned and appropriately wind-swept. I didn't mind how I looked.

Then for a while I sat on my bed and thought of Abe. Abe was the last visitor to the land of Kate. He was a grad student in Religious Studies at Yale Divinity. He was an atheist who studied religion, specifically the Greek Bible translations, in order to prove to himself over and over again that a belief in god, big or little *G*, was irrational. Conflicted, you might say. He was not a bad man, but he was what Milly called a *raincoat*. Practical, suitable, useful, and ultimately replaceable. We had dated sporadically after meeting at a translation conference in Milwaukee, and for a brief month or so I had believed, and so had he, that we might be a perfect couple, two professors at good colleges witnessing the work and times of the other's life. We *played* at being together, I realized now; he had been the male figurine in my adult dollhouse dream. Ken and Barbie. Kate and Abe. He wore leather sandals that made saddle sounds when he stretched to reach something off an upper shelf. It had ended like a small, flaming arrow landing point down in a lake. It should have been more of a show, but it slipped beneath the surface and was over. I didn't regret dating him, but I also didn't remember much about it. He was a bowl of mac and cheese. He was a shredded carrot on a green salad.

And what did that make me? That was part of the reason I felt reluctant to get involved again. Even with a broody Irishman.

After a little while, I pulled out a recent narrative I had come across at a home in Springfield. It was an account written by a daughter of her mother's final years in a nursing home. The mother had grown up on the Blaskets, had reached the age of seventeen before emigrating to America. In her final senility, the old woman had begun speaking in Irish again, returning to her childhood tongue as if the memory of it could no longer be suppressed. The daughter had transcribed as much as she could, but she hadn't known where or whom to contact about it. Through a string of connections, the narrative had surfaced into my hands. I could not read it fast enough, or deeply enough, or with anything but unbridled sympathy. It was the kind of academic gold that made careers.

Ozzie did not show up. After a half hour, I leaned back to

get the bedside light to fall more easily onto the page of my printout. After forty-five minutes, I closed my eyes. I woke with a jolt fifteen minutes later, temporarily confused at my whereabouts. When my head cleared slightly, I rose one last time to look around, to check my phone, but I had no messages from him. Part of me felt relief. That settled it. It had *not* been a date, and I had *not* been stood up, and now I could go to bed and fall asleep without worry. I did not need to end my sabbatical from men. I could concentrate on what had brought me to Ireland in the first place.

I tucked myself deep into the bed and finally closed my eyes. The house smelled of lemon cleaning soap. I had read once that Hemingway used to recall streams he had fished just before falling asleep. He would re-fish them, casting in his near dream as he had casted in life. It was a way to fall asleep, to enter the dream-world, and I found that I could trace my steps on the Great Blasket Island in the same way. I walked the center avenue and looked at the schoolhouse and church, and the wind came off the sea, and sleep rose up the chimneys that sang in the village and carried me away.

9

I admit it: I expected Ozzie to show up at breakfast with some sort of apology, a lot of nonsense about mistaken understandings, but he didn't. Neither did Nora send Seamus to take me off on another adventure. I was on my own. I needed to get back to the University of Limerick to move into my apartment and give myself some semblance of order, but I felt, absurdly, slightly abandoned by my guides of the day before.

At breakfast, Mrs. Fox fed me a hole-in-one egg and toast plate with Irish bacon on the side. The bacon tasted like ham. I ate and drank tea and studied the map of Ireland I had saved on my phone. I had already visited the Blaskets, I reminded myself. I hadn't expected to make it out there until spring, honestly, and so I felt a bit ahead of the game. Over a second cup of tea, I had a lovely scone with currant jam. When Mrs. Fox looked in to check on me, I asked her if she had any messages for me.

"None, dear," she said. "Were you expecting something?"

"No, not really. I just wondered."

"Did you meet Ozzie?" she asked, lingering in the doorway, a tea towel draped over her shoulder.

"Yes, he took us out to the Blaskets on his boat."

"That's what I heard."

She didn't say anything else, but I had the sense that she wanted to. Our eyes met.

"He's an interesting man, isn't he?" I asked, trying to stay noncommittal. It was impossible to know who was related to whom, how the trees of such a small town forest were arranged.

"He's a gallant lad," she said, her eyes remaining on mine, "even if he hops a fence now and then."

"How does he hop a fence?"

I sipped my tea. My background as an interviewer stood me in good stead. Two ears and one mouth was a rule I lived by. Listen more than talk.

"The usual way of young men, I suppose. Do you know the story of Androcles and the Lion? The one where the lion has a thorn in its paw? Well, Ozzie is a lion who never had the good fortune to meet his Androcles."

"And the thorn . . . ?"

"It's the war, of course. He went with you Yanks to Afghanistan. If you don't mind a bit of political talk, that war was a fool's errand from the start. That's my view of it, anyway. It's one thing to fight for your own country if it's under attack, but to go halfway around the world to engage in military action against a bunch of primitive societies, well. Forgive me if I've spoken out of turn."

"So you think he carries the war with him?"

"Yes, I do. It's hard to put such a thing down when you spent so much time carrying it."

"That's a big thorn."

"You'll not have to say that twice. Well, I am certain I've said more than I should. Ozzie is a nice young man, but troubled like many are. And handsome as the devil, which makes him irresistible to the girls about."

"Does he have a girlfriend, then?"

I felt myself blush as I asked the question. What in the world was I doing? What did I care if Ozzie had a girlfriend? I needed to have my head examined. I pushed at the last of my breakfast with my fork. Mrs. Fox switched the towel from her right shoulder to her left and brushed at the lint left behind.

"Girlfriend or acquaintance? In an earlier day, it was easier to know what a person meant to another person. Nowadays, I'm not sure what girlfriend even means. But he has an eye for the ladies, as he would. And with his good looks, he doesn't lack for opportunities."

"I'll keep a watch on him, then."

"With a good heart, though. Ozzie, I mean. He's done no end of charitable work in these parts. He's keen on dogs, too, you know? He's adopted a dozen dogs over the years. He tries to place them with families. No one would speak against that. Have you seen his place?"

"No, we just spent the day on the boat. With Gran and Seamus."

"Oh, you must see it. It's the grandest view hereabouts. You can sit and wear the sea as a tablecloth from where he lives."

I smiled at her use of *tablecloth*. She hung about for a moment longer, doubtless wondering what else she could tell me, then she bustled back into the kitchen. I imagined what Milly would say about the dog rescues. She would flip over that. She would say it promised a good heart, which might have been a fair assessment. In any case, it didn't matter. Ozzie was not on the menu. I did not need fried Ozzie or baked Ozzie or fricasseed Ozzie. I finished breakfast, thanked Mrs. Fox, and carried a cup of tea back to my room. I still felt sleepy and slightly jet-lagged.

I sat on the bed and spent a few minutes checking bus schedules. I needed to get to Limerick. I needed to check in with the administration at the university, and I needed to set up my apartment. The weight of travel, and my temporary dislocation, had begun to catch up with me. I wanted to set up a base of operations and work from there. I would feel better, I knew, when I could put my head down on a familiar bed.

I was still checking the bus schedule when my phone buzzed. My mother's picture appeared on the screen. I wondered at the simple proposition telephones gave us about the people in our lives: *green: accept, red: reject*. Two rings passed and fluttered before I could decide. At the three and a half rings, I punched green. Accept. Her voice sounded surprised, as if it had expected to leave a message and now had to deal with a live person.

"Kate? Can you hear me?" she asked.

"I can hear you, Mom."

"Are you already in Ireland? I didn't know your schedule."

"I am in Ireland," I said.

I was aware of giving flat answers to her questions, but that was an old story between us. Usually my mom had more to say than to hear.

"Well, good for you. That's wonderful. Ben sends his love, too. He's right here with me. We're going to Italy on Thursday. It's raining like anything there, but Ben loves Rome. He can't get enough of it. Even with the sun. There's much more sun in Italy than there is in Ireland, I suspect."

"I suppose."

"Now, listen, we gave some thought to visiting you in Ireland. Everything is close once you're over in Europe. Don't you find that to be true? We're looking at a boat, a sailboat, that Ben has his eye on. Really a gorgeous ship. It's owned by a group of investors, well, a corporation, really. They keep it for outings and such, to close deals, I guess, and they staff it with some Eastern Europeans. Anyway, Ben spotted it on one of his sailing newsletters . . ."

I heard Ben speak up. He had been listening. He always listened. He spoke loudly and Mom covered the phone with her hand, I guessed. Then she came back on.

". . . oh, he says it's a website. The sailing website. Not a newsletter at all. Yes, that's right, dear. Okay, yes. A Spirit C 65. Not a vintage boat, but a modern classic."

"I'm not sure you can have a modern classic, Mom. Classic connotes age."

"What's that?" she asked.

"Nothing. Just a quibble about words."

"Well, that's your field, darling. Anyway, it doesn't look like we can make it after all. We have to be back for the Adlars' dinner dance. The white dance. You know, they throw it every year, and that *has* become a classic."

"Absolutely."

She had heard my quibble about the oxymoron of modern classic. And she had rolled over it. My mom could be deaf or blind whenever it suited her.

"You laugh, but it is an event. And they raise a lot of money for needy causes. We have a table for ten we are hosting. I have to arrange the centerpieces. We give those away to funeral homes afterward. They reuse the flowers. I just learned that. Imagine that? All this time going to the white dinner dance, and I never knew the flowers were recycled in that way. It's made me proud of our little group."

I sipped my tea to steady my tongue. I wanted to bite the ceramic cup in half, to take a half-moon bite out of it like a great white snapping a chunk out of a surfboard. *Our little group* meant our little group of filthy rich old bastards. It meant a bunch of men—yes, the men were the breadwinners, corporate pirates all, some barely legal, some legacy brats who were handed reams of opportunity from their families, while the gals (yes, they were called gals) arranged social functions and put together centerpieces and consulted each other about outfits, and sweater swatches, and wallpapers and designers and gardeners and kitchen renovators and yoga instructors and dog trainers and security companies and golf coaches. *Our little group.* It was the group that my mother invaded and conquered after the death of my workaday, Irish firefighter father. It was the group she had joined before the death of my father, so that his last days flickered by with the knowledge that she had already gone to another man, leaving him behind to die as a cuckold. She couldn't wait. She saw an opportunity for a bigger, fuller life, she said when I confronted her about it in the wake of my father's death, and she took it. Like Sauron in *The Lord of the Rings,* she had sought the one ring to rule them all, a wedding ring from Ben Applegate, one of the best pirates to ply the corporate seas of central Massachusetts, one of the richest pirates, one of the catchiest catches to swim in her waters. Whatever our life had been, whatever my father's contribution had meant to her, had been eclipsed by the 173 acres of the Maxwell Country Club, by dinner dances and charity balls, by Ben of the bushy eyebrows and whale-printed trousers, tasseled loafers, argyle socks, and trips to Italy to look at classic, but new, wooden yachts.

That was my mom. And that was why we didn't do the daughter-mom thing very well.

"That's great, Mom," I said, because it was my turn to say something.

"Well, I thought I should keep you apprised of my whereabouts. In case."

"In case of what, Mom?"

"In case of anything, dear. In case something important comes up and you need to contact me. Or, for that matter, if I need to contact you."

"That's why cell phones were invented, Mom. It doesn't matter where we are."

"Please don't be snippy, Kate. We're all doing our best."

"You're right, Mom."

"This is just your bourgeois mother doing her bourgeois best, Kate."

"I know, Mom. Sorry. I'm just tired from travel."

She took a breath. We often took time-outs for breaths when we had a mother-daughter talk.

"It is exhausting, isn't it? Travel, I mean," she said after a moment. "And they've only made it worse. All the crowds milling and the suspicion. I really believe it's the suspicion that tires one out. People look at you as if you're carrying a bomb, for goodness' sakes."

I heard some quick talking in the background. Ben's voice spoke a little louder. My mom murmured something that I couldn't quite make out.

"Have to go, sweetheart," she said, coming back to speak directly into the phone so I could hear again. "Ben can't find his club covers. He took them off so he could clean his woods and now he can't find them."

I bit my tongue to keep from saying anything smart-assed. Golf clubs. Woods. Leaving a call to your daughter so that you could search for something insignificant for your semi-new husband. That summed up more than I could ever make her understand. And I felt like a whiny baby for thinking it.

"Love you, Mom," I said, to bring some warmth to her from my side of the ocean.

"Love you, Kate. Enjoy your vacation."

Not a vacation, I wanted to say. But then the phone clicked off and my mom went questing for the lost wood covers of Avalon. Whether she gave a single thought to the fact that I had journeyed to her first husband's homeland, to his heart, really, I couldn't say.

10

Elsa Bunratty showed me to my faculty apartment.

"We put you on the second floor," she said as we walked across the University of Limerick campus. It was a dark, overcast day, rainy in the way that Ireland was often pictured in the movies. *Windswept,* I kept telling myself. Elsa pushed her bike. She took her bike everywhere, she said. In fact, she told me, the women on campus had something of a bike society. I didn't know what to make of that, so I didn't say much in response. Her bike was the sort of English bike I always associated with vintage movies from the 1940s. It was black and solid, and a chunky chain-guard covered the center pedal stem.

She wore a gray skirt, tea length, and a soft cream cashmere sweater that rolled under her chin. A yellow slicker covered everything. She was beautiful in the way of Beatrix Potter, a woman I pictured in a cottage with a liver-shaped garden filled with tall, curious perennials outside her door. Maybe a cat. A fireplace, certainly, and a pot of tea ready whenever it was needed. A garden fence and a circular window that looked out on the River Shannon.

That's how I imagined her. In truth, she was a good bit more direct and serious. She was in charge of campus housing, big and little, faculty and otherwise, and it was, I gathered, an enormous job. She had agreed to walk me over—usually she would have sent one of her assistants, she said—but they had just renovated my apartment and she wanted to see for herself if the work had been done satisfactorily. She was my age, more or less, and I was glad to have her company. She put my small backpack in her front bicycle basket.

"We like to put women on the second floor. A bit more secure," she said as we passed a large stand of graceful pines. "On the first floor, students can be tempted to peek in and be a bother. That sort of thing. Just mischievous."

"Thank you."

"Not that there is a big problem. I don't mean to imply that. It's a precaution. It's quieter, too. You won't hear much noise from where you are, and you can catch a glimpse of the river from your kitchen."

"That sounds wonderful. I'm excited to see it. I've been dreaming about it from the moment I received my confirmation."

"You'll be comfortable. And if you're not, don't hesitate to contact me. I mean it. That's my job and I take it seriously."

"I'm sure it will be perfect for me."

And it was. She led me to a two-story building on the banks of the River Shannon. The building shared a common; a fountain took up the center, where a bronze statue of an archer pointed his bow toward heaven. I assumed this was a faculty common; around me, from what I could tell, other faculty members had set up shop for the academic year. When I asked her if that was the case, she nodded.

"We have faculty from twenty-seven countries," she said, shaking out her keys and fitting one of them to the lock on Number 86. "Some on a permanent basis, some on a year-by-year contract. It's a lovely arrangement. It makes for an interesting campus life. You never know who you might run into."

"Do they all teach?"

"Most do. Some do research as you are doing. We have a pub on campus—well, two, actually. You'll meet everyone in time.

You can get as involved in the social life as you like, of course. Some find it stimulating and some prefer to keep their own company."

She opened the door to a flight of carpeted stairs. I followed her up. I didn't know what to expect; the photos online had been difficult to piece together in any meaningful way. But as soon as we mounted the last step, I felt a knot of pleasure deep in my belly. The apartment, I knew beforehand, was a studio, but it was clean and freshly painted and the windows opened to the river behind the building. The River Shannon, which I couldn't help recalling the line from James Joyce's immortal story, "The Dead." *The dark mutinous Shannon waves*, he had called it, but from my window, when I pushed back the plain navy curtains, it looked anything but mutinous. Even in my first glance I saw white herons fishing the waters, their legs causing Vs in the rapids as they waded and cast their beaks down to spear a fish. It filled my heart with hope. It was as perfect as I could have dreamed.

"It's glorious!" I said. "Thank you, Elsa. Thank you for this."

"They did a good job," she said walking about and examining the paint job. "Nicely done. A few spots here and there, but life has a few spots, doesn't it? Yes, yes, I'll have to tell Bobby to compliment his crew. They turned this around quickly for me."

I couldn't fill my eyes fast enough. True, it was merely a studio apartment, not very grand, with a kitchenette on one side and a pullout couch on the other. But it was a foothold in Ireland, a place to be in the country I had always wanted to visit. Joyce's Shannon River ran past the apartment house, and central Limerick was a forty-minute walk along the quay beside the running water. Elsa had said the campus provided two pubs, and the buildings around me were filled with other scholars and teachers pursuing their own interests. If I were a plant, I decided, I had just been placed in the proper soil for me.

"Not bad," Elsa said, still doing her rounds, occasionally turning to me. "New curtains. Not very glamorous, I'm afraid, but they will keep the sun out when you need it out. In the cupboards, yes, here, you have pots and pans. All the basics. The one problem you may have is the grocery store. It's a good walk away and you'll have to carry things back. You can take a taxi, of course, but that's a cost. I'm assuming your funds are not unlimited."

"They're not," I said, following her inspection, my mind clicking off mental notes of what I would need, what worked, what could be augmented. It was all here; I really didn't need a thing more other than my books and perhaps a table in the library.

"A bike might be a good purchase. Let me see what I can dig up in surplus. We might have a few around. And I have friends who have extra bikes from time to time. You can get to market easily and you can run into town on the quay with a bike. I recommend it."

"Thank you. It's something I'll try, for sure."

She grinned.

"I love when you Yanks say *for sure*. It's such an odd phrase. What does it mean, *for sure*? And I love your accent. I could listen to it all day."

"I could listen to your accent all day," I said. "It's a dream."

"Well, we're matched, then. I am going to leave you alone so you can settle in. Austin will bring over your bags. Don't mind him. He's a little slow afoot, but he's harmless and well-meaning. Now I'll scoot. I'm sure you're fatigued from your journey."

"I am a little bit."

"Most natural thing in the world. All right then, here's your key. I'll leave it here on the counter. Settle in. If you want a quick bite, try the pubs. You can get fish and chips there and take that as a starting point. I'll be in touch, Kate."

"Thank you, Elsa."

She laughed at our formality, then she hugged me quickly and went down the stairs. I watched her leave. She swung her skirted leg over the lower crossbar and pedaled off, ringing her bike bell

at a student she passed, her hand lifted in a wave that might have
been to him or to me.

I scrubbed everything. My rational mind told me the apartment
had just been painted, but I knew myself well enough to understand I would not sleep or rest comfortably until my hand had
touched, and wiped clean, every surface in the apartment. Fortunately, it was a tiny space and I had it spic and span in a little over
an hour. I flipped the mattress in the fold-out bed, then sat for
a moment on the couch and looked around. The apartment had
good light, I decided. It was comfortable and easy and practical
and it was just what I needed. I imagined the heat worked satisfactorily and the water ran without a hitch. Everything considered, I felt more at home in a shorter time than I had expected.

University of Limerick, I whispered to myself. *A visiting
scholar at the University of Limerick. Not bad.*

After that, I burned sage and wafted smoke at the four corners of the universe. Ridiculous, I knew, but it was something I
had learned to do to sanctify a new home. An old hippie named
Esmeralda had given me my first sage whisk. She had been the
LNP hospice worker who had cared for my father over the last
months of his life. She wore her hair in long gray braids and she
dressed like an Arapaho from Haight-Ashbury, vintage 1971, but
she had the kindest eyes I had ever seen before encountering
Gran's eyes. She had been filled with hippie lore, tinctures and
vials of strange concoctions, bear grease and cat whiskers, for all
I knew, and she had dosed my father with them to set his soul
on its journey. I didn't believe a bit of it, but I liked the ritual
it lent to my father's weary decline, a moment of bright hope
in what we all knew was an inevitable parting. She used sage
whisks whenever my mother was dependably gone for the day.
She roamed around my father's bed, chanting and blowing the
smoke to the four corners of the world, and my father—when

he still had strength—said it smelled like campfire smoke and peat fires, and he held her hand afterward and thanked her. I came to like it, too, and when I received the fellowship from the Brady Milsap Foundation, signifying that I could go to Ireland and study the Blasket narratives, Esmeralda sent me a sage whisk and a rock charm and told me to burn the sage on the first best night.

So I performed my own little rite of welcoming. I cupped my hand around the smoke and blew it to the four compass points, carefully avoiding the blinking eye of the kitchen's smoke alarm. When I had satisfied the corners of the universe, I washed the smoke toward me, accepting its purity, feeling a fraud as I did it, but also happy. The smoke made me think of my dad, the softness of his final days when he became nearly transparent, a gentle man going to a gentle place. Before he had entered his final coma, he had talked a great deal about the Blaskets, about his heart's home, about the sound of water when it became no longer a sound, but a thought of its own, a reassurance that the sea was eternal and that it lived inside one as surely as it swept the beach clean each day.

I had just finished when I heard a knock. It took me a moment to understand the sound came from my door. Immediately I doused whatever embers remained in the clump of sage, then I spent a moment fanning the air with the dustpan I had used to sweep up. I opened two windows and called that I was coming, but whether the person might hear me or not, I couldn't say.

"Just a second," I called, glancing quickly in the bathroom mirror.

I looked sweaty and warm and slapped together like a pile of leaves. But there was nothing I could do about it. I went down the stairs quickly, sure that my sage ritual had sent a security officer to my door. Or perhaps a concerned neighbor. Luckily, the door had one of those fish-eye peepholes, so I leaned to it and tried to prepare my story for whoever might be outside.

It was Ozzie.

Oh, fuck, I thought.

To make it worse, he had a puppy in his arms. That wasn't even fair. It looked to be a Golden Retriever puppy, which is, without question, about ten times too cute for its own good. Ozzie held the puppy casually in one arm. Twice, while I looked, it tried to reach up and lick his face. *Of course dogs like him,* I thought. Probably kids, too, and widows and retired veterans. He had that way.

I considered not opening the door. I blew a little whistle of air out at my bottom lip. A half-dozen scenarios crossed my mind. Then, hardly knowing I was going to do it, I pulled open the door.

"How did you find me?" I asked, too harshly, I realized, after the words had passed by my lips.

"Hello, Kate," he said.

I reached out for the dog. I loved dogs. He handed me the puppy. I put my nose into the puppy's fur. One of the top ten smells, I reckoned. I tucked its sweet little paws into my open palm. The puppy craned its neck and tried to kiss me.

"That's Gottfried," Ozzie said, settling one hand on the puppy's head. "I just took him on this morning."

"Gottfried is a horrible name for a dog. It sounds like he's a flavor of ice cream."

"I didn't name him. That's what his guardians named him."

"It's still a ridiculous name. How do you even call him? Here, Gotty?"

"We haven't gotten that far yet."

"What are you doing here, anyway?"

I tried to calm myself. Why was I being so bitchy? Why wasn't I happy to have one of the few people I knew in Ireland stop by to see me?

Ozzie moved his hand softly on the dog's head and tucked back its ear. I kept the puppy close. I was aware of him petting the dog while it rested next to my breasts. Weird. And it was doubly weird that I had that thought. Then again, it had been a *long, long* time since Abe, since anybody's body had touched mine. I was probably hyperaware. I was also aware of Ozzie's size and looks as he stood just outside my door. Milly would have told me to grab him by his Irish sweater and yank him inside.

"I came to take you out," Ozzie said. "And to introduce you to Gottfried."

"Don't play that with me, okay? I'm not interested in a silly little do-si-do."

"I thought you might like to have a friend in a new city."

"You live in Dingle."

"I live in Ireland. It's not so big, you know?"

"I thought you fished for a living."

"I do fish for a living. But sometimes I like stepping off the boat for a minute. Are you going to insist on fighting every time we meet?"

"I might. I haven't decided."

"I'd rather not," he said. "I don't think I've given you cause to hate me yet, have I?"

"Not yet. But why would you say *yet* if you don't intend to give me cause?"

"I think you may have a fever. I think you may have beriberi."

"What is beriberi, anyway?"

"It's what you have. I feel sorry for you with your bad case of beriberi."

Gottfried chose that moment to kiss me again and nearly wriggle free of my grip. Ozzie took him. He put the puppy down on the ground and the dog ran right into my apartment. Naturally. Ozzie shrugged. He grinned. I hated it, but I grinned back.

And stepped aside to let him go after his dog.

Gottfried struggled to climb the steps. His broad little bottom weighted him down and he had to heave mightily to make it from step to step. I closed the door. For a moment, we stood side by side, watching the puppy climb. Then Ozzie took me and pushed me back against the wall and kissed me deeply, so deeply that I thought I might collapse like a folding chair when he let me go. It was a damn good kiss. I brought my hands up onto his shoulders and he kept kissing me. The grin came with the kiss. I felt a year of temperance, of celibacy, of schoolmarm scholarliness, wash away in the imprint of his body against mine. I kissed him back and, nearly at the same time, pushed his shoulders away.

"Get your dog," I said when my mouth came free of his.

"That's why I came to Limerick, Kate Moreton. I came all this way to kiss you."

11

I did not sleep with him. I wanted to, but I didn't do it.

It wasn't easy, because a part of me said, *why not?* Another part said, *don't you dare. You don't even know him.* Yet another part of me thought: *don't give into this guy so he thinks he can have his way whenever he knocks on your door.*

Good, sane thoughts. Added to that was the knowledge that I looked like a charwoman and smelled like cleanser.

We followed Gottfried up the stairs. I made Ozzie go up first because I didn't want him staring at my ass if I climbed the stairs in front of him. That's how crazy he had me. That's how the kiss had shattered my resolve.

We had a tense moment. We were both aware of the kiss. We were both aware of the dog sniffing the corners of the apartment. We were both aware of an enormous attraction that might have been my undoing if I had known him a tiny bit better. He was absurdly male standing in my tiny apartment. He filled it. He smelled like smoke and whiskey and wet wool and soap.

"Nice apartment," he said after an awkward silence.

We watched Gottfried sniff at the place where the floor met the walls. He was too cute.

"I like it," I said.

"I heard they take good care of people here. At the university, I mean."

"They've been very kind."

"Of course, the Irish like Americans. Not everyone does. I mean around the world. A lot of people find Americans arrogant and annoying."

"That's what I've always heard."

"Does this conversation seem canned to you?"

"How so?"

"Like we are filling in space because we just kissed and we want to kiss again? Like we are avoiding that?"

"You kissed me. I didn't kiss you."

"You didn't stop me."

"You're a bit bigger than I am."

"Did I read you wrong?"

I changed the subject.

"I would offer you something to drink, but I don't have anything at all in the place. I haven't been to the market yet."

"I could take you to the market. That might be a friendly thing to do."

"Do you have a car?"

"No, I came here on a magic pony, Kate. Yes, I have a car. It's not a great car, but it's car. In fact, it's a truck."

"What if I took a fast shower first? It's been a long day."

"That's fine. I'll walk Gottfried. He probably needs a little time. You know the River Shannon runs right behind this place, don't you? It's a good place to walk a dog."

"Yes, I knew that."

"James Joyce and all that."

"You know the story. I'm glad."

He nodded. We both kept staring at Gottfried.

"We probably have to have sex soon," he said, his eyes straight ahead, "or we'll be condemned to these stunted conversations forever."

"Do you think it's stunted?"

"Isn't it? We're watching a puppy because we're afraid to look at each other."

"I'm not afraid."

"You probably have little self-control. I'd probably have to make us both wait. I'll give you that gift."

"Does any woman ever go for this routine of yours?"

"What routine?"

"I don't know. The show up with a puppy routine. The slightly wounded Irishman routine."

"You're a hard woman, Kate."

"It would help to go to the grocery store."

"Okay, fair enough. I'll leave now, but I'll come back."

"Good."

"Gran says hello. She is quite taken by you."

"She's a love."

"Seamus says I should marry you. He says a girl with red hair signifies good fortune."

"He does, does he?"

He nodded. Then he scooped up Gottfried. He held him for me to pet for a second. Slowly, he bent past the dog's body and kissed me again. I kissed him back. Like a husband going off to get bread, I thought. Like a wife taking a shower to get ready for a casual dinner on a Tuesday night in marriage-land.

I expected his truck to be messy, but it wasn't. It was a red Ford F-150 and it was tidy and clean. I held Gottfried. He had started to get tired and he curled in my lap and rested. The earlier tension I had felt—*we* had felt—had dissipated. It probably had something to do with getting out of the apartment with a job to do. Ozzie narrated the roads to the market. As Elsa had said, it wasn't far. We pulled into the parking lot in under five minutes.

"Will Gottfried be okay in the truck?" I asked in the silence after he turned off the engine.

"Should be. The better question is whether the truck will be okay. He's got to learn to be by himself from time to time. He has to know he can count on me coming back."

"Are you going to keep him?"

"I'd love to, but the kennel is full."

"You have a kennel?"

"Not really. I take in dogs from time to time. But I'm not in a place to take care of a dog right now."

"How did you end up with Gottfried?"

"It's a long story. Not a good story, I'm afraid. He's kind of an orphan. Would you like to keep him?"

"I can't. Not in that apartment."

"I figured as much. Well, come on. Let's get your groceries."

Gottfried whined when I put him on the seat and closed the door. He raised up and ran his paws against the window. Ozzie bent down and looked at him eye to eye. Gottfried didn't get the message. He kept pawing at the window.

I realized, as we entered the store, that shopping with a man you hardly knew was a surprisingly personal thing to do. Not only was the store new and the products unfamiliar, but he pushed the cart for me and moved behind me so that he saw anything I purchased. I decided in the first minute that this would be a short trip and that I would only get the basics. Some other day I could come back and fill out a full shopping list, but for now I loaded vegetables and fruit into the basket, paper towels and soap.

"Are you a committed cook?" he asked.

"I like to cook. I won't kid you and say I'm very good."

"I like to cook, too. Would you like to get some things to cook for tonight? We can go out, of course, but it might be fun to stay in and cook together. Or I could cook and you could unpack. It would be my treat."

"I'd like that. Thank you. I'm not sure I have it in me to go out tonight."

"And I'll pick out some wine for us. You like wine, don't you?"

"I like wine."

"Then it's settled. Let me play chef for the night. That way we don't have to leave Gottfried in the truck while we eat."

"Thank you. That sounds wonderful, actually."

"Our first night together," he said. "How do you like that?"

"Our first dinner together," I said.

He looked at me and smiled. I smiled back.

Then it was all business, and I recognized, in no time, that he was more than an amateur cook. As soon as we had agreed to stay in for the night, he took over the dinner plans. Clearly, he was at home in a grocery store. He parked the cart in the vegetable section and spent ten minutes poking and prodding the produce. I had put carrots and a head of lettuce in the basket, but he lifted them out and replaced them with organic choices.

"I know who grows these," he said, hardly looking at me. "If you'll allow me."

He had obviously gone foodie on me. He refused to buy fish from the grocery store. If it wasn't fresh, he told me, meaning right off his boat, he didn't eat it. He settled on beef tips and asparagus and a rice pilaf. Simple but plain, he promised. He also promised me a pear tart for dessert. Then we spent a long time in front of the wine racks. To my relief, he wasn't a wine snob. He selected six bottles of wine, all moderately priced, plopped them in the cart, and then pushed on. I liked watching him shop. He took pleasure in the experience, sniffing basil and thyme, pinching the pears—*not ideal,* he said, *but serviceable*—and evidently imagining the tastes of each dish combining to form the whole meal. He wasn't fussy, only forceful, and I found it an attractive trait in him.

We had just reached the dairy section when Lollie found him.

I didn't know she was named Lollie, of course, until she introduced herself. She was tall and blond, with a pink bandana over her head. She wore a down vest and bright white sneakers

with her socks pulled high on her calves. She had just come from
yoga, she said, after she hugged him. He hugged her back. Then
they both turned halfway to me and we all knew that they had
once been together, had been lovers, and now I was in some sort
of place where she had been. She smelled of apples.

"Lollie is a nurse at the Limerick hospital," Ozzie said, introducing her more fully. "And she does visiting nurse stuff, too."

Lollie and Ozzie, I thought. They sounded like soft drinks.

"Nice to meet you," I managed to say.

"Kate is newly arrived on Ireland's shore," Ozzie said, suddenly sounding like a travel brochure. "Her family is from here."

"Welcome, then," Lollie said, and I hated that she felt it was
her place to welcome me.

And that she was blond and tall and wore yoga pants that
showed off a body that should have been licensed by the Irish
government. Lollie. Ozzie smiled at both of us. Then Lollie made
her getaway. She had a small basket clamped on her arm. She
switched it quickly and gave the smile of leaving.

"Nice to see you, Ozzie. And nice to meet you, Kate. Ozzie,
don't be a stranger. It's been ages."

"Far too long," Ozzie agreed.

Not nearly long enough, I thought.

"Still have your dogs?" Lollie asked, one step accomplished.

"No, the last one was farmed out a while back. I've just got a
new one in the truck if you're interested."

"Well, I'm afraid not. Not the right space for a dog at this
point, but I know where to come if I need one. He is so good
with dogs, Kate."

Then she walked down the aisle, her yoga pants whisking
slightly as she went. She sounded like a child's snowsuit as she
left. She stopped quickly halfway down, selected something from
the shelves on her left, made a tiny wave to us, then disappeared
around the endcap.

"I can't say I blame you," I said to Ozzie. "She's lovely."

"I'm sorry that happened. For what it's worth, it was a long time ago."

"You know, Ozzie. You seem like a good guy. And you're attractive in your own primitive way. When you kissed me at the door, well, I was fair game. But you know, I'm over here for such a short time, and the work I have to do is important to me. It is. Lollie just reminded me of that. Sorry. Not your fault, honestly. It's just not going to work on my end."

"It really was a long time ago, Kate."

"I believe you. But there are other Lollies out there waiting. Again, that's not anything I blame you for. I just don't want to be a Lollie."

"You aren't a Lollie. That's unfair."

"Maybe it is. Maybe it isn't. The point is, I'm not interested in the part. You don't need me, Ozzie. You have plenty to keep you busy. I'm sure of that. And sex is fun and I'm not a prude, and under other circumstances, well, who knows? But I'm not here for all that. Truly, I'm not. I need a clear mind and I need to concentrate on my work."

"I like you, Kate. I liked you from the start."

"I believe you. I don't think you're trying to trick me, Ozzie. Nothing like that. I simply don't have time for a distraction. I've got one academic year. I need to travel and absorb as much as I can. And I am going to spend as much time as possible in the library. That's always been my dream about Ireland, Ozzie. It's nothing personal."

"All this because of Lollie?"

"And because of her yoga pants. And her telling you not to be a stranger. And your damn good looks."

"You think I'm good looking?"

"Don't be desperate, Ozzie."

He laughed. I gave him credit for that.

"Well, I'll give you a ride back anyway. I'll empty this cart and you can grab another."

"Thank you, Ozzie. I hope we can be friends."

"Did you really just say that?"

It was my turn to laugh.

So that was what we did. I came out of the market with two bags of basic supplies. Ozzie carried one but handed it back to me when we arrived at the truck. He opened the door carefully and gathered Gottfried into his arms.

"Mommy and Daddy are getting divorced," he whispered to Gottfried.

"It's not your fault, Gottfried. We both love you.

"You'll have two homes now. And two Christmases! Think how fun that will be!"

Then he looked at me over the dog's soft head.

"I'm not done trying, Kate. I like you more than you know."

"Do us both a favor and let it go."

"I'll curse Lollie to her last days for showing up when she did."

"There will always be a Lollie with you, Ozzie. It's the weather around you."

"Not true. You wound me, Kate."

I put my bags of groceries in the back of the truck and took Gottfried from him. He held the door while I climbed in, then closed it softly after me.

12

"We've reserved you a carrel. You can leave your things there. It will save you the trouble of carrying books back and forth. I hope it will be satisfactory. We have eight visiting scholars at the moment. You'll be in good company."

I followed Agatha Thomond up the stairs of the University of Limerick Library. She was a short, tidy woman, with brown hair and green eyes. She wore tweed. She reminded me of a woman out walking the glens of Scotland, a shepherd dog beside her, a walking thorn in her hand, while rain pelted her and fog tried to undo her hair. I liked her immediately. She was a member of the Bicycle Society, I knew, because Elsa Bunratty had called and made the connection. Agatha had been on my list of contacts in any case, but it was good to have an introduction. Despite the tweed, she was approximately my age, perhaps a few years older.

She escorted me to a desk overlooking the wide public square outside the library. It was not a grand desk, merely a two-shelved plain table with a laminate top, but it was clean and bright and well positioned to look out and watch the world go by. A handsome lamp took up one corner of the desk surface, and Agatha flicked it on and off to check that it was in working order.

"The bulbs are always going on these things," she said, glancing under the brown lamp shade to check. "But this one seems to be in order. How will this do? Can you make this work?"

"Absolutely. It's perfect."

"Well, you're being kind. But it should do you. We've had no complaints. The internet is fulsome and reliable. The carrel is yours, day and night. No one else will even sit at the desk. That's one of our policies. People are remarkably good about it. It's a bit of an ethical piece of local lore. Honoring scholars and all of that."

"Thank you, Agatha. It's just right for me. I can look out and daydream and read to my heart's content."

"And you'll be traveling a good deal, I imagine," she said, and motioned for me to try out the seat. I did. It was a straight-backed wooden chair, solid and heavy. She watched me as I fussed with the lamp to get the light to fall on the desktop in a way that generated a sharp moon of illumination. I had two drawers on either side of my leg area. Someone had left a pair of scissors, a pack of yellow legal pads, and a tin of tea in the top drawer on the right side.

"Oh, that reminds me. You can have tea down in the cafeteria. It's quite good and reasonably priced. You could nearly live in this library. We even have a shower room down in the basement if it comes to that."

"I hope I won't need that."

She smiled. She had a kind, good face. I liked her enormously.

"Elsa asked me to invite you to our next Bicycle Society meeting. Can you ride a bike? We simply bicycle to a pub and drink wine. It's nothing fancy."

"Yes. I'm pretty good on a bike."

"It's a funny little group. Just we three, really. You haven't met Victoria, have you?"

"No, not yet."

"She works in grounds. Plants. She's in charge of the landscaping around here. You'll like her. She lived for a long time in Colorado with her mad boyfriend. Then they broke apart and she came back here. She's more American in her outlook than Elsa or I."

She smiled the type of smile that said she had delivered all the information she had and now, if I needed anything, it was my turn to talk. I didn't need anything. She nodded her head.

"Then I'll leave you to it. Some of the scholars write down their area of interest and tape it to the desk. It's a little tradition. You don't have to do it if you won't want to, but sometimes areas of research overlap and you'd never know you're sitting near someone doing work that influences your own. It's a good idea usually."

"Thank you. I'll do that."

"It's good to have you here, Kate. Welcome to the university library."

"Thank you. It's been wonderful already."

After she left, I sat for a long time and looked out at the common below. Students went back and forth, and a few boys rode by on long boards. It looked about the same as any college campus in the States. A small group of four played hacky-sack, a game I hadn't seen in a long time. The girls wore clothes you could see on any college campus: leggings and fleeces, sometimes with a scarf, sometimes with Ugg boots anchoring their feet. I realized, watching them, that I missed teaching. I missed the energy I gathered from young college students spilling into my classroom.

Later, when the sun had moved to cast long shadows into my window, I flicked on the lamp again and pulled out one of the yellow sheets from the legal pad. I wrote on it: *Kate Moreton, American, studying narratives of the Blasket Islands.* I taped it to my desk and turned off the lamp, then smoothed the note several times with my hands.

For two days I read. I read nonstop. I read deeply. I fell asleep in bed, a book suspended in my hand, the pages fluffing like a kind bird floating above me. I read in my carrel, concentrating and taking notes, and I read as I ate bowls of good soup in the campus pub. I read the account, haphazard as it was, of Maura O'Hailey, the woman from Massachusetts who, in her bouts with Alzheimer's, had suddenly returned to her mother tongue, Old Irish, the language of the Blaskets. I read about seals and cod and thatched roofs, and about men falling into the sea and disappearing forever, about the trawlers from the Isle of Man who came for the herring harvest, of nurses who visited the islands and found the inhabitants nearly starved and malnourished. I read about Robin Flower, a British researcher, who had spent his summers studying the language and customs of the Blasket Islanders, about the French who discovered bountiful lobster caches around the stony islands and traded rope and linens, beeswax and sugar, for the blue-green creatures who ended their lives in Parisian pots. I read until the world of the Blaskets felt more familiar to me than the world I inhabited, until the Blaskets became a dream I entered as easily as opening a door. I learned the family names, the names of deceased children, of women who had perished in childbirth. It was a pleasure—this consumption of prose—that I had only experienced in brief moments before. It was a scholar's compensation, the joy one could get only by living in books, the taste of pages on one's tongue.

I had the study-carrel area to myself. I wasn't sure why. I had gone quietly around the room, reading the names and concentrations of the other scholars. I told myself I did so to discover if my research interest overlapped with the interest of any other attending scholar, but the truth was more pedestrian than that. I was simply nosy. Three of the scholars, it turned out, had posted notes below their name plates to say they were away and would return on such and such a date. One scholar wrote that she was having a baby. Another scholar wrote that he had left on a drinking binge and didn't expect to be back until Christmas. I liked him for his honesty.

That still left two scholars. I formed the eighth. They had left no notes to explain their absences, and so each day as I sat in my carrel, I waited for one of them to appear. I knew their names: Carol Markman and Daijeet Agarwal. Carol Markman's research interest was Irish nutrition around the time of the potato famine. Daijeet Agarwal's interest was trout. While I found Carol Markman's area interesting, I found the simple declaration by Daijeet Agarwal more compelling: *trout*. Perhaps it was my fatigue, or my focus on the Blaskets, but I turned the phrase over and over in my head, playing with it, trying to make it make sense. *Trout*. Say any word long enough and it can become humorous, but trout was better than most. *Trout*. *Truite* in French. *Forelle* in German. I couldn't help conjuring an image of a man sitting at a table talking to a fish. Interviewing the fish. Shaking fins with the fish. I wanted Daijeet Agarwal to appear and explain his trout to me. But for my first two days, he was nowhere to be seen.

On the third day, on the Thursday when I was scheduled to attend my first Bicycle Society meeting, Daijeet Agarwal arrived. He was tall and round, a bear-man with feet that splayed slightly outward. He could dribble a soccer ball by merely walking to the window. He was dressed in jeans and a leather jacket, and he carried a well-worn backpack over his right shoulder. He smiled at me when he saw me, but he did not say a word. He sat down loudly at his desk and began pulling things out of his backpack. I tried to ignore him, but of course that was impossible. The space compelled us to be aware of each other. I looked out the window. Rain had come up early and stayed around, although the weather report called for clear skies later in the day. I wondered, absently, if the rain had chased Daijeet off a stream somewhere, derailed his trout studies, but I pushed that thought from my head and tried to concentrate on the Blaskets. My ears, however, picked up the steady thump of him emptying his backpack. Whatever he did with trout, it seemed to require a fair amount of equipment.

"You are the new scholar," he said when the thumping

stopped. "The Blasket Islands scholar. We heard you were coming."

I turned in my chair.

"Yes. Hello. I'm Kate."

"And I am Daijeet. An Irishman of the first order."

He smiled. He had a wonderful smile. And I was fairly certain he was not an Irishman in the sense that he meant it.

"Nice to meet you. You study trout?"

"Yes. Well, water, too. Oxygen and the carrying capacity of waters for rainbow trout. I work with the Irish government to increase fish production. At least that's our mission. It's not always successful."

"That's fascinating."

"To tell you the truth, I'm an angler, mostly. I like to fish, so I thought this would keep me near a stream. So far it has. I'm not here very often. I usually only stop in to check messages and whatnot."

"How about Carol Markman? Is she around?"

"No, she dropped out of her doctoral program. She came to hate it. She took off to Bali or somewhere in the east. She liked to travel more than study. A little bit of a party girl, I guess. I think it's just you and me this semester. And you needn't worry. I won't be here often."

"I don't require a priestly silence."

"I didn't mean that you did. My mother always said boys make noise to confirm they're alive. I think she was right about that. I have a station at a water lab in the north, up by Donegal. I spend most of my time there."

"Do you live in Limerick?"

"I have an apartment here. A tiny place. I'm officially part of the University of Limerick visiting faculty. I spend a good deal of time sleeping in my truck. I have a government pass to fish wherever I like. All in the name of research. I guess I am what Americans call a trout bum."

I liked him. I suspected his research was a good deal more complicated, and more valuable, than he let on. I envied him what I imagined to be the straightforward nature of his research. Water and trout. That seemed sensible. It raised the question of my own research. The narratives were unquestionably worthwhile. What I was less certain about was my own approach to the narratives, how I would turn them into a readable volume that would shed light on the women's experiences on the islands. That was a large part of what I had come to Ireland to understand.

But that was a concern for another day. When Daijeet finished rumbling around in his desk, he appeared at my elbow and asked me to tea.

"I'd love to have tea," I said, not entirely clear on his invitation. "Anytime."

"I meant now. Let me treat you to a cup of tea. It's the least I can do to welcome you. We can get to know each other a little bit."

I didn't want to stop reading, but I sensed it would be good to take my nose out of a book for a few minutes. Besides, I liked his way. I grabbed my wallet out of my desk drawer and stood. He held out his hand.

"We should meet properly, Kate," he said, taking my hand. "Daijeet Agarwal. Nice to make your acquaintance."

"Kate Moreton. Nice to meet you, too."

We hardly spoke as we went downstairs to the snack bar, but it was not an uncomfortable silence. Something about his presence was soothing. At the checkout counter, he insisted on buying my tea. I let him. Then we went to sit at a tiny round table near a large window looking out on the common. It took me a moment to realize we sat directly beneath our carrels.

"How did you come to study trout?" I asked him when we had settled.

"Oh, it's a funny story, really. I'm an Anglophile. Absurd, I know, for an Indian boy. We have cause to hate the British. I was raised in India by an aunt and my mother. My father died when

I was young, but he left behind a remarkable library. A British Empire library, I suppose you could say. I spent my days reading all sorts of British rot about the Empire, and Queen Victoria, and goodness knows what else. I became enamored of Sir Izaak Walton, of all people. Do you know his work?"

"Nothing except the name."

"Some call him the father of fly fishing. British to the core. His father died when he was a young man. He earned his living as an ironmonger, but was trained as a linen draper. He spent the last twenty years of his life traveling around and fishing with eminent clergymen. The balmy English, you could say. He published *The Compleat Angler* in 1653, about a half century after *Hamlet*. I don't know why, but I bought into it all. Maybe the search for a father, God save me. The old clergymen and Walton wading around the streams of England. And wearing the whole British getup, tweeds and unsuitable hats. It probably didn't even exist as I envisioned it, but I came up with my own interpretation of it. Like a boy playing Dungeons and Dragons, you could say, except I really did go out to the streams and teach myself how to fish. A kind older man named Emmet Peterson took me under his wing and taught me the finer points. He loved Walton's writings, too, so we were well matched. He taught biology in a secondary school, so that lit a fuse with me. I saw a way to teach and fish and go along. And here I am today."

"That's a wonderful story. What a different way into your field."

"Oh, it feels ridiculous sometimes. I often wonder why people make the choices to go into the fields they choose. But I do like the work and the field study. I'm not fishing with old clergymen, but I have a chance to wander around the British Isles and fish and take water samples. But I am talking way too much. I guess I've missed the company of my fellow scholars this semester without even knowing it. Tell me about your interest, Kate. I'd like to know."

I did as he requested. To my bewilderment, I found I had a great deal bottled up, too. I told him about my family growing up in the Springfield/Chicopee area of Massachusetts, about my father and his remembrances of his childhood, about my concentration on women's narratives of the Blaskets. Asked ten minutes before our tea, I would have said I couldn't possibly outline my area of interest for a virtual stranger. But I did. It had something to do with Daijeet's kind, soft eyes. And my own loneliness, I supposed. You couldn't live in books forever, I knew.

"Well, aren't we a pair?" he said when I finished. "What kind of deranged childhoods did we endure?"

He laughed as he said it. I laughed, too. We finished our tea watching the students walk by. He said if I ever wanted to go fishing with him some day, I should feel free to ask. He promised to bring me fresh trout and salmon. I looked at him and realized it was like having a bear promise to bring you food. A friendly bear. Yes, I told him. Please do.

SECOND LETTER

Kate—

Fall skies. Smoke and the pull of a fish deep in the ocean. Sometimes I climb to the top of the *Ferriter* to see the curve of the earth in the distance. It's possible to fall off the ocean, I believe. Rooks are clustered near my land these days and I have been watching them dive on an orchard, their beaks red and yellow with apple pulp. Two fingers of whiskey. When the rooks look up, they have black eyes. I imagine if I could see one closely enough, see their eyes, I could see a reflection of Ireland in them. Of grass and wind and stone. Here's what I thought when I met you: this woman is a bird you hear singing just before sunset. A hermit thrush. Maybe that's too much. That is too much. Try again: this woman is a fire on a cold autumn day. She is a burning of branches, apple branches, and the smoke that goes to the clouds. The rooks tell me we should try again. Try once. I am not perfect and I am not whole. I am spotted. But my blood tells me we would be right together. That we could be together in bed and sleep until the sheep sing to us and the stars dive into the light. Come be with me, Kate. I won't bite. I will meet you with honesty. Nothing needs to happen until you say it needs to happen. Until you can trust me.

Winter will be here soon. The season of bowls and spoons. We should spend it together.

Gottfried misses you. I considered tying this letter to his collar and tying him to your door, but that seemed hackneyed. Too cute. Or too something.

"And then I asked him with my eyes to ask again yes and then he asked me would I yes and his heart was going like mad and yes I said yes I will yes."

I hope that is your answer.

13

I read Ozzie's letter twice before I placed it on the small kitchen table facedown. Instinct, self-preservation, told me to burn it. A dart of headache registered between my brows. It was a good letter, if maybe a bit straining. It was a provocative letter. It was a come-hither letter. It was a see-I-am-a-soulful-wounded-man-come-mend-me letter. All of that.

And the last line was a quote from Joyce. I looked it up on my phone. I read it slowly and admitted Ozzie had good taste. A good eye. But, of course, it could also be a pose, a trap he used to lure women closer. It was a better trap than most, I granted, but my warning bells still tinkled.

I took a deep breath and glanced at the clock on the stove. It was 4:37. The Bicycle Society was planning to call on me at five. They had switched plans around to accommodate my newness. Instead of me joining them, they promised to swing by and pick me up. On bicycles.

I used the bathroom, brushed my hair, then texted Milly.

> **Going out with the Bicycle Society. If not back later, call police.**

Hardly a minute went by before she texted me back.

Fun. Play nice.

Ozzie sent a letter.

Dreamy or drecky?

Half and half. Romantic. Byronic. Idiotic.

Give him credit for trying.

*Daijeet Agarwal is my study buddy. He might
be a bear wearing spectacles.*

I need a study buddy.

Here they are, I texted when I heard them knocking downstairs. *Gotta go.*

"You're wondering," said a woman when I opened the door, "if we are prostitutes or something altogether different. I wish we were hookers, dear. Ladies of the night. They have better underwear than we do."

I didn't recognize her, so I assumed the speaker was Victoria, the landscape professional.

"We are the Bicycle Society," Elsa said. "May we come in?"

"You have to invite us in like vampires," Agatha, my friendly librarian, said. "Otherwise, we have to stay outside."

"Certainly. Please come in, won't you?"

I stepped back. Agatha touched my elbow as she passed. Victoria, tall, with wide shoulders and a masculine cut to her clothes, stopped directly in front of me. She had enormous energy. Her dark eyes looked out in sharp, appraising lines. She wore a fascinator in her hair. It caught the late afternoon light and sent it in a dozen directions.

"Victoria Willington," she said. "God-awful name, I know.

Sounds like a joke. British more than Irish. Most call me Vic, never Vicky. Nice to meet me."

"Nice to meet you, Vic," I answered, only catching her little joke on the last bounce.

She smiled. They came in like a well-ordered troop and went up the stairs ahead of me. Victoria, Vic, carried a bag that clanked. Wine, I imagined.

"They did do a good job, Elsa," Agatha said, looking around the apartment to inspect the paint job. "The painters. Nicely done. Was that Jim and his crew?"

"I believe so. Yes, I am trying to remember. Yes, Jim. No . . . Bobby. I don't remember for sure."

I hadn't reached the top step of my own apartment when I heard my kitchen drawers opening. Victoria went through them rapidly, looking for a wine opener, I imagined. She had set a bottle out on the kitchen table next to Ozzie's overturned letter. I had the odd sensation of being hosted in my own space. Elsa seemed to read the panic in my expression.

"We've terrified you, haven't we?" she said. "You must wonder what in the world . . ."

"You really should supply people with wine openers," Victoria said, closing the last drawer in frustration. "It's uncivilized not to, Elsa."

"I have a Swiss Army knife," Agatha said, digging into a pocket in her skirt. "We've used it before. Quit being such a bulldog, Vic."

"Oh, hand it here. I'll have the corks out in an hour or two. Bloody desperate corkscrews on these knives," Vic said.

"And we have tandem bike for you to ride, if you're still game," Elsa said. "You'll ride with Agatha. We've decided to amend the program today. We're just riding to Vic's house."

"Call her Aggie, for god's sakes," Vic said. "No one calls her Agatha."

"You and Aggie, then," Elsa finished and then glanced at Vic. "Are you quite through antagonizing everyone, Vic?"

"Not yet," Vic said, snatching the closest bottle off the table. "Not until I have a drink."

"She does calm down later," Aggie said, sitting at the kitchen table. "She's like a horse who has to run around the track a couple times before she's sensible."

I felt the tiniest bit overwhelmed, but happy, too, to have people in my apartment. To have friends or at least acquaintances. I had been terribly deep into my books. Before Vic could finally get the cork out, though, we decided to bike over to her house and drink the wine there. It wasn't far. They were all coming from work and I sensed they wanted to get to a familiar place. It didn't make sense to settle twice around a glass of wine.

I locked up and followed them downstairs. I tried to remember the last time I had ridden a tandem bicycle. It had been years. Aggie took the front and I took the rear. She looked back at me over her shoulder.

"Ready?" she asked.

"I'll do my best."

"It's only a mile or so. We'll be there in a jiff. We stay right next to the river, so no worries about traffic."

"I'm game."

It was beautiful. Vic zoomed in and out, laughing and taunting us, complaining that she needed a drink, and Elsa rode responsibly, in keeping with her nature. It was Thursday, almost the end of the work week, and I felt the pleasure of the day ending, the small lights coming on in the houses we passed. I was in Ireland, I reminded myself, biking along the Shannon River with some new Irish friends. White herons stood in the gentle current, scanning the river bottom for worms or shrimp or whatever it was they ate. The autumn air chilled me, but it felt good to have the breeze on my skin. I matched my pedaling to Aggie's pace and we sprinted along, doing better than any of them, ahead of the pack but part of it, too. The moon rose above the eastern horizon and sent a yellow light onto the water, the beams fracturing like fire the moment they touched the dark current.

We sat in Vic's country house. That's what she called it, although we remained in the Limerick city limits. It was a dream Irish cottage: dull gray stone covered in ivy, with multipaned windows and a mossy brick walkway to the front door. Milly would have called it a calendar house, one of those remarkable homes photographed to mark October or March, the kind of place that filled you with envy and a hope that life really could be like the cottage suggested. But Vic's nonchalance around it made it comfortable and welcoming. Near the front door she had a box full of walking sticks and boots. The fireplace was not enormous, but it burned nimbly. She had cat andirons, tall and thin, whose eyes glowed when the flames caught them in the right way. We sat under one lamp while the fire provided the rest of the illumination. If someone had told me I would land in such a cottage after a week in Ireland, I would have told the person she was crazy. But here I was. Life had moved quickly.

"Kate, you now know all the inner secrets of the Bicycle Society," Elsa said. "It isn't much, I'm afraid. It's Vic's fault, the whole thing. She made us exercise to feel good about drinking wine, so we combined the two at her suggestion."

"And no one has to drive," Aggie added. "That's key. Ireland is unbelievably tough on drink-driving."

"It's a good society," I said, settling more deeply into the loveseat that directly faced Vic's lovely fire. "Just the proper amount of secrecy. All societies should have a little secrecy baked into them."

"Lord, I like hearing an American voice. All that twang," Vic said, her backside to the fire. "We sometimes forget. I remember when I first moved to Colorado I couldn't get enough of the American accent."

"Is yours a Boston accent?" Agatha asked me.

"I guess so. New England, really."

"I get such a kick out of southern American accents. They sound as if they're chewing each word. I like the word *gumbo*," Elsa said.

Evening had fallen around us. Vic ordered Chinese food. It came in minutes, much to my surprise, until Vic explained the restaurant was only a block away. I got up to wash my hands and came back in time to hear Ozzie's name mentioned. It surprised me to hear it.

"You went to the Blaskets with him, didn't you? On his boat?" Elsa asked as we leaned forward to make selections from the white cardboard containers of Chinese food. "Ozzie Ferriter?"

"I did," I said, careful of what I said. Ireland was a small country. Ozzie was right about that.

"He's Nora Crean's grandson," Elsa explained to Aggie and Vic. "Great looking and a fisherman of some sort. He was soldier in Afghanistan, wasn't he, Kate?"

"He was, I gather. I don't know him well."

"Nora Crean is rich as Midas," Vic said. "She supports a dozen Irish charities single-handedly. She has New York money."

"And he runs a dog camp of some sort. I remember hearing that," Aggie said, passing out the chopsticks that accompanied the order.

"Rescue dogs, I heard," I said. "But he gave that up, I think."

"He is a good-looking bastard," Vic said. "I know who you're talking about now. I've seen him beside Nora Crean at openings and such."

"He's good to his grandmother," I said, taking an egg roll. "To Nora or Gran. That's what Ozzie calls her."

"Did he ask you out?" Vic asked, then she shook her head and laughed. "Of course he did! You're both beautiful! The question is, did you go with him?"

"Not yet," I said.

And that brought a small roar of laughter.

"Don't let them bully you," Elsa said. "You go out with whom-ever you like."

"But to come all this way and end up on a date with an Amer-ican," Aggie said, "is just too rich."

"He's half Irish, too," Elsa said, a beard of noodles cascading down from her chopsticks. "With a name like Ferriter? Do you know, they once had a castle on the Blaskets?"

"I did know that," I said. "It came up in my research."

"Oh, give him a tumble," Vic said. "Why not? He might prove to be a nicer guy than we're making him out to be."

"I'll put out feelers and see if any women friends have a line on him," Aggie said.

"Please don't," I said. "Whatever you find out I'll either like too much or too little, and neither position helps me."

"She's right!" Vic said, grabbing a bottle of wine and filling all of our glasses. "Good mental health, Kate. Not always easy to achieve in this group."

The fire chose that moment to send a spark onto the floor near Vic's boot. She smashed it down and twisted on it until she could be certain it was extinguished. I watched her, eating slowly, my mind drifting to a lecture I had heard in an anthropology class years before. The professor, Dr. Conahue, had been a mar-velous teacher who had spent years in Africa observing village and tribal life. She said that in Africa women engage in lam-entation sessions. It could take place around a river while they washed clothing, or in the process of pounding millet for their evening meals. In fact, Dr. Conahue said, wherever women con-gregated, they invariably created a lamentation session, where each individual could have a turn at airing her heartache or dis-appointment. I hadn't thought of that concept since I had been an undergraduate, but it seemed true to me in this moment. We were village women gone to the river to haul water back on our

heads. Meanwhile, we passed the time by complaining or specu-
lating about men. It didn't change much the world over.

That thought flashed through my mind in an instant. But it
left me wondering what to do about Ozzie. I wanted to ask their
opinions, but I was too uncertain of the reactions. What did I
want them to say? How did I want to see Ozzie? The entire matter was still upside down in my mind.

But I remembered him kissing me. I remembered kissing
him back.

We talked about the university after that. They filled me in
on people I should know, who could fix a computer, who might
process travel money associated with my fellowship. They also
gave me a thousand destinations to consider. Vic pulled out three
well-thumbed Lonely Planet travel guides from the bookshelves
beside the fireplace. Then, as suddenly as it had begun, the day
ended.

The fire went lower, and Aggie said she should be getting
back, was I ready? I said yes and that cued Elsa to stand.

"Thank you, Vic," I said, shaking her hand. "Thank you for
having me."

"Thank you for coming and joining us. It freshened things
considerably."

We biked back to the campus. The air was soft. We rode beside the River Shannon and three white swans watched us pass.
They stood on a sandbar and one dug at something on its side
with its pumpkin beak. A new web of moonlight threw itself over
the water and the current carried it only a second before tossing
it aside and continuing on its way.

I went back to my work the next day and for almost a week afterward I kept my head in books. I read and made plans for travel
and connected, for the first time, really, the scope of the Blasket
story as it fit into the Irish mainland. I read a good deal about the

actual day in 1953 when the boat came to remove the remaining twenty-two islanders. The seas ran at the shores so roughly that the islanders were forced to abandon their household goods—as meager as they were—on the strand where I had picnicked with Nora and Seamus and Ozzie. Only weeks later, when they traveled on a fair day to tend their sheep, did the islanders bring to Kerry the remainders of their belongings. The image of household furniture sitting on a beach and waiting to be claimed was a haunting one and I searched several catalogs and everywhere online that I could think of before I finally found a photo of that artifact. Some of that furniture, I realized, likely belonged to my father's people.

I began to dream about the Blaskets after that week of concentrated study. The dreams focused on small, trivial details. The flip of a felt roof when the wind brushed it back; the paint used to mark the sheep that roamed all over the island; the tuck of a gull as it bent to the wind and fell through the air with a loud, raucous call. Scattered dreams. I sometimes fell asleep at my desk and that, I knew, marked a cautionary line that I had crossed. My lifelong tendency was to immerse myself in a project to the exclusion of everything else. It made me a disciplined scholar and teacher, but it also pushed me toward reclusiveness. In the past, I lived in self-selected isolation, not antisocial exactly, but in too close comfort with my own company. It could be dangerous, I knew from experience. To counteract it, I forced myself to take long walks along the River Shannon in midday, rain or shine. I did stretching and light yoga beside my desk. It was during one of those yoga sessions, in the middle of a downward dog, that Daijeet returned.

I stood, flushed, embarrassed that my butt had been in the air when he arrived. If he noticed, he didn't seem to care.

"I brought you a salmon," Daijeet said, swinging a large cooler onto his desk. "Caught this morning. It's a good one, too. Twenty-three inches. You do like fish, don't you?"

"I love fish. Thank you."

I went to his desk and watched as he opened the top of the cooler. He had three fish inside on ice, all of them silver as clouds. He picked one up and held it for my inspection.

"Got this one on a midge," he said.

"What's a midge?"

"A tiny fly. You're supposed to be impressed by that."

"I am!" I said, laughing.

He set the fish back in the cooler. I saw again his resemblance to a bear, a chunky, rounded figure who happened to love all things British. Paddington, maybe, or Winnie. He pulled a roll of plastic bags from his pocket and set them on his desk.

"When you head home, just take one in a bag. I recommend you eat it right away. That's the way it will be best. You live on campus, right?"

"Yes. Dodge Hall."

"There you go. Take whatever one you like. I've promised the other two to some friends."

"Thank you, Daijeet. That's going to be a treat."

"I recommend cooking it as simply as possible. No sauces except maybe a little lemon. Fish this fresh deserves to be its own taste."

"You'd be welcome to join me, Daijeet."

He pursed his lips. He was adorable in a kind, gentle way.

"I have a date," he said. "With my supervisor at the fisheries division. It's a bad idea, I know, but he's too cute to resist."

He was gay, I realized. I didn't know him well enough to be surprised, or confused, but the truth was I hadn't twigged that. Understanding his inclination, however, I worried that he thought I had asked him to my house for dinner out of a boy-girl sort of impulse. I blushed. I felt my scalp get warm under my hair.

"That's exciting," I managed to say. "Have you known him long?"

"Just a few months. We've been circling each other like sharks. Technically, we work together, so it's dodgy whether he should ask me out. But we're not edgy, we two. We're old, pokey fishermen. No dance clubs for us, unfortunately."

"Well, I can't wait to hear how it goes."

"Neither can I."

He smiled and put the cooler next to his desk. I smiled, too, and went back to my desk. Out of some stupid impulse, I picked up my phone and texted Ozzie.

What's the best way to cook salmon? I texted.

The little legend blinked on to say the message had been delivered. But no message came back at me. Not that night, not that weekend, not until seven days later.

14

"Let me get this straight," Milly said over Skype, her smile leading her words. I sat on my couch and watched her. "You're mad at him because he took you at your word that you didn't want to get tangled up in his business, right? But now that you texted him, you expect him to text back."

"I'm sick of men."

"Which is why you're texting him."

"Don't be logical, Milly. I hate when you're logical."

"Just listening and responding," she said. "You sound a little lonely."

"Not really. I had lunch with the bicycle girls. They've been welcoming."

"But a man is a different proposition."

"Maybe. Probably not. Who knows?"

It was good to talk to Milly. We had missed each other for more than a week, leaving messages and trying to catch each other. She had gone to Western Massachusetts to help her mysterious benefactress install an art piece at Mass MoCA. They had been gone for three days and then had driven to Montreal on impulse to visit a lavender farm. She had seen fields and fields of lavender. It had been stunning, she said. It had been almost more than her eye could accommodate. Now she was back and we had set up a date to Skype. She wore a big, black sweater and heavy slipper-boots and her hair looked like squirrels had decided to winter there.

"You're probably horny," Milly said, sipping from a ceramic mug of tea. "That's half of the world's problem, you know? Everyone needs more sex. It would make us all relax."

"I have done a lot of research. That's coming along great."

"And you're still horny. Horny is not work-related, dearie. Horny is a different thing."

"And I need to travel. I need to get out of Limerick and poke around. I need to go to Dunquin, where they settled some of the Blasket families. They built them cottages."

"Call Fish-boy and tell him to take you places."

"His name is Ozzie."

"Fish-boy suits him better. You have two fish-boys, don't you? You have Ozzie and you have Paddington Bear. Did gay Paddington bring you more salmon?"

"I'm never talking to you again."

"Oh, sweetie. It just started snowing."

She turned away, then she lifted her laptop and carried it outside. I knew everything about her studio. I knew it had a deck overlooking a small, overgrown section of forest. She held the screen toward the line where the trees met a meadow swatch. I watched the snow fall. I knew exactly how that felt. I knew the softness some snow brought with it, and how it made a small ticking sound on leaves sometimes, and how the grass would turn white and pale in the moonlight. It made me miss New Hampshire. It made me miss the East Coast of the US and the inevitable winter that came and made everyone cross after they had all fallen in love with it first. I missed old Yankee men in red wool hats with ear flaps.

"First snow always makes me cry," Milly said, turning the laptop camera around to her again. "I wish you were here, Kate."

"I do, too. But I like being here. I guess I'm just a little topsy-turvy right now."

"Any word from your mom?"

"Just a text. She's in Italy looking at sailboats."

"Will she come up to see you?"

"Not as far as I know. She could change her mind, but it depends on Ben. Maybe they'll sail up here."

"You're kidding, right?"

I nodded.

"Mom is not a sailor type," I said.

Milly slipped back onto her couch. She picked up her tea again. In the same instant, a text-notification came in from Ozzie Ferriter. It flashed on my screen, then faded before I could read it. It said something about boats and out of touch and then it disappeared.

"Ozzie just texted," I said. "How's that for timing? That's some weird juju."

"What did he say?"

"He said he's been on a boat fishing."

"See?"

"My mother and I are both dating sailors. Lord save me."

"You're not dating," Milly said. "It doesn't have to be dating."

"Then it's just exercise?"

"Something like that."

We signed off a little later. I didn't read Ozzie's message at first. I didn't want the temptation of eagerly writing him back. I made myself get up and clean the kitchen. I had been lax about that. Then, on a roll, I cleaned the rest of the studio. It didn't take long. It occurred to me as I worked that maybe Ozzie had texted that he was going to drop by. After being deliberately careful with it, I grabbed the phone and read his message.

Was out fishing. Who r u?

I want to see Gottfried.

When?

This weekend.

He's busy but I'm free. Friday afternoon?

Yes, please.

The letter worked?

Maybe.

Three Friday afternoon. Anything you don't eat?

Zebra.

I'll have a day planned for you.

Is Gottfried really busy?

I'll bring him. He's a teenager already.

See you Friday at 3.

I put the phone down. I wondered what in the world I had done.

Inner dialogue for 2.5 days, nights before sleep, brushing my teeth, dull, quiet moments in the study carrel:

What are you thinking? What do you expect? He's going to want to sleep with you. Is that what you want? Be careful what you wish for. Jeans, probably. A top and a sweater of some sort. I need to shop. No, I don't. I am on a budget. A night bag? Who calls it a night bag anymore? This is ridiculous. He's cute, and he's tall, and he smelled like a lamb last time I stood next to him. He jumped on a donkey and jumped off. He has a boat. He has a truck. If you show up with a night bag, then he assumes you are planning to stay over. That was not the agreement. It's snowing in New Hampshire. I want to see snow. I should bring a backpack. I could put things in a backpack. Things I'll need and a book and a charging cord for my phone. A toothbrush. Hairbrush. I should tell someone where I am going. Elsa. She would understand. He quoted Joyce. He knows Joyce's work. That's a plus. That's a big plus. He doesn't seem military. He seems the opposite of military, whatever that is. Hippie. Not hippie. No one is a hippie anymore. Crunchy, maybe. Sleeping with Abe was like borrowing a cup of sugar from a neighbor. Is good sex good love? Is good love good sex? Argue clean, sex dirty, someone said. Gottfried is a teen. He's planning a day. That's good. Layers. I should bring layers. It could get cold at night. Will we be together at night? He said a day. Not sneakers. Trainers, they call them here. He kissed me against the wall. He kissed me hard. You asked him to take you out. You did. You can pretend you didn't, but you did.

He did not show up at three on Friday. He did not show up at three thirty, either. He showed up at 3:47, his hair wild, his clothes dirty from work. A dark stain covered his hands in spots and his jeans bagged at the knees. He wore a knee brace on one knee and something like wood chips dangled in his hair. He had a small leather case of some sort attached to his belt, and it took me a moment to see it contained a tape measure. So he had been building something. And time had gotten away from him. He showed up dirty for a date, which was a signal of some sort.

He grinned when the door opened.

I felt furious. I felt furious that I had devoted time to thinking about what I would wear, what I should bring, when he, in his own good time, showed up like a guy heading out for a beer with his buddies after work. We were out of balance already.

"Please don't look at me like that, Kate," he said. "I know, I know, I know, it's exactly what I didn't want to have happen. Exactly. Please forgive me. I know I look a mess, but I have a good excuse."

"This is a mistake, isn't it?"

"Being late? Or going out together?"

"Both. Everything. I don't know, Ozzie. What are we doing?"

"We're going to have an afternoon together. I'm sorry. I am. Please, let's start fresh."

Was this going to be the pattern? I wondered. If he couldn't arrive clean and on time for our first date, was it likely he would be better on our tenth or twentieth? And didn't I sound like the bitch of the north wind? I needed to check that, I realized. I needed to prune it back. Did my irritation come from putting too much emotional weight into this single date? Probably. I forced myself to take a deep breath. Ozzie grinned again.

"You look nice, at least," he said.

"I thought we kind of had a date."

"We do, Kate. We do. I was in the middle of something and I had to see it through. I should have texted. I apologize. It won't happen again."

"I sound like a shrew, don't I?"

"A little bit."

"You're not filling me with confidence."

"I get that. But I had a dream about you. In the dream, I could reach my hand through you. What do you think that means?"

"It means you should see a doctor."

"I mean it. I could reach straight through your body."

"That could be creepy. You're not driving a white van, are you?"

"No, just the old truck. It didn't feel creepy in the dream. It felt as if we couldn't be closer."

"I can't tell what to believe about you, Ozzie. You confuse me. What was on the other side?"

"What other side?"

"When you put your hand through me, what was on the other side?"

"A bologna sandwich."

"Seriously?"

"No, nothing really. Just air. We were up in the air."

"I don't need a big distraction right now."

"How about a small distraction? I could maybe do that."

He grinned again. Then we almost kissed. I saw it come into his eyes and I watched, unsure, as he stepped inside. We stood for a moment close together. I couldn't resist him. Not really. He knew it and I knew it and we were both doomed. He bent down and grabbed my backpack and told me someone in the truck wanted to see me.

"Gottfried?"

"Yes."

"Okay. Gottfried works."

"I really am sorry, Kate. Truly. It was inconsiderate of me."

"Yes, it was."

"That's a little shrew-y. I think maybe we should kiss. Just once to get rid of the date jitters. What do you think?"

"Maybe."

"It's bad form to talk about a kiss. We should just kiss."

"You're talking too much."

"How big a kiss?"

"Now you're talking way too much."

He kissed me. It was soft and gentle. I had to go onto my toes. When I came back onto my solid feet, I knew that I was lost. At least for now. At least for a little while. At least until he didn't show up in dirty Carhartts and dirty hands and have a for-god's-sake cute puppy waiting in his truck.

I ran up the stairs and checked the apartment one last time. Stove off, lights off, windows closed against possible weather. When I came back down, I saw him framed against the doorway.

I admit my heart did a small dance. He looked like the man you wanted waiting at the bottom of a stairway.

"Ready?" he asked.

"Ready."

He put his hand on the small of my back as he walked me to the truck. His hand could not have sent my spine more sensations if it had been a spider.

Gottfried met me at the truck door. He smooshed his head out of the small window space to give me kisses. I kissed him back, then gentled his head back through into the interior. Ozzie held the door open for me.

"Thank you," I said.

"Shove him over. Gottfried, give her some room."

Ozzie leaned across me. He pushed Gottfried slowly into a down position. Then, turning slightly, he kissed me again. This time it wasn't gentle. He kissed me and slid his hand onto my thigh and that was deliberate, and that was okay, and I put my hand on the back of his neck.

"Forgive me?" he asked.

"No."

"Good."

He pulled back and slipped out the door. I bent down and kissed Gottfried. I told him he was getting to be a big boy. And he was. He had clumsy big paws and a black, shiny nose. He still smelled like a puppy, so I left my nose buried in his neck fur. He nuzzled me back.

Then Ozzie slipped in and we headed out for our day, for sex, maybe, for I couldn't guess what. As we drove off, I saw the River Shannon glinting between the trees.

We made out on a cliff overlooking Dunquin.

We had stopped to let Gottfried have a break. We took him for a walk along the Dingle Way, a circular hiking trail that ran around most of the Dingle Peninsula. Ozzie knew about it. He said it would be a good place to walk a dog.

So we did. And it *was* a good place. The day had settled into an autumn bath of sun and wind and clouds. The Dingle Way on that part of the peninsula worked along a rugged set of cliffs that looked out over Dunquin. I knew Dunquin by reputation. It was the location of the Blasket Museum. I had planned to visit it, but I had been too fixated on my research. Ozzie said he knew someone who could give us a private tour. He said Bertie Janes, one of the docents, had been one of the last children to have been born on the Blaskets. Now Bertie earned his living telling the story of his birthplace. Nora Crean connected to Bertie in some way. Ozzie did not spell out the connection, but it sounded as if Bertie would be happy to help us.

We pulled over beside the blaze that signified the Dingle Way. Beyond the sign, the land gave way to blue-gray rock and sheer cliffs. Gulls and pippins and shearwaters flew in the up-breezes, swirling and diving out to the green waves. I knew about the birds and how the islanders often ate their eggs in season. The view could not have been cleaner or more vivid. A single trawler plied the waters and left behind great white angel wings of wake. Wind pushed my hair back and I stood with my arms crossed and watched as Ozzie bent to let Gottfried off leash.

"It's beautiful here, Ozzie," I said, and the wind crushed my voice and rolled it into a tiny ball. "Is that Tralee Bay?"

"Brandon Bay, I think, but they run together. It's the Atlantic, when all is said and done."

He bent and whispered something into Gottfried's ear, then let him go. Gottfried darted ahead then looked back, uncertain, his heavy paws resembling a pile of leaves on each foot. Ozzie nodded and reassured him that it was okay to run ahead. We followed after Gottfried. He clumsily moved along the dirt path, apparently having a difficult time believing he was free to run and roam as he liked. His body dangled between postures; he attempted to determine whether to zoom forward or stop and smell every odor that pushed toward him. In between impulses, he gazed back at Ozzie. He loved Ozzie, and it touched my heart to see their mutual devotion.

"You can see the Blaskets from here," he said, walking beside me. "From up on this point, anyway. You can see how they sit in the sea. I thought you'd like to view it. Beyond them it's all open ocean. Rough seas a good portion of the time. They think they're named the Blaskets from the Norse word, *brasker,* meaning dangerous place. But I suppose you know that already."

"I do."

"The government resettled many of the islanders to Dunquin. The government built cottages for them in Dunquin and they gave them a couple acres of land, but the islanders didn't like being away from the sea. That's what people say, anyway. There is quite a romance about the Blaskets. Paradise lost, and all that. But I guess I'm telling you things you know already."

"But it's good to hear them beside the cliffs like this. That's why I'm here. To see it with my own eyes."

"The seas are rough, I can attest to that. I was out one day for mackerel and a wave came from my stern and chucked me against my own wheel. I thought I'd broken my nose."

"And they went out in canoes. It's hard to believe."

"And they died regularly enough. It was a hard life."

"I can't imagine living next to the sea, then having it taken away. Even the voice inside your head would sound different. I'm not sure how you would form a thought without it afterward."

We talked, but it didn't mean anything. I might have recited lines from "Jabberwocky," for all it mattered. We had reached that strange point where men and women meet in their bodies and blood, reached that place in which words don't signify any longer, where whatever biology wanted from us had to happen. He couldn't have looked better: hair blowing in the wind, slightly mussed and dirty, frequently bending to whisper some new instruction to Gottfried, his jeans dirty and baggy. He sat on a flat stone that served as a bench and in front of us the sea ran all the way to Boston. I sat beside him. And then that inevitable moment arrived, that moment that is both thrilling and terrifying, when I expected him to kiss me, to lean over again as he did in the truck, but he didn't. He kept talking about the Blaskets. I couldn't take it. I stood and stepped between his legs and then he tucked me closer, his hand on my waist, and pulled me into him. We kissed. And now it was no longer cautious and tentative; I pushed my body into his and he slid his hand down to the back of my thighs and lifted me slightly. We kissed again and again, and there was no reason to stop, no reason to ever stop, and a wild flurry of thoughts pushed through my head. Research, job, Paddington Bear, my mother's sailboat, Dartmouth, Milly, the Blaskets, my father, and then I flatlined on all of that. I abandoned myself to him, I fell into him, into his body and his mouth and his hands, and a hunger I hadn't known I possessed a minute before began to pulse through me in great, boiling shudders. I may have made a small, desperate sound in the back of my throat. I may have grabbed his face and held it in front of me. I may have run my hands over his broad back and, simultaneously, let his hands run where they liked. And they did run over my body, touching everywhere and passing on, making my body move almost to capture the next place his hand would land. He whispered in my ear, something soft and sweet, and then darker, something about bodies, but the wind kept me from hearing it clearly. Then finally, unable to breathe exactly, he put his forehead against mine and held me solidly, his lovely eyes inches from mine.

"Nora said you'd be by. Come this way. We've just closed shop for the day, but I can run you through quickly enough. How is she?"

"Gran's fine, thanks, Bertie," Ozzie answered.

"Oh, that's good to hear. You're very welcome, my dear. It's

Kate, is it? Please call me Bertie. Everyone does. Glad to have a scholar visiting. So many people traipse through the museum without understanding a thing about it. Without understanding what it might mean to live in such a manner as the islanders did. So much, so much, so much to consider," Bertie said, backing up and waving his hand to suggest I let my eyes roam. "And this museum is merely a snapshot. Sometimes I think it's wrong to have a museum of anything, because it lets one believe that lives can be encapsulated in tiny displays. I mean, does one pyramid tell you anything about the Egyptian kings? I think not."

Bertie was a treasure. He was short, perhaps five-four, and as round about the waist as a bowling pin. His gray hair ran in a ring around his scalp, tail chasing head. He had a busy manner, like a cartoon mouse late for dinner. He wore a bright, red-checkered vest and dark trousers; a gold watch chain drooped in a shiny moustache across his potbelly. He glowed red; he had the fairest skin of any human I had ever encountered. He looked newborn, actually, as if he had reached the age of sixty or seventy without passing through the mandatory cracks and creaks of aging. He was fascinating to see and indisputably Irish. If he felt any displeasure at having to show around a nosy American tourist after hours, he did not reveal it.

Unfortunately, Ozzie and I could not keep our hands off each other.

But we had to. We had talked briefly about canceling the appointment, but Ozzie had insisted we keep it. Bertie Janes was not to be missed, he said, and it had been set up by Nora herself, and so with difficulty we had stopped kissing on the flat rock—I wanted him as much as he wanted me—and pulled ourselves together. We loaded Gottfried into the truck and drove the short descent into Dunquin, where the museum waited.

As I stood looking around the museum, dazed, I tried to shake myself. I had thought books and movies about people burning for one another was merely a Hollywood confection. Yes, a little passion, a little heat, but nothing that felt overpowering. But this did. This felt like wires edging toward a water-filled sink. I had never experienced anything like it.

Poor Bertie stood in the center of it. Perhaps he sensed it, perhaps he didn't, but Ozzie and I were aware of his sobriety while we felt drunk with each other.

He pointed to the sign at the entrance. It was in Irish.

Is ionad oidhreachta agus cultúir/músaem ar leith é Ionad an Bhlascaoid Mhóir a chomórann an pobal eisceachtúil a mhair ar na hoileáin iargúlta seo go dtí gur tréigeadh an Blascaod Mór sa deireadh in 1953. Anseo, leathslí timpeall Bhealach Cheann Sléibhe, tá radharcanna iontacha de chósta fiáin an Atlantaigh agus d'oileáin iomráiteacha an cheantair le feiceáil ar gach aon taobh.

"Do you read Irish?" he asked. "I won't judge you if you don't. You can be a Roman scholar without reading Latin. But I wanted to know."

I read the sign aloud to him. Not perfectly. Not without hesitation. And not without feeling Ozzie's boiling presence beside me. But I didn't do it badly.

With stunning views of the wild Atlantic coast and islands at the halfway point of the Slea Head Drive, the Blasket Centre is a fascinating heritage and cultural centre/ museum, honouring the unique community who lived on the remote Blasket Islands until their evacuation in 1953.

"Very good, very good indeed, Kate. Did Nora tell me your father lived on *An Blascaod Mór*?"

"Only as a little boy. My last name is Moreton. Do you know it?"

"I do, of course. Like wheat thrown into the wind, we were," he said, now leading us more fully into the hall that formed the center of the museum. "Now come along. I'll give you the Cook's tour. You'll have to return in full daylight some other day, so I can spend a few hours with you."

"I'd love that."

"You're mostly interested in the female narratives? Peig Sayers, of course, is from right here. She wrote a lovely book, as you know. But there are many others. We've been collecting oral histories right here at the center, as a matter of fact."

"I'm aware of your collection. I'm here to study them."

He smiled. And maybe he *did* sense how Ozzie and I felt for each other. We were like two teenagers rousted off a basement make-out couch by a sleepy parent. I blushed when he studied me. Ozzie moved away and pretended interest in a display I was certain he had seen many times before.

"You have Irish coloring, Kate," Bertie said.

Which made me blush even more.

We did the tour. Ozzie kept his distance. He knew a good bit about the history of the islands, but no one could match Bertie's comprehensive knowledge. I felt halved by having such a rich source standing in front of me, and the weak twitter I felt anytime Ozzie stepped near. Several times I had to rededicate myself to listening. At some point Bertie understood what was going on, and he smiled a kind, gentle smile and closed off the session.

"You're young," he said when we concluded the brief circuit of displays, "and this will keep for another day. Are you running up to Limerick or going to Ozzie's land?"

Neither one of us answered. We didn't know ourselves.

"I guess we haven't decided," I said. "This was our first stop."

"Promise me you'll come back when we will have more time together," Bertie said. "Now, run along, both of you. It's a beautiful Irish night and you don't want to spend it listening to me yabbering on."

"Thank you," I said. "It was wonderful."

We put down a few dates on my phone and I took his contact information. He smiled and held the door open for us.

"Best to herself," Bertie said to Ozzie, meaning to give his compliments to Nora. "And remember me to Seamus."

"I will."

We stepped out into the quiet evening light. Ozzie looked at me as we walked to the truck.

"Limerick, or my land?" he asked.

I didn't answer. I didn't have to.

15

Is it simple pheromones that attracts people to one another so violently? A blood chemistry, perhaps mixed with some unidentifiable trick of posture and body language? Whatever science has to tell us about attraction, it could not have overstated its case inside the truck with Ozzie. Our hands touched over and over and whenever we had to stop, I fairly climbed on top of him and kissed him. When we pulled off to take in an overlook, we held hands. It was absurd, and we knew it. We joked about it. We tried to push it away. But a wash of chemicals moved through my stomach and into my lower body and I could not resist finding him again, kissing him, wanting his skin against mine. Call it butterflies. Call it lust. Whatever you call it, it was real and unquenchable.

We drove toward his land, toward his dwelling, toward his bed.

Gottfried saved us over and over. His sweet, goofy head swiveled back and forth to see what we were doing, what we planned, who would be the one to lurch against his back and kiss the other. He made a good dog chaperone. Ozzie also tried to point out landmarks and things he thought I should note, but it was hard for us both to concentrate. *Smerwick Harbor, Slea Head,* he said in a voice that was not in keeping with what was going on between us, then we rounded the tip of the Dingle Peninsula and headed toward his land.

"When did you buy this land?" I asked, trying to clear my head, trying to be reasonable.

"About three years ago. Gran knew when it came on the market and she urged me to buy it. She said there will never be another chance to own such a thing. Not in our lifetime."

"Gran is your guardian angel."

"More than I can say. She has a bit of magic, you know? Good things follow her."

Then, for a little while, the passion I felt for him gave way to an appreciation of what he called his land. We bounced down an unpaved path and drove toward the sea. For a moment, I thought we actually might go into the sea; the road led us to a drop-off and I grabbed the dashboard before I realized Ozzie had it under control. It was simply a fold in the path, a bump that obscured the magnificent wash of land and water in front of us. As soon as the front wheels of the truck cleared it, the land opened, and I saw his place. He lived in a yurt, a round, circular tent that I had seen many times in Vermont and New Hampshire. A yurt was more than a tent, I knew, and Ozzie's yurt could not have been more perfectly placed. He had built a wide, level platform that extended slightly over the slope of the hill, as if the entire structure wanted to make sure it gained the best view of the waves below. From the deck, I saw, one could sit and watch the sunrise. The sea was, as Mrs. Fox of the Dingle B&B had said, a tablecloth for him. It pressed and moved everywhere around the site, and I could not swivel my head fast enough to take everything in. It was surpassingly beautiful, and I was glad when Ozzie did not try to discount its perfection or pass it off as unimportant.

"I'm a lucky man," he said simply.

"It's incredible, Ozzie. I had no idea."

"The yurt is temporary. Or at least, it's only what I live in now. I have the foundation in for a cottage. I'm building a traditional Irish cottage. At least, that's my plan. It's tough funding it and finding the time to work on it, but it's what I do right now. That's what I was working on and why I was late. I'm still sorry about that. I was in the middle of something and I couldn't put it down."

"Does it have a name? The land?"

"No, not really. Seamus said it was once called Sheepshead, but I don't know how reliable that is. Another old-timer said it was called Galleyhead when he was a boy. A family lived here for years, but they had a fire and they couldn't recover. The land sat empty for a long time over legal matters, a family dispute. If Nora hadn't known about it, I wouldn't have heard a thing. I've been calling it Crow Point."

"And where did you get the yurt?"

"Purchased it. I built the platform. I'm a fair carpenter. I won't pretend I am better than I am, but I can drive a nail. The yurt can be a studio or a guesthouse when the cottage is completed. I'll be a hundred years old by then."

"Oh, but look what you have, Ozzie. Look at what it is. The sea is everywhere!"

I looked at him. Who was this man? And how had I fallen into his life? He drove slowly up the last dozen feet until he parked and turned off the engine. As soon as the engine quieted, the land began to speak its own language. He smiled softly. His smile did not convey covetousness or pride at what he owned. He knew full well that he was merely a custodian. The sea felt humbling. Whatever you built, however you lived beside it, the sea had the last and final word.

I pushed open the door and climbed out. Gottfried scrambled out after me.

"You are a lucky man," I said, my eyes filled with the sea and the grass and long slope to the water. "To have this."

"I'm lucky if I can keep it and meet the payments."

He came and stood beside me. I put my hand through his arm. It felt natural. He pressed my hand against his ribs.

"I'd give blood if I had to," I said. "I'd do anything to keep it."

"Do you own your house?"

"No, but I have plans for a cabin. I bought some land I was looking at before the fellowship came through. My dad left me a little bit of money for it. It's pretty land in New Hampshire, but it doesn't compare to this. Six point seven acres. It was forested about three years ago, so it's mostly bald. But things grow fast in New England. It has a small brook running through it."

"It's good to have water near you. It keeps the fairies from wandering away."

"It's lovely land, Ozzie. Seriously. I'm glad I saw it."

"You make it sound like you're dying or going away."

"Not dying, I hope. But going away someday."

He turned and kissed me. The kiss grew and burned and I leaned back against the car to have a little of his weight on me. My mind explored the edges of everything that had happened and I had to force it back. I refused to think of Ozzie here with any other woman, or the possibility that he had played this exact hand before. Whatever was happening between us, I was glad to follow it.

"Come on, I'll show you inside," he said finally when we broke apart.

"The sun is going down."

"It does every day."

"Here, though. It sets behind us, but look at the light running across the sea. And the Blaskets are to the south and west. Do I have it right?"

"You have it exactly."

He bellied away from the yurt entrance to call Gottfried, who had been running back and forth across the long meadow to the sea. I was impressed when Gottfried came at his first recall. Ozzie squatted down and Gottfried crashed into his arms and lap, overjoyed at being beside his guardian again.

"He's hungry," Ozzie called. "Are you hungry?"

"Not at the moment."

"Seamus was right, you know? About your hair. It's Christmas ribbon. And it's getting redder by the moment beside the sea."

"One lies and the other swears to it," I called back, using one of my father's favorite expressions. "You have no shame."

He stood and looked directly at me.

"Come to bed with me, Kate Moreton. Please come to my bed. It's you I want, and I believe you want me."

I nodded and walked forward. Not even the fairies could have kept me from his bed.

It was savage. It was love. We hardly made it to his bed, a wide sea of a bed that overlooked the waves running to the shore below. Undressing, slowly undressing and teasing one another, was out of the question. It was too late for that. The entire afternoon had been foreplay and now he took me out of my clothes with complete assurance. We fell on the bed like a sheaf of wheat being scythed by a tractor blade. Our bodies collected motion, sensation, and brought it back time and again to something central and important in our kisses. He pushed his clothes away and once, stopped, smiling, to push Gottfried away as well.

"Go," he said to the puppy.

Gottfried retreated a few paces and sat, his head tilted quizzically.

"Not now," Ozzie said. "I promise, later."

Then we began again, continued again, resumed again. I felt him ready, felt him bursting, and his hands slipped into the right places, the places I needed his hands to be, and I arched to him, giving him everything, giving him a bridge to walk across to me.

I loved him in that instant. I loved everything about him and I knew, I knew, I knew, it was not love, not true love, but I had never experienced such a connection. Then his body came on top of mine and for a minute, an hour, a day, we kissed so deeply that I thought I might go blind. My body shook. Then he entered me. There was no preamble, no careful planning except that it had all been planning. I pulled him deeper into me and held him, and for a ten count, a million count, neither of us moved. He kissed me again and again, then he stopped, stopped everything, and he put his eyes on mine and said my name.

"Kate," he said. "I knew it would be like this."

"Yes," I said, because I knew it, too.

"Is everything all right? Are you okay?"

I nodded and put my lips on his throat.

Then it began to build again. I didn't know how that could be, how we could be peaceful for an instant, then build so rapidly back to greedy, wanton lovemaking in mere heartbeats. Behind him, the sun faded and gray night began to fall. I listened and heard the sea and a few last gulls began to cry at the fall of daylight. For a moment, everything mixed together: sea and Ozzie and sex and gulls and wind and light and water. Why had I ever considered denying myself this? I couldn't help wondering. I knew I could press this moment into my memory and hold it for the rest of my days.

After that, he guided me. He took me as he liked and I went with anything he suggested. My climax lingered and came forward, then retreated slightly, back and forth, and he controlled it by looks he gave me. He was accomplished. He was generous and kind and forceful and gentle. We worked in concert, I knew, and the night grew darker and we continued until he withdrew and told me to follow him.

"Follow you?" I asked, confused.

"We're going to swim now."

"Did you . . . ?"

"No, not yet."

I couldn't help thinking of Milly, of how she would hang on every element of this story. But I vowed that I would never tell her. This was ours alone. I held my hand out to him and he pulled me onto my feet.

"It's not far," he said. "You'll see."

I almost asked for a robe. For something. But then I knew that was exactly what we didn't need.

"Come on, Gottfried, you can come, too," he said.

We stepped naked into the night. The air felt glorious and clean. I was still proudly aroused and twice on the gentle descent to the water he stopped and kissed me. He put his hands in places that invited me to more and more and more, and then he held my arm tightly as we walked across the rocky beach toward the water. He refused to let us stop. He continued on and I felt the water rising on my legs, my breath shortening, and then, in one smooth motion, he dove forward. I dove with him and the sea moved and pushed around us, and he came to me and kissed me over and over, our lips and tongues tasting of salt.

"We have this, Kate," he said. "Not everyone has this."

"I know."

He lifted me, my legs around his waist, and carried me to the shore. Carefully, slowly, he placed me on the sand and entered me. Above him the stars moved and danced, and I closed my eyes.

"Now," he said, "oh, now, Kate. Be with me."

16

We made eggs and toast and a kind of Irish bacon I had never tasted before. We kept the door open and let the breeze come in and out as it liked. I wore one of his shirts, a blue-green flannel, and a pair of old socks he lent me. A tiny nervous voice woke inside my head and asked if this was not all a routine, a postcoital protocol that he had practiced and mastered with other women, but I tried to allay those suspicions. He owed me nothing; he had promised me nothing. We moved back and forth from the stove to the small table he had in one section of the yurt, while Gottfried studied us both. Ozzie tucked his iPhone into a player and we listened to Irish trad sessions mixed with American jazz. Now and then I looked out at the sea and saw the moon sending its lonely light across it.

"Do you like your eggs dry or runny?" he asked from the small tabletop range, his back to me while he cooked. "Be careful. There's a right answer."

"Dry."

"That's the right answer. Runny eggs are a sin against humankind."

"You have strong opinions."

"I like an orderly world," he said, turning to hand me the plate of bacon. "One more second and then we'll be ready."

"I thought you had more dogs than just one," I said when I

returned for another assignment. "I thought you ran a dog shelter of sorts."

"Isn't Gottfried enough? Do you hear that, Gottfried? Kate thinks you're not enough."

"Just trying to assemble the facts."

"Oh, I've been a way station for a bunch of dogs. I had some kennels for a while outside, but I didn't like leaving them alone. Now I help out when I can at the local shelter. They come and go."

"But Gottfried won't come and go, will he?"

"No, he's here to stay."

"Thank goodness."

Had a morsel of artificialness crept in between us? It reminded me that, beyond the crazed heat and lovemaking we had shared, we didn't know each other at all well. We could not be natural with one another, because we did not know how we fit together except in our bodies. We did not have the liberty, exactly, to touch each other, to giving the loving passes that couples could share. It made the cooking and the food preparation slightly formal. We were back to a first date, despite the fact that I walked around his yurt in a pair of panties and smelled his body on every inch of me.

"Ready, I think," he said, lifting two plates. "Take these over, if you would, please. I'm going to have a whiskey. Would you like a whiskey?"

"Sure."

"Bushmills. Do you like Bushmills or Jameson?"

"Is there a right answer again?"

"There is."

He clanked some glasses together and then came to the table carrying two jelly jars of whiskey. He had filled them almost to the top. It was more whiskey than I had ever drunk before.

"You have an Irish hand when it comes to pouring drinks, Ozzie. That's what my father would have said."

"Joy should come in full glasses."

"Are you feeling joyous?"

"I'm feeling I met a wonderful woman. I'm feeling I have miles to go before I know her."

He held the back of my chair. I sat. Then he touched glasses with mine. I drank a sip. The whiskey burned in a lovely way throughout my body. He sat down across from me. He took a larger drink and grimaced a little when he did so.

"As God is my witness, it's the doctor's orders," he said, putting his glass down on the table, then nodded to my plate. "Eat while it's hot, Kate. Don't insult the chef."

"I'm suddenly feeling shy," I said, because it was the way I felt.

"Well, we leap-frogged ahead a little, didn't we?"

"You call that leap-frogging?"

He smiled. He took another large drink and then bit into his toast. He looked handsome and tired and sleepy. He wore a heavy sweatshirt and a pair of shorts. Bare feet. The gray sweatshirt had OHIO STATE stenciled in red across the front.

"Do you think men and women live on different islands?" he asked.

"Depends what you mean by islands, I suppose."

"Oh, that we have trouble pulling the oars in rhythm."

"It felt like we had pretty good rhythm," I said, because I couldn't resist.

He looked at me and took my hand.

"Why don't you stay here a while and we can get to know each other?"

"Here? With you?"

"For a few days. You have time, don't you? I know you have to do research, but we can set you up here. Call it an experiment. I have to warn you, though. I don't have running water. Outhouses and swims in the ocean will have to do. I have a sun shower hooked up outside and that's fairly reliable when we have a sunny day. I manage to stay reasonably clean."

"It's tempting. But maybe we should try it day by day to make sure it works well for each of us."

"Look. I haven't liked someone as much as I like you in a long, long time. That's the truth. I'd like to see where it goes. We can stand on ceremony and you can go back to your apartment, but no one is keeping tabs on you. You can be here or there, right?"

"Right. I suppose."

"It seems like fate gave us a few free days. I'd like to know you, Kate. How are you feeling about it all?"

"Still shy."

"We can drive back to Limerick tomorrow and you can pick up anything you need or want. I have to go out fishing some days, and you can come with me if you like. Or better still, you can use my truck and take day trips around Ireland. You can visit Bertie. He really is a source you need to tap. You know how to drive a stick, don't you?"

I nodded. Neither one of us had eaten more than a bite. He drank off his whiskey and stood to get more. Watching him, I couldn't think. This was precisely what I didn't want to have happen. It would get in the way of my research, I knew, but another part of me, a deeper, more compelling layer, urged me to accept his invitation. I ran through a mental list of objections, but I knew I could make things work if I wanted them to. My schedule was my own.

"Eat and think. You don't have to decide this minute," he said, coming back with the bottle. "I promise to drive you back to Limerick the second you've had enough. No questions asked. But I think you'll like it here, Kate. I have some friends I'd like you to meet. And Gottfried would like it. I don't see any ragged edges to the plan."

He picked up my hand again. He held it as he ate. I ate, too. The sea air rolled into the yurt and made me feel a little crazy. I ate everything on my plate. Gottfried came and put his chin on my knee as I finished. It was two against one, I realized, and that was hardly fair.

We slept with the door open. The weather had been cool enough to kill off any last mosquitoes, and so we could leave it wide open to the sea and the wind that came up after sunset. The sea made its relentless call to us, but now it sounded far away, and lonely, and although I fell asleep in exhaustion, I awoke in the small hours to a pang of fear and worry. I had dreamed of something, something troubling, but I couldn't fix it in my mind to study it. I also had to pee. I slipped out of the bed and walked carefully through the yurt, afraid I would trip and wake Ozzie or knock myself out in an absurdly awkward fall. But when I reached the doorway, moonlight met me, and I slipped down the stairs of the yurt platform and squatted in the grass. I said a silent thank you to the camping trips my dad took with me. After finishing, I stood for a moment and looked around. Mist covered the slope of the hill down to the ocean. It was one thing, I realized, to study the Blasket Island narratives, but quite another to live as the islanders had lived. True, we had electricity in the yurt, but for the rest it was remarkably similar to the life any of the islanders might have experienced. We would live by moonlight and tides and wind. I was glad of it, calm and happy, and although I could not have said why I had accepted Ozzie's offer to stay, or why I wanted to be near him, I knew that I did.

"Your feet are blocks of ice," he said when I climbed back into bed beside him.

"I'm sorry. I tried to be quiet."

"How do I know you're not a fairy woman come to take my soul?"

"You don't."

"I suppose a fairy woman could manage warm feet, wouldn't she? Was it raining out?"

"No."

"I thought I heard rain earlier. Can you fall back asleep?"

"Usually. Sometimes it's hard."

"I fall asleep like a stone, but once I wake, I usually have to be sung back to sleep."

I felt my stomach drop. I wasn't certain I had heard him correctly.

"Are you serious?" I asked.

"Yes, you have to sing, Kate."

"I'm not going to sing, Ozzie. You're insane right now."

"I need you to sing an old Bing Crosby song. Something sappy and sentimental. It's the only way I'll get back to sleep."

I raised up on one elbow. In the dimness, I saw him smiling.

"You almost had me, you horrible man," I said, shoving him a little. "If I had started singing, I would have made you take me home."

"It's not too late to sing. Come on, we'll sing together."

"I'm not singing with you, Ozzie. Not now, not ever."

"Do you have a bad voice?"

"I have a terrible voice."

"I knew you did. You're very nasal."

I shoved him again.

"I'm not singing, but I am not nasal."

"How would you know? I think in this case I'm the better judge. Let's hear you sing something simple. Try 'Row, Row, Row Your Boat.' It will be like a sound check."

"You're ridiculous. You know that, right?"

"Are you better with 'Frère Jacques'? Maybe that would be less nasal for you. You might do better with that. Come on. I'll start, and you do the chase round."

"What in the world is a chase round?"

"It's the second part, usually given to the person with the weaker voice. The nasal voice."

"I've begun to hate you."

"Don't hate me. A poor carpenter blames his tools. It's not your fault you have a nasal voice."

"I do not have a nasal voice. Do you think I'm nasal when I speak?"

"You sound a little goose-ish. Like a duck with a beak that's too long."

He started singing "Frère Jacques." He sang it low and slowly gathered me in his arms. Each time he came to the end of a line, he paused, waiting for me to sing my part. He sang it twice through, then stopped and kissed my neck.

"If you won't sing me to sleep, I will be awake all night," he said. "It's not my fault any more than your duck voice is your fault."

"I do not have a duck voice."

"Well, that would be the only reason to withhold your chase round."

"Nobody on this earth calls it a chase round."

"What do you mean by chase round? You mean the part you don't sing?"

He sang again, softly, whispering it in my ear. When he stopped, I sang my part. It felt crazy and oddly embarrassing. I would have preferred to put on a small dance recital at the foot of the bed, but he was so adorable pausing and holding me that I couldn't resist. We sang the round three times, our voices blending, and it was dark and full of wind and sea sounds. On the last round, I buried my face against his neck and that started our bodies again. What before had been lustful and straining, now became something yielding and quiet. He pulled me on top of him and pushed the covers away and I fell against him, self-conscious for a time before he lifted me back with his strong arms and I knew the dim moonlight illuminated me.

"You're beautiful, Kate," he whispered. "You take my breath away."

"Tell me I have a beautiful voice. That's all I care about now."

He smiled. Then we didn't talk for a while. It was still intense and fierce, but we knew each other better now and we kissed with more knowledge and communication. I felt alive with him, happy as I had not been happy in what felt a long time, and we continued pulling together until some of the night had passed. When we finished, we did not move apart. We fell asleep in each other's arms, and we slept until the sun found us in the morning and called us away from our bed.

17

We lived this way:

We woke at first light and sometimes we went down to the sea with Gottfried beside us. The wind and gulls called to us and we fell into the sea face forward, diving as if we would swim across Dingle Bay, but the water took our breath and gave it back to us in short, exhilarating pants. At times the water tried to soothe us, to ask us to stay, but then the chill broke through that momentary idleness and sent us clambering onto the rocky shingle. Back at the yurt, wet and shivering, we poked the stove for more heat, and dried ourselves as we made black coffee, then we carried our coffee back to bed and watched as the sun filled the yurt. A small Plexiglas top capped the center of the yurt, and the light came there first, pulling at it as bear might pull at a honey jar to have it open. We held hands and drank coffee, and our legs twined together, and sometimes we turned on cello music, low and quiet, and other times we wanted only the gulls. On rainy mornings, when the clouds climbed off the sea and came to rest for a while on land, we read from an anthology of Irish poets, Yeats and Alice Furlong and Eiléan Ní Chuilleanáin, Biddy Jenkinson, Jane Wilde, Lady Gregory, the poems repeated or rejected by our own tongues. Sometimes, but not always, we made love again, our passion easy and welcome, a friend that visited for the morning, a promise of what we would turn to in the softening of the day.

In late morning, we separated. I pulled my books around me, plugged in my laptop, and I did the research I needed to complete. For long hours, I lived inside the books, lived on the islands I had come to love, my thoughts and musings teased by the wind and smell of salt. We left the door cracked open so that Gottfried could come and go, and I listened with half my attention to the sound of Ozzie's hammer as he worked on the cottage he built stone by stone, board by board. Later, depending on the day, I worked beside him, taking pleasure in the rock labor, the hoisting and twisting and sizing. Ozzie buried his hands in the building; he gave it everything. He worked quietly and orderly, moving carefully as if he knew such things cannot be hurried. He had in his head an Irish cottage, white-washed, with thick walls to take advantage of solar gain, and twelve windows all on one floor. He called the windows the apostles. The stones he gathered around his own land, Crow Point, pulling up rocks with a bright yellow spade and a rock sledge that he unsheathed from a harness on his back. He needed no real plans on paper. The design of the cottage had been in his head for a decade, he said, and it was only the letting it out that caused him any hesitation. Now and then he talked as he built, and sometimes he forced me to sing "Frère Jacques," and occasionally we had to ride to town to get lumber, or a bag of mortar, or a pack of metal pins he wanted for the walls. We rode with Gottfried between us, his size nearly doubling in those days, and frequently I treated Ozzie to a dinner, bangers and mash, shepherd's pie, a pale red Smithwick's or a black, foaming Guinness on the side. But we had lost the habit of being with other people, and we preferred, instead, to gather the groceries along with the building supplies and head back to Crow Point. Then we cooked something long and lingering on the wood stove, chili or stew, and when the weather came up foul we returned to bed and listened to the storm, rising only to stir the food.

Every third day, if the weather cooperated, Ozzie fished. He went for mackerel, but he went for much more. I have to say this now: he had a coiled spring inside him that tightened gradually until it needed to go off to the sea, needed to get away from everything, even away from me. I knew that need came from something that had happened in the war, or many things that had happened in the war, but I didn't ask him about it. I was not his confessor. I listened to anything he had to say about his time in Afghanistan, which was little, and I saw the spring inside him tighten and close and then I knew to leave him alone. He did not take it out on me; he took it out on himself, and twice, when he returned from being on the sea all night, I spotted liquor bottles on the deck of the *Ferriter.* He did not attempt to hide them, nor did he speak of them. It was as if he went away to a clinic, to a specialist only he could visit, and when he returned he appeared weak and still, exorcised of a demon that began to take life in him again the moment he set foot on land. I did not ask him about his drinking, or his time at sea, and I knew, instinctively, that I was not invited on these journeys. I did occasionally go with him to hand-line for a few mackerels, drifting off Crow Point's shore, but those trips were light and fun, picnics that he invited me to join. Sometimes we lay in the sun as the boat floated anywhere it liked, and we kissed until we had to either go back to land or have each other in the shade of the cuddy, our skin wild for one another, our eyes half sleepy from the sun.

Sometimes, late at night, I asked myself what I was doing in this man's bed, where I expected things to go, but I tamped those questions down as quickly as they appeared. What did it matter? I was drunk on him. I was drunk on the land and the sea and our lovely bed. And if he had to disappear now and then to turn a mirror inside on himself, well, what was the worry with that? Besides, my research went well. I wrote in a mindful haze, drifting in my note-taking and in my own prose. I knew the pleasure of scholarship and I sank into it, receiving joy from a well-turned phrase or a particularly sharp insight. I did not share my

work with Ozzie; it was as separate as his nights on the ocean. I
believed that living next to the water informed my work. It would
be deeper, I imagined, because of it, and I was grateful to Ozzie
for letting me stay with him in our secret hideaway. I wrote in
sustained chunks and lay in bed with the stove going to reread
my work. I sent it to no one, not even to Milly, for fear that letting another voice speak on top of it would sap the poignancy of
the women's narratives I sought to represent.

On those days when Ozzie went to sea, I took the truck and
traveled where I liked. I haunted the Dingle Peninsula, stopping twice to take a cup of tea with Bertie, who proved to be a
dear, dear man and a formidable scholar. But I also slipped over
to Kerry and Kinsale and Killarney, to Waterford and Cashel. I
made up itineraries for myself and charted out my travel fastid-
iously, taking Gottfried with me as a traveling companion. The
truth is, I welcomed Ozzie's departures just as I welcomed his
returns. We defied the stuffy notion of two people having to be
constantly next to one another. When we reunited, our passion
had been stoked by absence, and for days at a time we stayed
near the yurt and cottage as if it returned a strength we dissipated when away from it. From the library in Dingle, I borrowed
discs of old movies and we lay in bed to watch them, my laptop
propped on his belly, my head on his shoulder, the actors dancing on his body. He played with my hair and at times we kissed
and put the movie aside, but oftener we fell asleep and woke to
a white screen staring at us like a sea creature's pale dead eye.

Time passed. It ceased to matter as it once had. I returned to
Limerick to check my apartment, to gather books, and to answer
emails. I Skyped with Milly, and spoke with my mother, but their
voices sounded far away and small. Away from Crow Point, I felt
incomplete. Away from Ozzie, I missed a part of myself. When I
returned and met him at the door, he greeted me and kissed me
and told me he could put his hands through me, so desperately
had he missed me. We fell back into the bed and back into our

holiday from the world, and Gottfried watched us and came with us in the mornings when we swam and washed the night's love-making from our skin.

"I want to take you somewhere," Ozzie said one morning after standing by the door to look out at the sea. "The weather looks promising. Would you care to take a short trip?"

"Do I get to know where you're taking me?"

"Not right away. I want it to be a surprise."

I was in bed, lounging, a cup of black coffee burning a welcome hole in the center of my belly. Gottfried lay in the doorway, looking out at the sea. He seemed to want to do whatever Ozzie decided to do. It was calm and bright, a day stolen from the usual autumn weather for better purposes.

"What do I need to bring?"

"We may sleep on the boat one night. Bring a change of clothes and some warm things. You'll like it, I promise. Are you up for it?"

"I could use a break from my books."

"Don't bring any books unless you want to read them aloud. We're traveling back in time today. How does that sound?"

He turned and faced me. He smiled. It was kind, gentle smile.

"It sounds fine," I said.

"You may fall in love with me too much if you come with me today."

"I'm already too much in love with you, Ozzie. I thought you knew."

"And I with you, Kate. I'm great with you," he said, employing an Irish phrase.

He stood and looked at me. I couldn't take my eyes back from him. I wondered if he felt what I felt. I wondered if any human could know in the end what her love thought when their eyes were locked. I didn't think so.

We packed everything into the truck. Ozzie made us swing by the small grocery store on the road to Dingle to get supplies. He bought champagne and red wine and grapes and cheese. We stored them in a cooler, which we carried onto the boat. We lashed the cooler to the starboard gunwale. Then Ozzie pushed off. In less than an hour, we had gone from our bed to the open sea.

If I could take one picture and hold it forever of Ozzie, of Ozzie in our splendid isolation, then it would be from that morning on the sea. He stood at the wheel, happy, content, his old gray-green sweater hanging comfortably around him. He needed a haircut, but the unruliness of his hair made him even more attractive. He looked wild and free, the finest version of his many editions, and when he called me over and made me stand between his legs so that we could be one body steering the ship, I agreed happily. I was so in love with him, so lost to him at that moment, that I could have denied him nothing.

We traveled south. We passed Slea Head and kept the land on our port side. The sea had a mild chop, but that was all. I liked feeling Ozzie's alertness to the sea and its moods. He watched the birds to signal fish, and he watched the waves and the landmarks for signs of treachery. But it was not a day for anything to go wrong.

We traveled to Skellig Michael, or, in the Irish, *Sceilg Mhichíl*. I knew it by reputation; anyone who visited Ireland knew it. Obnoxiously, it had also been used in the final scene of a recent Star Wars movie, and the rumor was that it had now become too crowded to enjoy in season. It was a UNESCO World Heritage site, a place of surpassing beauty and historical importance. It had been built between the sixth and eighth centuries as a Gaelic Christian monastery. It was a stone needle in the sea, a place of such severe beauty that the monks had finally abandoned it in the twelfth century. For centuries, the monks had lived off the provisions from a vegetable garden supplemented by fish and birds' eggs.

"Thank you," I said when he revealed his plan to me. "It's a place I've dreamed of going, but I thought it was too late in the season."

"Not when you know a fisherman."

"Have you been to it before?"

He nodded.

"What's it like?"

"You'll see for yourself soon enough. You can't explain it. Nothing I could say would do it justice."

"It's such an extreme way to live. Incomprehensible, really. I almost envy their fixed belief."

"It could never sustain more than a dozen monks and an abbot. There's a hermitage at the back of the island where single monks lived for years at a time in silence."

"Except for the sea," I said.

"Yes, except for that."

It was not a long journey. Ozzie kept the *Ferriter* moving at a steady pace through the chop. For a while, I asked him more questions about the monastery, until he finally turned me into his body and kissed me. I knew what the kiss meant: it was not a moment to worry about research and knowing the historical context. It was, instead, a moment to witness something powerfully human. He was right about that, I knew, and when our kiss broke off, I felt myself ease into a comfort that claimed me.

At last the islands rose from the sea. They were rockier than the Blaskets, more severe and lonesome. Ozzie knew the landmarks. The Great Skellig supported a lighthouse. He brought the *Ferriter* around and in no time approached the dock. Clearly, the attraction had been shut down for the season. The slips that jutted out from the docks had been roped off. A steel gate stood across the walkway that ran, in summer, from the dock to the land. Someone had hung a CLOSED sign on the gate.

I looked at him. He didn't seem to give it a thought.

"We'll have to climb around the gate," he said, shutting down the engine as he backwashed it halfway into a slip. "Might be hard to bring Gottfried. Jump up to the bow and tie her up, would you?"

"Are you sure about this?"

"What could happen?"

"Maybe a fine. I don't know. You tell me."

"I'm a Catholic. They can't keep me away from a place of worship."

"Oh, you're that much of a Catholic, are you?"

"I am today."

I tied her off as he had taught me to do. Ozzie whistled as he shut down the boat. I stood for a moment staring up at the steps to the monastery. The steps were its most famous feature, I knew. People sometimes slipped and died on the steps when they tried to climb them in bad weather. I found it difficult to imagine the labor that went into building such a staircase. Perhaps they had used donkeys, but much of the work, I imagined, had been done by human hand. Digging and pulling, pulling and digging.

"The Vikings attacked here in the 800s. Bloody intrepid bastards they were, too," Ozzie said, coming forward. "I've always admired the Vikings. Greatest navigators of their time."

"Are we going to climb it?"

"We didn't come all this way to be locked out by a gate, Kate. If the Vikings can attack, the least we can do is slip around a few metal bars."

"It's a UNESCO site."

"It's a rock in the middle of the sea where a bunch of crazy religious men lived in filth and prayer. It's both more and less than what people say."

He had set his jaw. I had never quite seen this aspect of his personality. He seemed to take it personally that the authorities had closed the attraction for the season. I wasn't sure how to read the situation. I didn't doubt that he would get us to the top of the island. I wondered, though, if anyone would be waiting when we came down, ready to impound our boat or hand us a ticket. Ozzie didn't appear to care.

I decided I didn't care, either. I didn't come to Ireland to be timid.

"Okay, let's go. What about Gottfried?"

"We'll have to lift him around the gate. I think we can do it."

"Is Gottfried a Catholic, too?"

"As a matter of fact, he is."

We kissed. Perhaps it was my fault, but a little of the pleasure of the day had seeped away. I hated that I had asked so many questions and paused so noticeably at the closed gate that it had cooled the adventurousness of the moment. He had gone out of his way to bring me here, a place I dearly wanted to visit, and I had been overcautious and tentative. I felt his irritation running a thin line through his blood. We were different in that way: he jumped and then thought of the consequences, while I considered the consequence before jumping.

Gottfried salvaged things. It was a comical piece of business to hand him around the end of the gate. Neither one of us, I suppose, had quite taken into account how large he had grown. It was one thing to see him grow larger day by day; it was another thing to hoist him up in our arms and hand him around the outmost post of a fence, dangling over the water, only one hand free to cradle him. If Ozzie hadn't been massively strong, we never would have accomplished it. As it was, Gottfried perceived the danger and struggled more than necessary in our arms. Finally, Ozzie lowered him to the ground and he ran off, happy to be free, while Ozzie helped me swing past the gate post.

"Up we go," Ozzie said.

"Thank you. Thank you, Ozzie, for bringing me here."

"You're welcome."

"It's magnificent already."

"It's a remarkable place."

And it was. It was penetratingly beautiful, especially in this quiet season without tourists running everywhere. The famous steps ran up through the valley and went almost to the clouds. Oddly, I felt an almost overpowering need to kneel, or to show some outward sign of respect. It was not obeisance to a mysterious god, but to the human part of us that strived so urgently, and so doggedly, for connection to something greater than our mortal bodies.

Fortunately, Gottfried kept us from becoming too serious about our undertaking. He scouted ahead and then turned back to us over and over. He covered three times the trail that we did.

"There are no toilets," Ozzie said after we had started. "I mean, even in the summer. They have no toilets on the boats and no toilets on the island. I've always thought that was the strangest feature of the whole shebang."

"Why don't they? And don't talk about it or I will have to go for sure."

"I guess because it's a religious site. I don't know, honestly."

"How many steps?"

"Six hundred," he said without pause.

It took us a little over an hour to climb to the top. We could have made better time, but the scenery, the gain at each level of elevation, staggered us. It was more beautiful, and more austere, than anything I had ever experienced. In the summer, perhaps, with thousands of people climbing beside us, their cameras out, their kids running ahead, we would have missed something essential. But on this day, in the cool gray of November, alone as we were, the sense of something sacred was palpable. Except for the sea, it was silent. I found my eyes clouding a dozen times as we hiked.

We stopped at Christ's Saddle to rest, and for a long time we sat without saying anything. What was there to say? The labor of the monks humbled us.

At the top, we had the place to ourselves. The sea reached everywhere around us. The monks had built large stone structures, corbelling them so that each stone leaned inches inward from the stone beneath it. By building that way, the structures stood up and leaned inward, rising without mortar or anything to hold them except gravity. They had beehive shapes. The living, or residential, cells led to the larger oratory and to St. Michael's Church, the only building on the island to use lime mortar.

"Do you like it?" Ozzie whispered to me.

He had come up behind me and put his arms around me. The wind blew ceaselessly from the north. I felt if I closed my eyes I could be lost in the wind, lost in the vision of the sea. Gannets and puffins lived on the stony cliffs, but it was not the season for them. Still, seabirds flew and banked in the air, their calls echoing slightly as we stood and looked out.

"Thank you. I've never seen anything more beautiful."

"We're alone on this island, Kate."

"I know."

"I want to marry you here and now. Will you marry me, Kate?"

I turned in his arms to face him.

"You're not serious," I said.

"I am."

"Here? This minute?"

"We will marry here. We will know it in our hearts. We can have a ceremony if you like some other day, but today, here in this holy place, I want to marry you."

I searched his eyes. I began to shiver, but it was not the cold. I put my cheek against his chest. He was correct: we were as alone as two humans could be. A glance to sea told me no one had been alerted to our presence on the island. No one came toward us. I looked into his eyes again. Who was this man, anyway? And why did he want to marry me? For that matter, why did he want to marry anyone? What pulled him toward me and what could I give him in exchange?

Those thoughts raced through my head and they did not find their way to my lips.

"Yes," I said simply. "I'll marry you here."

"Thank you, Kate. I love you more than I thought it possible to love. I pledge myself to you. I ask for your pledge in return."

"I pledge myself to you, Ozzie."

He reached inside his Carhartt jacket and brought out a scarlet handkerchief. He unfolded it carefully.

"This is Gran's mother's ring. And now it is yours."

He knelt and kissed my hand. Then he slipped the ring onto my finger. He stood and took me in his arms.

"Nothing can remove this moment from us, Kate. Nothing will ever stand beside it and lessen it. Whatever the world brings to us, I am yours and you are mine. From this day forward."

He kissed me. Wind surrounded us and pulled at our hair. I clung to him and kissed him deeper and deeper, nothing sufficient, nothing strong enough to bond us as I wanted to be bonded to him. He picked me up and carried me to the rocky wall and we made love against the hard ground, the sea calling to us, the ancient rocks unyielding. We spent ourselves against one another until nothing seemed separate, nothing seemed mine or his. We forged a third body, a body we shared, and we urged and urged and urged together, sex and love and wind and ocean all tied together around us. I called out when I climaxed and he followed me down, down, until our bodies had reached a peace as calm and perfect and joyous as I had ever known.

Part 2

———

WHERE MY
BROKEN IS

18

For our honeymoon, Ozzie proposed a journey to circumnavigate Ireland.

"I've thought about doing it forever, Kate. We can outfit the boat and sleep in the coves when we need to. We won't go out to sea very far. It's rougher up north, but we'll be mindful. We'll be safe, I promise. I've thought it all out."

We had finished making love. It was the afternoon and light came into the yurt, filtered by the mist of the winter sea. We had tossed the blankets off, but now the air felt chilly against our damp heat. I gathered them up and tucked against him.

"I used to have a career before I met you, Ozzie. I have work to do. A little project called a dissertation."

"I know you do. I'll leave you alone in the afternoons so you can work. I promise. We'll travel in the morning when the winds let us. It's a journey, but it's not like traveling to China or going across the open sea. We can come in to port whenever we like. We'll have a good meal or two, clean up, then keep going."

We were married now. Married even in the eyes of the law. We had had a small civil ceremony with Gran and Seamus and the Bicycle Society women in attendance. Daijeet and his boyfriend, Andy, attended, too. My mother did not come, but she sent her best wishes and Skyped in the night before. She was in Hawaii with Ben, looking at real estate, and the flight was too far to make comfortably.

It didn't matter. I was now married to an Irish citizen. And I was hopelessly, madly in love with my husband.

"Around the entire island? Are you sure this isn't a crackpot idea?"

"Of course it is, but that's the joy of it. We'll start in spring and finish by late summer. We'll go as far as we can. As I said, it's something I always wanted to attempt. I'll put some work into the *Ferriter* to make her right. We can fish for our meals and get any kind of lobster or seafood we want in the ports. I've thought about it for a long time. We'll be explorers."

"Did Leif Erickson circumnavigate Ireland?"

"Well, he should have if he didn't. Will you come with me? Could we have that adventure together?"

I said yes. I couldn't resist. In that perfect moment with him, I would have said yes to anything. It had never entered my mind that I was a seafaring wife, a person who left solid land for any length of time. But the chance to circumnavigate Ireland would never come again; that was a certainty. And maybe, I thought in bed next to him, we *could* devise a plan that would permit me to work. I could take my books and write when I needed to, and in the afternoons we would pull into a hidden cove and bath in the water and sun. I trusted him on the sea.

"What about Gottfried?" I asked.

"I'm afraid we'll have to leave him with Seamus. He loves Seamus."

"He loves us more."

"It wouldn't be fair to take him, Kate."

"I know. I hate to leave him behind, though."

He nodded. He waited to let me understand that he would never take leaving Gottfried lightly. Then he went on.

"Let's leave May first. We'll leave here and go round to the eastern coast, then swing around the northern coast in high summer, then head down the western coast and arrive back in plenty of time for you to return to your teaching."

"Do people do this sort of thing? Is this something other people have done?"

"We'll find out. And if it ends up taking too long, you can hop off and get back for the start of classes. I'll bring the *Ferriter* back myself. Or I can pull it up onto land and get it trailered back to Dingle."

"You want me to abandon ship?"

"No, but I know you have to teach in the fall. I get that."

It was already late November. I tried to do the calculation in my mind, but I found myself giving it up as the numbers grew and twisted. Too many variables had to be factored into the equation. Nautical miles, knots, tidal changes, currents, wind, our endurance. I Googled the distance: seven hundred miles, roughly. It might not have been a trip to China, but it was long enough. Although I had done the usual activities growing up in America—skating, skiing, swimming, soccer—I had a short résumé when it came to outdoor adventuring. I liked the idea of circumnavigating Ireland, but it existed, when he first proposed it, as a purely theoretical plan. I couldn't tell, even in bed that day, how serious he was. People propose things all the time, daydream about what they could do in their lives, and in my experience they seldom follow through. But Ozzie did. And as I watched him prepare the *Ferriter,* pulling her onto dry dock and scraping the bottom then repainting it, as he renovated the small sleeping quarters below, and had Donny, the local mechanic, come in and retool the engine, I wondered if he was running to or from something. He drank with Donny, or anyone else who came by to see him, and I realized, as winter spread over Ireland and took the green grass down to a darker hue, that the trip was more than a sightseeing spree. All trips are internal, as someone once said, and I was not sure we were heading off on the same trip, or if we had ever been as joined as I had imagined.

December arrived. We had snow. We lived through Christmas in the yurt. I wondered what would become of the cottage.

He seemed to have lost interest in it now that he had the boat to occupy him. If we went for an entire spring and summer around the island, construction would stall. Whatever progress had been made on the cottage would be compromised by a long summer of abandonment. The trip to circumnavigate Ireland was impractical; at the same time, it was romantic and adventurous and I felt I could not bring up any of my worries without sounding overly cautious, the scolding wife. Ozzie detected my hesitation, my questioning, and twice we got into heated discussion about what kind of life we saw ourselves living. The discussions usually came after he had been drinking. His line of reasoning skipped like a stone skimming across water, landing sometimes with a bigger splash, something with nothing but a light imprint that pushed the weight of the rock away. The trip was important to him, but I couldn't help thinking about what came afterward. Where did we go from there?

"He has wanted to do this since he was a boy," Nora told me when I visited her for lunch in late December. We sat in her solarium, eating grapes and cheese and Irish bread. Seamus puttered nearby, pruning the profusion of houseplants that clung to every inch of sunlight that came through the leaded windows. "It's grown in him. I'm not sure why. He used to read books about Arctic exploration when he was a boy."

"I worry that he's risking something so that he can defeat it. I'm not against it, really, just wondering how it fits into what our lives might be."

"Is he drinking?"

I studied her. How much did she know about his drinking? How much did any of them know? And how deep was my ignorance around the issue? We had hinted at the subject before, but never addressed it directly.

"How much does he drink, Gran?"

"It's hard to know. He holds it well for the most part. Seamus would know better."

She called him over. He wore a navy apron over his white shirt and gray trousers. A pair of scissors stayed nocked against his fingers. She put the question to him.

"It's impossible to say how much a man drinks," Seamus said, clearly uneasy with the question. "Who can gauge that, in truth?"

I thought: *This is unfair to Ozzie.* To interview his closest relatives about his drinking, to cast doubt on his motivation for circumnavigating the island, was bad behavior. I closed the subject down and diverted them with a story about Gottfried. They let the topic go. But something had entered our relationship— Ozzie's and mine—that I could not control or properly combat. It contained no substance that I could point to and say, *Here, look at this.* We were out of step in some way that I failed to understand. I couldn't even say for sure if Ozzie felt it, too.

"What about the cottage?" I asked Ozzie one night early in February. "Will it be destroyed if we leave it all summer?"

It was a wild, wet night. Rain came through portions of the yurt, dampening the bed. We had the wood stove going, and it flickered and fought to stave off the coldness. I had never minded the rain before, or the wild weather, but now the yurt felt small and impermanent. An encampment. He had been drinking again with Donny, and I smelled the spirits on him as he sat and tried to read. I wasn't the first bride to wonder what came at the bottom of a bottle that he could not find at home with me. I knew there was something, but I couldn't put a name to it.

"The cottage will be fine," he said, his gaze locked to the page. "I'll cover it with cloths. Seamus will keep an eye on it for me. I'm sick of working on it anyway."

"I thought you liked working on it."

He looked up over the lip of the novel he was reading. It was *Brideshead Revisited.* He had read it once before, I knew. I lay on the bed and tried to stay dry. A white mist penetrated the yurt whenever the wind blew at full gale.

"I'd rather go to sea than lay bricks. Any man would."

"You're not laying bricks. There's not a brick in the entire cottage."

He looked at me. Then he put his eyes back on his novel.

"The cottage will be fine," he said, dismissively. "I'll get it done when I do."

How had this prying apart begun? And how did we stop it?

A reporter named David Robinson arrived one day in early March and asked about our proposed trip. He was a large, walrus-like man, with a moustache that twirled up in two curls on either side of his red lips. He drove a ridiculously small car, something like a French Citroën, and when he climbed out, I had first thought it was a joke. He came forward with his shoulder bag strung over his neck, his steps high to be careful of boards and stones and re-rod. Ozzie was down at the beach, bathing, and I sat on our tiny front porch, reading. It was a cool day, with a steel-colored light that took the grayness of the sea and spread it over the land. I was accustomed to Gottfried signaling any kind of visitors with a series of cheery barks, but he had followed Ozzie down to the sea, his bushy tail disappearing on the trail ten minutes before.

"Hello," David Robinson called when he was still some distance away. "Does Ozzie Ferriter live here?"

I stood and called back that he did.

The strangest moment occurred then. As he came forward, carefully to avoid the debris of construction, I saw our habitation from a different set of eyes. It was romantic, unquestionably, but it was also painfully unfinished. I watched him triangulate, checking before him, glancing at the yurt, peeking out to survey the ocean. We had beaten a path down, certainly, but it was not gracious or welcoming; it was like walking onto a construction site, and I wondered, as I tried to place him, how we had let it become so unruly. True, it was March, and the season remained more winter than spring, but I couldn't avoid feeling that I had

lost sight of a basic level of orderliness. It sent a prickle of understanding into my thinking that I tried at first to deny.

"I'm from over in Dublin," David Robinson said, finally
reaching me and holding out his hand, "and I came to talk to you
about your trip."

"We're still talking about it ourselves."

"You intend to go around the island? That's what I heard."

"That's the plan," I said. "Can I offer you anything? I have
tea water on."

"I'd love a cup. You have a magnificent view here. Breathtaking, really."

He put his hand to his forehead like an old mariner and
scanned the horizon. I saw that view through his eyes, too. It
was breathtaking. And we had let it become somewhat slovenly.
And the cottage, I knew, was not going to get built anytime soon.
That knowledge, highlighted by David Robinson's sudden appearance, made me unsettled. How had I lived here and not seen
it as his eyes saw it?

I gave him my chair and went inside to fix tea. Stepping into
the yurt, I saw the confusion there, too. Everything was scrambled. We had no proper dressers or armoires, so everything was
tossed randomly from one corner of the yurt to the other. Only
the yurt had no corners. It struck me as adolescent, suddenly,
two kids on a campout, or two young people sharing a college
dorm. I knew as I formed the thought that I wasn't being fair to
either of us, but the impression wouldn't fade away. How had I
failed to see it before?

I heard Ozzie return and begin talking to David Robinson.
Ozzie would be cold from his swim and would want to come
inside to warm up, and I felt an annoying embarrassment that
I had let the place become so hopelessly cluttered. It did no
good to tell myself that it was both our responsibility to keep the
place clean; I was enough of my mother's daughter, enough of

an enculturated woman to take on the responsibility of a clean house for myself. It was maddening and it made me cross. Forget being a scholar or a PhD candidate. In some nagging part of my mind, I was a wife of the Blasket Islands, neglectful about sweeping out the cottage when the village priest arrived for a visit.

Ozzie pushed into the yurt a moment later with David Robinson behind him.

"I've always wanted to see inside of one of these. Ah, they're larger than I imagined. Yes, I see," he said as he stepped through the doorway.

"You'll have to excuse the mess," I said, "it's a hard place to keep in order."

"Oh, you should see my flat," David Robinson said kindly. "You wouldn't know it from a bomb shelter."

I gave him a mug of tea, then went back out to read. I didn't know why I felt so ill at ease. I heard their heavy male voices talking back and forth, their confident patter about which coast would be more difficult, which currents the more taxing, and I put down my book and called Gottfried for a walk. He gladly followed me. Rudely, I did not tell them I was going or bother to say goodbye to David Robinson. I simply followed our usual trail down to the sea, but instead of continuing to our strand, I turned south and went down a trail I had taken a hundred times before. Gottfried trotted ahead of me, scouting the lumpy soil for voles. Wind covered the men's voices and soon the land obstructed my view back to the yurt.

I told Ozzie I had to get some things in order, speak to my dissertation supervisor, do laundry, clean up, answer emails, pay bills, a hundred things. He dropped me at my tiny apartment in Limerick. He didn't ask if I wanted him to stay with me; I didn't invite him. The relief I felt when at last he left, waving from the truck as he backed up, Gottfried's head bobbing a little at the motion, was remarkably piercing. I couldn't wait to recover a missing portion of my life. I couldn't wait to take a long, warm bath.

I felt strange without Ozzie near, but also supremely at peace. How easy life was, I admitted, if one had only to take care of oneself. I found an open bottle of wine on my countertop, sniffed it to check it, then poured out a glass and carried it with me to the bath. I ran the bath as hot as I could stand it and climbed in, sitting on the side until I could gradually feed myself into the warm, waiting water.

I locked my mind down. I told myself not to think of Ozzie or the boat trip or anything else. I pushed myself deeper into the water and sipped at the wine. The wine was horrid, but not quite turned, and I didn't care anyway. I got out of the bath and tiptoed into the kitchen, dripping, and poured a second glass full to the brim. I carried it back and submerged in the bath again, relieved beyond measure to have the warmth of the apartment, the four solid walls around me.

And solitude. That didn't surprise me, entirely, but it stopped me for a moment to consider why I hadn't asked Ozzie to stay. He might have liked a day or two in a different setting. He was my husband, after all. But we had both tacitly understood we needed to be apart for a time. I wondered what that meant. I wondered a great deal about that.

I went out to dinner at Cupcakes, a small restaurant that specialized in cupcake desserts. It was more of a café than a restaurant, but I had been in there twice before and I felt comfortable as a single woman dining alone. It was not the sort of restaurant Ozzie would patronize. He would have found it artificial and silly, but I enjoyed it. They had a good shrimp salad that I liked, and an excellent red curry that had no business existing in a restaurant called Cupcakes.

A young waiter seated me at a table in the back corner of the restaurant. It wasn't busy. I asked for another glass of wine, then simply sat for a moment experiencing the pleasure of clean hair, clean nails, clean everything. I smelled good and felt good and the bath had made me boneless and sleepy. I smiled when the waiter brought the wine and I ordered curry. Then I opened a notebook I had filled about the Blaskets, about medical care specifically, and I read over what I had recorded, pleased with the depth of my note-taking.

When the waiter brought my curry, he brought me a second glass of wine. I looked up, puzzled, and he pushed his chin toward a man sitting at the small bar at the front of the café.

"With his regards," the waiter said, clearly uncomfortable carrying the message.

Not once in my life had I been sent a glass of wine by a man, and I flushed red. I had no idea what the protocol was in these situations. Ridiculously, I picked up the first glass of wine with my left hand so that he could see my wedding ring, the one Ozzie had placed on my hand at Skellig Michael. I thought that would do the trick, but he merely smiled and raised his glass to me. I looked down at my notebook, embarrassed and confused.

When the waiter came back to my table carrying the curry soup, I nearly asked him to remove the wineglass. But that seemed churlish and juvenile. Men bought glasses of wine for women and women bought glasses of wine for men. I knew that.

Still, I felt mildly uncomfortable accepting the wine.

The lovely haze I had when I entered the restaurant now grew thinner. It troubled me to have to eat my soup with someone watching. I had lost my anonymity. I kept my eyes down, but I peeked enough to know that the man remained at the bar. I saw his reflection in the mirror; he was dark and square, a block of wood chipped from an old bookcase. His hair was short on the sides, longer on top, and he wore an expensive-looking suit without a tie. His shoe, up on the bar rail, was a black loafer.

Not that it mattered, but he was not my type at all. I tried to imagine what Milly would call him. If Ozzie was some sort of pickup truck, this man was an expensive sedan with tinted windows. I kept my head down and ate my curry, which was delicious.

Then suddenly he stood beside my table. I detected motion, nothing more, and for an instant I thought it was the waiter. When I glanced up, I saw him. He stood respectfully, waiting for me to look up, his glass of wine in his hands.

"Did I overstep?" he asked. "I apologize if I did."

"Thank you, but I'm just not interested."

"In wine? Or in the strangers who send the wine?"

"Both. Each. I appreciate the gesture. But thank you, no."

"How do you like glass?"

Now he was overstepping. I looked down, hoping he would back off. But he didn't move. It made me uneasy. But it also— and I hated that it did—made me a little flushed and nervous. As if I wanted his attention. As if I wanted his glass of wine.

"I'm here for a glass exhibit," he said. "I'm going to leave a ticket here, on the edge of the table. My name is Jonathan. I'll be there tomorrow. It's quite a famous exhibit and you might enjoy it. Here, and I apologize again."

He slipped a ticket more solidly onto the table. He smiled when I glanced up and it was not the worst smile in the world.

"I won't be attending," I said.

"But just in case. Ask for Jonathan. Most people know me."

He left. I saw him stop at the bar, pay, then take off. He did not look over to me. In an instant, he was gone.

As soon as he left, I felt anxious and guilty. But why? I hadn't done anything. I couldn't prevent someone from sending me a glass of wine or approaching my table. Yet I wondered if there had been something in my demeanor, my posture or my glances, that had invited him to approach me. If that were the case, what was behind that? I wondered. Peculiar. I finished my curry and finished the glass of wine Jonathan had sent to the table. Counting the two glasses I had consumed in the bath, that made four. Two was my usual limit. When I stood after paying the bill, I felt slightly light-headed. I looked for a long minute at the invitation to the glass exhibit. I took a step away from the table, then stepped back and picked up the ticket and stuck it in my notebook like a bookmark. It burned my arm when I tucked the notebook against my body.

19

As if serving penance for picking up the ticket from the table, I spent the next day in a flurry of errands and organizing. I sat at the small kitchen table in my apartment until two in the afternoon, answering emails, arranging bills, Skyping with Milly and with my mom. It felt good to get things in order. My dissertation director happened to be beside her computer, and we wrote back and forth a number of times, catching up. I felt plugged in again. It was something I had to remember to do more often. It made me think about the summer, and how it would be to live on a boat for months at a time. But I dismissed those thoughts when they came and forced myself to concentrate on the job at hand.

Around three, I went for a long walk. It felt strange not to have Gottfried with me, but the River Shannon had a wonderful color at this time of year, and I walked along its edge until I felt fatigued. I wasn't going to the glass exhibit. I wasn't. That was clear in my mind, but I still felt uneasy about the message—had it been a message?—that I had sent out into the world. What had this Jonathan character seen in me? What sort of opportunity did he think he had? It vexed me.

When I made it back to the apartment, I found Ozzie waiting. He and Gottfried were upstairs. Ozzie had a bottle of Bushmills on the table and two small glasses beside it. He poured out a glass for me and pushed it toward me. When he looked at me, I saw his eyes had emptied of something I had always found there. I sat across from him. My heart beat too fast.

"Are you leaving me, Kate?" he asked.

He had been drinking, I saw. I guessed that this was not the first bottle of Bushmills.

"I'm not leaving you, Ozzie. Why would you say such a thing?"

"You've changed. Is it the trip?"

"The boat trip?"

"Was there another trip I should know about?"

I squared my shoulders. I sipped the whiskey. It burned but felt good going down. Ozzie sipped his own drink.

"What do you mean I've changed?"

He shrugged.

"You had more gladness before. I can't put a finger on it. Do you feel you've made a mistake in marrying me?"

"No, Ozzie. No, that's not it."

"But there is something?"

"I don't want to get into all this, Ozzie. It's true, I've been feeling something. But I'm unsure what it is, and I don't want to talk about it until I know."

"The whiskey will loosen your tongue."

"I don't think I'm going to drink enough of that to loosen anything."

"You know, it would be kinder to call it a mistake and end it cleanly, if that's what you're feeling. No blame there. Anyone can make a mistake."

"And what about you, Ozzie? What are you feeling?"

"I'm more in love with you now than ever."

"You say that too fast."

"It's true, Kate. For all my faults, I love you. I always will."

He poured out more whiskey for both of us. It felt strange to be having such an important conversation in this tiny apartment that didn't truly belong to either of us. It felt like having a life talk in an airport waiting room. But now that we were in it, deep into a sort of frankness we couldn't always capture, I decided to speak plainly.

"Are you happy, Ozzie? Are you glad you married me?"

"I am. I think, though, the marriage signifies something different for you. I'm a wonderful figure to be in love with, but to be a wife to me as a husband, maybe that's the problem."

"What do you mean?"

He took a deep breath. Clearly, he had given this thought.

"Oh, to be a wife to a man like me can't be easy. I'm not as dependable as I should be. I rattle around. I'm not on a clear path. But you are, Kate. You are. You have purpose. You're building a career. I'm hoping to drag you off to the ocean for the summer. That's an adventure, but it's not building toward anything."

"Does anything build toward anything?"

"Don't do that, Kate. You're not the cynical type. We've only talked a little bit about children. About starting a family. For all our talking, we haven't been plain with one another, have we?"

"I suppose not. Not as you mean it."

"We better start being plain, or we will end up hurting each other."

"What about you, Ozzie? Am I the wife you wanted?"

"Yes."

"You answer too quickly. You're sure about that?"

He nodded. He put his hand on Gottfried. The whiskey continued to burn, but not as much as it had before.

"Kate, I didn't expect to find you. In some ways, maybe, I wasn't ready for you. But I love you, yes. I have no doubt about that. And, yes, you're the wife I wanted. You're the woman I've searched for."

"How is it that we haven't talked about all this before?"

"We have talked about some of it. But we are still courting each other and showing our good sides. Maybe the boat trip made us both realize we need to understand each other better. It put some pressure on us both that we didn't anticipate."

I nodded. He wasn't wrong. Maybe that had been the sand in our gears. I sipped more whiskey. I studied him, then asked what I had wanted to ask since I first met him.

"Tell me about the war. If you mean what you say, tell me. You've always held it back. What happened there? What wounds are you carrying?"

"I can't talk about that, Kate. I made a promise to myself that I would never talk about it."

"But you should be able to talk to me. I'm your wife."

"You're the last person I want to tell. The last. I want your good opinion."

"I'd love you no matter what."

"Would you? How do you know that, Kate? How do you know I didn't do something monstrous? Something unforgiveable? There are acts that don't deserve forgiveness."

"Is that why you drink?"

He looked at me. Carefully. He lifted his glass and sipped it. Despite the crazed, nervous feeling I had in my gut, I wanted to hear everything. I wanted to know everything at last. I wanted everything on the table, to be organized, to fit together in a way that made sense. It was foolish, but that's how I felt.

"It's too easy to point to one thing and say that's the reason I drink. Or why anyone does anything. Life doesn't have many straight lines, Kate."

"Fair enough. But how much do you drink? How much when you're away from me?"

He squinted. I knew the question hurt him.

"More than I should."

"That's too vague."

"Do you want a number? A bottle count? I don't have one."

"To the point of . . ."

"Foolish drunkenness? Is that what you are wondering? Yes, sometimes. Sometimes I am the worst cliché of a drunken, maudlin Irishman."

"Do you really fish?"

He laughed.

"I do," he said. "I do fish, Kate. I like to fish, only it doesn't pay much. You know that. I sell most of it off the books, so I do better than some. Some months are quite good. Restaurants know me."

"Where is the money? You don't put it in a bank, do you? You'd be taxed on it if you did."

"Do you know the red stone?"

He had pointed out the red stone to me at least three times. It was a dark, ruby-colored stone halfway on the walk to the sea from our cottage. Except for its distinctive color, there was nothing exceptional about the stone. It was easy to miss.

"You keep it there?"

He nodded. We didn't say anything else for a moment. I wondered how I had been so blind. So gullible. So willing to put everything aside and believe that love, this madness I had felt since I met him, covered all, removed all, formed its own island protected us from the world.

"So the long and the short of it is, Kate, that you've married a drunken fisherman."

"That's not who you are, Ozzie."

"Yes, it is, Kate. That's a large part of me. Don't turn away from it. I apologize that I didn't make it clearer to you sooner. I do. It was unfair. I didn't hide it, but I didn't parade it before you, either. I won't apologize for my life as it, but I apologize for not telling you. You made a decision on slanted information."

"I made my decision on love. On my loving you."

"I believe you love me, Kate. I know that. What I don't know is whether I can be the husband you want and need. That's the part that is unclear to me."

"It takes time to know things, Ozzie."

"We have time if we want it, Kate. But if it seems a bad bargain, then we'd be better to end it quickly than stretch it out."

"How did we start talking about this?"

"We've always been talking about it, Kate. Just not in words. There are no villains here. Just humans trying to be good at a difficult thing."

He came around the table then and knelt before me. He kissed me. The kiss continued, and maybe it was the whiskey, or maybe it was the level of feeling that we had admitted to, but in a minute, we were in bed, clawing at each other. It was afternoon and the light came in quietly and the wind carried the scent of the River Shannon on its skirts. We kissed over and over until nothing mattered but that. We did not manage to remove all our clothes. Twice I began to wonder what this meant, how it fit into the words we had just spoken, but then he took me in a new way, kissed me more deeply, and I clung to him and began to cry.

20

We left May first. It was a bright, brilliant spring day. The sun cracked into a thousand pieces of sparkling glass on the soft waters of Dingle Bay. Gran and Seamus came to see us off. I knelt for a long time before Gottfried and whispered my love to him. Then I hugged Gran and Seamus, kissed Gottfried one last time, and stepped on board. Ozzie had already thrown off most of the lines.

"Your hair is red as fire, Kate," Seamus called to me as the *Ferriter* moved slowly away from the pier. "You're as Irish as you'll ever be. They'll sing odes to your parting."

"Thank you, Seamus. It's an honor to be told that by a *Tylwyth Teg* like you."

A *Tylwyth Teg* was a Welsh fairy. His eyes widened and he laughed.

"Travel safely," Gran said. *"Go n-éirí an bóthar leat."*

She took something from her pocket and tossed into the water behind us. She had cast bread crumbs on the water. I knew the Bible verse by heart: *Cast thy bread upon the waters: for thou shalt find it after many days.* She nodded to me when our eyes met. She trusted her grandson to me.

Then we were launched, alone on the ocean except for the shipping that passed this and that way on the day's labor. We had set out at first light and we watched the sun climb above the ocean rim and spread itself wider and wider. The scent of the land came to us in small, fragrant pants. I stepped close to Ozzie and realized that whatever became of us I would always remember this moment, this exact moment, when we left Ireland on a journey for no other purpose but to be together in love and adventure.

"How do you like it so far, my love?" he whispered into my ear as he told me to stand with him at the wheel. "The world can't catch us here."

"Thank you, Ozzie. Thank you for this. I never want the world to catch us."

"You dream of a thing and you hope one day to see it. To live it."

"*It's a mad, mad plan,*" I said, quoting a movie line we had been saying to each other over the last couple weeks as we readied the *Ferriter.*

He nuzzled my neck.

"You're my mad, mad plan," he whispered. "You're all of it."

I took the wheel for a time while he fixed breakfast. He went below and I steered the *Ferriter* into St. Finian's Bay. Our GPS system was top-notch, but Ozzie had also taped a large navigational map to the back of the cuddy so that we could see where we traveled, what landmarks reached from the island to us. I glanced to see how far it was to Dursey Head. We planned to spend our first night in Bantry Bay, well guarded by the glove of land around us.

"Hope you're hungry," Ozzie said, carrying up our breakfast. "I made coffee black as the inside of a cabbage. Seamus was correct, you know? Your hair is on fire this close to the ocean. You look like a fairy woman at the helm."

"I feel like a fairy woman right now."

He looked to check our bearing. Then he handed me a small plate full of olives and cheese and sliced tomato. He had scrambled eggs with chives.

"A little chop coming up. We might get a blow later. But we're right on course."

"Did you always love the sea, Ozzie?"

"No, but I've always felt the sea loved me. Isn't that a strange thing?"

"Not strange at all. It's a marvelous thing."

"We should make an entry in the log after we eat."

"I'll write it, if you like."

"That would be fine. How's this for your breakfast?"

"Lovely."

"Did you see Gran cast bread upon the water? She's an old witch, my gran."

"She loves her grandson. Loves him more than she could bear if she lost him."

He nodded at that. Then he served me breakfast at the wheel. *This is how it's going to be,* I realized now. We were going to travel, and see, and watch, and look at the land from the ocean. We had made our own island, an island so perfect we needed next to nothing from the world.

When we finished breakfast, Ozzie cleaned up and then took the wheel back. The sun had risen in the sky and the heat of the day had begun. We passed a pod of seals, then watched a flock of guillemots or gannets diving into the sea. The breeze ruffled Ozzie's hair and I watched him and felt a gush in my stomach for how handsome he was. My handsome, handsome husband.

"It's a mad, mad plan," I whispered to him as I hugged him from behind.

He took my hand and kissed it. We traveled east with the wind and the sea carried us softly away from the sun.

THIRD LETTER

My Darling Husband:

Don't be cross with me when you see I haven't written a proper log after breakfast. I am too in love with you to write down what we had for breakfast, or how many miles we travel at what speed. I will be better in the future, I promise, but right now I want to tell you how much I love you and why and what it feels like to stand beside you and pilot this boat around our beloved Ireland. We have a mad, mad plan, we two, and my plan is to stay next to you and form a life that will satisfy us both. Thrill us both.

This lovely boat is our island. If we were wise, we would never leave it. We should stay here under the sea's spell and refuse to touch ground ever again. You knew that. You gave it to both of us. We married on Skellig Michael and the sea was our priest.

I know I am ridiculous sometimes when I fall into these moods of love. I almost can't bear what I feel for you. Even this note is too flowery. You will laugh at it, and laugh at me, but my heart feels like it wants to burst when I am with you.

I feel sometimes we have a small creature between us—not Gottfried, although I love him, but something small and more delicate, a tiny goat or a dove—and that we must be careful to treat it properly, to avoid inadvertently stepping on its limbs. I've lost my mind, I know, but I hope you see what I mean. Neither one of us contains our love, but we share it as we would the care of that

small animal, so that it trails after us and depends on us and waits
to come forward. I don't know what I am saying. Forget the animal.
This is supposed to be a log. We are going east and then north, and
the current will carry us northward at least for a time. You said that.
Underneath us the sea is urging us to stay, to remain, to drift away
from land to live on our island forever.

Oh, I am mad, mad, mad for you, Ozzie. Ozzie is a ridiculous
name, you know? It is. It sounds like a furniture polish. But I love it
with you, and I love to say it, and love to call your name when you
are deep inside me and we are nothing but that heat and desire and
closeness.

Right now you are standing at the wheel and you are so
handsome you take my breath away. The wind plays with your hair.
Your hands are large and heavy. No one else can ever claim this
moment. No one else will ever be on this island with you. I am yours,
Ozzie. As you are mine.

P.S. We ate eggs and cheese and tomatoes for breakfast. Black
coffee. Black as the inside of a cabbage, you said.

21

We anchored deep in Bantry Bay that first night. The stars came out and we decided to carry our bed up to the main deck and sleep there. Ozzie checked the anchor lines and made sure our running lights worked properly, while I worked on the bed. I made it up with fresh sheets and plump pillows; a good bed was one demand I had made when Ozzie had proposed the trip. We needed to sleep on a decent mattress. I bought the mattress to fit our belowdecks quarters, but we knew we would carry it up on mild nights to sleep beneath the stars.

"Well, our first night, Kate, what do you think?" Ozzie asked when he came back to help me with the bed.

"I think it's magical. I think it's everything we hoped."

"Do you think you'll get tired of it?"

"Not for a long time."

"I'm going to have some whiskey now. Shall I pour you a glass?"

"Wine, please."

"Coming right up."

He disappeared down belowdecks and returned a moment later with our drinks. We had already eaten. In the morning, he said, before we resumed our travel, he would put over hand lines for mackerel. Bantry Bay was known for its schools of mackerel.

"Cheers to us," he said, clinking my glass.

"To us."

We drank. The wine coated my tongue and tasted of land and plants.

Later, in bed, we studied the stars. I had never seen more stars. They stretched across the sky from horizon to horizon. Without the engine throbbing below us, the *Ferriter* had become a soft, pliant canoe set out on a calm sea. Water lapped against her sides and chucked under her bow. I liked hearing those sounds. Part of me wondered how I had come to this, to this place, with my husband beside me and all of Ireland waiting to be explored. Every journey holds a beginning, and this was ours.

A little later, as we drifted toward sleep, we heard dolphins blowing nearby. Ozzie whispered that they sometimes came around boats to inspect the passengers. They were nosy about humans.

"Kate, take off your clothes and stand up naked so they can see you," he whispered urgently. "They need to examine you. They'll keep us safe if you do."

"I would not get out of this bed for anything on this side of heaven."

"The dolphins are a kind folk, but you shouldn't trifle with them. They like to see a naked woman in starlight from time to time."

"They'll have to find another boat, then."

"You discourage me, Kate."

"How about a naked man? Don't they like the sight of a naked man?"

"They do," he said. "But not half as much, I'm afraid."

"Well, then, go. I'll stand naked tomorrow night and we'll be half protected tonight."

"Are you telling me to leave our marriage bed?"

"I'm only advocating for the dolphins."

"They run the mackerel up against the shoreline and corner them. It's a cruel business. They could use the sight of a naked woman to cheer them up."

"Would a naked woman cheer up a school of mackerel?"

"Oh, no. Mackerels are the accountants of the sea. They only look down at their ledgers. They write in chalk."

Mizen Head, Clear Island, Galley Head, Seven Heads, Old Head of Kinsale. Each night we navigated to the lee side of what sea was running or wind was blowing and there we anchored. Ozzie was an excellent captain, solid and seaworthy, and he had been over most of this part of the coastline for years. He knew small coves and inlets and places where fresh water came rushing out from the land. The weather held fine. For weeks we lived on a small wooden boat in a vast, empty ocean. In the afternoon, wherever we were, Ozzie chased me downstairs and told me to work. I went halfheartedly. How could dry, bookish work compare to navigating the Celtic Sea? Eventually, however, I gained a rhythm with the work. It wasn't easy to concentrate, but when I managed to cross the barrier of the everyday world and merge with the memoirs of Blasket Island women, I felt more connected than ever before. Perhaps the sea influenced me, or inspired me, and I grew to look forward to the slow leaving of the Blaskets, the return to life abovedecks, the sea, the wind that blew constantly from the west greeting me as if I had been gone for ages. Then it was cocktail time, drinks on board, drinks while we aimed the *Ferriter* to her night's rest and our place beneath the stars. We made love in the open air, the sea everywhere, the moon rising and casting our skin in gold and silver.

Sometimes at sunrise, but more often in the afternoon, we pulled in close to shore and spent the day sunning and swimming. We were in no rush. That had become clear quickly to both of us. It was not a race to circumnavigate the island; we could do it stages, or over years, and we had no one to answer to but ourselves. We swam naked and it felt cold and wild to be out in the middle of the sea, close to shore, yes, but still not on a beach or anywhere that let us merely walk free of the ocean. We swam as water-creatures, almost, and we rose after our swims and lay for a long time in the hot sun, collecting the heat into our bones so that we could carry it into the evening. Sometimes we didn't move. Other days, we kept going, not caring, driving the *Ferriter* into the night and picking up the stars one by one from the black water. I became better as a pilot. Ozzie made sure I took responsibility for half the navigation, and I found I enjoyed that part of it more than I would have anticipated. I liked looking at maps and planning our journey; I liked finding a tiny bay where we could anchor for the night and sleep without worry.

We were almost to *Dún Laoghaire*, near Dublin, when the first true storm caught us. We had been tossed around a bit on several occasions, but this time the signs of incoming weather proved unmistakable. Ozzie listened to the radio through most of the morning, not liking what he heard, but not, I felt, overly concerned. Around noon, the sky grew dark and furrowed, and the sea began lisping against the keel. Ozzie stood beside me, the first worried look I had seen on his face since we had begun.

"We need to either go out farther to sea, or move toward land," he said, his eyes passing back and forth from the water to my hands on the wheel. "We can't stay here. The running tide will push us against the land and we won't be able to fight it."

"Should we go out farther to sea? What do you think?"

"I'm not sure. The sea might make up our minds for us. We'll have to take the waves as they come to us."

"Do you want me to turn away from land?"

I didn't want to; every impulse told me to head toward land, to what I had always known as safety, but I knew the sea had its own rules. The trick, at least in part, was to take the waves on one's shoulder. Rise with the swell, then down into the trough. Ozzie had explained that much to me. The *Ferriter* was not a ship for open water, I knew. Not in an authentic storm. The clouds and sky began moving faster and faster above us. The water around us turned a gray, solemn hue, the color of mice or the greenish mold on bread, and the aerometer on top of the cuddy sang like a boy shouting into a fan. Wind began driving us from every direction. We had to raise our voices to be heard.

"I wish I knew how far we are to Dublin," he said, eyeing the water, the clouds, the spray foam. "I make it about ten miles, give or take."

"We could turn back to Wicklow, couldn't we?"

"We're five miles out from Wicklow. If it's ten to Dublin, we can run for it. By the time we come about and turn our flanks to the sea, we could be in trouble."

"What do you think? I trust you, Ozzie."

"We're in a pickle, Kate. I won't pretend we're not."

"It came up fast."

"The bad ones do."

"Can the *Ferriter* handle it?"

"I hate to ask it of her. With the open back, the fishing platform, you run a risk of being swamped. It's not a blue-water boat."

"It's really getting ugly."

"If we run to sea, we have no chance of help or assistance. Toward land, at least, we could run her aground if we needed to."

"You mean just run into the shore?"

"We may not have much of a choice if it comes to that. It wouldn't be ideal."

The swells had grown to more than ten feet. I had never been in a sea like it. I knew from conversation with Ozzie that ten feet was nothing; the waves could grow and grow until they were the teeth of an enormous saw blade running furiously at us. The sky, especially, looked foreboding. I noticed the gulls that usually followed us had gone to land. We saw no other ships, no other spots of life on the ocean surface. The sea had become a blue-green desert.

"Let's run to Dublin," Ozzie said, throttling the engine higher. "It might be a mistake, but it will leave our options open. I'll take the wheel, Kate. I'm going to open her up. It could get rough for a time."

"Should we radio our position to someone?"

"We will soon if it gets worse."

"Are you afraid, Ozzie?"

"It's a mad, mad plan we have, Kate."

We kissed. A quick seal for the decision we had made. The waves ran at us and threw us up and down over the troughs, but we kissed anyway. Then it all became serious. Deadly so. He told me to go around and batten down anything that might have shaken loose. He shouted over the wind that I needed to be careful. The sea could take me off the fishing platform in no time. Afterward, he wanted me to go down to our quarters and check things there. Turn off the gas that ran our heating furnace and our two-burner range; tie down anything that might come loose and crash about. Stow everything as much as possible.

I did as he asked, but going onto the fishing platform terrified me. As soon as I thought I could predict how the sea might move the *Ferriter*, it quartered a different way. Twice the waves sent us skidding on the water and we flew down the side of one wave and crashed the bow into the oncoming wall of water. It was quickly becoming too great a sea for us. Even I could see that. A wave broke over our starboard side and rocked us on our beam. The engine labored beneath us, churning the water, but occasionally having difficulty catching a purchase in the froth of the gray sea.

"Come back, Kate," Ozzie yelled when I had nearly finished lashing down a brown tarp we sometimes set up as a sun shade. "Don't worry about the small things. If they blow over, so be it. You're going to get washed over."

"Coming."

At that moment, a wave grabbed me. It crashed onto the center of the fishing platform and suddenly I was knee deep in water. It happened so quickly, and with such force, that it toppled me and threw me against the opposite gunwale. Then the wave swirled and emptied through the gunnels. I crawled back to the cuddy, my right shin throbbing. Ozzie hadn't seen a thing. He had been concentrating on the approaching waves.

I climbed to my feet. Only when I had my balance again did it strike me fully how close I had come to being washed overboard. I would have been dead in minutes. No one could stay afloat for long in such a crazed sea.

I went down below, shivering. We were good housekeepers when it came to keeping the mess and tiny sleeping quarters in order, but the waves had taken everything and given them a good shake. One shelf of books had come loose from the wall and now books lay everywhere. A Pyrex pie plate had broken into a thousand pieces and crunched under my shoes as I scrambled to secure anything that looked wobbly. At the same time, I knew it was a fool's task. Nothing could keep the sea from shaking things loose. I did my best, still frightfully cold and scared, and when I came back up to check on Ozzie I saw his face held a determined, fierce expression on his features.

"Are we all right?" I shouted.

"I don't know."

"I don't want to die, Ozzie. For the record."

"Neither do I, Kate. All we can do is keep going. I'll radio our position in case . . ."

"Why didn't we know this was happening? This storm?"

"We knew some of it. We just didn't know it would be this bad."

Probably not true, I thought. Ozzie probably did know, but he ignored it. Or put it on a back bench in his mind. I hadn't paid attention to the report. It had been on him. I knew that line of reasoning was no help; it was less than help, actually. But I found myself resenting him for putting us in this situation. It seemed to tie into a recklessness I had always recognized in him. That recklessness could be attractive, but it could also be dangerous. I felt like kicking him. I felt like kicking myself.

We forged ahead. We could do nothing else. Although it was an odd notion that came and went with the waves, the *Ferriter* seemed to comprehend the precariousness of our situation. The engine kept up a steady thrum, but at times it seemed to miss the water in the wrenching waves and then the prop spun for a shrill moment in plain air. That sound came as a horror. Each time it occurred I thought we were headed over. Ozzie stood his ground, his legs wide to brace himself, his hands never leaving the wheel. I knew enough to understand that one wrong turn could put us broadside to the waves and that would be our end.

The entire world grew wet and gray and horrible. I had to resist the panic that sought to take me over. I couldn't do a thing to help, really. I stood beside him and watched him navigate each wave, the run up a thrilling, terrible climb, made worse by the knowledge that we would sled down the opposite side. If possible, I hated the descent more; the following sea caught us and pushed us and then we broke our bow into the next wave. Over and over and over again. I wondered how the *Ferriter* could take it. I knew it was good boat, a stout boat with oak bracing, but it was not really made for these conditions. In the end, it was a working boat designed to stay close to shore on calmer days; it was not a pleasure cruiser. Ozzie did not like to run the engines as fully as he had to, and I saw him glance back a dozen times, a thousand times, at the small betrayals the engine made against the water. If the engine quit, I knew, we would be goners.

"I should have shown myself naked to the dolphins," I shouted, trying to keep my own spirits up as much as anything else. "It's my fault."

"I tried to tell you, Kate! It's the lack of gratitude they can't stand."

"Is this really our honeymoon?"

"I guess it is!"

"Couldn't we have gone to a nice hotel? Maybe in Paris?"

"It never occurred to me, Kate, but you might have a point."

He smiled at me. His eyes held such power in that moment that I almost felt heat from them. He loved this! He loved the excitement of handling the boat against the ocean that wanted to whisk him away. How had I failed to know that? How had I not understood that essential part of him? He wasn't panicked or terrified. He was glad to be in such circumstances, his blood wild and running through his veins, his hair blown back, his hands heavy and strong on the wheel. It was not bravery. *I* was brave, because I feared our situation but carried on anyway. Ozzie felt no such fear. He thrilled to the danger, to the chance that everything could be taken in a moment. He was not brave, I realized, but driven by forces that I could not comprehend. He needed to put himself, and me, in peril, to satisfy something he probably didn't even acknowledge in his heart.

"You like this, you fucker!" I yelled when I had a moment longer to study his face. "You're happy right this minute!"

"What are you talking about, Kate?"

"You like this! You want to tempt fate. You do! Holy fucker, you put us in this spot deliberately!"

"You're crazy, Kate."

"Am I? I don't think so. You stupid bastard!"

"Quit talking like a mad woman, Kate. You *are* off your nut."

But I wasn't. I knew I wasn't. He was fully alive. I had seen glimpses of that expression before, but never the full bloom of it. It was a carnal, avid face, one that revealed a side to him that I hardly recognized. He didn't want to kill me, but he also didn't want to take steps to protect me, either. He had heard the weather report and he decided to ignore it. Maybe it wasn't as conscious as that, but the possibility that he had simply absorbed the information, had put it away so that he might ignore it, and had gone on about his day—that knowledge disturbed me. He was willing to risk both our lives in some inchoate desire for sensation. I couldn't help linking that to his drinking, to his push to feel more and more without end. He was a stranger, suddenly standing beside me.

We continued for nearly two hours without knowing whether the next wave might kill us. I felt nauseated from the motion, but also from the understanding I had gained. Carefully, after a grueling hour and a half, he took the center passage into the Dublin port. Incredibly, the sea calmed and became tame as it had ever been as soon as we rounded the outmost jetty. Ozzie looked at me and smiled. I dropped my hands. They had grown tired of holding the handles near the cockpit.

"We made it, Kate!" he said, smiling and reaching for me. He took me in his arms but I pushed away.

"Jesus Christ, Ozzie."

"What?"

"You could have killed us!"

"It was a storm, Kate. When you go to sea, sometimes storms come up."

"But you knew! You heard the weather report!"

"What are you talking about? No one called for that kind of sea."

"I don't believe you."

I went belowdecks, wondering if I needed to vomit. What had just happened? Did I simply panic and blame it all on him? I couldn't say. I didn't want to be a timid jerk, a whiny scaredy-cat who came unglued at the first rough weather. But it had been more than rough. We had been lucky to escape. And when we finally pulled into a berth in Dublin harbor, I came up from our mess and jumped out and walked away, not sure what I felt, not sure where I needed to be. *Fuck him,* I thought. The stupid, stupid motherfucker nearly killed us. I wondered if he wouldn't always be half drowning and pulling me down as he went.

22

To be on land, to be safe, felt almost better than I could believe. My knee hurt horribly from hitting it against the gunwale in the wash of sea water that had almost taken me overboard, but otherwise—except for a continuing wave of nausea—I felt fine. In the pit of my stomach, something churned and blistered me. It had something to do with Ozzie, something I had always known but failed to address. *I saw him.* I saw him now. It felt as if some final understanding about him had descended on me without my acquiescence. It lodged in my guts and I kept walking, limping, really, to get it out of me.

It was evening. Lights had already flicked on all over Dublin. I had difficulty reconciling that on the sea just beyond the jetty you could lose your life. That I could lose my life. How did one resume one's life after an afternoon like that? I had never had my life so clearly in the balance for such a prolonged period. I didn't like it. I found no pleasure in it, although I remained convinced that Ozzie did.

I walked, limping, my knee hurting more than I had realized. I had no idea where I was going, or what I hoped to accomplish by being apart from Ozzie, but I knew I needed to breathe different air. I was halfway down the first pier when I remembered that my phone and money were back on the *Ferriter.* I stopped and put my face in my hands. That was how I was standing when Donald O'Leary called to me to see if I was all right.

I looked up. It was just dark enough to make his presence obscure on the pier. He had been doing something on a boat, a boat much like the *Ferriter*, and he seemed to be calling it a day. The trunk of his car stood open. He smiled. He had a comfortable, easy smile.

"I'm all right," I said. "Thanks."

"You look a little the worse for wear. Sorry to say so."

"I'm okay."

"A Yank?"

I nodded. He came around the tail end of his car. He was not tall. He carried too much weight around his belly and he reminded me, in that dim light, of a groundhog or squirrel who had magically learned to walk on its hind legs. His eyes squinted. His right hand was missing. In its place was a bright silver pincher prosthetic, a mechanism that obviously he used to grab and pull when he needed to. He wore a Munster jersey over a pair of stained jeans. I knew Munster was not the Dublin team in rugby, but I didn't know whether it mattered. The Irish were mad for rugby.

"Can I help? You don't need to be scared of me. I'm local here."

"Feeling a little seasick."

"You were on that boat, I saw."

"Yes. We came up from Wicklow."

"That's a good sea running."

"Yes, it was."

"Well, you made it to port. That's what counts."

"Yes, I guess so."

That was it. He smiled and then went back to loading something from his boat to his trunk. I looked around for Ozzie. Wherever he was, he wasn't coming after me. I suspected he might need a drink. Several drinks. I recalled that I had a clump of bills, not too much but enough for dinner, maybe, stuck into the pocket of my jeans. I limped over to where Donald—I didn't know his name at that point—stood beside his car.

"Are you going anywhere in town where I could get a bite to eat?"

"You need a ride?"

"I don't know Dublin at all, I'm afraid."

He looked past me at the dock where the *Ferriter* remained bobbing on the still water of the port. I knew he was trying to assess the situation. Why would a lone woman step off a boat and ask for a ride to town? I didn't know the answer myself.

"I'm headed home now, but I could drop you somewhere," he said. "If that would be a help."

"It would, actually."

"Just give me a minute and then we'll be off."

I considered running back to the *Ferriter* for my phone, but I did not want to engage with Ozzie. Not for a time. It was better to let it settle. All of it. I still felt keyed up from surviving the run up the coast, but I also felt exhausted and empty and close to tears. I realized, when Donald came back from the boat one last time and held out his hand that he must have thought I had a fight with whoever remained on the *Ferriter.*

"Donald O'Leary," he said. "Pleased to meet you."

"Kate Moreton."

"Do you know where you want to go?"

"Not really. I only have a few bills in my pocket."

He appraised me.

"Fight?" he asked.

There was no point in hiding it from him.

"Something like that," I said.

"Well, we'll fix you up. Come along. My wife likes Yanks. Her uncle lives in Rhode Island. Do you know Rhode Island?"

"Only a little."

"She wants to go to Rhode Island in the worst way. It's her El Dorado. I can't shake her out of it."

"We all have funny notions."

"Isn't that the Sunday truth?"

I climbed in the car. It was small and not particularly tidy. It smelled like fish. As soon as Donald turned the ignition, the radio blared out. It was too loud. He quickly reached over and decreased the volume.

"Sorry," he said. "My daughter had the car last."

"No problem."

"Why don't you come home for dinner with us? It's my daughter's birthday and my wife is cooking shepherd's pie. She makes a wonderful shepherd's pie."

"That's kind of you, but I couldn't impose."

"No imposition at all. Honestly. Then I could bring you back when things cool down. We've all been in these situations. It's good to give them time."

I thought for a moment, then nodded. It wasn't fair to Ozzie to disappear as I had, but it wasn't fair for him to put us in such danger. I still felt angry at him, intensely so. To go back to him in that moment would have caused more fighting. Maybe it was the wrong thing to do, I couldn't say for certain, but I didn't particularly care what Ozzie thought in that moment. He had almost killed us both.

"Thanks," I said. "I'd love to come to dinner. It might be just what I need. I've been on the boat a long time."

"Good. Glad for the company. My wife will be thrilled."

Donald O'Leary put the car in gear and drove slowly down the dock. The tires caused the wood planks to thump softly beneath us. As easy as that, I left the *Ferriter* and its reckless captain.

I *would* have called Ozzie if I had my phone. I would have. Or I would have texted him. I wasn't trying to make a statement and I wasn't trying to hurt him. Not consciously. I felt more than a little shell-shocked. We had almost died, I realized over and over. That understanding came at me in pulses. One wrong turn, or one rogue wave, and we would have been ducked under like a toy boat in a child's bathtub. Besides, I did not intend to stay in Dublin for long. I had no clear idea why I had asked Donald for a ride. Maybe to shake the salt off me. I couldn't say. I felt confused and shaken. His kindness had offered me the only compass point I could see.

Donald O'Leary was a lamb. He was a soft, gentle man who said I could even sleep over, but I said no, not that, and he repeated his willingness to run me back to the dock afterward. It wasn't far. I let him believe that Ozzie and I had just come through a large fight, which wasn't entirely untrue. I knew just enough to know that I wasn't thinking clearly. I felt edgy and still not entirely solid in my stomach.

"Have you been to sea . . . ?" he asked when we left the dock area.

"We ran up from Dingle."

"That's a long way."

"We're planning to go around the entire country."

"That's an even longer way."

"It's seven hundred miles."

"Is it? I never knew. Live and learn."

"It was good until we came into that weather."

"Farther north, the seas will get larger. On average."

That was the last thing I wanted to hear. Before I could answer or say anything else, an enormous weariness settled over me. Fatigue dripped from the crown of my head down through my body. My head snapped forward as I fought sleepiness. Whatever adrenaline had sustained me through the storm had at last given way. I was vaguely aware of Donald looking over at me, and then I fell asleep. I should have been embarrassed, but I was too tired to resist.

The next thing I knew, Donald's voice called softly for me to wake.

"We're here," he said. "Kate, we're here."

I woke and sat up. Just on the other edge of sleep, the waves still lifted me and threw me backward. For an instant, it had felt as if we were going over into the gray water.

"Yes, yes," I said, stumbling awake.

"You're tired."

"More worn-out than anything else."

"Well, we're here. Please come in."

I climbed out. We had pulled into the driveway leading to a small house. Lights shown from the windows. It was a modest home, but it was entirely welcoming. Someone had planted a lovely perennial garden beneath the largest window. I saw day lilies and delphiniums, large, bearded irises, and Shasta daisies. The combination of the light emerging from the window, and the tranquility of the garden, pulled at me. It made me realize I had been lazy about planting a garden near the cottage. Maybe, I reasoned, I had been unsure how permanent my living in the cottage had been. Everything I saw in my heightened emotional state seemed to give me something to interpret.

"What a lovely garden," I said, still standing beside the car.

"My wife is the planter. She has a green thumb."

"How old is your daughter?"

"Seventeen today."

He opened the trunk of the car, grabbed a few things, then led me to the front door. He pushed inside and held the door back for me and I entered. Whatever misgivings I had about going with a strange man to a strange house disappeared the moment Donald's wife, Lucy, came out from the kitchen. I looked closely, but I did not see her react for even a moment at a stranger's appearance in her home. Her husband had brought someone to dinner; the guest was immediately welcome. She possessed a wonderful, cheery smile that broadened across her face the moment she realized I was a Yank. She was short, like Donald, with soft shoulders and auburn hair that she kept long and piled high on her head. She wore jeans and a Munster rugby sweatshirt. She carried a dish towel in her hands with a jar that she held out to Donald the moment he cleared the doorway.

"Would you open this?" she asked him, then held out her hand to me. "I'm Lucy, Donald's better half."

"I'm Kate."

"She just came in on a boat and was headed for the city proper and I gave her a ride," Donald said, twisting the cap off the jar. Pickles, I saw. "I thought she could do better for dinner here with us."

Did they exchange a look to explain me? Maybe. But if they did, they did it so masterfully that I couldn't say for sure where it began or ended. Lucy trusted her husband. If he needed or wanted to bring someone home, they would be hospitable first, then explain later. I felt a tiny stab at seeing their understanding of one another. *This is what being truly married means*, I thought. Compared to them, in some way difficult to define, Ozzie and I seemed like teenagers in the first flush of passion.

"Well, you're welcome, Kate. We're glad to have another person at dinner. Did Donald tell you it's our daughter's birthday?"

"He did."

"She'll be right back. I sent her to the market for a few last things. Come in, please. We're informal people. We usually entertain in our kitchen."

"That's where I prefer to be."

"We're having shepherd's pie. It's my daughter's favorite."

"It smells delicious."

I followed her into the kitchen. I liked her more than I could say. She possessed a no-nonsense air, undermined, in a charming way, with that lovely Irish sparkle of amusement at life's peculiarities. Donald came in to set down the opened jar, then excused himself and went to clean up. Lucy grabbed an open bottle of wine from the kitchen counter and cocked it toward me.

"Would you like a glass of wine, Kate?"

"Love one."

"Have a seat at the table there. I'll set another plate in a moment. Our daughter is quite full of herself today. She's certain that by turning seventeen she is nearly independent and separated from us once and for all. As parents, she's let us know we are impossible in many peculiar ways."

"She sounds just right for her age."

"Oh, she's that, all right. You'll get a kick out of her. Now tell me, did Donald say you came in on a boat just now?"

She poured the wine into a jelly jar and brought it to me. I thanked her. I felt sleepy again, but this time it was a comfortable, warm sleepiness. I liked being in their home and I liked the gentle confusion of a family dinnertime. Lucy—or Donald? But I couldn't imagine Donald decorating—had hung white, cheery curtains over the windows. A two-foot-tall statue of the Virgin Mary stood on a corner shelf by the back door. Her kitchen was functional and tidy. I liked that she gave me wine in a jelly jar, not a fussy wineglass with a stem and base.

"We came up the coast from Dingle," I said, tipping the wine toward her in thanks. "We're planning to go around the country."

"By sea?" she asked, her eyebrows going up.

"That's what we thought. The storm today might make us think better of it."

"Well," she said, going to the sink and running a large ladle under the faucet to clean it. "It's an ambitious project, I'll say that."

"It may be too ambitious. We didn't have a good day."

"I'd not imagine that you would. You're with a fellow?"

"A man named Ozzie Ferriter."

She nodded, then stuck out her lower lip to indicate she didn't know him, hadn't heard of him. At that moment, the back door opened and a beautiful young girl, obviously their daughter, barreled inside. She had her phone held out in front of her. The light from the screen turned her skin slightly blue, but there was no mistaking her beauty. She was stunning. She had rich brown hair and gray eyes. She wore leggings and a baggy shirt, but even that informally dressed, she was model-pretty.

"Say hello to Kate," Lucy said, taking a paper bag from her daughter's outstretched hand. "Kate, this is our daughter Helen."

"Happy birthday, Helen," I said. "Many happy returns of the day."

Again, if she wondered at my sudden appearance in her kitchen, on her birthday of all days, she hid it wonderfully well. She put her phone at her waist and held out her hand. I shook it.

"Are you a Yank?" she asked.

"I am."

"I'd like to go to America. I love your accent."

"I want to go to Rhode Island," Lucy said behind her. "Have you ever been, Kate?"

"I've been a couple times, actually."

"It's the smallest state," Lucy said. "Small things welcome you in ways large places don't."

"Mom, that's ridiculous," Helen said.

"Maybe ridiculous, but that's my experience in the world."

Donald appeared. He had taken off his jacket and changed his trousers. He grabbed Helen and kissed her. Helen pretended to fight him off a little, but it was easy to see she enjoyed it. I tried to remember my seventeenth birthday, but that felt like ancient, ancient history.

"They're making a round of Ireland," Lucy said to Helen, by way of explaining my presence. "Circumnavigating, I guess you could say."

"It's a mad, mad plan," I said and felt a pang about abandoning Ozzie at the dock.

"It sounds great to me," Helen said, her eyes bright with youthful enthusiasm. "We should do that, Dad."

"I can't get you on the boat as it is," he said, going to the fridge for a beer. "You'd think I was asking her to pitch coal all day."

"It's a long way," I said. "Maybe I'm just realizing that."

"I wonder if anyone else has done it?" Donald asked to no one, pulling out a beer.

Then Helen spoke to Siri.

"Has anyone circumnavigated Ireland?" she asked.

She studied the screen when Siri gave her the results.

"Looks like more people than you might think," she said. "There are two Australians who did it by kayak just last year."

"I knew something about that," I said. "But we aren't doing it to break new ground."

"Well, it sounds like a grand adventure in any case," Lucy said. "Now, Helen, help me serve. Donald, you keep an eye on her wineglass."

It was a friendly, warm meal. The shepherd's pie tasted better and fresher than any I had eaten since arriving. When I asked about the recipe, Lucy said she made it from mutton raised by a friend of theirs; she did not trust the supermarkets except for basic staples. A thick layer of mashed potato and creamed corn coated the top of the stew below. It was delicious and nourishing and I didn't object when Donald poured me another glass of wine. I was charmed by the entire family. They teased each other in gentle ways, but their love for one another was evident in every tick of the clock. The food was plentiful and they seemed happy to have someone else to include in their circle. Helen asked me a dozen questions about the States that I could barely answer. Lucy laid out for me her entire connection to Rhode Island. Donald, for the most part, remained silent, but always attentive.

They served cake for dessert and Helen blew out seventeen

candles. She looked lovely sitting behind the candlelight. I don't know why, but I felt teary watching her. She was loved and effortlessly embraced by the two people closest to her. She had her fondest birthday wish whether she knew it or not.

Presents. A pale gray sweater that matched her eyes. Ear buds. A homemade coupon for a "movie night" with her dad. A first edition copy of *The Wind in the Willows*, her favorite childhood book, that her mother had come across in a thrift store. When it was finished, she went around the table and hugged them both. For good measure, she hugged me. Their inherent kindness had been planted and harvested in their daughter.

"You're welcome to stay," Lucy said when Donald said he could run me back whenever I liked. He looked tired and I was certain he was not far from falling into bed. "We could fix you up and have Helen sleep out here."

"Thank you, but I should be getting back. We usually leave early in the morning."

"This storm isn't leaving," Donald said, standing to get his keys. "It's going to get bigger before it gets smaller."

"Well, I guess we'll sit it out then."

Lucy leaned close to me as we neared the door to leave.

"Are you safe?" she whispered.

"Yes," I answered, shocked that she could think me in the position of an abused wife. But why not? I had all the symptoms.

"Be back in a shake," Donald told his women. "Keep the lights on."

We left after some more goodbye-ing. The car felt cold and damp after the warmth of the house. Donald drove me back without much comment. I thanked him and told him he had a lovely family. He smiled and nodded.

"If it comes to it," he said when he dropped me back at the dock, "you always have a place here."

I leaned across and hugged him. In that moment, his door jerked open and Ozzie reached in and yanked him out by his collar. It happened so suddenly that my arms remained out-stretched from my body. Then I saw Donald snap against the hood of his car, and I heard Ozzie's hand slap against flesh. I screamed for him to *stop it, stop it, stop it,* and he did. He walked away, weaving with drink, and I hurried around to help Donald back to his feet.

23

Donald was not hurt badly. He had been humiliated, and shocked by the sudden violence, but he stood beside the hood of his car and smiled at me. It was a smile to tell me he was all right, it was not my fault, he could take it.

I didn't want him to take it.

"I'm sorry. I am so, so sorry. I am sorry I got you involved in this."

"I'm fine, Kate. I've had worse. He didn't have a heart for it."

"But you were so kind . . . and I repay you with this."

"You didn't repay me. He did."

He nodded in the direction of the *Ferriter*.

"If you'll wait one minute, I'm going to get my things," I said. "Then if you'll let me, I'm coming to spend the night at your house."

"I'll wait," he said. "I should go on board with you."

"No, let me take care of this. It will be all right, I promise."

But I didn't know if it would be. Ozzie had never been anything but kind to me. I had never seen him act violently toward anyone until this night, although I occasionally heard stories of past altercations. They were muted stories, little worrisome legends that followed him. He had always been exceedingly tender with me. If anything, he had been careful of his strength around me, protective in a good, honest way.

I hurried. I stepped onto the *Ferriter* and immediately went belowdecks. I didn't see Ozzie. I didn't sense him on board, either. That was curious, but I didn't have time to worry about it. As quickly as possible, I filled a bag with as many things as I could remember to take. I grabbed my computer. I grabbed my notes. My hands trembled as I stuffed things inside the bag in no order whatsoever. My mind asked over and over how it had come to this. How had I ended up on a boat in Dublin with a man who could not feel life unless he risked it recklessly? Who drank beyond what was good for him? Who jerked a man out of a car and slapped him so quickly, and so horridly, that I saw in my husband the soldier, the trained killer who carried a memory of actions in war that plagued him? How had I been so blind to miss all the tell-tale signs?

As soon as my bag was filled, I hoisted it onto my shoulder and climbed off the boat. Still no sign of Ozzie. The bag made me unbalanced and I nearly fell on the uneven dock boards as I returned to the car. Maybe that was an omen, I wondered.

"Was he there?" Donald asked.

"No. I don't know where he is."

"I saw someone walking out that way," Donald said, pointing toward an area where lobster pots had been stacked. "It might have been him."

"Please, let's go. I'm sure he's ashamed of himself. We'll have no more trouble with him."

We went. As we pulled slowly away, I put my hands over my face. I didn't cry, although I wanted to weep. My stomach filled with butterflies, poisonous ones that landed on each thought and fluttered there. My hands continued to tremble. I felt apart from myself, if that made any sense: I was watching a girl from a low-budget television movie, a girl whose husband raged and fumed until she had no choice but to leave. It was bad television, bad drama, bad life.

198 J. P. Monninger

"Would you please drop me at a hotel?" I asked, my voice tight with emotion. "I can't face your family. Any kind of hotel whatsoever. I don't want Helen to see me like this."

"She would understand. Sincerely, Kate."

"Please," I said. "I'm embarrassed and shaken. I have my wallet. I can manage, honestly. I'd prefer it. I don't want to explain anything to anyone right now. Everyone will be kind to me and that will only make it worse. Honestly."

"Are you sure?"

"Yes, I promise. I'm humiliated. I just want to be alone. I'm sorry. I'm sorry for everything."

He didn't say anything to that. He stopped at the first stop sign we came to and told me he was thinking of hotels nearby, what might make sense.

"Maybe I should drive you a little distance from here," he said, "in case he comes looking for you."

"I think he's done for the night. I really do. He was drunk. He was angry at me and angry at himself, probably. He's not like this."

Donald looked at me. I sensed the evaluation. He didn't buy my assessment.

"Well, still, I know of a place," he said finally.

He drove for twenty minutes or so until we seemed to enter the outskirts of Dublin. We parked beside a small B&B called the Coat of Arms. It was a dull, brown building with a poorly kept façade, but I didn't care at that point. I wanted to be alone. I wanted to be away from everyone. Donald waited while I ran inside to see about vacancies. A sleepy-eyed boy named Martin told me I could have a choice between two rooms. I told him to give me the one he would pick. He did. I signed the register, gave him my credit card, then went out to say goodbye to Donald.

"I wish I could apologize even more," I said. "I wish I could make it go away."

"Well, it was a bad act, but he didn't seem like he wanted to hurt me. He's a strong man. Don't torture yourself about it."

"Would you do me a favor and not mention it to your girls?" He smiled.

"Well, I can't promise I can keep it from my wife. She can wring anything out of me. But Helen doesn't need to know. If anything comes up, and you need a place to stay, you come and find us, all right?"

I hugged him. But it wasn't a warm hug anymore. He was tired of me, tired of the problems that trailed after me. His left eye had swollen a little along the edge where Ozzie had struck him. I hurried into the Coat of Arms. Martin led me upstairs and opened the door to my room. It was a basic guest room with a white comforter on a full-sized bed, a chest of drawers, and a small writing table. A tight bathroom extended off the window side of the room. I accepted the key, told Martin it was fine, then closed the door after him. I flipped the bolt on the door and then stood for a long minute in the silence, the whir of my blood filling my ears with the sound of the sea.

I fashioned a desert in my head. A desert was the proper anti-dote for the sea.

It sounded ridiculous, I granted, but it was the metaphor that sustained me. I grew a wide open, dry land, with pale cacti and shimmering waves of light and heat. I wedged that image into my head and left it there, a harbor of safety and quiet that allowed me to retreat to it whenever I needed. Everything—meals, travel, other voices—everything had to accommodate itself to my dry, white land.

Ozzie did not get to come to the desert. He did not get to be there. He was too loud and too liquid to live there.

What I did was this: I took the train from Dublin to Limerick. I got a cab from the station to my apartment. I turned off my phone. I went into the apartment and I slowly, method-ically unpacked. It did not take long. I pulled the kitchen table into a better position against a southern-facing window, so that I could get the sun all morning. I showered. I took a long, long shower. Then I did some yoga stretches and fixed tea. I did not feel sleepy. I felt that I had a desert to live in, and I made myself dry inside, quiet and light-filled.

When any thought of Ozzie, of what would become of us, of what needed to happen started to intrude, I shut it away. I sent it to the desert. I wanted to be a mystic, a holy woman wandering the desert, fixed and focused on my work.

For a day, I did nothing but reread everything I had gathered or written about the women's narratives on the Blaskets. I reordered things, put things in new packets and manila envelopes. I charted every correspondence, every set of notes into an Excel spreadsheet.

If I had been too sloppy, if I had gotten off the track, then the simple solution was to restore the track, to get back on it, to regain order where chaos had threatened.

I took a cab to the grocery store on the second day of my return. I stockpiled food and bought myself two dozen yellow tulips. I stored the groceries carefully, as one would in a desert, then put the yellow tulips in jelly jars near my desk-table. Later that day, I burned sage again. It was ridiculous, more ridiculous than ever, but it brought me serenity.

On the fourth day of my return, someone knocked on my door. I sat for a long time and waited for whoever it was to go away. I made no sound. Eventually the person left. I looked out the window to see who it had been, but the person had gone off in a different direction, one that prevented me from seeing who it was.

I kept my phone off. I detached from everything electronic.

I did more stretching and yoga. I edited my Blasket piece. I watered the tulips. They did not belong in the desert, but they comforted me anyway. I had just returned to my desk for an afternoon session of writing and research, when someone knocked again. This time the person didn't wait. I heard a jingle of keys, then suddenly the door opened.

"Hello?" someone called up the stairs. "Miss, are you here? Is anyone here?"

Tentatively, I walked to the top of the stairs and looked down. It was a campus security officer. He was a young man who held his hat under his arm while he put away his pass key. His zippers and pockets and lanyards made noises whenever he moved.

"Hello? Yes, what is it?" I asked. "Is something wrong?"

"We were asked to check on you. A woman stateside, your friend Milly, she called campus security. She said she hadn't heard from you in a number of days. She said it was unlike you. We didn't know if you were here."

"I'm fine, thank you."

"She was persistent . . ." he said, leaning a little to use the light to inspect me. "Everything all right, then? You're not sick, are you?"

"Just working. I'll call her. Thank you, though."

He paused, sizing me up. Then he nodded.

"If you require anything, please let us know."

"Thank you. Everything is fine. I appreciate you looking in on me."

But it wasn't fine, of course. Healthy young people don't have security officers checking on their status. I lifted my hand to say goodbye to him. He backed out of the doorway. I returned to my desk and put my nose against the tulips. They smelled of gardens.

"Now what?" Milly asked.

I had told her the entire story on Skype. I had tried to tell it calmly, flatly, without tipping the scales one way or the other. I drank tea and laid out the whole ordeal. She listened, drinking tea on her end, her hair pulled back, her hands coated with flecks of paint. She had been up late, working. She had apologized for getting a security guard to check on me, but she had been frantic that I had been lost at sea. It was our habit to text nearly every day, even when I was out on the *Ferriter.* My absence had caused her concern and she had tracked me down like a mama bear.

"I don't know, Milly. I haven't thought that far ahead. For now, I work. I get back to the reason I came here. I research."

"You're married, though, Kate. It's not like breaking up after a fling."

"I know."

"And Ozzie hasn't been in touch? Is he still circumnavigating the island?"

"I don't know."

"You haven't talked to him?"

I shook my head. She puckered her lips and blew air through her mouth.

"Kate, you have to talk to him. Is this a pride thing?"

"Whose pride? His or mine?"

"His, yours. What does it matter? Are you finished with him?"

"I don't know."

"But you love him. You had a wonderful time on the boat, didn't you?"

"We had a wonderful time, yes. We did. For a while. And I love him deeply. But I'm afraid he's broken, Milly. I'm afraid I've fallen in love with a piece of pottery that's beautiful, but you know it has a hairline fracture at its base and that it won't hold up. It won't be able to fulfill its function. It's no longer a bowl. It's simply pretty clay. Does that make sense?"

"Yes, except that Ozzie is not a bowl. Or a piece of pottery. He's a man. He's flawed, I guess, but we all are."

"I know that. I know I'm flawed. Seriously flawed. But that look on his face when we were in the storm . . . I can't forget that. That's a serious thing, Milly. And the drinking. He's carrying a wound from the war that he won't get fixed. Or he can't get it fixed. He won't talk about it or address it. And it haunts him."

She sipped her tea.

"Better to cut it off now then to keep thinking the bowl will mend itself?" she asked. "To use your metaphor."

"I don't know. Maybe. He's so charming and he's so beautiful that he still takes my breath away. He can quote Yeats. He's the dream guy in so many ways, but he is hurt and wounded. I'll never forget him pulling Donald from the car and slapping him. I can't forgive that."

"He was jealous and drunk. He'd just come through a violent storm and his wife left the boat."

"I know. I know that. I've been over that a thousand times in my head."

Then I told her about the desert I had fashioned in my head. She smiled. It was an indulgent smile.

"That's a very Kate thing to do," she said. "Living in a dream desert."

"All I can do is wait for a while. I think we both are using this time to assess our relationship. That's my guess. He's not the sort to run after me. If I need time to sort things out, then he will leave me alone. From his way of thinking, I'm the one who left the boat. I canceled the trip."

"He has a point. Don't get angry with me, but he does."

"You're supposed to be on my side, Milly."

"I'm supposed to be a neutral witness, my dear. You don't need a cheerleader. You need a friend who can tell you what she sees in any given situation."

"Fair enough."

We signed off a little later. I finished my tea and rinsed out my cup. I reviewed the conversation while my hands remained under the stream of water. Did I really see things the way I had told Milly? Was that a fair assessment? Did I expect too much from Ozzie? Were we sufficiently different to be doomed from the start? I wondered. I wondered about it all.

And what about me? Was I some sort of coward who gave up at the first struggle? But it wasn't the first struggle, I reminded myself. If I was honest about things, if I could be clear for a moment about things, I had always had reservations about Ozzie's suitability. He was a man who jumped on the back of a donkey for the hell of it. He drank.

And when he wanted to, he turned me inside out.

I went back to my desert. I worked. I began taking long, wandering walks along the River Shannon in the afternoon. It was good to walk. It was orderly. Work, walk, work. My dissertation had taken on greater strength. I felt solid in all ways except one.

At night, though, I thought of Ozzie. I thought of him on the *Ferriter* by himself. I thought of him heading into the north seas around the top of the island. Donald had said the seas were rougher there. From the tip of Ireland, the currents rolled into the Arctic. Ozzie would like the wildness. He would like testing himself against the sea. And if the crack in his base withstood that, if he did not break apart like pottery, then maybe he never would. Maybe that was why he went to sea.

24

When I had been off the boat for a week—with no sign or word from Ozzie—Bertie Janes contacted me out of the blue and invited me on a fortnight archeological dig on the Great Blasket Island.

"We have a mind to explore the site of the *Rinn an Chaisleáin,* or Castle Point. It was the castle owned by your husband's people."

"Ferriter Castle?"

"Yes, what's left of it. There are no physical remains to speak of. The stones were carried away to build a Protestant soup kitchen and school in 1840. But you know all this, I imagine?"

"I know most of it."

"Well, we don't expect much to come of it, but it's probably worth investigating to be certain. People have dug there before, but you'll have the best of the island's weather, so it should be pleasant at any rate. It's a camping situation, so I don't know how you feel about that."

"I'm fine with that. I'd love it. It's a dream for me."

"The dig, if you can call it that, is being run by a Swede named Sixten. Honestly, I don't know if that's his first or last name. He's a linguist primarily, from what I can gather. A large man, a veritable Viking. He's bringing with him a team of volunteers, some Irish, some Swedish. It's a hodgepodge of researchers, but he has permission to be out there for two weeks and I immediately thought of you."

"Thank you, Bertie."

"Ozzie is welcome to come as well. His boat might be of use."

"We're not seeing eye to eye at the moment, I'm afraid. Think we might need a little time apart."

Bertie made no comment; he let it pass. After a moment to take stock, he filled me in on the details of the expedition. I had three days to get ready. The permit had just gone through. That was the reason for the short notice. I needed to bring my own sleeping bag and tent. We would prepare our own meals, taking turns on kitchen detail; the island canteen had recently started up its summer schedule for the tourist trade and the staff had enough to do without feeding our team. We had to be independent. Sixten had already engaged a local company to resupply us with food. The Irish government had given him a permit for two weeks. Bertie, as the Blasket Island museum curator, would visit several times through the weeks to supervise our findings. That was nonnegotiable.

"The government is touchy on the subject of a Swede coming to dig for artifacts on Irish soil," Bertie concluded after we had talked for some time. "But I was only half joking about the Viking part. The Vikings likely attacked the Blaskets as they attacked nearly everywhere. They were greedy, adventuresome folks. They especially liked to plunder churches. I gather Sixten has money from the Swedish government to look for traces of Viking monkey-business. They plundered Skellig Michael, but they may have visited here as well."

"It all sounds exciting."

He fed me more details, then paused for a moment before commenting on Ozzie.

"I've known Ozzie all his life, Kate," he said softly. "Since he was a boy. Do you know the Irish expression of a man having a wind inside him? It means he has difficulty settling beside a fire.

Ozzie has a wind inside him, Kate. He always has. I feared for you when I saw you with him, not because he's not loveable and kind, but because he has a wind inside him. Those kinds of men are difficult for the women who love them."

"Thank you for saying that, Bertie."

"Some might say a man with a wind inside him is the only kind of man worth having."

"Do you have a wind inside you, Bertie?"

He laughed. Then he laughed harder.

"Afraid not. I'm couch-sitter, an observer. I wish I were a little bit more of a Viking, but I'm not. I read about the exploits of others. How about you, Kate? Do you have a wind inside you?"

"I thought I did. Now I'm not sure. I feel rather timid these days."

"You two seemed well matched. Well, it's a long life, Kate, so you never know what will happen. Give it time. Where is Ozzie, anyway?"

"I'm not sure. He might still be circumnavigating Ireland."

"Well, he has always been an intrepid lad. Good for him. Now, if I've answered all your questions, and you mine, I should let you go. Say hello for me if you speak to your husband. It's difficult not to love him in spite of himself."

He said he would email me final instructions. Meanwhile, he repeated that I should arrange to borrow a tent and a sleeping bag if I didn't have one. Bring work clothes. Prepare to work in the soil, he said. Camping.

It was a lovely and needed distraction. It turned out that Daijeet had everything I required. He was a veritable outfitter for outdoor adventures. In fact, he pressed on me more equipment than I needed; I began to feel like the neophyte Girl Scout who wanders off into the hills with a backpack too stuffed and loaded to carry properly. But it was okay. I took pleasure in packing my backpack with the necessities of a two-week camping trip.

I cooked Daijeet a salmon—that he caught and filleted—as a thank you for his generosity. We had a wonderful dinner together.

Twenty-four hours later, I found myself standing at the Dingle dock, the same dock where I had first met Ozzie and Gran and Seamus. The day came up foggy and overcast, but it was summer now and warm. Mid-June. The sea looked gray and calm. My instructions mentioned that we would board the tourist boat, the one that made a regular circuit to the island. It had been commissioned for our party.

Fifteen minutes after I had arrived, three white vans pulled up beside the dock. It would have been impossible to miss Sixten. As soon as he swung out of the van, he began calling out orders. He was at least six and a half feet, with a large curly beard and a wild head of hair that barely stayed contained under a ridiculous rain hat. The rain hat had a large brim with a blue ribbon tied above it. It was a horrible hat, a woman's hat, really, and it made him look like a grandmother who had slipped into the garden to cut some roses. The hat was impossibly at odds with his size and gender. It protected him from the sun, I supposed. He possessed reddish-blond coloring, auburn and freckled, and was probably prone, as I was, to burning. His belly was spectacular, a large cliff of flesh that he carried before him like a mother chimpanzee carrying a mature baby, but it did not look fat so much as formidable. Everything about him spoke to food and consumption and appetite, a Scandinavian King Henry VIII, and his energy in those first moments nearly bowled me over. But he beamed a happy, bright smile at anyone who caught his attention, and he seemed to be always on the verge of laughing at a good joke.

"Summer camps, boys and girls, summer camps!" he called, getting the word *camps* a little wrong. "Let's go, time is wasting. Let's be at it."

The crew was already at it. In no time, they unloaded one of the vans and started on a second one. They stacked everything on the deck in the slot allocated for the tourist boat. Once the boat arrived, it would be a simple matter to put it on board. Gas stoves, shovels, picks, buckets, coolers, all new. Seeing the newness of the purchases, I felt slightly less intimidated. I stepped forward when Sixten had a moment and introduced myself.

"Ah, the American lady. Bertie's friend," Sixten said. "Welcome, welcome. The more the merrier. Isn't that the saying?"

His voice came up as if from a barrel.

"Yes, I'm Kate Moreton."

"Nice to meet you, Kate. Time not to make formal introductions now. Just lend a hand when you can. The boat should be here any moment. Yes, I can see it now. It's make the traverse."

Transit? It didn't matter. I went and helped the crew unload the remaining equipment. I introduced myself when appropriate. We were all too busy to make full connections.

A half hour later, the boat was packed and we pushed away from the dock. As easy as that. I sat on the starboard gunwale and watched Dingle drop slowly into the sea behind us. It was difficult to talk over the engine sounds, and the raucous shout of the gulls, so the crew contented itself with smiling and nodding at one another. I nodded, too. Someone passed around a plate of sliced apples and cheese. I took a piece and ate it. It was my fourth time across Dingle Bay. The first three had been with Ozzie, but now he was no longer beside me. I forced myself to go to my self-imposed desert. Clear thinking, I told myself. Deep breaths.

I pitched my tent on the green slope of a hillside overlooking the lower village, where years and years ago, at the end of the sixteenth century, the Ferriter family had leased lands from the Earls of Desmond and Sir Richard Boyle after the dispossession of the Desmond Geraldines. I only had the history fresh because I had read it the night before to prepare for our undertaking. Besides, in a way I was a Ferriter, though only through marriage. I had kept my own name, Moreton, though at the bank and in the grocery stores occasionally someone called me Mrs. Ferriter. It was a proud name, as purely Irish as I could have it. I wasn't sure, honestly, whether Sixten knew my connection to the Ferriter castle or not. It didn't matter in any case.

A pup tent. Again, I sent a silent thank-you to my father and to Daijeet for teaching me how to set up my tent. In fact, I was skilled enough to lend a hand with other peoples' tents, and I even proved somewhat useful when we came together to set up the community tent. This was a larger canvas affair, with stakes and poles, that we were told would be our meeting place, our place to review any artifacts we found, and the place where we would eat our dinners, such as they were. Little by little, I got to know some of the team. Most were affiliated with a university in Ireland or Sweden; two linguists, one male, one female; one ethnographer, female; a weapons expert—he said he expected to recover Viking ax heads; a male grad student who seemed to be a boy of all work, and Sixten and his second-hand man, Grover. Grover, who looked like a smaller version of Sixten, but thinner and more streamlined, was the techie. While the crew set up the large tent, Grover and Sixten launched a drone and spent a good hour circling it around the dig site, happy as boys, both of them taking turns piloting the buzzing helicopter.

"Ya, ya, ya," Sixteen said, calling to Grover when Grover checked the returning images on his laptop. "Good, good, good."

"Bigger circles," Grover called back. "Bigger and bigger."

And it was right at that moment, right when the sun had grown weaker in the western sky, and the drone buzzed above us, and the male grad student hammered stakes into the ground to support the large, central tent, that I saw Ozzie's boat.

It was too far off for me to recognize it at first, but then my eyes adjusted to the softening light and I finally claimed it from the western glow. I recognized its shape and the way it sat in the water. I felt my heart begin to thump in my chest, and I couldn't help walking away from the settlement we made. I climbed the hills—the same hills women had climbed for centuries to regard the sea and watch for boats—and put my hand like a visor over my eye ridge. Yes, it was the *Ferriter.* Watching it, I felt a wild mixture of emotions: fear and anxiety, joy, pleasure, anticipation, defensiveness, shame and lust. Part of me wished his boat would go away; another part of me wished he would throttle forward and arrive at the island dock as quickly as possible. My legs trembled. I felt light-headed and absurd, a high school girl seeing her crush coming down the hallway from chemistry class.

My desert place didn't help. Nothing helped.

I waited until I saw what Ozzie intended. He seemed not to be certain what he wanted to do, either. But then the *Ferriter* bent its wake toward the Great Blasket Island, and Ozzie came forward at a good pace. I raised my hand to wave, then withdrew it and put it against my throat. I watched the *Ferriter* and waited until it had come within a quarter of a mile before I began walking down the hill to meet him.

25

The timing could not have been worse.

The day-trippers, the tourists who had taken the ferry out to the island, had assembled on the dock, waiting for the ferry to fetch them. They looked tired and wind-burned, most of them ready to be back on the mainland, back to food and comfort and a soft bed. Two boys pointed at Ozzie's boat, thinking it was the ferry, and that caused a small undulation in the crowd. Then people realized it was the wrong boat, and they went back to their impatient waiting. The ferry, someone said, was late.

The day's quiet was almost upon us. I had to ask for space a dozen times as I made my way through the crowd. A few people regarded me with annoyance; they assumed I was angling for a better spot for boarding. I pointed at Ozzie's boat, telling anyone who would listen that I was meeting *that* boat, not their boat, but they were mostly too tired to care about my excuses. A little girl even held out her foot to trip me. I gave her devil eyes and stepped past.

Ozzie brought the *Ferriter* around to the shallower side of the dock. He backed the engines expertly, then softly swung the tail into the pilings. He handled the boat masterfully. He always had. He stepped onto the gunwale, then onto the dock. He tied the boat off before it could drift even a foot away. He left the proper amount of slack for the tide. Then he stepped back on the boat and helped Gottfried climb onto dry land.

For a moment or two, neither of them saw me. Maybe the crowd on the other side of the dock distracted them; maybe Ozzie needed to give Gottfried a chance to do his business. Either way, they seemed preoccupied. Then, finally, Gottfried saw me, and he came forward wagging his tail, crouching a little as was his habit, his soft manner making him ready to turn over to expose his belly.

"There's my boy," I whispered to him, gathering him in my arms. "That's my good, good boy."

I didn't dare raise my eyes to Ozzie. The glimpse I caught of him told me that he looked off to seaward. Fortunately, we were saved by the ferry blowing its horn. The crowd bunched together, and the ferry slowly rounded the piers and came into docking position.

"Could we walk him, Kate? He's been on the boat a while."

I nodded and stood. I took the leash from Ozzie. I needed something to do with my hands. I could barely catch my breath.

We didn't say anything. We walked Gottfried and concentrated too much of our energy on him. For his part, he behaved as he always did. Once he spotted a roaming donkey and shied away, slanting his body comically to escape and woofing under his breath.

When the ferry finally tied off, we turned and watched the crowd board her. It didn't take long. It was the last run of the ferry for that day. I guessed the crew was ready to be home to their suppers as well.

The ferry tooted its horn and then backed its engines. In no time, it passed through the secluded harbor and headed in a straight line for Dingle. We watched it go.

"They say you can get pregnant on the Dingle ferry if all else fails," Ozzie said, his eyes lingering on the boat. "It's tried and true."

"That sounds like a convenient wives' tale for men."

"You have little faith, Kate."

Our eyes still hadn't met. We might have been strangers discussing a sunset.

We walked slowly back to the *Ferriter*. It was a fine evening, soft and warm. A few minnows darted around the dock pilings. Ozzie stepped down into the boat and coaxed Gottfried to join him. Given the height difference of the pier and the boat deck, I had to look down to see him.

"I've come to apologize, Kate. I behaved badly."

"Thank you. I appreciate that."

He smiled up at me and squinted a little at the last sunlight.

"I don't think I'm like that, honestly, but then I have the proof of what I did to weigh against it. I have thought a lot about that. About everything. I'm not as good a man as I'd like to be. As I'd like to be for you. I'm afraid you saw a side of me that makes me ashamed."

"I'm sorry, Ozzie."

"I tried to love you, Kate, as I know how."

"I know you did. I believe you."

"I love you still, but I feel we've stepped out of the spell, haven't we?"

"I don't know, Ozzie. I'm not sure."

He smiled and then handed me a box. I knew what it was: my books, a few clothes, odds and ends. It was heavy and I put it down on the dock.

"I want to be the man you need, Kate, I don't think I can be. Not yet. I have some things I need to examine. Some dark places. It was being with you, and with everything that happened . . . it put some light on things I'd rather not inspect too closely. But I need to. Things that occurred even before you. I can't ask you to wait, Kate, but I can ask you to keep your heart open to me. If you want to."

I nodded. I couldn't speak. He smiled and reached down to pet Gottfried.

"The old sailors say there is a current out to the east of Ireland that is made of ice and gold. And if you sail in it, it won't release you until you've gone so far north that the icebergs surround you, make you lose your bearings. The white bears come out then and point in different directions, and soon you're lost and become a ghost ship sailing on a current of gold and white. It's a matter of going too far out. We might have been lost, you and I. But I've brought you back to shore safely and I discharge you, Kate. *Slán leat.*"

I had difficulty speaking. Part of me could not believe what we were doing. Was it over? Had we ended just like that?

"*Slán leat,*" I repeated the Irish farewell.

He climbed back on the dock to throw off his ropes. Then he jumped aboard. I watched every move he made. I watched for hesitation, for a change of mind, for anything. Could this really be happening? I wondered. Was this what I wanted? Was this the right thing after all?

The *Ferriter* moved slowly around the piers, then bent to the incoming sea and headed back to the mainland. I did not cry to see him go. I was too numb for that, too shocked that it could end this simply. I walked to the end of the dock and watched the *Ferriter* go into the darkening night. I whispered the single line from Browning that I had learned in high school. *O heart! oh blood that freezes, blood that burns.* In all the years of knowing it, it was the first time I understood what the poet had tried to say to us.

Part Three

—

SUNFLOWER
SEEDS,
NOT MILLET

FOURTH LETTER

Eileen Silverman
Provost
Dartmouth College

Dear Doctor Moreton:

Your teaching assignment for the academic year is as follows. You will be teaching a 2-3 load in a combined English/Social Science appointment, with all the attendant responsibilities of a full-time faculty member. Your rank will be Assistant Professor. Please feel free to contact this office if you have questions about your appointment. Consult the faculty handbook for additional information regarding your position and the responsibilities therein.

All best wishes for continued success in your academic career.

Cheers,
Eileen Silverman
Dartmouth College

26

"So you've met someone?"

"I wouldn't say met someone."

"What would you call it, then?"

"Okay, yes, I met someone."

"A man?"

"Yes, a man."

"One doesn't take such a thing for granted any longer. Genders match up in all sorts of ways."

I wondered, absurdly, where Dr. Kaufman had found the scarf that wound around her throat. It was a wonderful color, a mixture of russet red and a silver glimmer that heightened the gray tones of her hair. It was *always* a wonderful color with Dr. Kaufman. As my mother would have said, she was a woman who dressed to advantage. She was sixty-two. She had a trim figure, a former dancer's body, with slim antelope ankles and shapely calves. She sat in her large, comfortable swivel chair and I sat in mine. Between us, a lovely French door opened onto a winter landscape. She had hung a cylindrical bird feeder from a garden trellis and the birds came and went, carrying off their black seed prizes or stopping for a moment to dive on the ground and peck at the treasure there. The garden itself was immaculately kept; all the strands of withered day lilies and tired peonies had been either bobbed back to a manageable length, or braided into a French twist. Everything about Dr. Kaufman, including the garden, seemed to reveal an inner tranquility, a sense of order and calm. She was French. She came from the Bordeaux region in France. She had read everything, seen everything, traveled everywhere. She was every woman's dream "after" picture; if, finished scrambling through years in a whirl of confusion and missteps, the after photo of our own lives would have portrayed us as something like Dr. Kaufman, any woman would have accepted the terms of the contract and signed on. It felt like sinking into a warm bath to be in her company, to be her client, to talk, as I did once every other week, to her wise ear and stare into her pale blue eyes.

"He's a visiting professor. His name is Lawrence Barthelmes. Dr. Barthelmes. You might have seen him on television."

She inclined her head. I knew that gesture. It meant, no, no she hadn't seen him on television, she rarely watched television, modern pop references to American television were never going to interest her. The only reason I had risked such a reference was due to the fact that Lawrence Barthelmes was a well-known economist who might have appeared on a show sufficiently weighty to have interested her.

"Where did you meet him?" she asked.

"At a faculty tea. A wine-and-cheese affair."

She smiled. She glanced at the birds, then returned her eyes to me.

"We were introduced," I continued. "Nothing much to it."

"And you like him?"

"Maybe. Yes, I guess. As a person, I suppose. He has a lot of energy. He's a bit full of himself. He's kind of a star right now in that world."

"In what world?"

"Economics."

She inclined her head again. It meant go on if I liked, otherwise she would watch the birds.

"He's divorced. We talked a little about that."

"About divorce? Or about your situation?"

"Both. Both of our situations."

"Does he know you are not divorced?"

"Yes, but I didn't dwell on it."

"I imagine you wouldn't."

She had said many times that divorce was not separation. Divorce was its own category. I saw the calculation in her eyes. She found my open-ended situation with Ozzie unnecessarily messy. She would not come out and condemn my murky status, but she had made me understand that the nebulous quality of my arrangement with Ozzie—or my lack of arrangement—might cause me and others pain. She had wondered several times why I did not file papers and close the books between us. It was a fair question. It had been two years.

"You had a date?" she continued.

"We met for a drink. We've gone out twice since then. You could say we hit it off."

She nodded. That also meant *go on*.

"He has a child. A little girl named Sylvie. She stays mostly with her mother. They live in New York City."

"Where does he live?"

"In Brooklyn. His appointment is at Columbia, but he has been a visiting professor here at Dartmouth for the last year and a half. He spent a semester at the University of Texas. Then he came here."

She nodded. I knew what the nod meant.

"You're wondering where he finds time to be with Sylvie," I said, proud that I could anticipate her question.

She kept her eyes on mine.

"I admit, I wondered, too. But he flies in a lot. We're going down this weekend, actually. It's a little early, a little soon to do that kind of trip together, but he has to be there. Wants to be there. He's been invited to speak on one of the Sunday morning talk shows. You know those, don't you? No? Well, Sunday mornings a bunch of experts talk about the issues of the day. He'll be on *Meet the Press*. I know you don't follow those things, but it's a big deal. Not just anyone is asked. We'll fly back Monday morning. I have to teach that evening."

She shifted her position in her chair. I knew that meant one of two things. Either we approached the end of our hour, or she was not entirely comfortable with my assessment of the situation. It might have been both things. It felt strange to hear myself describe my new relationship with Lawrence aloud. I was aware I was making it sound more permanent, more solid, than it merited. I wondered what that meant or indicated about my psychological landscape. Dr. Kaufman had told me more than once that we had all the answers already; the trick was to listen to ourselves carefully. What was I trying to say about Lawrence?

"Do you think I'm making a mistake to go to New York with him?"

"Do you?"

"No, I don't think so. I hope not. He's very talented."

She nodded.

"And after Ozzie, well, you know."

"What should I know?"

"It hasn't been easy for me to . . . trust new people."

"Because?"

"Because of what happened. How it happened."

"Have you heard from him?"

"No."

"Why, then, does Ozzie have anything to do with your decision to go to New York with Lawrence?"

"He doesn't. I didn't say he did."

"You brought him into the conversation."

"As a reference point."

She nodded and raised her eyebrows.

"Okay, maybe I didn't need to reference him. Maybe he has

nothing whatsoever to do with my decision to go to New York with Lawrence. Is that your point?"

"I'm not making a point, Kate. You are. And we are out of time, I'm afraid."

"So the fact that I brought Ozzie into the conversation when discussing my feelings for a new man is telling?"

She smiled. We were done. A red cardinal landed on the ground beneath the feeder. Of course she had a red cardinal visit, I thought as I stood. Of course Dr. Kaufman didn't settle for common sparrows or chickadees. I slowly swung into my coat and took a deep breath.

The Dartmouth campus in early winter looked beautiful. By the time I left Dr. Kaufman's office and walked the half mile to the Dartmouth Green, the lights around Hanover, the town that supported and surrounded Dartmouth College, had come on to chase away the first darkness. I had an hour and a half before my class, and I had planned to spend it in the library, prepping, but I found myself walking slower and slower. Something felt broken inside me. My internal compass had lost its bearing. When I reached the Dartmouth Green, a wide grass swath that stretched from the Baker Library to the lip of Hanover's Main Street, I felt light-headed and empty. I tried to remember when I had last eaten, but that was a dodge. It wasn't food I needed. I stood for a moment beneath a street light. Was this a panic attack? I wondered. I had never experienced one before, but if this wasn't a panic attack, it certainly was doing an estimable job in approximating it. My breath came in short, desperate pants. I stuck my hand in my pocket, thinking I should call Milly or the police or someone. I even drew my phone out and began to dial Milly's number when I stopped at the sight of an old dog approaching me. It was a Golden Retriever, an ancient fellow, with a white muzzle, and I squatted and invited him into my arms. He came slowly and softly, tired with his walk, maybe tired of life, but he placed his gray head against my chest and I put my face in his fur and began to weep. I hadn't known I had such feeling inside me a moment before, but the smell of his fur, the sweetness of his aged body against mine, evoked something in me that I couldn't control. I touched his warm ears, petted him gently, aware that I was making a small scene. A few people passed by; a young woman in leggings jogged past and seemed ready to pause if I needed help. I held up my hand and nodded to say I was all right. But I wasn't, and I cried against the old dog's kind head, unable to stop.

"Are you okay, lady?" a young boy asked me.

I looked up. A boy of about ten stood staring at me, a leash in his hand. He was obviously the guardian of this old dog. I nodded that I was okay and wiped my sleeve across my eyes.

"What's his name? Is it a boy or a girl?"

"His name is Clobber."

"Clobber? He doesn't seem like he can clobber much anymore."

"He's fourteen. He's older than I am."

"He's a sweet dog."

"He sleeps in my bed every night. He always has. I have to lift him up onto the bed now, though. Mom sometimes has to help."

"I'm sorry I'm crying like this. I've just had a funny kind of day."

"My mom says that's why they invented wine."

He smiled. He knew it was a joke and that maybe he shouldn't be ratting out his mom by telling me she drank wine. He was beyond cute.

"Did you ever have a dog?" he asked.

"I had one once. His name was Gottfried."

"What kind of dog was he?"

"A Golden like Clobber, I guess. I miss him. I miss him every day."

"My mom says the way to prepare yourself for when a dog has to leave is to be as good as you can be to the dog today. Like, you shouldn't be lazy about taking him out for his afternoon walk because, well, you never know."

"Your mom is very smart."

"Clobber has a good life."

"I bet he does."

I bent quickly to Clobber's ear and whispered that he should say hello to Gottfried. I told him that petting him meant some love went off into the world to Gottfried. Then I kissed the top of his old head and stood.

"Thanks for giving me a minute with Clobber."

"That's okay. Clobber likes meeting new people."

"You're a good kid, too, you know?"

He smiled. He bent forward and hooked his leash onto Clobber. A little snow began to fall, and I watched them walk away, boy and dog, the boy matching his steps to the sweet slowness of his friend.

27

I heard Milly's Jeep chugging its way up the steep dirt road that led to my cabin. She was coming over to help me pack, to dress, to talk. I peeked out to make sure it wasn't Lawrence. He was due at three. It was only one o'clock now, but I had to be certain. Our flight left Manchester at 5:10. It was only an hour and a half down to New York City.

Milly backed the Jeep around until she had it facing downhill. Her Jeep Wrangler was perennially unreliable and more than once she had used the hill to jump-start it back to life. She banged out of the door a moment later, a huge purse over her shoulder. She wore enormous mukluks on her feet and a long, colorful kaftan over everything. She was on her way home from jazzercise, her latest craze, and I could not quite match the hermit Milly with the spandex Milly. But she was full of contradictions and it did no good to try to fit her into a slot.

"Getting ready to shack up with Lawrence?" she called as soon as she pushed through the door, her voice making it into a musical line. "Ready to go, girl? Ready to get your freak on?"

"No one says *freak on* anymore, Milly. You sound ridiculous."

"I said it. I said it just now, so surely someone says *freak on*, right?"

She dumped her purse, her car keys, her cell phone onto my kitchen table. Then she went right to the range and put on a teapot. I stood in the doorway leading back to my bedroom. I couldn't help smiling. When Milly was up and in good spirits, no one was more fun to be around.

She made a little grinding motion with her hips and bit her bottom lip. She wiggled her eyebrows at me.

"Gross," I said.

"You're getting laid."

She said it in the singsong voice we used as kids when one of us taunted the other.

"Do not torture me, Milly. I am in no mood. Come and help me decide some things to wear."

"Do you have to go to the TV thing with him?"

"You mean *Meet the Press*? It's not a TV thing, Milly."

"What do you call it, then?"

She followed me into my bedroom and flopped down on my bed. Some cold air still clung to her. She kicked off her mukluks and pulled the comforter over her legs. She resembled a young Elizabeth Taylor, a little unkempt, a little prone to letting her garden go wild, but her eyes captured anyone who came into their line of vision. Every man she had ever dated had bent over backward trying to describe her eyes. They were green and sharp and thrilling. Bartenders bought her drinks and older men asked her to dance at weddings.

She fluffed the pillows behind her. She punched one to make it just right.

"I still can't believe you do Jazzercise," I said.

"Got to keep the body moving and beautiful."

"But Jazzercise?"

"Old-school, kitten. I like dancing to corny old tunes, so sue me. Get started now. Give me a little fashion show."

I did. I pulled out things, paired them together, put them back. I held up different outfits to my chest, looked in the mirror, looked at Milly, then put them back again. It wasn't easy. What made it difficult was not knowing precisely what we would be doing. I knew we would go to the studio, wherever that was, and

I knew we had plans to take Sylvie to see the tree in Rockefeller Center, but otherwise the itinerary was wide open. Being ready for everything meant you were never quite right for anything. The eternal dilemma.

The tea kettle went off about halfway through the process. I made us both tea and brought a cup to Milly. She sipped and watched.

"Did you buy new underwear at least?" she asked when I began folding things and stuffing them in my overnight bag.

"Maybe."

"New man, new underwear. That's the rule."

"I don't know him very well."

"Well, you're about to."

"You have a one-track mind, Milly."

"What's he actually talking about on the show?"

"Tax policy."

"Ugh. That's dry."

"Not when he does it, I guess. He says tax money is the tributary stream of democratic life. It fills the public lake."

"Oh, jeez. Where did he get that? Off a bottle cap somewhere?"

"I guess people like what he has to say. Or how he says it. I looked at a few of his talks on YouTube. He's pretty engaging."

She sipped her tea. She smiled.

"You look beautiful right now, Kate. In this light. He's a lucky man. This weekend will go great."

"Do you think so?"

"I mean, you never know. But you have to try, right? You like him. He likes you. That's a basis for something or other."

"You make it sound like mixing a cocktail."

"Well, in a way it is. Give it a shake and see what happens. But drink slowly."

I finished putting the last few things into my bag. Then I circled the bed and climbed in with Milly. It was cold outside,

somewhere in the low twenties, but the cabin felt warm and dry.
I had purchased it after returning from Ireland. It was a gift to
myself, an attempt to make my life more stable. The finances
pushed me to my limit, but I was able to swing it in the end. It
was a simple structure, a one bedroom log cabin with a wood
stove and a wide back deck. I loved being in it and I loved Milly
being there beside me.

"I'm scared," I said.

She grabbed my hand.

"It will be okay. It will be great," she said.

"I don't have a great track record."

"Don't think of it as a record. Think of it as bouquets that
have shared their beauty, but then fade. But they were beautiful
once."

"You're a poet, Milly."

"No, but you know what I mean. Just because something
doesn't last forever doesn't mean it has no meaning or worth.
You have to keep trying."

"You don't. You hardly ever try that sort of thing."

"That's because I am a cynical bitch who keeps life at a distance. The messy parts, anyway."

"And you do Jazzercise."

"And I do Jazzercise."

We stayed there until we finished our tea. The light changed
from midday to afternoon light. When Milly left, her Wrangler
started right up. She clunked down the hill, and forty-five minutes later, Lawrence pulled into her place.

His apartment was small. He smiled when he held the door open
for me, one arm out. We carried our bags up from the Uber ride.
I had a vague idea where we were located in Brooklyn, but it was
only vague. He had mentioned Prospect Park as if he thought I
would surely recognize that as a landmark. I didn't. The apart-

ment had a brick wall, a window that overlooked the street, and a black couch facing the window. Modern. A statue of a woman in a yoga pose, another of a man raising an ax, all done in wire. Indirect lighting. The kitchenette bled into the sitting area. The bedroom, from the way he motioned to me when he said the word, was back and off to the corner. It, too, looked out on the street.

"Wow," I said. "Great."

"Do you like it? Of course, Brooklyn is hipster right now. Everyone wants to be here. I should grow a long beard and go mountain man. That's the style on the streets."

"I've seen that. Not sure you fit the part exactly."

I put my bag down. And my purse. We were here. Whatever was going to happen between us was probably going to happen here. I had to get my mind around that. I told myself I was a Doctor of Arts and Letters, a woman with a well-launched career, and I did not need to be timid or bashful. But I *felt* timid and bashful. I felt a little out of my element.

"There's a great Thai place right around the corner. I thought we could have dinner there. You like Thai food, don't you, Kate?"

"I do."

"They make the best drunken noodles I've ever had. Tomorrow I need to get a haircut. And if you didn't mind, maybe you'd give my wardrobe a look. I don't want to look too newly trimmed, but, you know."

I looked at him. He didn't need a haircut. In fact, I had the strange sensation of *seeing* him for the first time. Maybe it was because we stood on new ground, or had traveled on a plane together, but I had a new understanding of his appearance. He was tall and lean, extremely lean—*Like his wire statues?* I couldn't help thinking—with eyes that strayed a tiny bit to the side. An alligator profile. He wore black clothes, tailored to fit his chest and legs, and a navy pea jacket that he wore buttoned to his chin. He was handsome. He was. But he was not the sort of handsome that usually drew me. I went for the rougher, flintier types. He was trim and well kept; the shirt that he wore under the peacoat had a silky shimmer to it that caught the light in ways I didn't usually associate with a guy. He was dark; he told me he needed to shave twice a day to look his best.

"How about some wine?" he asked, dropping his bag and stepping behind the small kitchen island. "I should have a decent vintage around here. Let me look."

"Thanks, I'd love some. Is the bathroom . . ."

"Through there," he said, and pointed to where it had to be located unless the apartment was larger than I imagined.

I stepped through the tiny attached hallway, wondering as I did so what the protocol of this situation might be. Did I carry my bag to the bedroom and plunk it down? How did we play house, exactly? I felt out of practice. I felt rusty. It was true that I had consummated two brief flings—very flingy, very brief—but it had been a long time since I had been with someone to whom I felt well matched. Although he wasn't exactly the flavor, maybe, of the man I expected to be with, he was suitable and smart and ambitious. He was somewhat anti-Ozzie, which I didn't take as a bad thing.

In the bathroom, though, he had a black-and-white photo of himself with Noam Chomsky, the famous linguist and social activist from Harvard. They both smiled at me as I used the facilities.

"Noam Chomsky," I said when I came out.

"Oh, yes, a bit of a hero of mine. Great man. I don't agree with all his politics altogether, but I never questioned his sincerity."

He had two tall glasses of wine set out for us. I took a seat on one of the stools. He stayed behind the island.

"To us," he said, toasting. "To getting to know one another."

"To us."

"How hungry are you?"

"Not famished. How about you?"

"Maybe let's have a glass of wine, then mosey down to the restaurant."

"That sounds great."

But before we could mosey anywhere, my phone buzzed. I looked quickly at the number, expecting to see Milly's address staring back at me, but instead the number said Broadman Publishing. I didn't know anyone from Broadman Publishing. I knew the publishing house, however. It was an academic press, a branch beneath a larger publishing house with a famous imprint, and I recognized it because colleagues had published books with them.

I held up a finger to Lawrence and slid the accept bar to the right.

"Hello?" I asked.

"Is this Kate Moreton?"

"Yes. Who is this?"

"My name is Edna Barrow. I'm an editor here at Broadman and I was calling about your doctoral thesis. Do you have a minute?"

"Yes, I guess I do. Can you give me one moment?"

"Certainly."

I pushed the mute button and looked at Lawrence.

"A strange thing. Broadman Publishing . . ."

"Take it, take it. You can jump in the bedroom. Go ahead."

I did. I pushed the mute button and said hello again. A black and white duvet covered Lawrence's bed. It looked like the tile floor of a diner. I sat on the corner of the bed.

"A friend recommended your book to me," Edna Barrow said. "I've read it and loved it. I am a bit of an Irish junkie. I was wondering what plans you had for publication."

"Well, I don't have any plans, honestly. Not beyond what I've already done with it."

"I see. Well, we see some potential here. Interest in Irish

works is always strong. You've captured the poignancy of the Blasket Island move, the expulsion. I called your office and they said you're in New York for the next couple days. Would you have any time to meet to discuss the possibilities?"

I felt out of my element, but I knew enough to fake it.

"Sure. That would be great."

"How about coffee tomorrow? I have an evening appointment, but the morning up until noon or so I am wide open."

We made a date for ten. I asked her to text me the restaurant address. It felt a little awkward to be making a date with someone else when I was here with Lawrence, but opportunity had knocked and I had answered. Or something like that.

"She wants to discuss my book," I said when I stepped out of the bedroom. "That's out of the blue."

"Congratulations," he said, although his eyes stayed on the screen of his laptop. "Hold on, I'm just finishing things here. It's about the appearance. My agent."

I sat and sipped my wine. I felt a bubbly thrill in my stomach. Although my dissertation had been well received, and I had defended it skillfully, I felt, it had been read by a mere handful of people. Maybe ten, all considered. Maybe one hundred, if I squinted my eyes and pretended a little. It was an academic volume on an academic subject. I was pleasantly surprised and grateful to hear it had somehow made it into the hands of an editor at Broadman Publishing.

"Ready?" Lawrence asked, folding the laptop shut. "Are you hungry now?"

"I am."

"My agent really thinks this could put me on another level. Speaking tours and that sort of thing."

"That's terrific."

"I hate to say it, but I am feeling some pressure. I have a couple things I want to prepare . . . but, you know, make them sound off-the-cuff, so to speak. Casual."

"I get that."

"Well, drink up. Two-minute walk, tops. That's what I love about Brooklyn. So much diversity."

I drank off the rest of my wine. I watched, waiting to see if he would circle back to the call about my book. But he busied himself rinsing out the glasses and corking the bottle. He ran a dry dishcloth around the sink to make it shine.

"So glad you're here, Kate," he said, helping me on with my jacket. "You're going to love this place."

28

We didn't sleep together.

Or rather, we didn't *sleep* together. We *slept* together. As in the same bed. As in the same room. As in touching, but not *abracadabra*.

To his credit, he didn't pressure me. He didn't assume. He was a gentleman, although he was enough of a guy to bait the trap anyway he could. Late in the night we had a nice talk about teaching, and about books, and he asked me about the Broadman editor at last. It had taken him a while, and I suspected it would always take him a while to show an interest in anyone beside himself. It was nearly acceptable in his personality. It was like having blond hair or a funny ear lobe. He couldn't do anything about it. Besides, he was about to appear on television for the first time, and I accepted that it was a big deal. It's just that it wasn't the *only* deal. I wasn't sure he got that.

In the morning, we had coffee and then made plans to meet Sylvie and her mom near Rockefeller Center. It felt a little stepmom-ish, but what choice did I have? He gave me solid directions to the restaurant where I was to meet Edna. We kissed goodbye. Doing the couple thing reminded me of trying to learn the steps of a complicated line dance that you wanted to master, but still felt clunky doing. You had to watch each step as you took it.

But it was good to be in New York City. It felt lively and smart and vibrant. A young man on the street corner played a gorgeous cello piece; another fellow beat on a white five-gallon bucket with drumsticks, doing a kind of scat chanting unlike anything I had heard before. I took a subway to midtown, then crossed three blocks and found Edna sitting at a small white table in a small white window in a small cute restaurant.

"Kate?" she asked when I stepped inside.

She stood and shook my hand. I liked her immediately. She was about my age, her hair two shades blonder than mine. Strawberry-blond. She wore a fleece, running shoes, and leggings. She held a cup of tea in front of her. I had a suspicion that she was Irish in her ancestry, and that some of the interest in my book came from that heritage. She motioned me to a seat and I squeezed in as a waitress fluttered by and took my order. I ordered tea and a croissant. Edna ordered a poached egg with rye toast.

"Are you down long?" Edna asked. "In New York?"

"No, just the weekend. We're flying back on Sunday."

"Oh, nice. Sometimes I think that's the way to handle New York. Think of it as a mad affair and only dip into it once in a while."

"But you live here?"

"I do. I was raised here, actually. Born and bred."

"Isn't that a strange phrase? *Born and bred.* What does it mean to be bred in that context?"

"I guess it means by birth and upbringing. I guess I never thought about it."

Then she said many kind things about my book. She said she found it compelling. She said she thought its audience could be enlarged without great difficulty. She said she thought it needed a rewrite with a more commercial slant in mind. Not too commercial, she added quickly. She pointed out two or three places where I might focus more sharply on a particular strand within the narrative. I was impressed with the closeness of her reading.

I was impressed with the kind but serious tone she adopted. Her recommendations were excellent. She had a vision for the book that I hadn't quite met. Her critique was a little like suggesting we move the couch over there, the end table over here, but it also suggested the room might have a different purpose. I saw my own work in a different light.

She paused when the waitress came with our food orders.

"So how does that strike you, Kate? That was my takeaway. I admire your work on this and I think the subject has a broader appeal than you might know."

"I appreciate your comments," I said, so pleased that I had trouble forming coherent thoughts. "I didn't expect anyone outside of my field to take an interest."

"With the proper handling, Kate, we think it could be a bigger book. It's hard to predict these things, but it has support in-house. Ann Grisham liked it very much, and she is in charge. We'd like to come up with a better, stronger title. And the cover could make all the difference. The Ireland angle is appealing on all kinds of counts."

"Are you . . . ?" I asked, then stopped because I felt myself blanch.

"Yes, we're offering a publishing contract. We'll do the best we can moneywise, but it won't be much. Nothing to retire on, but it's possible the book will do well. People have made careers writing history. Think of Doris Kearns Goodwin or Ron Chernow. Some books cross over and snag a more general audience. We think your book has a chance to do that."

"I'm blown away. That's not a very elegant way to put it, but it's how I feel."

"Well, it's a great subject and the treatment is excellent. I didn't know the first thing about it when the book came onto my desk; about the subject, I mean, but when I dug into it, I found myself entirely absorbed. As you can imagine, I see plenty of books that have something admirable, but not precisely what we need."

"How did you even come across my dissertation?"

"We scout dissertations. And we pay attention to scholarly publishing. We've dug out a number of good titles from research doctorates. It's how we stay in business. And I had a friend in Hanover who had caught wind of it. Do you know Amy Eisen?"

"Name doesn't ring a bell. I'm sorry."

"Doesn't matter in the end. It landed on my desk and I read it and loved it."

"I'm flattered. Truly. And thrilled."

"Well, I'm glad," she said and began eating her egg and toast. "It would make a very strong entry into the market."

My hands shook as I broke apart my croissant. I felt enormously, over-the-moon pleased. I had difficulty sitting in one place and eating with proper table manners. But Edna was charming, and she did most of the talking. She told me she would prepare her notes and send them to me. I could look them over and see whether the book, the adaptation of my book, made sense when I had time to consider it. From that point, if we were of a mind, we could go forward. She told me that Broadman was a solid publishing house with strong financial underpinnings. She told me that editors at Broadman tended to stay in place, not like many other publishing houses, because history and scholarly work demanded different muscles than more purely commercial publishing.

When we finished, we stood. Although I felt as if I wanted to hug her, hug everyone in the restaurant, we shook hands instead. She said she was going to meet people for a run around the reservoir. I told her I had a date at Rockefeller Center.

"They put up the tree, didn't they?" she said as we stood for a moment outside the restaurant. "I always love that."

"You know, I've never seen it in person."

"Oh, you'll love it. It smells good, for one thing. And the lights are pretty."

"Thank you, Edna. You're made my day. You've made my year, actually."

"It will be a good book, Kate. Together, we'll make sure of that."

She turned and walked north. I watched her go, my heart soaring. More than soaring.

I saw them from a good distance away. Lawrence and his ex had the we-were-once-a-family-but-now-we're-trying-to-be-kind-strangers-with-one-another look. I didn't know a great deal about their breakup, but Lawrence had repeated many times that they were being mature and reasonable about it. By their outward appearance, I wasn't sure he saw the situation the same way his ex did. She held her hand out on Sylvie's collar, keeping contact, while the little girl pointed at things on the extravagant tree. The ex also had her cell phone out and seemed locked on to it. Lawrence, meanwhile, scanned the crowd for me, I guessed. It was a lot to walk into it, but after the talk with Edna—and a quick, squealing call to Milly, *abook!abook!abook!*—nothing could bring me down. And Sylvie, from my quick glance, was nothing but darling.

"There she is! Hi," Lawrence called as I approached them. "Hi, Hi," he said too many times.

"Hello," I said, wondering if he would try to kiss me hello in front of his ex and child. To my relief, he didn't.

"Beth, this is Kate. Kate this is Beth. And this is Sylvie."

Beth peeled her eyes off the screen for the briefest moment and said hello. Sylvie turned and tucked herself against Lawrence's leg. She held the side of his trouser leg between her fingers. I fought the impulse to squat down and try to make better contact with Sylvie. All in time, I thought. Or maybe never, but not right now.

"Okay, I'm going to run. You'll have her back by seven?" Beth asked.

"Yes. We'll grab something to eat, then scoot uptown to you."

Beth clicked out of whatever she was doing on her phone. She squatted and kissed Sylvie.

"Bye, pumpkin," she said.

Sylvie, on cue, flung her arms around her mother's neck. It was hard to know who wanted the contact more. Beth kissed the girl on the cheek and then petted her hair.

"Just a few hours," she said, standing. "Daddy wants to show you the tree."

"I see the tree!" Sylvie said. "I already saw it."

"Well, there's more to see, I'm sure. And Daddy will take you to a good dinner."

"Not pork chops."

"No, not pork chops," her mother assured her.

Sylvie looked at me. If she thought she could get away with sticking her tongue out at me, she probably would have. I smiled. Children could be intimidating as hell, I realized.

Beth kissed Sylvie again, then darted off into the crowd. Lawrence held Sylvie's hand. He looked at me and smiled.

"It all takes a little getting used to," he said, then whispered, "she'll warm up."

But she didn't. Not really. We walked around Rockefeller Center and admired the tree. I couldn't help thinking that any child would have been more comfortable with her hands in the hands of both parents. Whether that was fair or not, it seemed to be what Sylvie wanted. But I wasn't her mom. I was a stranger with a peculiar relationship to her father that she couldn't possibly understand. I wasn't sure I understood it myself.

The tree, though, was spectacular. It was tall and dark and

beautiful, and seeing it made me miss my tiny cabin. It made me miss New Hampshire. And deep down I had a pearl of delight slowly growing and becoming stronger in my belly. A book, I told myself.

We got cocoa in the restaurant just off the ice rink. It was crowded, but the crowd was jolly. Sylvie did not want marshmallows in her cocoa. She did not like the Styrofoam cup they served it in, and I sat with her while Lawrence talked to a counter person to get a ceramic mug. I watched him. Sylvie watched me. I tried to coax her into talking, but she simply stared at me, unhappy in everything around her.

"There we go!" Lawrence said triumphantly when he returned with the mug. "A mug for my princess."

"Thank you, Daddy."

"How are the skaters?"

My phone buzzed. I had it on vibrate. Under normal circumstances, I wouldn't have answered it. But I was away from home and it seemed important to make sure the cabin hadn't exploded with its propane gas feed or that a tree hadn't fallen on top of it. It also occurred to me that it could be Edna calling back with additional information. Something. I pulled it out and checked the screen.

Incoming call, it said.

Nora Crean.

29

"I have to take this. Sorry."

Lawrence nodded. He dabbed at Sylvie's chin to rid it of a stream of chocolate. The café was loud; it was a tourist trap, really. Maybe to Sylvie's young eye it felt magical. For her sake, I hoped so.

I stood and walked outside. I waited until the third ring before accepting the call. I said hello, but for an extended interlude no one spoke on the other end. I heard the crackle of a long distance call. Then I heard Nora Crean's voice, older, somewhat reedier, but unmistakably Nora.

"Kate?"

"Hi, Nora. Can you hear me?"

My eyes began to water. I loved Nora Crean.

"I'm calling you about Ozzie. We fear he's dead, Kate. We just received the news."

I felt the words in my stomach. I felt them punch me over and over. For a moment, I thought I might vomit. I leaned forward and held on to the metal railing around the skating rink. I couldn't reconcile the news I had just received with the sight of so many people in colorful clothing sailing around the white rink. I closed my eyes and tried to concentrate on Gran's quiet voice.

"I'm sorry, Gran . . . tell me, did I hear you correctly?"

"Yes, Kate. He's gone."

"How?"

I could only speak that one word.

"The *Ferriter* went down. Lost at sea."

"I can't . . ."

"I know, darling. It's terrible to deliver such news on the phone, but I didn't know how else to get hold of you. We're just getting the information now. None of it is clear at the moment. I thought you'd want to know. I thought Ozzie would want you to know."

"Yes, of course."

"I know you'll have a thousand questions, Kate, but I'm afraid I have few answers. This has just happened. Would it be too much for you to fly over?"

"No, of course not. No . . . I just . . ."

I couldn't catch my breath. I couldn't feel my feet or legs or the pulse of blood in my wrists. Ozzie dead. *Ozzie was dead.* It couldn't be. In the haze of my grief, I tried to picture my calendar. I could leave by the middle of next week. I could free a few dates, cancel a dozen student appointments and make accommodations. Pack a bag, get on a plane. It was Saturday. I could be in Ireland late Wednesday night. That's what my internal calendar told me.

"I'm so sorry to drop such news on you this way, Kate. If there were another way . . ."

"No, I had to hear, of course. I just can't take it in."

"None of us can. Seamus informed me that there are some legal matters as well. You are still married. Legally, I mean. You're needed as next of kin. It's horrible, I know. Everything is upside down right now. Please be patient with us."

"I understand. Yes, I think I can get there by Wednesday. Would that be early enough?"

"Yes, of course. There's no rush in that sense, Kate. Nothing can be done on this end."

"I'm so sorry, Nora. I know how much you loved him."

"And how much he loved you, Kate."

"Yes, I know."

She paused. Then she said she had to go. She said Seamus could pick me up Wednesday night, but I declined the offer. I didn't want him waiting for me at the airport late into the night. She told me to come and stay with her. I accepted. I had stayed with her a number of times in her grand old mansion. It felt like the right place to be.

"Travel carefully as you can, Kate," Nora said as we readied to end the call. "There is no need for haste. What's done is done."

"I understand."

"He never got over you, Kate."

"And I never got over him. I tried to deny it, but that's the truth. It's devastating news."

We ended the call. I stood for a long time watching the skaters. I stood so long that eventually Lawrence and Sylvie came out to fetch me. Lawrence carried my coat over his arm. He held it for me and I slipped into it. I had tears in my eyes.

"Bad news?" he asked. He studied my face.

"I'm afraid so. My husband, my ex, died at sea. Is missing. They don't know yet."

But he's not your ex, I could hear Dr. Kaufman say. *That's the point.*

"I'm sorry, Kate. Are you okay?"

I didn't know how he thought I could be okay, how anyone could be okay hearing such news, but I shook my head and let it go. I supposed he meant to ask if I felt faint or unsteady in any way. It was just a way of checking with me. It was merely a social convention.

"I have to go to Ireland. I have to get there."

"What can I do to help?"

"Nothing. Nothing really. I have to go tie up a bunch of loose ends back home and then book a flight. There are some legal matters, I guess."

"At least the semester is winding down. You'll have some time."

"Yes," I said, "there's something to be happy about. But there are still a few weeks to go."

"I'm sorry this happened, Kate."

"So am I. Sorry to have to go."

"That's okay. I understand. We understand, don't we, Sylvie?"

Sylvie had her eyes on the skaters. She had the glazed look of a child who had just consumed a cup of cocoa.

"I'm going to leave from here," I said. "Would you bring my bag back to Dartmouth?"

"Of course."

"Tomorrow is such a big day for you, I'm sorry."

"It's okay. Life always gets in the way of itself."

"You're a poet, Lawrence."

"I'll show you the clip when you get back. Or I can email it to you."

There he was again, always in the center of the camera shot.

"Bye, Sylvie," I said, squatting to be at her eye level. "Nice meeting you."

She sank back against her dad's trousers again. I stood and kissed him on the cheek.

"You must have loved him a lot," Lawrence said when I pulled away to depart.

"For a time," I said, "he was my sun."

"Of course, the feelings return. That's only natural," Dr. Kaufman observed. "Deaths are crisis rites. They are in every culture. That's why we ritualize them."

"I've been fanaticizing about not going. About putting my head in the sand and pretending nothing has changed."

Dr. Kaufman smiled. She didn't smile often.

"When do you leave?"

"Tomorrow night. I've got my classes all set for a while and whatever committee work I am supposed to do is done. I'm fine that way."

"The boat is missing. That makes it more difficult. The uncertainty."

"Yes, I received two phone calls from an Irish solicitor. I have to meet with the authorities. It's complicated because they have no body. He was lost at sea."

She nodded. The birds were less active on her feeder today. It was warmer than it had been last week. Maybe the birds found food elsewhere. She wore a different scarf today. It was as beautiful as the last one I had noticed, a dark, mysterious green that reflected the color of her eyes. I wanted to ask her if she would go scarf shopping with me or at least give me the name of her store.

"You're going back to his world. The world you built together."

"I know."

"You're older now. Wiser?"

"Maybe. Maybe not. Does anyone become wiser?"

"We'll let the philosophers handle that one. You could see this as a chance to heal."

"I've thought of that."

"To bring peace to a chapter of your life."

I nodded. I *had* thought of that.

"I'm hoping it helps me understand what happened between Ozzie and me. In our marriage."

"That's a lot to hope for."

"It is. But it feels like a natural piece of punctuation. His death, I mean."

"Death often is."

She remained silent after that. I knew she didn't like guiding the conversation. As Milly said, all therapists are counterpunchers. They punch only after you throw a punch. For a little while we sat and watched the birds. I liked watching them. I could see their appeal. It was rewarding to see them, to try to identify them, but it was also cathartic to watch them dash away. They flew off into trees and into the dark winter afternoons.

"I feel as though I still love him," I said. "That I've always loved him."

"I'm sure you have those feelings."

"But I mean really love him. That I had been some sort of idiot to end things with him. I felt like I had to end it almost out of some strange political stance."

"Political?"

"Maybe social is a better word. Social proprieties. He was drinking. And he could be a jerk. I had this idea that he had to be this one way. This one way that suited me. And that if I settled for anything less, then I was shirking my responsibility to women everywhere. Isn't that crazy?"

"Not crazy. Maybe not useful."

"You've met couples where the man is not exciting at all. And the woman is much more accomplished. More present. And sometimes you ask yourself, what is she doing with him? It's such a horrible question. What is anyone doing with anyone? I had some strange feeling projected onto Ozzie that he had to be something. Something that matched me. If he didn't match properly, then we didn't belong together."

"An idealization?"

"Yes, you could say that. Yes, I suppose so. We were so much in love that I felt overwhelmed. When I think back to it, I can barely breathe."

"And now he's lost. Both figuratively and in reality."

I put my face in my hands. I couldn't cry. I felt too furious with myself. With Ozzie. With life. How could we never get things straight? Why did the dresser drawers always get scrambled and messy despite our good attempts at order? Why did things always slip away, not in a grand fashion, but in small, negligent ways that left one grabbing for the meaning of it?

"Our time is almost up, Kate. Maybe you should keep a journal when you're in Ireland. It might provide a sounding board for you. A place to reflect."

"Maybe I will."

"I'm sorry about Ozzie. I know you're in pain."

"I am."

"Time will pass, and the pain will soften, but it does no good to know that now."

"Thank you."

I stood, my mind already flashing forward to what I had to do to get ready. Teach a class, grade six papers, call for an oil delivery, cancel my mail, and on and on. Details. I stood and put on my coat.

"Do birds come to any feeder you put out?" I asked her, my mind glazed and still. "They're comforting."

"They'll come if you put it in the right place. Like us, they need to feel safe when they dart in for nourishment."

"Maybe I'll do that when I get back."

"I recommend it," she said.

FIFTH LETTER

Robert Smith, Barrister
Peal, Simmons, Hassleton
77 River Liffey, Dublin, Ireland

Dear Ms. Moreton:

As we discussed by telephone, you have been designated the
executrix of Oswald Ferriter's estate. Although he is at this time still
legally missing, not declared dead, it would benefit us to have a brief
meeting at this juncture to secure your legal standing. Please, at your
leisure, review the enclosed documents. When you have finished,
contact our offices and we will set up an appointment to review the
intent of Mr. Ferriter's last will and testament.

With our heartfelt condolences,
Robert

30

Seamus met me at the Limerick airport. I suspected he would, because he was Seamus. I saw him before he saw me. He looked older, less steady on his feet, but when he spotted me finally, his face grew merry. Gottfried sat patiently beside him on a purple leash. They waited just outside the terminal doors. Gran had texted me to be on the lookout for them both. She couldn't keep him away.

It was late, three in the morning, and I could not imagine how long he had waited. It was cold, and he likely waited outside to keep company with Gottfried. Or he wanted Gottfried to be the first thing I saw when I set foot on Irish soil. It was one of countless acts of kindness he gave freely to me. He always had.

I felt myself choke on seeing Gottfried. He was the same good boy. I dragged my pull-behind duffel through the automatic doors and began to cry as I approached them both. The crying took me over. I thought I had cried things out, was ready to be in control, but the sweetness of them standing patiently waiting for me wrenched me deep inside.

"Hello, you two," I said.

I hugged Seamus for a long time. He hugged me. Then I went down on my knees and put my hands on either side of Gottfried's head.

"Oh, you darling, darling dog," I whispered. "How did you let this happen to our boy?"

He licked my face. I hugged him. I cried harder.

"The car is just over here," Seamus said after a little while. "I have a driver. My eyes aren't up for night driving."

"Thank you, Seamus."

"How's the dog look?"

"Perfect," I said, standing, my hand still dangling on Gottfried's head. "As dear as ever. And so are you."

"Sorry we're meeting under these circumstances."

"So am I."

"Nora was going to try to wait up for you, but I don't think she can quite manage it. Night wearies the old."

"But not you?"

"I've made a bargain with the fairy folk to stay young."

"They seem to be holding up their end of the bargain."

He led me to the car, where a young man sat asleep behind the wheel. Seamus rapped sharply on the window beside the boy's head and he jerked awake. Seamus motioned for him to wind down his window.

"Are you awake enough to drive, Johnny?"

"I am," the boy said, rubbing his fists in his eyes.

"This is Kate Moreton. Johnny Lewis."

"Hi, Johnny."

"You might think about getting out of the car and helping the lady with her bag," Seamus said. "You're going to have to learn that sleep is not work."

Johnny scrambled out and stowed my bag in the trunk of the old Plymouth. Then he held the door open for me. Gottfried waited while I moved across the seat, then he jumped in beside me.

"I'm going to sit up front to guide the boy through his troubles," Seamus said. "Nora had some food packed for you. You'll find it in the little basket there. She was worried you wouldn't eat on the plane."

"That's too kind."

"I hope Johnny didn't eat it in his sleep. He has the appetite of a gladiator."

"I am a little hungry, actually," I said. "The food on the plane wasn't great."

"It never is."

Seamus walked around the car and climbed in beside Johnny. I watched him, wondering how many years ago it had been when he came with the same automobile to take me to the *Ferriter*. Four years? Three? I kept my hand on Gottfried's soft fur. He was the best company of all.

"How is Gran?" I asked as the car finally began to move.

Seamus watched everything Johnny did. It couldn't have failed to make Johnny nervous.

"She's taken things as well as she can, I suppose," he said, talking over his shoulder. "It's a hard turn of events, that's certain. It still doesn't feel quite real to any of us."

"Where was the *Ferriter* lost?"

"Off the coast of Italy. I'm not sure of the name of the village."

I sat forward. I had assumed the *Ferriter* had sunk somewhere off Ireland.

"In Italy?"

"Off the coast."

Then he spoke to Johnny, pointing out something to help him navigate a roundabout. Johnny nodded.

"I didn't know. I simply assumed it was here. What was he doing off the coast of Italy?"

"Rescue work."

"You mean, like coast guard work?"

I was confused.

"No, the refugees. He took his ship down to help in the Mediterranean. You know, the crossings. The Syrians and the West Africans. They're all trying to make it to Europe to escape whatever hell they're living in, and of course their boats are terrible. Ozzie was involved, but I don't know much else about it."

"I had no idea."

"Why would you? You haven't been in touch, have you?"

"Not for a long time. Not since we separated."

"Well, it's not the kind of thing you post in a letter or email. Careful there, Johnny. Not so fast. Easy as you go. It's not as if he took a new job or moved to New Zealand. You can't drop it casually into correspondence."

"He died off the coast of Italy?" I asked again, hardly comprehending.

"Yes, by all accounts. It's still an unsettled death, but witnesses have confirmed the boat's sinking."

"Did they recover the *Ferriter*?"

"No, gone and lost. The only mercy is that he was alone when she went down. Large seas took him."

"I am sorry, Seamus. This is another shock."

"Aren't we all? Sorry, I mean. Life takes some queer turns, that's certain."

"No one loved him more than you."

He didn't say anything to that. He looked ahead, the light from the road sometimes illuminating his profile. I put my face into Gottfried's fur and breathed his scent until I could go on with the world.

I slept later than I dreamed of sleeping. When I woke, I had a moment of trying to remember where I was. Gran's house, I realized slowly. It was a lovely old place, out of date by decades, but still wonderfully warm and calm. Gran favored wallpaper. Every room, just about, had a different design, and it was the image of a lady in a full skirt, being handed out of a carriage by gentleman in a top hat, that finally placed me in Gran's guest room.

I showered quickly to get the airport feeling off me, then tiptoed downstairs in the fluffy robe Gran always made available to me. I found Gran at work in her greenhouse that extended off the south side of her mansion. The greenhouse was fitted with a railing that she could cling to, and a deftly designed sliding chair that she could move as she liked along the rail. She could prune and sit, sit and prune, and when she needed to stand, she had the handrail to assist her. She did not stand often any longer and rarely alone.

The air felt warm and thick when I entered. Plants grew everywhere. Gran saw me and smiled. I crossed to where she was and hugged her. She kissed my cheek. Her lips and skin were as soft as milkweed thistle.

"Did you sleep well?" she asked. "Those flights can be horribly fatiguing."

"I slept well, thank you, Gran."

"Ring that bell over there on the table. Gloria will bring you coffee and something to eat. She makes wonderful muffins. She won't tell me if she makes them from scratch or uses a commercial product, but they're good just the same. You'll like her."

"I'm not very hungry."

"Coffee, then. Just ring the bell."

I rang it. In a few minutes, Gloria came into the greenhouse. She was a tall, stout woman, with brown hair cut short. She wore a colorful smock over a pair of jeans. She carried a bouquet of silverware she had been polishing, apparently. She wore bright yellow rubber gloves. She looked to be in her late forties, square-jawed, her feet in brown moccasins.

"Gloria, this is Kate. Kate, Gloria."

"Nice to meet you, Kate. I won't try to shake your hand with all this mess going on," she said, and held up the silverware. "Trying to get ahead of the game."

"Gloria, please bring Kate one of your excellent muffins when you have a moment. Blueberry, is that all right, Kate?"

"That would be wonderful," I said, giving in to Gran over the muffin. It was easier that way.

"And black coffee. You still drink it black, don't you, Kate?"

"I do. Thank you."

Gloria nodded and turned to go. Gran pointed with her shears at a small tree she had been pruning as Gloria left.

"This tree is called a *Metasequoia*. Do you know anything about them?"

"I'm afraid not."

"I just learned about them myself. Their common name is Dawn Redwood. They're cousins to our west coast sequoias and redwoods. Botanists thought they were extinct until a Chinese biologist found one survivor in the Szechuan Province. They can live in water or on land, and they shed their needles like a tamarack. Their discovery was as unexpected as it would be for someone to find a living dinosaur. Now they have spread round the world again. I love plants with stories, don't you?"

"I don't know them as well as you do, Gran. But I like hearing them."

"Well, if you'll assist me, let's sit at the table where we can have a proper talk. Seamus told you some of the details, I'm sure. It's been a painful few days. I've dreamed of him every night since we got the news. Vivid dreams. It's almost as if he were in the room with me."

I held her arm as we edged slowly to the wicker table at the center of the greenhouse. She walked less steadily than she had before, and I noticed age had advanced on her in subtle ways. Her hair was pure white and her earrings, brass and diamond, looked too large on her delicate face. Moving beside her, I tried to calculate her age, but I could not get my mind to still. I had to brace her so she could sit. She plopped down the last few inches. Someone had placed a large cushion on her chair to help her.

"There we are. I don't like people to eat off their laps unless it's a picnic and can't be avoided. I never have. I'm probably getting too fussy in my dotage. Now let me look at you. You look beautiful, Kate. You've matured. You're no longer a girl, are you?

But you are still fresh and lovely. Lovelier, really. You've grown into your beauty. Not all women do, you know? Some resist it."

"Thank you, Gran. You look well, too."

"Oh, I look like an old sea turtle. A tortoise. I have a new hairdresser and she has tried to pep me up with this highlight business that is supposed to make the gray more attractive, but I don't think it's working. She tells the most scandalous stories, though, so I go to her whenever I can. She knows more about divorce than anyone I've met."

"Tell me about Ozzie, Gran."

She looked at me. Her eyes filled. Before she could start, Gloria returned with coffee and a muffin. Both things smelled delicious. She set them on the table before me and tucked a bright white napkin beneath a heavy fork. She had also brought me orange juice.

"Thank you, Gloria. This looks wonderful."

"Hope you enjoy it," Gloria said, then she whisked out of the room.

"She's a little shy with new people," Gran said, putting the shears down in front of her. "I'll tell you what I know, Kate. It isn't a great deal."

"Seamus said the *Ferriter* went down off the coast of Italy?" She nodded.

"Near Sicily. I don't know the details. I'm not sure anyone does. Apparently refugees land in Sicily all summer long. It's called the boating season. They're taken into custody and permitted to stay, from what I understand. A storm came up and the boat went under. He was known to Italian officials as someone who helped refugees land on Italian soil. I'm not certain they were happy with him. Politically, it's a situation fraught with difficulties on all sides. There is some talk of him having enemies. Ozzie was never the one to keep his opinions to himself when he saw an injustice."

"Who reported it? How do they know . . . ?"

"Those details are hard to gather. The refugees are a drain on the sluggish Italian economy. That's one spear of the argument. I don't know, dear. It feels as though it belongs to another world. It's a complicated political issue. A humanitarian issue, really."

"But why was he down there in the first place?"

She looked a long time at me. I could hardly contain the sad, nervous flutter in my stomach. I reached forward for the coffee Gloria had brought. It was dark and hot and it centered me. I had the sense that I was going to be told a truth that might be difficult to hear. I was certain of it.

"He was paying for his sin, Kate," Gran said slowly. "I thought you knew that. That's always been his cross to bear."

"What sin?"

"The sin of war. The sin of killing. The sin of arms."

"He refused to talk about that. He never told me what he did in Afghanistan."

"He couldn't talk about it. It was too much for him. Did you know he watched two boys be killed by an order he gave?"

"What order?"

"Oh, it was a commonplace order. Nothing remarkable in the least. Apparently, some boys had gotten in the habit of playing soccer near one of the military compounds. Ozzie told them they had to go somewhere else to play. It was policy not to have children too close to the compound. He loved children, so it was not out of meanness that he told them to go. Some of the soldiers had provided the boys with soccer balls, which was a great treat for the children. The boys had to move away and later that day they were playing and the ball took them into a booby-trapped field. The two boys chasing the ball were blown up, their parts thrown onto buildings and into trees. Ozzie knew the boys. His order brought about their deaths."

"Oh, lord," I whispered. What could be said against such news? Gran let the understanding fall on me slowly.

"Imagine knowing you had a hand in the death of two boys.

How do you resume your life, Kate? That was the sin he carried. We all have a sin. Maybe more. He returned from the war changed. He knew it, too. He knew a light had gone out of him. You brought it back."

"I didn't know."

"He swore me to silence about it. He told me the story on the condition that I never tell anyone else, but I suppose that promise is finished now. He carried a great weight, Kate. A weight he could not support. He took medicine. I don't know what all it was, but he worried it deadened him. And, of course, he had other stories inside him, I'm sure. How does a man so full of life reconcile himself to bringing about death in the world?"

"And that's why he went to help in the Mediterranean?"

"Yes. I suppose. The sin of killing can only be countered by the promise of life. I suspect that was the calculation in his mind. It's always risky to say a person did this or that because of *A* or *B* or *C*. Ozzie lived with pain, and that order in the war about the boys added to it. How could it not? That was only one thing, though, Kate. He was a soldier. A ruthless one, I've been told. What do they say? There is a victim on either side of a bullet. He was good at what he did. He endured a family history, as we all do, and he had his own turn of mind. It's always hopelessly complicated to imagine another person's life. What is acute pain for one person may not be as painful to another. One can't predict these things. One can only live with sympathy for us all. For every human we encounter."

I put my face in my hands. I didn't know if I wanted to cry or scream. I felt shallow and hollow, emptied of everything essential in my blood. During our brief marriage, I had been so intent on my own needs, my own petty academic career, my need for tidiness, that I had never seen what he needed from me. I had never understood his pain. Not really. Not fully. I had clung to a vision of what a marriage should be, what it had to be, and I had lost the reality of what it had been in everyday life. I loved him, yes,

I knew that. I knew that absolutely. But I had not given love, had not seen him all the way around, and that was my sin, I realized. I would live with that forever.

"I feel so foolish," I said when I could speak again. "I feel as if I didn't know him at all. Not really. Not the way I should have known him."

"He loved you, Kate. That's all you need to remember."

"I need to remember more than that, Gran. That was my mistake the first time. I was a trivial, foolish girl who thought another human being had to match me somehow. Some ridiculous way. I hate that version of myself. I hate it."

"We all learn as we go. I carry sins, too, Kate. More than I can name. The trick is to forgive ourselves. Ozzie wasn't able to do that. Perhaps his sins were too great. What one person can support proves too much for another. We are all of us doing our best."

"I didn't see him, Gran. I didn't see him clearly. That's what pains me. I was shallow and vacuous."

"You saw him. You saw a portion of him as he saw a portion of you. A side or facet. We mustn't paint him as a saint, either. He would be the first to tell you his faults. He never blamed you for returning to America, Kate. He understood. It hurt him, certainly, but he understood your reasons."

"I don't know if I had any reasons. Any reasons at all. I think he let me end it so I wouldn't be troubled by him. I don't know if any of my reasons . . ."

"You had your own life to pilot. Don't blame yourself over it. My husband used to say we all have our own sails and sometimes our boats cross and one sail steals the wind from the other. Ozzie had a large sail and perhaps you worried he would take all the wind you needed for your own course. Now have a bite to eat and drink some coffee. Life goes on. The lawyers are going to want to see you at some point during your stay. Except for a few personal things he left to Seamus, you have whatever it is he acquired in this world. He never stopped thinking of you as his wife."

The steam from the coffee wound up into the beams of sunlight slashing into the greenhouse.

"It's too much," I whispered.

"It is that. East of the sun, west of the moon."

"What's that?" I asked.

"Oh, it comes from a story I used to read to Ozzie when he was a little boy. About a polar bear and a fisherman. Nordic, I suppose. That's where the story took place. East of the sun, west of the moon. It was a saying Ozzie and I shared and loved."

Her eyes moistened at the memory. I took a deep breath and sipped my coffee. It was good coffee, deep and rich and hot.

"His estate, when all is settled, should come in at 1.7 or 1.6 million euros. We're still going through his holdings. Nora Crean suggested we look to see what it would entail to declare death in absentia. It's a legal tactic to have him declared dead before the mandatory seven years. We're still discussing that, but it's common enough. He was a modestly wealthy man, Ms. Moreton. I'm told he didn't live like a wealthy man, but he was well heeled despite all of that. He kept his assets fairly liquid. No massive stock positions. He had the land on Dingle, but you know about that. He also acquired some land in Ontario, Canada. A stretch of lakefront property. It's thirty acres of forest. I think that's all the real estate in his portfolio."

I sat in the law offices of Peal, Simmons, Hassleton. It was an office filled with leather upholstery and a massive grandfather clock that ticked heavily to remind us all of our mortality. An historically significant firm, Gran had assured me. Robert Smith, a conventional man with a conventional name, sat across from me at a wide oak table. He was tall and thin and reminded me of a bird leaning forward to seize a worm. The center of his scalp was empty of hair; two patches above his ears, like parentheses, grew in compensation for the missing center. He wore a solid gray suit with a blue tie pulled tightly against his throat. Mid-forties. His hands on the paperwork moved like accomplished pets obeying any instructions he gave them.

"I understand this is a great deal to hear in one meeting, Ms. Moreton. You have a lot to take in. Do you have any questions about what we have gone over so far?"

"Please call me Kate."

He nodded. I had already asked him three times to call me Kate. Informality went against his grain. I supposed that was an admirable trait in an attorney. A person stuffy over social niceties would be careful with paperwork.

He smiled and tapped his fingers on the paperwork in front of him.

"Very good. You can read the documents in your own time. I'm only trying to give you a sense of where you are positioned."

"I'm shocked, honestly."

He pursed his lips. He nodded.

"His parents left him a good sum of money upon their deaths. It was held in trust by his grandmother. The money grew. He was not someone who tended his money carefully. He let others do it for him, and that worked out splendidly in this case. Of course, his grandmother is well known and is an important personage in her own right. She had good people managing the money."

"I am stunned. That wasn't my perception of Ozzie."

"If you'll permit me to wax philosophical for a moment," he said, leaning still farther forward, "money is a fascinating thing. I don't mean the paper and coins, but the resource itself. I've spent my working life watching people's approaches to money. Some people are like the dragons of our mythical past. They sit on their pile of gold and know the weight of every doubloon. They threaten anyone who comes near their hoard. Others— and I would say Mr. Ferriter falls into this category—see it as a larder. A few cans of food on the shelf that they can go to if life makes them hungry. He did well for himself, but not in a way that signified anything to him. Cans on a shelf, that's how I think of it."

"Thank you for the metaphor, Robert."

He spread his hands to say I was welcome. In many ways, he was a perfect parody of a lawyer. I liked him. I felt I should ask more questions, but I didn't know what was left to discover.

"This will all take some time to transfer," he went on. "Documents to file and that sort of thing. Are you in need of any money at the moment?"

"Not in a significant way."

"Our firm could advance you something against your future holdings. Keep that in mind. We have all of your information. We'll be in touch as soon as we have more to report. For the time being, you have a true picture of what was contained in his portfolio. I hope you're satisfied. It's not a curse, you know, to receive a bequeathal. Enjoy it. I'm sure that was Mr. Ferriter's intention."

"Yes, thank you. I'll do my best. Cans on a shelf. I will remember that."

I stood. Robert stood. He was at least six-three, I imagined. A button of his suit jacket caught on the edge of the table and clicked when he stood to full height. He smiled.

"Pleasure meeting you," he said, sliding the packet of information he had compiled across the table to me. "The keys to the cottage are inside the packet. If there is anything else we can do, please don't hesitate to ask."

We shook hands. As I left, nodding and smiling at the lawyers and assistants who nodded and smiled at me, the grandfather clock chimed four o'clock. I counted each chime. And when I stepped back into the Dublin street-life, the sound of the chiming would not leave my head.

31

I brought Gottfried to the cottage with me. He rode in the front seat of my rental. Seamus had insisted on driving me, or at least insisted on having Johnny drive me, but I answered back with equal force that I needed to do this on my own. Nora hauled him in and told him to let me do what I needed to do. In compromise, he told me I should take Gottfried to keep me company. I was happy to do that. I felt eager to get away, to be alone with my thoughts for a moment, and without much more argument they let me go.

I remembered the drive and the directions easily. I hardly had to concentrate. When I steered down the grass path that led to the shelf of rock overlooking the sea—our shelf, where we had once lived as husband and wife—I realized at once that things had changed. For one thing, the drive was no longer dirt alone; Ozzie, or someone, had put in a proper gravel driveway so that mud and sliding grass would no longer be an issue. It was the first of a thousand improvements, I noted, because as soon as I had gone another twenty yards or so, I spotted the cottage.

This was how Ozzie had dreamed of the cottage, I realized. This was how he had pictured it in his mind all those years before. His hands had finally brought it to life, etching its outline against the pale evening horizon, the sea a flowing skirt that spread below and spoke to the white cottage that we had planned to share.

I began to cry. No weeping, no shouts of anguish. Instead,

it felt as if my insides had given up something valuable and irreplaceable; I had misjudged him. I knew that simple fact with every inch the car covered. The promise of the cottage had at last been fully realized. It was a dream cottage, whitewashed with rounded windows, and a roof made of rushes and felt. Clean lines. Humble shapes and colors. A home on a hill overlooking Dingle Bay and the Celtic Sea.

"He built this," I whispered to Gottfried. "I think he built it for us."

I put my face against Gottfried's soft head and hugged him. But Gottfried moved impatiently. He wanted to go find Ozzie. I swung open his door and he jumped out. I followed him. The scent of the sea moved everywhere. Gulls flew near the path down to the beach and the wind threw them back to land until they cut against it and darted seaward.

I had seen no photos of the cottage transformation. Ozzie had remained silent and distant. I had sent him a Christmas card after our second year apart, wishing him well, sending good thoughts to Nora and Seamus and Gottfried, but the card came back unopened. He had disappeared from my life as cleanly as a surgical cut. And what had I done about it? I had assumed it was for the good. A grown-up decision. He had been a passion, certainly, but was he the man for me in the long run?

Now I wanted to spit at myself. I reviled myself. I hated how I had boxed him in, made him into one thing so that I could persuade myself that I knew best.

"It's beautiful," I whispered to Gottfried, but he was already sniffing down by the path, hoping, I supposed, that Ozzie would come striding up, his hair wet, his skin tasting of the cold, cold sea.

It *was* beautiful. It was elegant and charming, a re-creation of an earlier time. I walked slowly toward it in the late light and felt myself coming home. Every inch, every angle of the building, spoke something about Ozzie. I pictured him here, working,

working, working, slowly shaping this cottage out of the surrounding rocks and sod. I had doubted him. Meanwhile, he had been sitting on a small fortune. He could have hired builders, he could have had the building completed in a brief season, but that was not his intent. He wanted to build something with his hands. I knew now that it had been part of his reclaiming the goodness of life. Balance the cottage against an IED blowing children's limbs into the trees on a bare Afghanistan plain. Find in the curve of the rounded windows the symmetry and calm the war had taken from him.

I opened the door with a key from the packet given to me by Robert Smith. The door opened on easy hinges. I stepped through and saw the perfection of the interior. Another woman may not have found it to her taste, but its simplicity, its clean, unobstructed lines fit me in every molecule. One of the things I had loved about the Blasket Island stories was the description of the cottages. Like this one, they had been clean and spare, with bare floors, sometimes dirt floors, and a bright, useful fireplace against the back wall. Ozzie had carried out that motif to perfection inside the house. Five stick-back chairs ranged around a circular oak table. The chairs, I imagined, could be rearranged so one might sit by the fire. It was a cottage that contained incredible stillness, a stillness that could be interrupted by the gladness of the occupants. The sea outside waited and grabbed color from the tall grasses that ran down the hillside toward it.

I had let this all go. I had let Ozzie go.

I called Gottfried inside and ran a pan of water for him. Ozzie had left firewood beside the hearth. I found paper and crumpled it together and lit a fire. I squatted beside it, watching the flames climb. A foolish girl had once demanded perfection from her mate, had not been strong enough to stand beside him despite his goodness, his love of life, his appetite for living. It pained me to think of it; it pained me to picture her, so self-righteous, so certain of all that she knew. I added wood to the fire, and then, when I was certain it had caught, I pulled two pillows from off the bed and set them beside the hearth and spent a long time watching the flame push back the gathering darkness outside. Gottfried came and settled next to me. I put my arm over his shoulder. I could no longer cry.

When I woke, I was hungry and thirsty and disoriented. Moonlight fell through the windows. I did not turn on a light. Instead I fed the fire more wood and stepped outside to give Gottfried a moment. As I waited for him, a voice came up out of a place in my heart. It filled me until I couldn't contain it. At first it felt absurd, but then it gathered force and clawed its way through me, and it carried with it the force of the women in the Blaskets who keened for their men lost at sea, for their children who died in difficult births, for the old whose heads became as light and soft as the pillows that held them in their final beds. I cried out in a long, painful voice, in a voice that was only part mine, and I watched the clouds move over the moon and I heard the sea that listened and took my sound into its waves.

SIXTH LETTER

Théid mé suas ar an cnoc is airde
Féach an bhfeic mé fear a' bháta.
An dtig tú anocht, nó an dtig tú amárach?

(I went up to the highest hill
To see if I could see the boatman.
Will you come tonight, or will you come tomorrow?)

32

I found his note by chance. I had spent a week alone in the cottage with no company except Gottfried. I had done little except sleep and make fires and take long walks. I ate without appetite. I read Yeats, as we used to read him together. Twice Seamus called, and once Nora, and I spoke with them calmly and rationally, although I did not feel that way. On the third day, Lawrence called, but I did not have the heart to answer. He left a warm message, wishing me well, hoping things worked out as best they could, and then he spent a few minutes filling me in on his appearance on *Meet the Press*. It had gone better than he imagined, better than he could have hoped, and his phone had lit up messages and requests for speaking engagements. It was amazing, he said, what an impact a single television program could have . . .

I deleted the message before he finished leaving it.

I talked to my dean, too, and my department chair. I arranged to shift the focus of my class to an online structure. I knew, as I spoke to them, that they understood I was about to do a terrible job finishing my classes. I couldn't help it. I went several times to a B&B and paid a flat twenty-euro fee to tie into the internet. But I couldn't lather up any enthusiasm for the coursework, and the students detected my state of mind. My courses limped to an uneasy pause.

I searched the cottage, too, for glimpses into Ozzie's life

there. He did not leave much. He had a table where he kept bills and odds and ends, a bookcase with perhaps two hundred volumes of every sort, and an armoire with some of his clothes. I wore two of his flannels as nightshirts; the second one, the one I did not wear, I kept folded under the pillow where his head had laid, so that I could have more of his scent.

I spent a day and a half researching everything I could about the loss of the *Ferriter*. I could find next to nothing; it had been one of many losses in that horrible migration of West Africans and Syrians and Eritreans from Africa to Europe. I knew little about the migration paths, the dreadful capsizings, the tales of children living on toothpaste. I recognized some of the pictures that had gone viral: a dead Syrian child facedown in the wash along an Italian beach, a horrid photograph of an open boat's gunwale dipping into the waves, a photo of an ancient-looking grandmother staring steadfastly into the camera, her eyes empty and exhausted.

Without truly meaning to, I formed a plan in my mind to go to Italy. At first the idea started as a buzz in the back of my head. Slowly I realized I could do it. I could travel to Italy and see what Ozzie had seen. I could ask about him and about the *Ferriter*. I didn't have any illusion that I would be Nancy Drew, a shrewd girl-detective gathering clues, but I understood I had to go. I had to see whatever I could and I needed to do it now, before his memory faded in people's minds. As much as possible, I needed my eyes to see what his eyes had seen.

The day before departing for Italy, I discovered he had left a message on the upward-facing surface on the bottom half of the cottage's Dutch door—the level board where you would lean your elbows if you looked out with the top half of the door open. I had opened the door a dozen times without noticing the small message left in black script. It was composed so that it resembled the wooden grain of the door and it said, *I went up to the highest hill / To see if I could see the boatman. / Will you come tonight, or will you come tomorrow?*

I put my finger against the script. I didn't cry. But I knew he had meant the message for me. He had waited for me here. I read the script and looked out at the sea. I read it over and over until it burned a spot in my memory that scalded me.

I nearly forgot the red rock. I had seen the rock a thousand times, but I had never turned it over to determine if Ozzie had been serious about stashing money there. I took Gottfried for a short walk and brought along a spade to pry the rock up. It was a heavy rock, about the size of a football on top but wider below, and it had settled in its place. Grass had grown around it, so I had to stand on the shovel blade to get its nose beneath the weight. Gottfried wanted to help, and I had to push him away so I wouldn't cut his paws when plunging the blade into the soil. Using all my weight and strength, I turned the rock over. The hole beneath it was empty. If it had ever been Ozzie's hiding place for money, it was no longer. I rolled the stone back in its place. Grass reached up to reclaim it.

I locked the cottage. Afterward, I stood for a long time looking out at the bay. I knelt next to Gottfried and put my arm across his back. *Will you come tonight, or will you come tomorrow?* Everything I knew about love seemed sealed inside those words.

"It feels strange to talk to you via a computer like this," I said.

Dr. Kaufman nodded.

"At first it is. But many of my clients prefer it. It's better than a phone. At least we can see each other."

"Yes, I suppose so."

She paused. She always paused rather than introduce a subject. It was my time, my topic. I sat on the edge of my bed in my Dublin hotel, laptop on my knees. I was flying to Rome the next day. I had said my goodbyes to Seamus and Nora. I had said my goodbyes to Gottfried. I was going to Italy without a clear plan, except that Milly, my kindest, dearest, sweetest friend, had agreed to meet me there if she could swing it. I would pay, I said. It was Italy. And I needed her. But even with her committing to meet me, I felt scattered and a little bit crazy. That was what I told Milly. That was what I told Dr. Kaufman.

"Crazy isn't really a useful word, though, is it?" she asked. "Probably less than politically correct. I don't think we refer to people as crazy any longer. That's behind us, thank goodness."

"I mean confused. Distraught. A thousand things."

"It's understandable."

"I keep wondering if I am now a widow. Am I not a widow until he is officially pronounced dead?"

"I think that is probably true. I don't know, honestly."

"I keep wondering how to get the answer to a question like that. It's extraneous to everything I'm doing, but I can't seem to let it go. I even asked Siri, but she didn't answer anything intelligible."

"Is it important to call yourself a widow?"

"I don't know why, but it is."

She didn't say anything. I wanted to ask her to turn the screen so I could see the birds. I went on.

"It feels as if I would have some standing in his life. Or in his death, I guess I should say."

"What meaning would that have for you?"

"I don't know. A social meaning."

"As in the approval of society?"

"I know it sounds ridiculous. It's probably just a way to feel I am still attached to him."

She stared at me. She didn't say anything.

"He left everything to me."

"You've told me. How does that make you feel?"

"Horrible. Honored. Angry. Sometimes I feel it wasn't fair of him to leave me everything. The rest of my life, I will have a part of him with me. I'll never be done with him."

"Do you want to be done? A moment ago, you wanted to determine if you were his widow."

"I don't know what I want. I miss him. I wonder if I didn't make a terrible mistake in leaving him."

She didn't say anything to that. She looked placidly into the screen of her computer.

"That expression, *You don't know what you've got till it's gone?* It's from a song."

"*They paved paradise, and put up a parking lot,*" Dr. Kaufman said, deadpan. It was uncanny to see her mouth a pop-song lyric. I waited for her to smile, but she didn't.

"Yes, that's it. That's what I wonder. I regret the way our marriage ended. I regret that I didn't see him clearly."

"It's always easy to second-guess from a distance. You acted on the information you had at the time."

"Did I? I had this remarkable man in my life, my husband, and I ran away at the first glimpse of unpleasantness. Of incompatibility. I had some sort of tidy idea of the way my life should go, and I bent everything to fit it. That's what pains me. I feel like I was a spoiled little girl who failed to see what was in front of me. I had a passionate love and traded it for a pair of slipper socks."

She waited. I felt teary and dizzy. I tried to remember when I had last eaten. I found it hard to keep track of such things. Milly would help me with that. She would take me under her wing.

Will you come tonight? Or will you come tomorrow?

"Do you know Somerset Maugham's *The Painted Veil?*" she asked after a few moments. "If you haven't read it, you should."

"Why? What's it about?"

"It's a story very much like yours. A young woman who is frivolous and adulterous is carried away by her husband to a remote region in China. She is bored and listless and unhappy with her station. She yearns for her former life in society. Her husband is not the equal of the man with whom she carried on an affair. Her husband lacks the panache of her former lover. A plague comes and it attacks a local school—well, the whole area, really. Out of boredom she has gone to work in the mission school and there she begins to hear a different account of her husband than the one she has imagined on her own. To the nuns and health workers, her husband is nearly divine. He is a good man. The traits she has difficulty accepting in him are the traits that make him a tireless worker on behalf of the poorest factions of society. In time, she realizes she has fallen in love with her husband now that she sees him truly."

"What happens?"

"I am not saying you are frivolous or adulterous, by the way. Don't mistake me. But it's a story of reappraisal, similar to your own circumstances. Should I spoil the ending for you?"

"Yes, please."

"He dies. It's literature, so of course we need that drama. The final scene is quite interesting. She returns to London and happens to run into her former lover. She passes him in the street and she hardly bothers to notice him. He's not a fraction of the man her husband was and now she knows it. She has learned to value other things."

"As I must do."

She gazed directly into the screen. Remarkably, her eyes glimmered with tears. I had never seen her exhibit any emotion in all my sessions with her. She spoke softly when she continued.

"Look, Kate, you can't blame yourself. Our inexperience is a box that we can't escape except by experience. Ironic, isn't it? Ozzie played his part, too. Maybe he wasn't quite ready for the kind of life you had imagined. That kind of compromise that couples must learn to do, that's a perspective we gather along the way. You're what? Three years older now? You wear different eyeglasses today than you did then. Kierkegaard says, *Life can*

only be understood backwards, but it must be lived forwards.
That's the human condition. It's the source of our unquenchable
anguish."

"Thank you, Dr. Kaufman. That's more than you've ever said
at one time before."

Now she smiled.

"Sometimes we therapists can share perspectives that might
be useful. You can borrow my eyeglasses for a moment. You're
grieving your former husband and the dissolution of your marriage. Those are not small things."

"No, they are not small things."

"Step by step. Be charitable with yourself. We're all doing our
best. You and Ozzie and everyone else."

I nodded. I finally asked if she would point the computer
toward the window so that I could see the birds. She did. We
signed off a few minutes later.

33

I landed in Rome with no plan to speak of, except to work my way south. I thought of renting a car, but I wasn't sure I could drive confidently in Italy. I found a train—the Leonardo train—to take me into the center of town. I had never been to Rome, but I loved it at first sight. It was warm, for one thing, and the sun created beautiful mosaics everywhere I looked. It was different from Ireland. Ireland was butter; Italy was olive oil. Motor scooters buzzed everywhere, and the streets contained a lovey languor, an invitation to sit over coffee and watch the world pass. I loved the fashion, the men in tight-fitting suits and heeled boots, and the women in black trousers with fabulous tops, and purses that picked up their outfits and carried them to a logical conclusion. Yes, Rome. It was the first bright thing I had experienced in weeks.

I took at room at the Villa Duse. I splurged and asked for a room at the top of the hotel, with a terrace. If I was going to have a brief stay, I figured, I might as well spend it properly. Besides, it was off-season, and the room was moderately priced. A young man with Elvis sideburns carried my bag to my room. I gave him a tip—how much? I was never good at that—and then closed the door after him. I opened the doors to the terrace and stepped outside. Rome greeted me with warm winds and buildings that had stood vigil for longer than anyone knew.

I ran a bath and stayed in it for a long, long time. When I got out, I dressed in jeans and a black sweater and went out to find something to eat. If possible, my love affair with Rome grew in the half light of early evening. It was the hour of the *bella figura,* that period of time in early evening when locals parade and present themselves. I knew about it only from books, but when I sat at a small table at the Café D'Angelo, I watched the promenade with pleasure. I ordered a prosciutto mozzarella tomato ciabatta with basil pesto and a glass of Antinori Villa Antinori Classico Riserva Chianti from an older, whiskered waiter, who took my order with boredom dripping from every sigh. But he was competent and quick, and in no time I had a succulent meal in front of me, steaming, and a glass of excellent wine.

"Anything else?" he asked me in English.

"Nothing, thank you."

"Prego."

I sat and ate and watched the people, and in my deepest recesses I tried to imagine Ozzie here. Ozzie in Italy. It did not quite fit. It was not his natural habitat. He was a north man. He would only come to Italy with a purpose in mind.

I was drinking my wine when my phone buzzed with a call from Milly. I didn't want to be an obnoxious American who spent her meal time talking on the phone, but at the same time I wanted to speak to Milly. We still hadn't confirmed final plans.

"Where are you?" she asked when I answered.

"In Italy. In Rome. At an amazing little café."

"Can you wait another day there? Maybe a day and a half?"

I felt my stomach roll.

Will you come tonight? Or will you come tomorrow?

"Are you coming, Milly? Please say yes."

"I am. I just booked. I'll be there tomorrow evening, I think."

"Are you serious? Oh, Milly, how can I thank you? You don't know how much this means to me. I don't know if I could do this without you. I feel a little alone in the world right now."

"I sensed that, Kate."

I had to stop speaking for a moment. Milly was coming to join me. With Milly by my side, I could do anything. I felt grateful beyond words.

"You'll love it here, Milly. I've been here half a day and I already love it. It's everything you want it to be. And it's warm."

"I can't wait. It will be an adventure."

"We'll go south, but we can stay and see Rome for a day or two."

"I'd like that. But I know you only have so much time. I know you're eager to find out what you can about Ozzie."

I pinched the bridge of my nose. I nodded before I spoke.

"He's dead, Milly. I'm only going to see if I can find a trace of his memory."

"I know, sweetheart."

"We'll have a stay in Rome, and then we'll go south. Joy and sorrow mixed. That's life."

"Yes, that's life. It's damn hard, but it's life."

I broke down. I cried over my meal and I heard on the other end of the line Milly's patient breathing. When I finally composed myself, she gave me her flight information, asked me a little bit about what to bring, and said she couldn't wait to see me. I promised to message her my hotel address, then signed off. The waiter returned and looked at me.

"The food is not that bad, is it, Signora?"

He meant that it had caused my tears. He meant it as a joke. He poured me a little more wine.

"The food is excellent. Sorry. It has been an emotional time."

"Don't be sorry. Have a sweet tonight. Treat yourself well."

"Yes, please. Recommend something. And coffee, thank you. Black coffee."

He brought me zabaglione, a pale light custard that was a café specialty. I Googled it on my phone down by my lap after he served it. It had been invented in Florence during the sixteenth century in the court of the Medicis. That seemed the right kind of dessert for my first night in Rome. I put my phone away and took deep breaths. Milly was coming; I was going to go south to see what I could see. The world would keep spinning. Ozzie had gone east of the sun, west of the moon.

The night had grown darker. How strange it all was. I was in Rome, and I was the widow—was I?—of a man who had left me wealth. I was drinking fine chianti and eating zabaglione, a dessert I hadn't known an hour ago. Life seemed too random, too unpredictable to be trusted, and I thought of the *Ferriter* on the ocean on our passage to Dublin, the wave slashing me against the gunwale, the sizzling sound of water as it spilled past me and invited me over the side and into the gray-green water.

I ate slowly, relishing every bite. Then I paid and walked slowly back to the hotel. A young man sitting on a scooter made a kissing sound at me. I ignored him. I went up to my room and I left the terrace doors open as I fell asleep. Soft breezes pushed the white curtains back and the sound of scooters sounded almost like crickets.

Milly texted every step of the way.

Just landed, she wrote from the airport. *In love with three Italian men already.*

Later: *On my way. Coming to the hotel. The driver knows it.*

I went down to the lobby and waited. I brought a book, *The Autobiography of Peig Sayers of the Great Blasket Island,* a book that usually filled me with serenity, but I couldn't focus on it. I sat on a green, overstuffed chair that rested too close to a potted fern. I got up and moved to a second chair, this one next to a window that looked out on the street. I checked my phone for messages. And again. And again.

And when she finally arrived, I nearly missed her.

I would have missed her arrival entirely, except I luckily recognized her stride as she went across the small lobby to the check-in desk. I let out a dog-yowl of happiness and surprise and unnamable emotion. It was Milly. Presto-chango, she was there. She turned and propped her small pull-behind bag on the ground beside her. It tipped over, and the handle made a loud whacking sound on the tile floor. She started to reach down to put it right, but then she stepped away and waved it off. It could wait, she said with a shrug. She walked toward me with her arms expanding to hug me. She looked a great, happy bird landing or preparing for takeoff and I stepped into her arms, put mine around hers and then we both began laughing.

Who knows why?

Nerves, eagerness, sadness, joy, happiness. A collection of feelings that expressed themselves, somehow, in a deep, deep laughter. We hugged and hugged and wrestled each other gently from side to side. Then she pushed me back and wiped her eyes with her sleeve and smiled brightly.

"We're in Rome!" she said.

"I know."

"Rome, Italy."

"I know, I know, I know."

"It's a dream. I've always wanted to come here."

"I have, too."

"I couldn't help feeling . . . it was the oddest thing. I thought, I am a grown-up. Kate is a grown-up. Grown-up ladies fly to Rome and meet each other. They just do. I think we're grown up now, Kate. What do you think?"

I thought it was marvelous to see her, to have her beside me, to feel her kind, bubbling energy. I grabbed her arm and held it in mine and scooted her bag after us as she registered at the desk. They gave her a key to our room, and then I whisked her away. She smiled at everything. She wore skinny jeans and fabulous blue-black boots. Her eyes, as always, drew people's gazes to her. People checked her and wondered if she was someone famous. She looked as if she could be. Her energy lit up the world around her.

Stepping into our room, she went immediately to the terrace and looked out. She took a bunch of deep breaths with her hands on the cement railing, then turned to me and took me in her arms again. This time it wasn't a bear hug, but a hug that was quiet and calm and dignified.

"I'm sorry," she said. "I'm sorry about Ozzie. I'm excited to be in Rome, but I also remember why we're here. You lost your husband."

"He wasn't my husband," I whispered.

"Once someone is your husband, he always will be. You two were still married."

"Only on paper, Milly. I want it to be true, but it isn't. We were estranged. Isn't that the proper word for it?"

"You were married in your hearts. That's what counts."

We broke apart. Our eyes stayed locked on each other. Then she made a funny face, and then held out her arms to indicate *Look at us, look at where we are, look at where we find ourselves!* I nodded. It was a million miles from New Hampshire.

"Are you exhausted?" I asked.

"A little. I feel dried out, mostly. Flying is inhuman."

"There's water in the fridge. We'll share a bed. We can spend a night or two here, then go south, Milly. It will be fun."

"Are you sure? I don't know if that's a good idea. You're not in the mood for fun. You're in mourning, for god's sake. This isn't a vacation."

"No, of course not. But we may never be back in Rome again. We need to experience it a little. Ozzie would even tell us to do that. I thought we could have one perfect day in Rome."

"One perfect day? One perfect day, you say? I like the sound of that. Well, if that's the case, then I am not sleeping. I'm going to pretend the flight never happened. One night and one day. Then we go south to see what we can find out. What about your classes?"

"My classes are falling apart. They're in shambles. I am doing a horrible job with them. The semester is almost over, thank goodness."

"Any problem with that? Pushback from the administration?"

I shrugged. I didn't know. I wouldn't have blamed Dartmouth for firing me. I wouldn't have blamed my students for reporting me to the dean. I didn't intentionally put them in this position, but the fact remained that that's where we were. I couldn't side-step that. I had already prepared myself mentally for accepting whatever outcome had to occur from my absence. That was life.

"They can't be happy with me. It's not what you do to climb up the tenure ladder."

"But life sometimes gets in the way. They must understand that."

"Life always gets in the way. That's what I'm learning."

She smiled. She nodded. There was little she could say to make things right back in Hanover, New Hampshire.

"I'm going to take a shower," Milly said to cut away from that topic, pulling her bag into the bedroom. "We'll play things by ear. I'm here for you, Kate. When you say we go, we go. No questions asked. We can go right now if you want to."

"A day."

"Okay, a day. One perfect day. And a night," Milly said and wiggled her eyebrows at me.

"You're such a witch."

She stepped toward me and hugged me with one arm.

"I love you, Kate," she said.

"I love you, too, Milly."

"We're grown-up ladies in Rome."

"It appears so."

"Amazing. Simply fabulous."

34

If I could have ordered online a girlfriend who would be sensitive, fun, lively, quiet, attentive, self-reliant, and ready to do anything I asked, Amazon would have delivered Milly by drone and dropped her on the terrace without ruffling the curtains. She emerged from the bathroom wearing a white robe, her hair tucked into a fluffy azure towel, her phone packed already with the addresses of restaurants her friend, Jennifer Donnelli, a native of Rome now studying at Dartmouth, had told her she must visit. Milly held the phone up.

"Here's what I think. Seafood, maybe pasta. Good meal. Then we go out and find the best bar we can afford. We drink a post-dinner martini, or maybe cognac, I don't know. What does one drink in Rome after dinner?"

"Sambuca?"

"I thought only old Italian ladies in Sons of Italy weddings drank Sambuca."

"Stereotype much?"

She waved my prissiness away. She plunked down on the bed, her finger zooming across the phone screen.

"We only have so much time, so we have to streamline everything. I plan to be making out with an Italian boy later tonight, so that's just the way it is. Before that, though, we need to see the city from Capitoline Hill. Jennifer says it's a must. And then the

Roman Forum. She says night in Rome is pure theater. How is this sounding so far? Too much?"

"It's sounds like the perfect start of a perfect day in Rome."

"That's what I thought!" she said gleefully. "I agree! We probably have to see the Spanish Steps and Trevi Fountain . . . maybe we can get a boy on a motor scooter to take us. Isn't that the dream? Buzzing around Rome with two boys who should be in school somewhere?"

"Too much," I said.

"Okay, okay, okay, I got carried away. I know. But we do need to see the Trevi Fountain and the Spanish Steps. Maybe Porticus Octavia, too. Jennifer ranks it a *B*. She says see it if we have time, and it's over by the Coliseum, so we probably should."

She looked exotic sitting in her towel, her face lit by excitement. She was transformed from New Hampshire Milly to Italy Milly. Water dripped down her shoulders. Her eyes had fatigue etched into the skin around them, but I didn't doubt she could keep going for days. In traveling to Ireland, I had lost track of her emotional rhythms. She was certainly in an up phase.

We left the hotel at eight twenty, a time we assumed was late enough to be chic. We dressed well, but not extravagantly. We walked in sensible shoes, giddy as schoolgirls at the sights and sounds and smells. Milly kept my arm locked in hers and she filled me in on the New Hampshire gossip, who was dating whom, who had broken up, who had gone into a rehab center, who was definitely getting divorced. I listened, half drawn in and half aware that I, too, probably lived on the tongues of gossips in Hanover. *Did you hear about Kate? Kate Moreton? Her ex-husband, or was it her husband, anyway, some man she was with years ago drowned in the Mediterranean Sea.* Then they would move on. I would be forgotten, a mere juicy item, but the consequence of the little spurt of gossip would stay with me for years. Real people lived inside of gossip. I patted Milly's hand and she got the message and changed the topic, glancing at her phone to chart our way through the Roman evening.

We ate at Ristorante Crispi 19, on the Via Francesco Crispi. It was a gorgeous restaurant, with a dark wooden doorway and crisp white tablecloths, and Milly said we wouldn't be able to get a table during the regular tourist season. We paused at the entrance, slightly timid, but a tall, gray-haired man wearing a beautiful navy suit stepped out for a cigarette and saw us. He clicked his lighter and blew a stream of smoke up to the heavens.

"Table?" he asked in Italian.

"Si," Milly answered.

"Americano?"

"Si," Milly said again.

"Good food. I'll take you in . . . two more puffs."

We watched him smoke. Milly tightened her hand on my arm. The man was out of central casting: tall, distinguished looking, happy to enjoy a cigarette on a warm evening. He was as good as his word. He took two more puffs, then extinguished the cigarette on the cobblestone ground beneath him.

"We go," he said, holding out his hand to show us the way. "Nice table."

We passed through an intimate, cozy dining room. It was crowded, despite it being off-season. Our gentleman led us to a tiny table near the center of the room. He held our chairs out for us and pushed them under us when we sat. Milly caught my eye and smiled. From an American man, holding out chairs and being mildly chivalrous usually seemed strained; the Italian gentleman who seated us did not give it a moment's thought. It's what one did.

"Your waiter, Emilio," the gentleman said, introducing a broad, bustling waiter who might have popped up through a hole in the floor so quickly did he appear at our gentleman's shoulder.

"I am Emilio," Emilio said, smiling, "Americanos?"

"Yes," Milly said. "Americanos."

"Good, good, good," Emilio said. "Delicious dinner ahead. Full speed ahead."

We did not order well. Or rather, we did not order fluently. We settled finally on a seven-item fish tasting menu, with wines selected by Emilio to compliment the dishes. It limited our decision-making and gave us a chance to absorb the ambience of the restaurant.

"What is it about Italy?" Milly asked, her eyes roaming around to pick up all the details she could discover. "It's beautiful, of course, but it's silky somehow. American seems like a coarse, cotton napkin by comparison."

"The climate, maybe."

"Everybody eats outside . . . the cafés, and the lights. I don't know. At least in New England where we live, everything faces inside."

"I once read that Europeans go out to be social, and home to be alone. In America, we do the opposite. We go out to be alone, to climb a mountain or kayak a river, but we go home to be social. Strange, isn't it?"

Before Emilio returned with our first course, Milly leaned across the table and took my hands in hers. She shook them slightly and got me to meet her eyes.

"How are you feeling? Is this too much pretend?"

"No, no, I like it. I like being here with you, Milly. It's just . . ."

"That the man you loved drowned in the Mediterranean."

"Yes, I guess so. It's not as if there's anything I'm going to be able to do about it. Or know about it, really. I just feel I need to go to wherever he was in his last days."

"I understand. Are you numb?"

"A little. Sometimes. More haunted than anything else. Does that make sense?"

"By Ozzie?"

"By Ozzie, by how easily I let it slip away. By how I didn't fight for our marriage as I should have. I was hasty."

"But you had your reasons, didn't you?"

"I had my reasons. I'm not even sure I made the wrong decision. It's not about the decision. I remember talking to a friend who got divorced, and before she did, she went to hours and hours of couples' counseling with her soon-to-be ex. She knew she wanted a divorce, but she went anyway. She wanted to be sure she had done everything she could. She wanted to sweep all the corners. She didn't want to wake up five years down the road and realize she had made a horrible mistake. Or that she hadn't investigated every possibility."

"I get that."

Emilio returned with two other younger waiters in tow. They pushed a small service tray. Emilio poured us wine while the other two busied themselves with our first fish course.

"Pan-fried cod fillet with polenta mousse, anchovies, si? And fried capers with candied tomatoes . . . yes?" Emilio asked.

"Yes, wonderful," Milly said, letting my hands go as she sat back. She repeated a line that she had obviously memorized. "There's no cure for love but to love more."

"It's good to be here with you, Milly," I said, raising my glass.

"To a perfect day in Rome."

We saw the lights of Rome from Capitoline Hill. We saw the Coliseum, lit up and beautiful, and we strolled over to the Porticus Octavia, admired it, then continued on, walking in a delicious haze of food and wine and travel. It felt good to be in Italy. Winter was advancing in New Hampshire, and Ireland had been damp and cold, but Rome invited us to take our time, to see everything, to absorb life carefully. We did. We walked the mile from the Coliseum to the Spanish Steps along the Via del Corso and the Via Condotti, and then we stood for a long while watching the night scene spread out against the Spanish Steps. We watched jugglers and flame eaters and sword swallowers, and we watched some of the Italian kids flipping their skateboards on the wide plaza spreading out from the steps. Milly clutched my arm and laughed at every new, shimmering moment of beauty. It felt good to be among people, to be simple tourists with no responsibility but to watch and admire. After the Spanish Steps, we walked to the Trevi Fountain. It's impossible to see such places without realizing you are familiar with them from movies and documentaries, and it is impossible to stand in front of the Trevi Fountain without feeling like a silly tourist. At the same time, the Trevi Fountain, with its exquisite sculptures, the water spilling over charging horses, feels like a tribute to all that is good in humanity. Beauty, grace, whimsy. I backed Milly onto a bench and together we sat for a long time watching the water play with the lights, the push of tourists and Romans stopping by to toss coins into the fountain.

"Do you want to make a wish?" Milly asked me after a while.

"I don't think my wish can come true."

"You never know. What would you wish?"

"Oh, you know. For a second chance, I guess. For a chance to fix things with Ozzie."

"I'd wish to pet a koala bear. I've always wanted to do that."

I looked at her to see if she was serious. She was. I started laughing. It was such a wayward thought that I couldn't stop laughing when she bumped her shoulder into mine.

"You want to pet a koala bear? That's what you would wish for?"

"Why, is that strange? I think they're cute."

"They are cute. I wouldn't mind petting one, but you'd use your chance at the Trevi Fountain to wish for that. I love you, Milly. I love your koala wish."

"I'm going to go to Australia and pet a koala one of these days."

"I hope you do!"

"A koala wish makes as much sense as anything else. Unless you want to wish for more wishes. That's always the best wish."

We waited until the crowds thinned before taking a bunch of pictures in front of the Trevi Fountain. The lights had switched from white to gold. It was slightly gaudy, but also dramatic. Milly said the changing light was in keeping with the Renaissance-Baroque character of the fountain. She asked a young Asian girl to take a few pictures of us together, arm in arm, in front of the fountain. The girl took a dozen. We thanked her and then left. It was nearly midnight.

"Are you ready to go dancing?" Milly asked.

"I'm not, Milly. But you go ahead if you want."

"I am not going dancing," Milly said. "I am going to climb into bed and sleep and wake to a perfect Rome morning."

"I'd like that."

"As long as we can tell everyone we went out dancing, okay? Our secret, right?"

"Absolutely."

We talked about art in our Uber home. We talked about Rome and how it would be to live there, what it would mean to have so much antique beauty around one. It seemed impossible that people got to live with such grace and art surrounding them. We talked about the *bella figura,* and about the *dolce vita,* the sweet life, and about how New Hampshire, as sweet and pure as it was, sometimes felt like a wilderness of cold and bright, brittle days. At some point exhaustion kept us talking, and after we paid the Uber driver and climbed to our room, we opened the windows as wide as possible and fell into bed with the night pawing restlessly against the white sheer curtains.

I was asleep only an hour, maybe two, when I woke and told Milly I had to go.

"To the bathroom?" she asked, drunk with sleep.

"No, to the south, to find what I can about Ozzie."

"Yes, of course, yes."

Whether she heard me or not, I couldn't say. I climbed out of bed and sat on the railing of the terrace and watched the night deepen and clutch our little neighborhood of Rome in darkness. Motion still made its claim from the streets, but I could no longer be a tourist. I was sorry that I couldn't play with Milly for a day, couldn't give her that, but I needed to search for traces of him. My students had been sending notes and work through email, and I had let it stack up like dishes in a sink. It was time to do what I had come to Italy for; I couldn't postpone it any longer. I sat and watched the city churn beyond my terrace, the black buildings outlined against the brilliant lights that sometimes caught their reflections on a car window or mirror and sent a beam or two toward the sky, and I tried to picture Ozzie here, tossing his life into the sea, trying to win back his soul after having lost it in the senseless Afghanistan war.

I went up to the highest hill to see if I could see the boatman. Will you come tonight, or will you come tomorrow?

I was done with waiting. My stomach felt sick with waiting.

35

Porto Salvo in Gaeta is the southernmost town on the Italian peninsula. It is part of the Bovesia Greek-speaking area of Calabria, and it occupies a hilly formation that descends gracefully toward the Ionian Sea. Fishermen leave the harbor early in the morning and return in midafternoon, birds following them, and sell their catches directly from their boats. Local restaurants buy the fish and carry their purchases homeward in small cars or motor scooters. Across the street from the main harbor, a fish market runs until late afternoon and sometimes into the evening. It is all cobblestone and white flashing fish. The air, heavy and moist, never arrives without the scent of the sea embedded in its core. Light from the water falls against the buildings and the sides of boats, and old men mend nets in the afternoon light with bone needles the size of clothespins.

Milly's friend, Jennifer, had booked us a room in a private home she knew about in Porto Salvo. It was a stunning stone building overlooking the port. A stout, elderly woman in a black dress came at our knock. Her face shone white, a moon suspended on a magician's black tablecloth. Her dress came to her knees. She wore black boots on her feet, the sides toothed with bronze zippers.

"Signora Rici?" I asked, absurdly trying to make my voice sound Italian.

Signora Rici was the contact person Jennifer had used to make the reservation.

Signora Rici nodded. She backed away, pulling the door open.

"In here," she said in English. "Follow, please."

We stepped inside. She shut the door behind us. I put my bag down out of the way. Milly moved forward, took things in, then turned to me with her eyebrows raised.

It was a stunning apartment. The southern end gave way to French doors that stood open to take in the sea air. White curtains blew back and lolled against the stone walls. Everything in the apartment had been done tastefully. It was modern, with clean lines, and the blond furniture worked in pleasant juxtaposition against the dark granite color of the walls and floors. For a moment, the voice inside my head told me it was too extravagant, too expensive, but then I recalled my settlement from Ozzie. I also remembered that I wanted Milly to have some pleasure in her surroundings. If she had come all this way to be beside me, I couldn't be stingy. I felt a weight drop off my shoulders as I gave in to the apartment. We wouldn't be here too long, I noted to myself. It was fine.

"*Bene?*" Signora Rici asked, moving her hand to indicate the apartment.

"*Moto bene,*" Milly answered, then she spoke in English. "Very beautiful. It's a dream."

"*Si,*" Signora Rici said. "Only good dreams with the sea so close."

"Oh, Kate, I could die happy after this."

Signora Rici walked me to the edge of the terrace. It was the most beautiful terrace I had ever seen. It was made of stone, for one thing, with ancient tiles on the floor. Some of the tiles had cracked and splintered, but that only made them more beautiful. A vine—bougainvillea?—climbed everywhere along the stone railing. Beyond the railing, nearly beneath us, stood a busy portion of the fishing docks. To say it was colorful would have been a gross understatement. The boats road merrily dockside, and more boats, hundreds of boats, bobbed in the quiet bay beyond the wood piers. They all pointed in the same direction, westerly, because the wind had pushed them in that direction on their anchor lines. Everywhere else on land, people hurried to transact their business, yelling and laughing, shouting about the night before or the night to come, filling the air with happiness.

"It's absolutely beautiful, Signora Rici," I said. "Thank you."

"Good. You comfortable here? Nice, nice. Now, if you like, some coffee? You can take here on the terrace."

"That would be wonderful," Milly said.

She put her arm through mine again and kissed my cheek.

"Local boy will go for groceries if you need them. Antonio. You ask and I will send you Antonio."

"Thank you," I said.

"Now coffee," Signora Rici said, and bustled away.

We roamed around the apartment like curious puppies, fumbling and stumbling over our enthusiasm. It was beautiful. Every aspect blended with the next until it achieved a precious harmony. I vowed to buy Jennifer a bouquet of flowers when I got back to the States. It was an incredibly fortunate booking.

"It's beautiful, Kate," Milly said, dropping her bag on the bed in the second bedroom. "Thank you for inviting me. It feels so good to get out of New Hampshire for a while. And to this!"

"Thank you for coming, Milly. You're a friend to do it."

"I propose we rest for an hour after coffee. It will be siesta time anyway. Then we can see what we can discover. We'll check the list of places you have."

"It's probably pointless."

"You may not find what you need, honey, but the search isn't pointless. It's far from pointless."

"I can't turn away. I have to do it. I have to see a little of it with my own eyes."

"Of course you do."

When Signora Rici reappeared with coffee, we took it at a wrought-iron table with matching chairs on the terrace. Someone had spread a paisley runner across the circular surface of the table. The sun found us, but it was sliced by the shade thrown by the building itself. By moving the table around the terrace, you could sit all day in perfect comfort. I felt myself caving slowly downward. Perhaps it was the weight of Ozzie's disappearance, or perhaps I had been traveling so much that exhaustion finally seized me. I felt wrung out. I thanked Signora Rici and picked up the coffee in both hands. I held it tightly for its warmth.

Milly carried her coffee to the edge of the terrace, then turned and asked me a question that seemed to be troubling her.

"Do you ever wonder if you could come to a place like this and never leave? Just change your life entirely in one fell swoop? This place makes me believe I could do it. It makes me think I could eat sunlight. I know, I know, I'm getting carried away. I know I'm being silly, but I find Italy appeals to me so deeply, I can hardly separate myself from it. I always thought I would love it, but didn't know I would feel this way about it. Southern Italy is known as the Mezzogiorno. Did you know that? It expresses a way of life, really. I could live here. I really could."

"You can't live here. I need you in New Hampshire."

"It's so bloody cold there," she said, coming back to sit with me after casting another look at the sea. "Months and days of little light and cold. Constant cold. We could live here in southern Italy, in the Mezzogiorno, and eat pasta every night. And drink great wine. Wouldn't that be something?"

"I'm more drawn to Ireland, honestly."

"Because you're a redhead!" she said, and laughed. "You like freckles and white skin. Give me a swarthy man anytime."

I sipped my coffee. I tried to be lighthearted, but it wasn't in me. Milly reached over and held my hand. She could read me better than anyone.

"Say what's in your heart, Kate. You've traveled a long way to be here."

"It's all mixed up."

"I know, but talk a little. I'm kidding around about swarthy men and redheads while you're on a fact-finding mission to learn about your ex-husband's death. Forgive me. I'm just excited about Italy."

"I know, sweetheart. Don't worry about that. We don't have to go about on eggshells. Ozzie is dead. His grandmother is heartbroken and his dear friend, Seamus, is devastated. I'm not sure they'll recover. He was their world, really. It most ways, they have a greater claim on his loss than I do."

She nodded. To my relief, she simply listened.

"I have a cottage overlooking the sea, too. Our cottage. I am not sure I can stand being there without him. He's in every wall and chair. He made it beautiful. It's a cottage anyone would love."

"I'm glad, honey. I'm glad you have that piece of him."

"He came down here. I don't know why. Or I should say, I know why. I just don't know how he plugged into it, so to speak. How did he know what to do or where to go? I've read enough to learn a little, but it feels overwhelming. Some people say anyone with a boat can make a difference. The immigrants are so desperate to leave Africa that they take to sea in horrible conditions. It's like the Cubans crossing over to Florida, only more tragic."

"I've heard that. We've all heard that. But most of us don't join the rescue operation. He did. Or at least you think he did, right?"

"I think so. I'm not even sure of that much. Americans tend to think of the Mediterranean as a little pond, but of course it's a sea like anywhere else. On the nights in the cottage, after I had the news about Ozzie, I read parts of *The Odyssey*. Ozzie had an old school copy with his margin notes. I think I read it to see his handwriting as much as anything else. But anyone who takes to the sea around here should read *The Odyssey* first. That story is filled with storms."

"What happens to the refugees when they arrive?"

I knew Milly was being my therapist. At least a little. I squeezed her hand to thank her.

"Well, that's quite a controversy, as I understand it. I don't know a lot about it, but I think the Italian government made it a policy to accept all immigrants who arrive here. But then, of course, how do they become part of the society . . . the social fabric? And some of them refuse to reveal their identities, because once they do, they will be required to show additional papers at the border. Many of them want to get to Germany. But I don't know, Milly. I am just repeating things I've heard. Don't take it from me. I feel more and more that I don't know anything."

"Have you had any time to catch up a little with your classes?" she asked gently. She knew that I hadn't. It was her way of nudging me to not abandon everything.

I shrugged. I couldn't bring myself to face that failing on top of everything else. I finished my coffee. I knew she was trying to talk me into a calm place, but I couldn't concentrate.

"I think I need to sleep for a while, Milly. Would that be okay?"

"Of course, honey. Are you hungry? I could go down and get us something to eat. Or we could send for Antonio."

"I can't stay awake. Go and explore, Milly. Take some time for yourself. When I wake up, we can make a few visits. Now that I'm here, the idea seems silly. The searching idea. I remember when I was little, someone stole my bike from the back porch. I was certain that I could figure out who it was and track them down. I'm afraid I'm that same naive little girl."

"Come on, let me tuck you in."

She led me back into the house, then across the central living space to a master bedroom. It was a quiet, peaceful room with a large canopy bed. She opened the window to let in air and then adjusted the curtains so that the sun would not strike me. I slipped out of my shoes and almost fell into bed.

She came to sit beside me and took my hand.

"I am so sorry about Ozzie. I know how deeply you loved . . . at least, I think I understand. And he surely loved you."

I sat up and hugged her. We stayed that way a long time.

"Lord, we're a pair," she said finally and pushed up to stand beside the bed. She wiped her tears away with the heel of her hand. "Okay, I'll be back in a while. You sleep. Rest, sweetie."

She tiptoed out of the room and closed the door after her. The noise of the fishing pier still reached me, but it sounded far away and of no concern whatsoever.

I dreamed of the Celtic Sea. I dreamed of being on the *Ferriter* with Ozzie. He shouted to me to look to starboard to see dolphins. And when I did I spotted Sylvie, Lawrence's daughter, skating on the ocean. She held a hot chocolate in her hand and sipped from it. She stared at me balefully, and sipped in rhythm to the waves that undulated beneath us. Then I heard voices far away, and I knew I was waking, knew the world had begun to intrude on my sleep, but I wasn't over my fatigue yet. I heard Mrs. Fox, the innkeeper in Dingle, tell me to make my breakfast, to find the rolls under the napkin, and then I was making love with Ozzie at Skellig Michael. *We were married,* he whispered. We *are* married, so I was a widow, I realized. I should never have questioned that. I saw, in my dreams, the shingle on the Great Blasket Island, heard the chickens clucking in the thatched roofs of the village cottages. Then Ozzie appeared again, this time riding a donkey, the donkey smiling at me with his long face and lips.

Will you come tonight, or will you come tomorrow?

"What time is it?" I asked, suddenly coming awake. I sat up and looked around. A breeze carried the ocean's scent in on its

back. In two clicks I remembered where I was. I pushed back
into the pillows. I had pulled the bedspread over my legs as I
slept and now I kicked it off. The dream clung to me. I was still
in a half sleep when I heard someone knock softly on my door.

"Kate, are you awake?" asked Milly, stepping inside the room.

It was evening, I realized. The sunlight came at an angle and
seemed tired of its work.

"I'm awake."

She came in quietly and opened the window wider.

"You slept straight through the day. I was worried you
wouldn't be able to sleep tonight if I didn't wake you."

"I'm glad you did. I was just coming awake anyway."

"You must be exhausted. Stress and emotions . . ."

"I'm okay, Milly. Honestly."

She fluffed the bedspread down by my feet. Her bracelets
jingled. Then she smiled at me.

"You must be starving," Milly said. "I found a trattoria close
by. This place, this town . . . it's beyond anything."

"Give me a minute. I'll be right out."

Milly left and closed the door gently. I checked my phone. A
thousand emails and messages from students. A note from the
department chair at Dartmouth. I didn't open the messages. I
put the phone under the pillows and went into the bathroom
to wash. For a long time, I stood looking in the mirror. I didn't
primp or do much of anything. I simply stared at myself.

This is you, I thought, my eyes meeting my eyes.

*This is who you are. This is Kate Moreton, widow, heiress,
cottage owner, cabin owner, failed professor, failed wife, daughter, friend to Milly, friend to Gottfried, fatherless, cruel, insensi-
tive, redheaded.* I didn't much care for the eyes staring back at
me. I bent my head to the sink and splashed water on my face. I
kept splashing long after there was any need for it. Then I dried
my hands and face.

I took a deep breath, straightened my clothes, and stepped back out into the living room to join Milly.

"There she is!" she said. "Oh, you look rested. I'm so glad you closed your eyes."

"I still feel sleepy as a possum."

"Are possums known for being sleepy?"

She sat at a wicker table near the center of the apartment. She had closed the terrace door against the evening chill. She worked to open a bottle of wine. She had a bowl of calamari and a few bread twists in bowls ringed around her.

A motor scooter revved outside the terrace and someone yelled a greeting in a happy tone. I smelled the gas of the scooter mixing with the fragrance of the sea. That, I realized, was the scent Ozzie had experienced in the instant of his death.

36

I knew nothing.

Worse, I had the mistaken notion that I *had* known something about the human tragedy taking place on the Mediterranean. I was a professor; I was accustomed to researching. That was my stock in trade, my single gift. I had done what most of us would do: I had Googled a thousand sites, read articles in magazines, watched YouTube broadcasts of Italian Navy vessels pulling refugees from rusted fishing trawlers. Seeing it, I believed I knew something. I was wrong. Deadly wrong. It was far graver than I was prepared for.

It took three days to confirm that I was in the wrong place. Or rather, that I needed to go to Pozzallo, Sicily, the place where the Italian Navy took refugees it saved from the sea. Our days on the mainland filled with increasing futility: each morning we went to a new office, a new official, and asked—in broken Italian, naturally—if the person could tell us anything about a ship going down. *The* Ferriter. *Ozzie Ferriter.* How painfully ignorant I was. Milly knew I was being ignorant, but she accompanied me anyway, nodded her encouragement, told me maybe the next place would provide some information. She knew better. A small seed in the center of my brain knew better, too, but I could not give it any water or light. To do so would be to make it grow and I could not permit that.

Despite everything, we had good moments: a lunch on a sailboat converted to a tiny restaurant. Fresh squid and handmade pasta and with zucchini and basil, the light from the sea crackling, the waiter charming, the scent of food mixed with the sea smells making it sharply poignant. We acknowledged the absurd incongruity: we had come to find out about a man's death in the face of vast human tragedy, and yet we sat and enjoyed a sumptuous meal, exquisitely prepared, in the luxury of a boat that never left the dockside.

Then, almost in penance, we plunged again into the Italian bureaucracy, trying to get answers to questions we could scarcely form. Who were we, anyway? By what right did we approach these various functionaries and ask—demand, really—information that they could barely unwind from the spool of human suffering they confronted daily? It was hopeless. It was also ignorantly arrogant.

"We should go home," I said when we finished our rounds on the third day. Our search had been ineffective again that day. Pointless. Almost ridiculous. My stomach felt empty and sick. We sat near the pier outside of our apartment and watched the fishermen clean their boats for the next day. I wanted to be a fisherman. For the first time, I understood Ozzie's desire to be on the sea. It was a simple life, a good life, a demanding one, but it was straightforward. I envied the fishermen, their good-humored shouts, their brightly painted boats. I could not look at them without remembering the *Ferriter*.

"Kate, we need to go to Sicily. Everyone tells us that."

"It seems like chasing a firefly."

"That may be. But we have to turn over all the stones. We need to go."

"I'm fumbling around like an idiot."

"Not like an idiot. Like a woman who wants to know what happened to the man she loved."

"I don't know why I'm putting us through this. Putting you through it. It's selfish."

"Do you know what *pot-invested* means in poker?" she asked, squinting against the late sun. Then she smiled. "Of course you don't. Why am I asking? You don't know the first thing about poker."

"Do you?"

"I used to play with my uncle Lenny during summers in Maine. He taught me with a penny jar. Pot-invested means you are playing a hand and you have to bet enough that to go forward is economically more prudent than to withdraw. You are pot-invested. You've put so much in, you might as well see the out-come."

"And I'm pot-invested about Ozzie down here?"

"Well, aren't you?"

"I guess so."

"To leave now, well, it would be folding your cards. You might as well see this to the end. Then you'll know what you know."

"Or don't know."

"Or don't know. Right. That's possible, too. Likely, even. But you've got a lot of pennies in the pot. You might as well call the bettor. See his hand."

"Look at you with your poker metaphors."

She looked at me, then laughed. We were both tired. There comes a time on any trip that the idea of returning home be-comes more inviting than to stay and go forward. Maybe we had both crossed that line. We didn't talk much as we watched the sun go down. I reached over and held her hand at the end.

We packed that night and caught an early boat to Sicily. There was nothing else we could do.

By luck, we became friendly with a young Syrian man named Karam on the crossing to Sicily. He sat down beside us on the starboard side of the *Cicogna*, a trim vessel that cut through the waves rapidly and with a minimum of side-to-side motion. Karam worked as a translator for an Italian agency, a branch of

Save the Children, that helped refugees in myriad ways. He was a young man, affable, with long hair held back in the front by a headband. He wore blousy trousers and dark brown sandals, and his phone never left his hand. His sideburns were thin, but he wore them long, like muttonchops, and they bled into a scraggly beard that covered his chin more than his cheeks. Two teeth had been knocked out or extracted on the right side of his face, and he frequently reached his hand up to cover that loss.

"Big controversy," he said in English, when he understood the purpose of our visit to Sicily. "*Mare nostrum,* right?"

I knew the phrase. It meant *Our Sea.* It derived from ancient Rome, when the citizens spoke of their love and dependence on the sea. Now it held a different meaning. It was used in the press to speak about the Italian emphasis on welcoming refugees. The conservative elements in the Italian government pushed back against it.

"I suppose it is," I said. "I don't know much about it."

"Oh, yes, big controversy. Arguing back and forth. Tick-tock. The conservatives, the right wing, you say? Yes, the right wing, they say if you let people in it encourages others to make the journey."

"And what do you say?" Milly asked.

"I say humans don't go on boats, creaky boats, unless they are desperate."

His English was excellent; he had been to school in England. He had been moving, he said, since he was eight years old, first with his father, then with a distant uncle. His father had died of pleurisy. His mother had been killed in a motorbike crash in Syria. He was rootless, he said, a citizen of the world, not of one country.

We bought him coffee and an array of pastries. We asked him to tell us everything he could. And he did. He had a great deal to say. He talked about injustice, about the cruelty of the Syrian government to its own people, about the poverty in Eritrea and

Mali, African nations that had become more religiously conservative in the past decade. He talked about the financial cost for each refugee, how many of them had paid a human transporter—he did not call them smugglers—roughly two thousand dollars for passage. He saw no solution nor any feasible end to the migration.

"People are like plants," he concluded, drinking his coffee, "they go toward light, not to darkness."

"Could you take us to a center?" I asked. "Would you do that for us?"

He nodded. It was easy, he seemed to imply, but probably useless.

"I'm sorry about your man, your husband," he said. "There are some who help. Most, most people, they look away. They worry about their own share of sunlight. They don't care if others wither as long as they prosper. Your man did not do that."

"No, I guess he didn't."

"That means he had a good heart. If you find nothing else here about him, you at least found that."

Milly engaged him after that. They talked about art and about music and I felt myself drifting toward sleep. I put my head against the railing and closed my eyes. I concentrated on smelling the sea, hearing the gulls, letting them transport me back to the *Ferriter*, to the night when Ozzie told me to strip and let the dolphins see me. I thought about our bed, warm and safe on the dock, and the stars everywhere, small white lights, and the north-flowing current that had promised to keep us away from land forever.

CIE in Italian stands for *centro di identificazione ed espulsione*.

CDA stands for *center for first assistance*.

CARA stands for *identification centers for immigrants without documents*, asking for political refugee status.

Like any institution, like an army, like a hospital, like a police force, the refugee crisis created its own vocabulary with a thousand acronyms. Several times as Karam spoke to us after we had landed, I glanced at Milly to see if she understood his explanation. It was clear from her expression that she was as confused as I was. We followed him, trying to piece things together. It felt like something that would take a long time to understand. Despair grew in me with every mile we crossed.

We stopped at a grocery store and loaded our taxi with water bottles. As many as it could carry, Karam told us. We paid. Afterward, we went to the camp at Pian del Lago, Caltanissetta, a tent city that had been constructed under a motorway. It had been closed and reopened more times than Karam could count. It had no water. Refugees set up tents on wooden pallets, but there were no sanitation facilities and no sense of hope. The odor was horrible. The police, Karam said, chased people off, or offered to relocate them, but there was nowhere to put them. They stayed, sometimes for as long as a year, many of them drifting in and out as their circumstances changed. Many of them waited for papers so that they could continue to Naples or Palermo.

"The water," Karam said, climbing out of the taxi into the dense heat, "will help them to trust you."

What had we expected? How dare we dip our toe into such a pool of human suffering and not be prepared to help to our last breath? I felt pampered and spoiled, a wealthy American dabbling with good works. Ozzie had gotten it right: this was worth dying for.

Children found us first. They came shyly, then with more confidence once they saw the water. Milly squatted and held out bottles to the smallest of the group. The children came forward, smiling, unsure, and I squatted beside her and did what I could. A few older men appeared behind the children and watched, both to protect and to ensure that children did not receive something that might be squandered in their inexperience. Karam had warned me that the refugees would be careful not to say too much if I asked them directly about Ozzie, or about anything, really. A misspoken word could have devastating effects on their chances of survival. They were cautious and wary, children and men alike, and when Karam called out in as many languages as he knew if anyone had heard or known of a boat called the *Ferriter,* the men pretended not to hear. They came forward for water instead.

When we had handed out all the water, we followed Karam into the heart of the camp. The children followed us in a listless, bored way. They were accustomed to European visitors, people who arrived, took photos, made short television videos, then left. From their side of things, that's all we were.

Karam spent most of our visit on his phone, only narrating occasionally.

"The population changes so quickly that it's hard to keep track of anything," he said, scarcely looking away from his phone screen. "New waves of people come almost every week. Some go away. Many die. Don't hope. You should never hope here."

"Don't say that," Milly said, her eyes taking everything in. "Don't say there's no hope."

Karam shrugged. It was a worldly shrug, suggesting we would learn.

We found nothing. Or, rather, we found heartache and despair and hundreds of people milling about. A few children played soccer on one section of the compound, a portion of a chain-link fence forming a goal. We asked if anyone knew anything about a man named Ozzie, or even the *Ferriter,* but we got nothing in return. It was not productive. The distance between us—two westerners asking questions through an interpreter—was too great. Karam, for his part, did not dig. He accepted whatever anyone told him and repeated the replies to us without inflection. He did not seem interested in our search. He showed no initiative or curiosity. Maybe, I considered, he found the centers depressing and a reminder of a fate he had escaped by sheer luck. The scale of the migration, the scope of what Ozzie had confronted, coated me like a mist.

We dropped Karam off in the center of Pozzallo in the late afternoon. He made it understood by his hesitation to leave us that he expected a gratuity. I gave him some money. He pretended surprise. Then he kissed our cheeks and went away, his phone like a dull light leading him away.

"Who guides souls into the underworld?" Milly asked, watching him depart. "That's our Karam."

"I don't remember."

"I guess we should get a room. Do you want something to eat?"

We stood in the middle of a plaza with people passing by, scooters buzzing on their way. Over there, in the camp, life went on as a desperate struggle. Here, in the town proper, daily commerce continued on as if nothing had changed or would change. I felt light-headed and furious and a thousand other emotions I couldn't name.

"I couldn't eat. Not right now."

Milly stepped in front of me and put her hands on my shoulders. She looked me directly in my eyes. In fact, she chased my eyes with hers until I could not look away. When she spoke, she moved her forehead until it nearly touched mine.

"We need to go home now, Kate. Soon."

"If I leave, then he really is dead."

"I know. It's not good, but you can't keep visiting detention centers forever."

"I need some word of him. Someone to say they saw him and they knew him."

"I understand."

"Is everyone around me thinking I am cracking up?"

"No, Kate. It's not like that. You're letting go. It takes time."

"I let him go before."

She didn't say anything to that. She couldn't. That was the truth.

"This searching is only going to make you sadder."

"Maybe I deserve to be sad."

"No one deserves to be sad, Kate. He came with a boat. He wasn't in these camps. Maybe the Italian Navy knows more about it than these people. You can't ask more of these people. You can't accomplish anything right now. Even if you found out something about his death, about the boat . . . where would it lead you? I'm sorry, sweetie, I'm looking out for you. If you want to come back here and work on the behalf of these people, then, yes, by all means. I'll give you a send-off party. But that's not you right now. Not now. You're grieving, sweetheart. You lost the love of your life. And all the king's men, and all the king's horses . . ."

I felt myself breaking. She was right, I knew, but I couldn't catch my breath to tell her so. In the middle of the plaza, with life all around us, I felt myself divided. I wanted to go with Karam, to be led by the soft light of his phone, to go into the underworld where I would pass a few coins to the ferryman and cross the River Styx to search for Ozzie, my Ozzie, the man whom I had cast away without knowing what I possessed.

37

Lawrence sent me tulips when I returned. I put them in a vase, then put them on the porch to let the ice have them. I watched each morning as they grew more and more pale, the sunlight and frost turning them into shadowy bells. I decided I did not speak Lawrence. I decided I was better off alone.

I turned into a monk. Or whatever the female equivalent of a monk might be. A nun. I woke each morning at five and did yoga sun salutations in front of the wood stove. I bent and twisted and fasted. Then, around seven, I drove the short commute to Dartmouth and camped in my office, meeting with students, apologizing, putting my contacts there back in order. Dean Fitzgibbons, my dean, came to see me on a dull winter afternoon. Classes had almost finished for the semester, and when he came in, he shrugged out of a wonderful vicuna jacket. He was a bit of a dandy. Everyone commented on it. The vicuna coat was his trademark. He was fifty and slender, with a good head of John F. Kennedy hair. He swept it all back and kept it there. He was a handsome man, impeccably dressed, and always well-mannered.

"You're back," he said, sitting in the chair usually reserved for my students. He did not bother to be asked to sit.

"I'm back."

"You were gone a long time, Kate. Maybe a third left of the semester."

"I know it. And I apologize. I'm trying to make it up to the students now."

He nodded. He smiled.

"It's kind of a sticky situation. We've had complaints. Students pay a good amount of money for classes. For your class."

"I understand."

"Dartmouth has standards."

It was my turn to nod. Clearly, the question on the table was whether I met that standard.

I said what I could.

"It won't happen again. I promise you that."

"Is that a promise you can keep?"

"I believe it is."

He crossed his legs slowly. Being around him was like being near a fine automobile, oiled and primed, never rushed.

"Students like your classes. That's not an issue. If they didn't, I suppose we wouldn't be having this conversation. It's this last semester that is concerning."

"I lost my way a little."

I decided on the spot not to tell him why or how I had lost my way. Maybe he knew, maybe he didn't. I couldn't share that with him, although perhaps he expected me to.

He nodded. He seemed comfortable in the chair. He seemed to need to sit for a moment. I knew the various deans around campus kept up a relentless schedule. We could all use a minute to catch our breath at this time of year.

"I had an office in this building when I first came here," he said, looking at my office as if checking its value on the real estate market. "It's a bit nostalgic to be back, especially at this time of year."

"I can imagine."

"I love the solstice. All the darkness contrasted against the lighted buildings. And everyone is ready to go home, but there is something wonderful about being here, too. It's poignant. I was young here."

"I like it, too. The solstice."

He sighed. He had excellent hair.

"You have a strong start to your career, Kate. Don't let this happen again, okay?"

"I won't."

He started to rise.

"What's that picture?" he asked, pointing with his chin at a photograph I had blown up. It was a picture of the cottage in sunlight, the grass rolling in the wind toward it.

"It's a cottage in Ireland."

"Yours?"

I nodded. I still couldn't trust myself to talk about it.

"Pretty place."

"It's heaven."

He left shortly afterward. I fixed myself tea from an electric teapot. I sat with a cup of green tea and turned down the lights. Christmas was here. Dean Fitzgibbons was correct: the season stirred up all sort of emotions. I turned and looked for a long time at the cottage.

Will you come today, or will you come tomorrow?

I was still sitting in the near darkness when our department assistant came to my office door with a FedEx package.

"Knock knock," she said. "This just came for you."

Her name was Lily. She was short and plump and had read everything in the world. She knitted constantly and had been married to Thomas, her man, since high school. He was also short and plump. They were the happiest couple I knew.

"What is it?"

"I don't know. Maybe it's a Christmas present."

She smiled and left. I took out a penknife from my desk drawer and opened the package. I knew by the second cut what it was. A small note from Edna Barrow slipped out of the package and fluttered onto my lap.

> *Dear, Kate:*
> *Here is a cover of your beautiful, beautiful book.*
> *Hold it and enjoy it. More to come.*
> *Edna*

The cover portrayed a chicken sitting on the roof of a thatched cottage, and in the eye of the chicken was a map of the Blasket Islands. Underneath it was my name. Two blurbs, both from historians I admired, appeared on the back. The logo from Broadman Publishing. I gazed at the cover until my tea was cold and flavorless. A book. My book. I held it against my chest and watched the darkness move across the campus. Little white lights.

"Congratulations," Dr. Kaufman said when I showed her the book cover the next day. "That's quite an accomplishment."

"It feels good."

"You should be proud."

"I am. I think I am. I can't help feeling it's part of my bargain with Ozzie. For Ozzie. That I gave up Ozzie to have this. This inanimate thing."

"That seems like a harsh way to look at it. It's not either-or, is it?"

It was midday. The birds seemed to be on lunch break. I didn't know what I felt, honestly. That was why I kept my appointment to see Dr. Kaufman. Sometimes it helped. Sometimes it cleared my mind.

"I was so unforgiving. So unyielding. It had to be my way or no way."

She looked at me. She didn't add anything to the conversation.

"I suppose I should stop talking about him, shouldn't I?"

"Talk about what you need to talk about, Kate. I don't have a lot of *shoulds* in this office."

"I just can't picture how I am going to go forward with a man. With any man. Not for a long time, anyway. Ozzie took that away from me."

"Sometimes, Kate, you talk as if other people were in charge of your life."

"And that's a mistake?"

"It's simply not accurate. For better or worse, we're all in charge of our own lives."

I nodded. I knew what she said was true, but I couldn't digest it for the moment. Didn't want to digest it. It was easier to imagine I was buffeted by winds I didn't create. I took a deep breath and continued.

"My teaching is back on track. That's one positive to come out of this situation. I was able to sort that out. The students forgave me and so did the administration. That's on the plus side. On the negative side, Nora, Gran, had a fall in her greenhouse. She's in hospital now. She's Ireland to me."

"I'm sorry to hear that. I hope she has a speedy recovery."

I wanted the birds to reappear, but they didn't.

"Does anyone get true clarity about anything, doctor?" I asked eventually. "I've always wondered."

"How do you mean?"

"Do we ever know exactly what we want? Or even what we need? Can we ever see our lives for what they are?"

"What do you think?"

"I don't know. When I was with Ozzie, he was everything. Then I let him go. He was the same person at both ends of that spectrum. I don't understand it. Everything seems to move and change and I'm not sure how we're supposed to be a fixed point."

"Who says you have to be a fixed point?"

"I do. I guess I do. Back in the day, people didn't have so many options. You married someone nearby and you built a house on your parents' property and you made the best life you could. Now you can go anywhere. You can go to Ireland or southern Italy. You can meet a thousand people. Men, women, it doesn't matter. It almost feels as if it's too much. Expecting to settle on one life, one person, is foolish."

"That's a cynical view."

"I'm not sure it's my view at all. Not at all. But it's part of my view. It's the truth of modern life. You can go online and swipe left and right over someone's picture as if you're at a grocery store and people are set out on shelves. You can marry someone a world away. I don't know if such infinite choice makes us happier."

I knew she wouldn't say anything to that little treatise. She didn't.

I continued.

"I had someone. And I let him go. I didn't see him for what he was. That's what pains me. That's the mistake I made."

"Often mistakes don't feel like mistakes as we make them."

"I know. I thought I was being wise and mature. Now I don't know. Now I think I should have tried harder."

She smiled softly. Our time was over. She didn't have to tell me. I stood and I swung into my coat.

"I put up a bird feeder," I told her. "It turns out I like watching them."

"They never disappoint."

"Do you use millet?"

"Just sunflower seeds. If you use millet, you'll have a pile of it by spring."

"And suet?"

"Yes, suet is essential. You'll get a better variety of birds. Woodpeckers especially."

I looked her in the eye.

"I think I'm finished with these sessions, Dr. Kaufman."

"Are you sure?"

I nodded.

"I think so, too," she said. "If you think so, I think so, too."

38

Two days after Christmas, I received a call from a man who introduced himself as Jackson Sawton. He had a rough, raspy voice. I nearly hung up on him until he mentioned that he was the caretaker for a cabin in Canada that belonged in Ozzie's holdings. His mention of the cabin rang a bell for me, but I couldn't place it at first. I was distracted and thought perhaps he had called to sell me something. We had one of those odd, forced conversations in which neither one of us was certain he or she was speaking to the right person. But then we teased it out.

"Up here in Ontario," he said, his voice evincing a French-Canadian lilt. "You know the place?"

"Cabin?"

I couldn't pin down what he meant. Not at first.

"You are Miss Moretown, aren't you?"

"Moreton."

He had heavy breath on the phone.

"The bank says your number is the one to call. I'm calling about some people living in there."

"Was this the cabin owned by Ozzie Ferriter?" I asked, finally nailing it down.

"That's right. That's the one."

"And what were you saying about it? You're the caretaker?"

"I am. Some people are living in it and they look to be planning to stay a while. I wanted to know if they had your okay to do that."

"What kind of people?"

"Nice people. But I received no notice of anything, so I wanted to make sure."

"Well, let me look into it, please. I'll get back to you. Thank you for calling. Sorry about the misunderstanding at the beginning."

"She'll be apples," he said.

I didn't know the phrase, but I liked it.

I took down his number and his address. I sent Nora a message and she sent one back saying the cabin belonged to Ozzie and that, if I didn't mind, it would be worthwhile to set eyes on the place, regardless. She didn't know much about it. I replied that I would go and take a look. I was happy to do it. It got me out of town for New Year's and afforded me an excuse to miss any additional holiday obligations. The holidays felt empty for me. I had no plans to blow noisemakers and celebrate the New Year.

It felt cleansing to travel north. I didn't want easy and warm days, days with too much food and cheer. I wanted something sharper and more challenging, and when Jackson Sawton's call came, it gave me a task, a simple, verifiable task. The cabin, once I fully understood the connection, was part of Ozzie's legacy to me. He had mentioned it a few times in an off-handed way. So had the attorney, Robert Smith, when we discussed Ozzie's holdings. I had glanced at the location once on a Google map, but that was about all. It was located almost due north from Hanover, and from what my papers said, it was on a lake nearly inaccessible except by boat. Deep in Ontario. During winter months, you could snowmobile there, or take a dog team, or helicopter in, but you couldn't drive.

I wrote back to Jackson Sawton at his number and said I was arriving in three days.

It took me four days. I felt lazy and sleepy. I drove eight hours a day, but on the third day I got caught in a winter storm and I had to lay over in a motel called The Buck Rack. It was a comical place, with vibrating beds still available for fifty cents, and a motel mini bar that included Budweiser and Labatt. I liked it. I ate breakfast in a diner the next morning and called Mr. Sawton. He answered on top of a whining saw or drill, and he only turned off the machine when he realized it was me.

He gave me directions to his shop.

But my phone gave me spotty coordinates, and I had to stop twice to ask if I had the right road. I did manage to stay on route each time, but the stops became more primitive. Pines surrounded me. I drove on a white road through a white land and only logging trucks kept me company.

Mr. Sawton's shop was located in a Quonset hut on the outskirts of a small settlement. An old sign above the door said Sawton's Auto. The sign hadn't been painted in decades. Jackson Sawton hadn't been painted in decades, either. He wore a Carhartt mechanic's jumpsuit, bronze-colored, over a heavy navy sweatshirt. He was tall and thick, his hands as heavy as branches when he took mine in his. He hadn't shaved, and his beard grew pepper and frost in the bristles. He wore a red plaid hat, a cliché of a backwoodsman, with ear flaps that folded halfway down. The ear flaps gave him the appearance of a dog, its ears cocked to listen.

"*Bien venue,*" he said, speaking a patois of French and English. "Glad you came to see."

He brought me into the shop and told me to sit. He had a few chairs arranged next to an enormous Glenwood stove. The stove burned like a sun. A boy of about eighteen sat in one of the chairs. He stood when I came near. He backed away as if I brought contagion.

"That's Helmet," Jackson Sawton said. "Odd jobber around here. He's going to run you up to the cabin. Not far. He's got a spanking new machine."

"Okay," I said, not sure how I felt about it, but not sure of much at the moment.

"That's Hel-met," Jackson clarified, perhaps seeing my trepidation. "Not German like that. Helmet. It's a nickname. Everyone calls him Helmet, guess he's always driving one thing or another and is always wearing a helmet."

"Of course. That makes sense."

"Hunters reported it back in the fall," Jackson said, drawing a handkerchief out of a back pocket and wiping his fingers with it. "The cabin, I mean. The occupants. Regular little tribe moved in. I went up to see them, but they said they had permission. We have a Mountie named Evans who rode out to see them, too, but he didn't evict them. They made a case for belonging."

"How do they live?"

"Oh," he said, sitting for a minute in one of the chairs. He waved to another chair for me to sit. Helmet kept his distance. "Oh, they do okay. Hunt, I suppose. And they had a bunch of supplies brought in. Two or three times, actually. Course, if you know what you're doing, it's a nice little cabin. You can hole up there in the winter and not need a thing. They just go pogey."

"What's pogey?"

"It's what we call relief. A government check. A lot of the fishermen over to PEI and Nova Scotia, they go pogey off-season. It's a way of life, isn't that right, Helmet?"

Helmet nodded.

"Keeps money flowing. Primes the pump. As I say, Helmet will run you up. You couldn't have a better guide. He lives on his machine most of the winter. It's heated and everything else. It's a dandy."

"How far is it?"

"What? Twelve miles, Helmet?"

Helmet held his hand out in front of him and shook it softly as if putting a spell on us. More or less, he meant. Approximately.

They had a snowsuit for me to wear, borrowed from a woman

slightly larger than I was. Snow boots and my own helmet. I looked ridiculous when I was finished, but I felt warmer. I stood beside the wood stove while Helmet went outside to warm up his machine.

"He's a good boy," Jackson said to me in a low voice. "No worries about that boy, I give you my word. Real quiet, though."

"I wasn't worried."

He nodded. Maybe, I thought, a woman heading off into the woods with a man she didn't know should worry. Maybe so.

Helmet buzzed his horn.

"That's the signal he's ready to go. He'll have you out and back in no time. You'll like the ride. And the setting where the cabin is, well, it's some kind of pretty."

"I'm glad to hear that."

"My advice is to just check in. Don't be too definite. You're the owner of the property, so you can have them out if you want them out. You get Mountie Evans to take care of that, although it's hard to evict people in winter in Canada."

Helmet buzzed again.

I felt like an astronaut in a space suit. I put on the helmet and then swung up behind Helmet. With another sort of man, it might have felt slightly intimate to reach around him and hold his waist, but Helmet seemed almost part of the machine. I might have been a backpack filled with canned beans for all he cared.

I don't know what I expected, but I didn't expect the beauty that waited for me. We took a trail that ran parallel to the last of the road, then veered off to the left and entered true forest. I tried to keep track of directions—did we go west or north?— but I quickly gave that up. It was too much. Instead, I looked over Helmet's shoulder and watched the trail spin below us. The machine's seat was heated, and my body felt warm and pleasant. Helmet drove with authority; he did not gun the engine to show off, but he also kept the machine moving briskly along the trails. We saw no one. The sun came out from the behind the clouds from time to time, but mostly the day remained silver and cold, one of the shortest days of the year.

We came across a small rise overlooking a lake, and Helmet stopped and pointed. I saw the cabin immediately. A stalk of smoke bloomed from the chimney. A wide porch, covered with snow and an enormous stack of wood, circled the building. It was not a log cabin, but something made of brown wood and a black roof. Someone had already lighted the evening lamps. It was a postcard cabin. The lake below it ran for hundreds of meters in either direction.

Helmet nodded. I nodded back. He gave the machine gas and we glided down the hillside and onto the lake. The ice stretched and yawned beneath us, but he didn't hesitate. He brought the machine expertly up and off the lake and stopped near the shore-line, a short walk remaining up to the cabin.

"I'll only be a minute," I said. "I'll keep it short."

He nodded. He turned off the engine. The silence that took the place of the engine sound could not have been deeper.

I removed my helmet and felt the cold press on my ears and throat. It was the farthest point north, I realized, that I had ever visited. Jack London knew this kind of cold, I couldn't help remembering. The English professor in me tied the experience to a book.

My boots made high, squeaking sounds as I crossed the short dooryard to the cabin. The metal roof had guided the snow straight off the downward eave and into a large pile, like a breast-work, that circled the house below the porch. Someone had cut a notch into it as a path to the porch. A pair of withered pumpkins stood on either side of the notch, tiny lampposts that had decayed and folded down in the snow. Two red candles remained embedded in the white frost.

I called out, *Halloooo,* then knocked on the door. I couldn't know the protocol of knocking on a remote cabin door in Canada, although I assumed they had heard the snowmobile arriving.

No one answered. I knocked louder.

"Come in," a voice called.

I pushed open the door and stepped inside. Five children sat around a table in the center of the cabin. They were Syrians, or refugees. I knew that at a glance. They were the brothers and sisters, the cousins and relatives of the children I had given water to in Sicily. They had been coloring large sheets of paper while drinking hot chocolate. Kerosene lamps illuminated the interior. A bright wood stove burned in the corner. It was warm and beautiful inside. The children's eyes were soft and curious, a shade or two nearer to fear caused by my arrival than children should be.

"We were passing by," I said, feeling my way, aware that by standing in the doorway I was letting the heat out. "We thought we'd look in."

The children did not say anything. Occasionally they glanced at one another to get a reading. My entrance had turned them into conspirators.

"What are your names?" I asked, closing the door softly. "May I sit down for a moment?"

The children moved to the side, shoving together like the shuttle of a loom, although a chair stood positioned at the head of the table where I could sit. The children seemed timid as deer. Two of them had severed arms, one chopped above the right elbow, the other missing his entire left arm; a girl, the smallest, had a horrible burn across her chin and neck. They were drinking hot chocolate, that was all. It was a long winter night. The oldest—a girl of about ten—pushed away from the table at the other end and nodded her head in greeting. As the oldest, she accepted her responsibility.

"I am Sana," she said.

I smiled. I felt my body beginning to cave down. There was a connection here to Ozzie, but I couldn't identify it. I couldn't name it. I put my hand on the back of a chair and sat for a moment. I looked around. I couldn't make anything clear in my head. I couldn't take anything in. Something about the picture, the setting, struck me as familiar.

"I can only stay a moment," I said, hardly able to speak. "I am with a boy named Helmet. He's waiting outside."

It was a stupid, blathering comment, but it was all I could think to say. Sana nodded. She had no idea what I was doing there, what I wanted, but she kept her eyes steadily on me. She had a kind, beautiful face. The other children watched me. They had stopped coloring.

"Who owns this cabin, Sana?" I whispered.

"We do," she said.

"You don't stay here alone, though, do you?"

She shook her head. She did not plan to tell me a thing if she could help it.

"Who stays with you?"

"Our friend," she said. "Elma. She's older."

I had made them profoundly uncomfortable. They had answered enough questions, I was sure, to last them five lifetimes. A wind blew against the cabin and the wood stove flickered brighter. I sensed if I made a sudden movement to snatch at any of them, they would have run off like water. I had never been in the presence of children so obviously wounded.

"Who is Elma?" I asked carefully. "Is she here now?"

She didn't answer. She didn't say yes or no. She would not volunteer unnecessary information, I realized. These children had learned the safety in silence.

"She couldn't have gone far," I said gently. "Elma, I mean. It's too cold, and I didn't see any tracks outside. She didn't go across the lake, I don't think. We would have run into her. Where are you from?"

That caused them to look at each other rapidly. We stood at an impasse. She wanted me gone. She wanted her safety. She did not trust strangers easily. Why would she trust a stranger with her business? Before anyone answered, a woman stepped out from what I took to be a bedroom at the rear of the cabin. She was a heavy woman, about sixty, who wore a red plaid shirt loosened around her belt line. Her hair was gray; she wore it in a bun at the back of her skull. I noticed a bright, silver crucifix around her neck.

She appeared harsh and disgruntled, but when I looked closer, I realized she had been sleeping. Her eyes were red and misty, as if she were slightly ill or suffering from allergies. Despite that, she studied me closely. Then she smiled. She had a wonderful smile, an Irish smile. It changed everything it touched.

"You're Kate, aren't you?" she asked, nodding at the correctness of her surmise. "You're his Kate. You're exactly as he described you."

I nodded in return. But I hardly knew what I had just agreed to.

She walked forward and almost picked me up from the chair. She folded me in her arms. Over her shoulder, I saw the children watching us. They looked stunned, but they had also begun to smile. When I began to stiffen and tried to pull away, she only hugged me tighter.

"I knew some day you would show up here. Ozzie said as much. He predicted it. Oh, you're welcome as anything, Kate. Welcome as the springtime flowers in dear old Donegal, am I right? Isn't that the song? This is Ozzie's doing. We miss him so, of course. This was his plan, you know? He likely imagined it a different way, but he knew he wanted us to meet, I suspect."

She let me go. She had begun to stare at me with the sort of attention one has when one is in on a secret that the other must guess to understand. I tried to put the pieces together, but they didn't fit easily. Who in the world was this woman? And how did these children factor in? I couldn't take it all in.

"Help me understand," I said, putting my hands out as if

calming a pillow into place. "I don't . . . Who are you? To Ozzie,
I mean? Who are these children?"

"Oh, yes, you must be tops and tails. Yes, of course you are.
My name is Elma McCoin, Kate. I'm with Catholic Charities
from Ireland. I'm a sister, a nun. These are children that Ozzie
collected from the camps and boats. They're orphans. He got
them to us and we brought them here. It's a step along the way
for them. It's a long story, as I'm sure you can imagine."

I sat and put my hands over my face. I couldn't think, couldn't
process everything that had happened. Elma turned to Sana and
asked her to put on the tea kettle. She spoke to one of the boys
and asked him to go out and invite Helmet inside. Elma scooted
the children down the bench and sat and took my hand.

"The Lord is good," she said. "Children, remember this day.
Today you are seeing a miracle. Kate is here and she is the wife
of our benefactor, Ozzie Ferriter. We pray for him every night,
Kate. He's first in our prayers. The children owe their lives to
him."

"I don't understand," I said, then broke.

I began to weep into my hands. It was far too much to absorb.
As I cried, I heard the door open and Helmet came in, led by
one of the boys.

"You're in time for dinner if you wish to eat with us," Elma
said, and placed her hand on my shoulder. "We eat simple food,
but it's ample. Young man, you're welcome, too. We have lentil
soup and bread. We're warming it now."

Then she bent close to my ear and whispered.

"I'm sure you have many questions, Kate. Spend the night,
why don't you, and see what Ozzie has made possible in this
world. These are his children, when everything is said and done.
He has their lives in his palm. We thought we had lost him, but
you see he is returned to us through you. Nothing is lost to God."

39

I accepted the lentil soup and I accepted the invitation to stay the night. Helmet refused, but told me he would pick me up at noon the next day. After dinner, by lantern light, Elma read to the children in English. I noted that she did not preach to them or force them to say grace. They were Muslim children, I gathered, and although she spoke of God often, she had the wisdom and respect to refrain from proselytizing for Jesus. She read them *The Wind in the Willows*, the same book Donald and his wife, Lucy, had given to their daughter on her seventeenth birthday years ago in Dublin. Elma was an excellent reader, as many Irish are, and she held the children mesmerized with her voice. They clustered around her as she sat in the lone easy chair by the wood stove. I sat on the outside circle, not quite sure of my place. Besides, I could not recover from the cabin being my first real link to Ozzie's experience in Italy. It did not seem real, and therefore, nothing in that small cabin felt solid.

By eight thirty, the children were in their pajamas. I helped where I could, but the children were not ready to accept me fully and I did not push it. They were darling; they clearly loved and depended on Elma. They slept in bunk beds in two back rooms. It was fiercely cold away from the wood stove, but they had enormous down comforters on their beds, and they climbed in and burrowed down until only the tops of their heads remained visible.

"Good night, my little sled dogs," Elma said as she made the rounds and kissed them good night. "Sleep deep in the blankets."

"Good night, Elma," they called. "Good night."

Before we returned to the sitting room, Sana spoke to me.

"Are you really his wife?" she asked at the last moment.

She asked that with her eyes fixed on me.

"I am by law. But we have not seen each other for some years, I'm sorry to say."

She seemed to have no opinion about that. She squirmed deeper in the covers until only her eyes remained.

I put my hand softly on her hair and brushed it back. She did not pull away.

"Would you care for a drop of good Irish whiskey?" Elma asked when I returned to the wood stove. "I don't usually indulge, but this is a special occasion. And besides, my social life here revolves around the children. It's nice to have an adult to speak with."

"I'd love a small one."

She poured us two glasses. One of the children made a sound of slight distress, and she stopped mid-pour and went to check on him. She returned in a moment.

"Our resident bed wetter," she whispered. "He always worries before he falls asleep. Abdul Ghafaar, Servant of the Forgiver. Poor lamb."

"I am surprised he is the only one," I whispered back.

"Oh, there are others. Just not as consistent as Abdul. He's the little lad with the severed arm."

She handed me a glass of whiskey. I touched her glass with mine. Before she sat, she put more wood on the fire. The cabin was warm and tidy. I admired the way she handled the children. There was no question of her love and caring for them. When she resumed her seat, I told her so.

"Well, thank you. They are dear children caught in troubles not of their own making. Each has a story. Horrible, horrible stories. You'll forgive me if I don't go into detail about them. Their injuries are their own. Someday they may want to tell of their experiences, but we in our religious order believe as much as possible that their ordeals are not for our fund-raising or lurid interest. Does that make sense, Kate? It's a line we draw. A sister I know calls it poverty porn. You know, the child with the swollen belly on the telly? That kind of thing."

"I understand."

"Sorry to be dogmatic."

"I'd like to hear more about the children. And about Ozzie."

She sipped her whiskey. I did, too. It burned all the way down to my toes.

"It's a long story, Kate, but in the end, he found a way to remove some of the children from the worst of it. Some of the children are held for ransom and exploited that way. Some are held and raped. Very few make it through in one piece, physically or emotionally. I'm sure you know the broad outlines. It's on the news."

I nodded. I sat up straighter.

"He used his boat to linger around the edges of what occurred on the sea. I don't know all of it, but one day he showed up with two children in tow. We took them in, pending authorization . . . all of that official nonsense. He showed up two days later with four more. Our Reverend Mother had a long talk with him and told him she could not take any additional children without approval from the government. But which government? That was the question. About a week later, Ozzie showed up with a half dozen more."

"Didn't anyone miss the children?"

"Certainly. But not all. Many of them had no parents, or the parents were being held, or remained back in their mother country. These children are messages in a bottle, that's all. The parents send them off because there is no hope for them where they are. The situation . . . oh, what's the sense of trying to frame it into a sensible explanation? It's an immense human tragedy. That's the long and short of it. Ozzie cut through that, and the Reverend Mother assisted him up to a point. He made enemies, but he was a capable seaman and military man. We didn't ask too many questions on our side of the equation."

I felt the whiskey in my bones. I took a large sip. Elma poured us each a tad more, then corked the bottle and put it on a high shelf above the door to the bedrooms. She listened to the back rooms to make sure the children had settled.

"They always fall right off," she said softly when she returned. "It's later in the night when the memories get them. Bad dreams. Don't be alarmed if you hear them crying."

"Was Ozzie allowed to take the children? I don't think I quite understand."

"No, no, he wasn't allowed to do a thing. There are no rules in that kind of human theater. But these children . . . they had no one else. He stepped in and removed them from whatever danger confronted them. He worked with a small squad of men, from what I understand. It was a guerilla action, so to speak, but only to remove the children. He made enemies and the Italian government was not happy with his involvement. We heard a buzz about it, but we ignored it to the extent we could. He didn't explain his tactics to us and we didn't ask. It was obvious the children required care."

"How did they come to the cabin? Why here? This seems so far away."

"There have been reprisals. The children represent a loss of money. The girls might be groomed for sex work. For that matter, the boys, too. It's a horrible predicament. Once we had the children in our possession, we removed them to safe houses. Ozzie gave us permission to use this cabin. We have established a network here in Canada that is quite extensive. Sometimes new children arrive, sometimes the children here move on. And the quiet . . . living here they have routine and quiet. It does them great good, believe me."

"And the *Ferriter*? How did the *Ferriter* go down?"

She shrugged and sipped her whiskey.

"A boat on the sea. It happens. Maybe it was sabotaged. We don't know. Fortunately, he didn't have children with him at the time. That was his last report, anyway. He had radioed in shortly before he went down. Then he went silent and the worst was feared, as they say."

"I still can't put it all together."

"It's a lot. Let it settle on you. That's what we tell the children. Don't resist it, but don't let it become too comfortable a garment to wear, either. Everything takes time. Time is the proper bandage for most things."

At her prompting, I told her about my trip to Sicily and the detention camps. I told her about the taxi full of water bottles and Karam and about the cottage. She listened to everything, nodding when my information matched something she knew. Watching her, drinking now and then the burning dregs of whiskey, I realized she represented the missing parts of Ozzie that I did not know. I saw him through her eyes; I saw him through the children's eyes.

"He was a brave man and true," she said when I finished. "While others talk and fill up the air with their voices, he stepped in and took action. I'm sorry for your loss, Kate, but I'm even sadder for the loss that these children, and others like them, just experienced with his disappearance. I told my fellow sisters that in heaven Ozzie would be the man to help you step from the boat to face St. Peter. He has the sea inside of him. He had a great heart, you know?"

I nodded. I couldn't speak.

She reached over and took my hand.

"He loved you, Kate. He talked of you often. He regretted his behavior with you. He regretted that he couldn't be a better husband. He tried. He did. I believe that. What do they say? A woman marries a man thinking he will change to fit her. And a man marries a woman thinking she will never change. Both are foolhardy. There was more to Ozzie than you might have seen, and likely more to you than he saw. You were young. That's a condition you can't help. Take some comfort in knowing you loved a good man. These children pray for him. We'll pray for you, too, now that we know you."

A few moments later, she rose and tiptoed to the door leading to the bedroom. She listened to the children's sleep. I turned and faced the wood stove. Flames tore at the logs and consumed them. It was warm inside and cold outdoors.

Snow and ice. Helmet's quilted jacket and the sound of the snow-mobile. The children waving from where they played king-of-the-hill on the mounded snow dumped around the cabin by the metal roof. Sana hugging me. Elma waving and promising to keep me in her prayers. Then Sawton's Auto, a brief explanation, *It was fine, it was fine, no problem, the people are welcome to stay there as long as they like. Do what you can to assist them, Mr. Sawton,* I said. My body shivering at the cold, at the new understanding of where Ozzie had been, what he had accomplished.

I drove afterward in a trance. I did not turn on the radio. Window down to feel the cold. To feel it burn me. Sleep in a Vermont rest stop, fitful and harsh, my body unable to get warm. Trucks pulling in, pulling out. A brief snow squall at dawn and the snow running like live things under my tires. The *Ferriter* in the mist of snow somewhere, diving down, down, going into the sea like an arrow. Sana's eyes. Abdul's single arm. Then New Hampshire at last, the day perched like a white bird on an old fence, Ozzie reading Yeats, the door open in the yurt, Gottfried shaking his head and the clink of his collar hitting his water bowl.

Lovemaking in the sea, in our bed, on our island of covers, the dolphins waiting for me to stand naked in the starlight. *Will you come today, or will you come tomorrow?*

Then home again. The cabin and the long driveway up, up, until I carried things inside, bags and a sack of grapes, cheese, light the fire, get the fire going, get the heat up, get the lights on, check my phone. More messages from Nora, from students, from the department assistant. A note about my book, a timeline for its publication. I stayed on one knee next to the wood stove and watched the wood catch, little by little, each flame climbing like an exploding star, like a golden vine, the wind following me home and singing a little in the stove pipe. The cabin shaking a little in the wind that followed me from the north, and I stood and closed the stove and for a long time waited in the middle of the room, unsure of everything, unsure of how the next five minutes could possibly pass.

40

In early January, Milly made me go sledding. She called it sliding. She arrived at my house with a pair of Flexible Flyer sleds
bungeed to her Jeep and honked like a crazy woman until I
clumped out to join her.

"This is the stupidest idea you ever had," I said, climbing into
the passenger's seat. "It's minus six degrees."

"You have to be young, Kate, or you'll get old. You're dressed
like a six-year-old, by the way. Where did you get a snowsuit?"

"This is not a snowsuit," I said, bending the visor mirror down
to inspect my outfit. "This is winter wear."

"Come on. Get into it. This will be great day."

And it was. She cranked the Go-Go's, a vintage band she loved,
and pounded on the steering wheel for the short trip to the sledding hill. She knew of a back road where the snowmobiles had
packed down the road into a veritable sheet of ice. She parked at
the bottom of Lieutenant Bennington Hill, hooted twice, then
scrambled out to untie the sleds. She stood on the doorframe,
wrestling with the knots, her mittens in her mouth. She looked
lovely and wild; she wore a cashmere scarf tied over her head and
her hair, windblown and unkempt, flew like a flag signaling joy.
She kept trying to talk around the mittens, but her voice came
out muffled.

She handed me one of the sleds.

"Where in the world did you get these?" I asked.

"From Denny Han. He's a cook at the Italian place over in Hanover. These belonged to his kids. He says the kids don't use them anymore and we can borrow them whenever we like."

"I haven't been sledding in a million years."

"When people start saying how long it's been since they've done something, that's a mark of them getting old. I make a point, don't I, Kate? I do. And by the way, I have decided to underline every time I make a point. That's my new thing."

She handed me the next sled. Then she slammed the door to the Jeep.

"We are never getting old, Kate. I've just decided. I make a point."

"Oh, good grief."

You can't predict the giddiness of doing something like sledding. It was the last thing I felt like doing. It was bitter cold, for one thing, which only made it more delicious. We had to pull our sleds up a long, narrow trail, one carved out of the surrounding snow by snowmobiles, and our boots made squeaking sounds from the temperature, and the cold did not seem so horrible. It was good to move, to force my body to respond, to breathe air that cut through every wayward thought. When we arrived at the top, Milly made me turn 360 degrees to take in the view. It was a spectacular view, all whites and blacks and blues, and the afternoon sun had begun to step quietly behind the mountains.

"What do you say, Kate? Are you ready?"

"I'm ready."

"I forget. Are we supposed to sit on it or ride it on our bellies?"

I didn't answer. Instead I picked up the sled, held it to my chest, and ran as hard as I could down the first ten feet of incline. Then I dove, tucking the sled under me as I had done as a ten-year-old, the muscle memory as automatic as it had been a thousand years before. It was like riding a bike. I let out a shout, felt my body hit the sled, and then, like mercury, I began sliding down the hillside.

I heard Milly squeal and run after me. Then I heard nothing except the runners sizzling against the snow. I bent the steering yoke to go left, then right, then straight. The snow and ice passed under me with blazing speed. I knew I could trail my boot toes in the snow—that was how you braked, I remembered—but I wanted more speed, not less. More snow, more cold, more everything. I lifted my feet up perpendicular to the sled, and I hit the fastest part, the steepest angle, and I found myself laughing, shouting back to Milly, happy to see a downy woodpecker flap away from a tree bole where it had been feeding and dart, like a darning needle, across the gray quiet of the afternoon.

I had almost reached the bottom of the run when I heard my phone signal a message.

I pulled my phone out of my side pocket and rolled until I was on my back as I halted. That was something else I remembered: winter afternoons, usually in snow, watching the night approach, the sun pull away as if going off to visit a sick relative. Winter. We were a week or two past the shortest day of the year.

Milly coasted up next to me.

"Get off your phone, you jackass!" she said to me. "Phones are poison."

But it was too late. The message came from Seamus.

Ozzie alive, it said. *Come quickly.*

On Crow's Point at sundown, I made a fire in the cottage fireplace. It was January and chilly. The wind blew and tossed the grass. Each time the wind struck the cottage, Gottfried lifted his head. I kept him beside me on a blanket in front of the fire. We were promised rain by the weather people. Starting at midnight, the reports said. Days of rain ahead.

Ozzie was due. Thirteen days, almost fourteen, had passed

since I had received the news. They had been unendurable, but necessary. I had not spoken to him. I knew from Nora how Ozzie had progressed. He had been found in an Algerian detention zone that housed African emigrants. He possessed no identification after the loss of the *Ferriter*, and he had been unconscious a good deal of the time. With so many humans in movement, one more, especially one not able to speak to his own interests, concerned no one. Even now, his circumstances caused difficulties. Police matters. Money exchanged, petty bribery. If it had not been for Nora's political influence, it would have taken months to effect his release. He was weak; he had been given up for dead when they had pulled him out of the water, but had been nursed to health by a fellow prisoner. He was still weak. For political leverage, Nora, in poor health herself, had traveled to Africa to oversee his release. He was quiet a good deal of the time, Nora reported. He was not broken, she said, but was contained, perhaps hiding, perhaps contemplating what he would do with his life now that it had been given back to him.

I would have gone to him, but there was no place to go. He was in transit, however slow that transit might be. He said through Nora that he would come to me. He had told Nora he would come to me in our cottage. He would not be too long, he said. He asked me to wait. Nora confided in me that he did not want to present himself in his weakness. He wanted to regain some of his strength.

Will you come tonight, or will you come tomorrow?

At the next gust, I bent and kissed Gottfried's head. It failed to settle him. I wondered if he needed to go out. He didn't usually react to the weather. I had been reading Robertson Davies, a Canadian writer I loved. I put the novel aside. It was late. I had been lost in reading.

"What's going on, boy?" I whispered. "You okay?"

He couldn't settle. I placed the screen in front of the fire and put on my rain jacket. Gottfried climbed quickly to his feet. He had already had his last walk for the night, but I didn't mind getting outdoors. I loved the winter smells the rain brought. When I opened the door, Gottfried sprinted outside. That was unusual. Ahead of me, the moon rolled like a white penny on the sea. I tried to remember the name for the winter moon, but I couldn't call it to mind. *The Hunger Moon* was my best guess.

"Not too far," I told Gottfried. "Stay close."

I heard his tags clinking, but he had already darted away. For the first time, I had a moment of unease. I checked the driveway and saw only my car waiting in the moonlight. I wondered if an animal had come onto the property. Sheep sometimes wandered onto the hillside leading to the sea, and Gottfried liked to chase them. That wasn't a good trait in an Irish dog, so I hurried my step to make sure he had not found a flock nearby.

The rain started in that moment. It came all at once, a strong downpour, and clouds moved over the moon. The rain brought up the sweetness from the grasses. I broke off a handful from the meadow and held the green to my nose. I closed my eyes and inhaled.

Gottfried began to bark. It was difficult in the wind and darkness to detect his location, but it sounded as if it came from below me, down by the beach. I called to him, but he didn't respond. I hurried down the slope of land and stopped midway when I saw a boat not twenty meters from the sand.

I couldn't move. I could think of no explanation for why a boat—and it looked to be a fishing boat, its outline like that of the *Ferriter*—would hold its position so close to the land. A wind pushed at me, trying to force me back to the cottage. I saw Gottfried down by the water. He ran back and forth, occasionally dipping into the sea, his indecision marked by loud barks he emitted, the sound slashed and pulled apart before it reached me fully.

I needed a light; I needed to be sensible. I remained for a long time watching. Then, throwing the grass away from me, I ran down the final slope to the beach. I stripped my clothes as I went, past caring, past knowing, past understanding anything real. As soon as I had removed my last bit of clothing, I dove into the sea. It was cold, cold as winter glass, and I felt the impact of the frigid water on my skin and down in my core. When I surfaced, Gottfried was beside me. He swam straight out to sea, his head an arrow in the water, his puffing breath eager and excited. I reached and touched his back and for a moment I let him pull me.

Then I swam. I swam into the Irish sea, into Dingle Bay, into the waters that I loved. I swam to my husband. The boat could not be far, I told myself. The moon emerged from the clouds again, and I did not permit myself a glance toward the place where the boat waited. I could not risk that. Instead, I put my face into the water and I opened my eyes and let the salt burn me.

When I looked up, Ozzie stood on the starboard gunwale, his face fixed in a smile. He looked almost the same, but taller and thinner than I remembered. It was not the *Ferriter*, but a friend's boat, the *Molly Mae*, belonging to Eldrich Payson. Ozzie had come by sea, not by land.

"Are you still my wife?" he asked me.

His voice was easy to hear over the water. Eldrich had turned off the engine. I treaded water ten feet from the boat. Ozzie kept his eyes on mine.

"Are you my husband?"

"I am," he said.

"Then I'm your wife and always have been."

"I don't believe a word of it. You're selkie. A fairy woman. I knew it when I met you."

"Come for a swim, then, Ozzie."

"In the winter? I do it at my peril. You have no mercy on me."

He dropped out of his clothes. He stood for a moment in the penny moonlight, Ozzie, my husband, and then dove into the sea. I dove down to meet him, my hands reaching out until they found his. For a moment, we stared at each other through the sea; the world had become a green apple and the tide pushed us toward the open ocean. Deep in the water, I looked up and saw Gottfried's small body paddling on the surface, and I begged him once more to keep his boy near, my husband, my love.

Ozzie pulled me against him, once, twice, and my skin turned into a flame. We kissed. Then slowly we rose together, side by side, each of us swimming through the blue-green water toward the moon.

SEVENTH LETTER

Dearest Milly,

It's spring in Canada at last. At night, we hear the frogs, and the loons came back last week. The beaver at the end of the lake is trying to dam the river, but he seems to be losing the battle. We wake early and sleep early and live in an easy rhythm of our own making. No internet, no routine outside communication. It's heaven. This cabin has restored us, Milly. We spend all day in each other's company. We swim in the water, which is frigid, and eat simple meals. We take a four-wheeler (you would love that) into town and get our supplies. When the agency brings children, as it is scheduled to do again soon, we are supplied by a tiny caravan of side-by-sides. It's all quite woodsy and lovely. You can eat pancakes here and not feel guilty for the extravagance. We are talking about tapping our own trees next year for maple syrup. We are both becoming expert anglers, and I have even tied my own flies.

Ozzie is recovered fully now. He is building a bunkhouse for the children. We hope to be able to have more children stay with us. I am working on my second book. Well, reading for it, mostly, but you know how I love research. I make a nest of books and only leave it to swim with Ozzie or make dinner together. Sometimes we go down-lake to cheer on the hapless beaver. I dangle my fingers in the lake and watch Ozzie paddle as the stars come out above him.

Our old pal Gottfried got quilled by a porcupine two days ago.

We removed all the quills we could, but he did a good job of it, and we worry we overlooked something. He is a dear old soul now and the children, when they are here, cannot keep their hands off him. I think he does more good for them than anything we can do. I sometimes believe he knew all along that Ozzie and I needed to be together. He is wiser than either of us.

I want to get this in the mail, so I won't write at length now. I miss you. I can't wait until you come for a visit. We will have long talks and walks and you will sleep like a log, I promise. As I write, I hear Ozzie finishing for the day. We usually meet for a swim before dinner. We read by the fire, try to keep from falling asleep, then go to bed and sleep the sleep of lovers. When I think how close I came to losing him, I can barely breathe.

I love you, Milly. Come soon. Come and stay and see my life through my eyes. And let me see your life through yours.

When Ozzie's life was saved, he told me an Irishman cannot drown when he can see the moon. I tell him I believe we are on an island, an invisible one, and the only ocean is our own indifference. If we stay near to one another, hold fiercely, then the sea is only a noise to sing us to sleep. We are foolish, of course, but we have learned that all lovers need an island. I have such hope for him, for me, for us, for you.

Missing you, loving you . . .
Kate

Acknowledgments

Although I wrote *Seven Letters* in a small New Hampshire cabin, it would not reach a single reader without the work and dedication of many people. No brief acknowledgment here can thank adequately all those who have edited this novel, designed the cover and look of its pages, carried it out into the world, promoted it, and introduced it to its potential readers. For all and any of you that I have missed, sincere thanks.

Thanks to my agents, Andrea Cirillo and Christina Hogrebe, whose opinions and guidance are given with grace and kindness. The team at the Jane Rotrosen Agency has always made me feel welcome and valued. Thanks to everyone in that small, lovely Manhattan brownstone who meet my requests and hopes with kindness and understanding.

Thanks and gratitude to Jennifer Enderlin, publisher at St. Martin's Press, and to all her wonderful staff. I always feel I am in exceptionally good hands at St. Martin's. A writing life is only as good as the people around one, and I am fortunate indeed to have landed among the hardworking people at St. Martin's.

Part of this novel was written while on sabbatical from Plymouth State University, our little college in the White Mountains of New Hampshire. I appreciate the time and support the university extends to me. I first learned about the Blasket Islands while teaching at Ireland's University of Limerick as a visiting professor, and I became haunted by the accounts of island life.

I encourage any readers who find something of interest in this novel to pursue the works of the many memoirists who recorded the rhythms of seasons on those austere islands. They provide a window to a lost world, and I wish to express my gratitude to those writers whose penetrating works I read on background.

Thanks to my friends and family. Thanks to Susan Shapiro, who often read sections of the novel and gave me truthful insights about what did and didn't work. It's wonderful to be able to talk aloud about a process that is often so internal. She also gave me lemon cookies.

Finally, thanks to the readers who pick up this book and spend a few hours with it. All novels are co-created in the pen of the writer and the mind of the reader. Thanks for listening to my story.